Wicked Surrender

SARA CRAVEN
CATHY WILLIAMS
DAPHNE CLAIR

MILLS & BOON

Published in Great Britain 2013
by Mills & Boon, an imprint of Harlequin (UK) Limited,
Eton House, 18-24 Paradise Road, Richmond, Surrey TW9 1SR

WICKED SURRENDER © by Harlequin Enterprises II B.V./S.à.r.l 2013

Ruthless Awakening, The Multi-Millionaire's Virgin Mistress and *The Timber Baron's Virgin Bride* were first published in Great Britain by Harlequin (UK) Limited.

Ruthless Awakening © Sara Craven 2009
The Multi-Millionaire's Virgin Mistress © Cathy Williams 2009
The Timber Baron's Virgin Bride © Daphne Clair 2009

ISBN: 978 0 263 90567 0
ebook ISBN: 978 1 472 00146

05-1013

Harlequin (UK) policy is to use papers that are natural, renewable and recyclable products and made from wood grown in sustainable forests. The logging and manufacturing processes conform to the legal environmental regulations of the country of origin.

Printed and bound in Spain
by Blackprint CPI, Barcelona

RUTHLESS AWAKENING

BY
SARA CRAVEN

Sara Craven was born in south Devon and grew up surrounded by books in a house by the sea. After leaving grammar school she worked as a local journalist, covering everything from flower shows to murders. She started writing for Mills & Boon in 1975. She has appeared as a contestant on the UK Channel Four game show *Fifteen to One* and in 1997 won the title of Television Mastermind of Great Britain.

Sara shares her Somerset home with several thousand books and an amazing video and DVD collection.

When she's not writing, she likes to travel in Europe, particularly Greece and Italy. She loves music, theater, cooking and eating in good restaurants, but reading will always be her greatest passion.

Since the birth of her twin grandchildren in New York City, she has become a regular visitor to the Big Apple.

CHAPTER ONE

As THE train from London crossed the Tamar, Rhianna felt the butterflies in her stomach turn into sick, churning panic.

I shouldn't be doing this, she thought desperately. I have no right to go to this wedding. To stand in Polkernick Church, watching as Carrie gets married to Simon. I should have kept away. I knew it before the invitation came. And even before it was made forcefully clear to me that I wouldn't be welcome. That I should keep my distance.

So how can I be on this train—making this journey?

Ever since the engagement had been announced she'd been dreading the arrival of the elegantly embossed card, and had already drafted her polite letter of regret with the same excuse— the shooting schedule on the next series—that she'd previously used to get out of being a bridesmaid.

And then Carrie had phoned unexpectedly to say she was coming to London trousseau-shopping, and would Rhianna meet her for a girls' lunch?

'You must come, darling.' Her voice had been eager, laughing. 'Because it might just be the last one now that Simon's got this job in Cape Town. Heaven knows when we'll be back in the UK.'

'Cape Town?' Rhianna had heard the sharp note in her voice and cursed herself. She'd made herself speak more lightly. 'I had no idea that he—that you were planning to live abroad.' *Nothing's been said...*

'Oh, it wasn't planned,' Carrie had said blithely. 'Someone Diaz knows had an opening in his company, and made Simon an offer that was too good to miss.'

Diaz...

Rhianna had repeated the name under her breath, tension clenching like a fist in her stomach. Yes, she'd thought dully. Painfully. It would have to be Diaz. Making sure that Simon was removed to a safe distance. Out of harm's way. Regardless of the damage already done, which would be left behind.

Diaz—twitching the strings from across continents and oceans to make sure the puppets danced to his tune, and that Carrie, his much-loved young cousin, would walk up the aisle of the twelfth-century church in the village to be united with the man she'd adored since childhood.

The perfect match, she'd thought, her throat tightening. And nothing would be allowed to prevent it.

She should have made some excuse about lunch, and she knew it, but she'd been torn between the pleasure of seeing Carrie again and the anguish of keeping silent while the other girl talked about Simon and her plans for the wedding. Of making sure that not one word, one look or one hint escaped her.

But, dear God, it had been so hard to sit opposite Carrie and see her pretty face radiant with happiness. To see the dream in her eyes and know how hideously simple it would be to turn that inner vision into a nightmare.

How simple, and how utterly impossible.

'So you will be coming to the wedding—you promise faithfully?' Carrie had begged. 'You'll introduce a note of sanity into the proceedings, darling. A rock for me to cling to, because by then I'll need it,' she'd added, shuddering. 'With the respective mothers already circling each other in a state of armed neutrality. I reckon there could be blood on the carpet before the great day dawns.'

And Rhianna had agreed. Because the only reasons she was left with to justify her absence were the ones she could never say.

But mainly because Carrie was her friend. Had been her first real friend, and shown her the only genuine kindness she'd ever known at Penvarnon. She—and Simon, of course. Which was how the trouble had first begun...

And now Carrie, who loved her, was here to make innocently sure that wild horses wouldn't keep Rhianna from attending her wedding.

But wild horses didn't even feature, Rhianna thought, her mouth twisting harshly. Not when they were up against the arrogant power of Diaz Penvarnon.

Against whose expressed will she was travelling to Cornwall. Defying his mandate.

His anger had been like a dark cloud, waiting in the corner of her mind to become a storm. A tangible thing, as if he were still standing over her, his lean face inimical.

'Don't say you weren't warned...'

As she remembered, her mouth felt suddenly dry, and she uncapped the bottle of mineral water on the table in front of her and drank it down without bothering with the glass the attendant had brought her.

Pull yourself together, she thought. You'll be in Cornwall for three days—four at the outside. And once Carrie's wedding is over you'll be gone—for good this time.

Besides, Diaz probably won't even be there. He'll be back in South America, arrogantly confident that his commands will be obeyed in his absence.

The rest of the occupants of that big grey stone house on the headland might not relish her presence, but there was no one who could really hurt her any more, she thought, her mouth tightening. No one to look down on her or treat her like an intruder. That section of her life was in the past, and she would make sure it stayed that way.

Because she was no longer the housekeeper's unwanted niece, the skinny waif that the daughter of the house, Caroline Seymour, had inexplicably and unsuitably decided to befriend and had stubbornly refused to give up in the face of concerted family opposition.

She was Rhianna Carlow, television actress and current star of the award winning drama series *Castle Pride*. An independent woman, with her own life and her own flat, who didn't have to dress in clothing from charity shops and jumble sales any more, or say thank you to anyone but herself.

She was a success—a face that people recognised. A few hours ago she'd seen some of the other passengers in this first-class carriage nudging each other and whispering as she'd taken her seat at Paddington.

She knew from past experience that it would only be a matter of time before someone asked her for an autograph, or permission to take a picture of her with a mobile phone, because that was generally what happened. And she would smile and acquiesce, so that the person asking the favour would go away saying how lovely she was—how charming.

And another brief performance would have been given.

But that was the easy part of being Rhianna Carlow. Because she knew it would take every scrap of acting ability she possessed to stand in silence the day after tomorrow and watch Carrie become Simon's wife. To hear him say, 'Forsaking all others…' when he knew that she, Rhianna, would be in the congregation, listening to him, angry, hurt—and above all, anxious for Carrie.

When every nerve in her body would be urging her to cry out, No, this can't happen. I won't let it. It has to stop right here—right now. For everyone's sake.

And weren't you supposed to be cruel in order to be kind? she asked herself restlessly. Wasn't that one of the relentless clichés that people trotted out, usually to justify some piece of deliberate malice?

But could she stand up and tell the truth and see the light slowly die from Carrie's bright face when she realised just how fundamentally Simon had betrayed her?

It would be like, she thought dispassionately, watching an eclipse of the sun, knowing that this time it would be permanent and there would be no returning radiance.

Carrie had always been a sunshine girl, lit from within, fair-haired and merry-faced, drawing Rhianna, the outsider, the dark moon, into her orbit.

Compensating over and over again for her aunt Kezia's unrelenting coldness, and the aloofness bordering on hostility displayed by the rest of the family at Penvarnon House.

From the first day that was how it had been, she thought. When she'd stood, an unhappy twelve-year-old, shivering in the brisk wind, at the top of the flight of steps that led down to the lawns, knowing guiltily that already she'd broken her aunt's first rule that she should never—ever—stray into the environs of the house and its grounds.

Knowing that her home was now a chillingly neat flat, converted from the former stable block, and that if she wished to play she should do so only in the stable yard outside.

'Allowing you here is a great concession by Mrs Seymour, and you must always be grateful for that,' Aunt Kezia had told her repressively. 'But it's on condition that you confine your activities to our own quarters and not go beyond them. Do you understand?'

No, Rhianna had thought with a kind of desolate rebellion, I don't understand. I don't know why Mummy had to die, or why I couldn't stay in London with Mr and Mrs Jessop, because they offered to have me. I don't know why you came and brought me away to a place where no one wants me—least of all you. A place with the sea all round it, cutting me off from everything I know. Somewhere that I don't want to be.

She hadn't meant to be disobedient, but the minimal attractions of the stable yard, with its cobbles and long-unused row of loose boxes, had palled within minutes, and a half-open gate had beckoned to her in a way it had been impossible to resist. Just a quick look, she'd promised herself, at the place where she'd be spending the next few years of her life, then she would come back, and close the gate, and no-one would be any the wiser.

So, she'd followed the gravel walk round the side of the looming bulk that was Penvarnon House and found herself at its rear, confronted by lawns that stretched to the very edge of the headland. And racing across the grass towards her had been two children.

The girl had reached the foot of the steps first, and looked up, laughing.

'Hello. I'm Carrie Seymour, and this is Simon. Has your mother

brought you to have tea? How grim and grizzly. We were just going
down to the cove, so why don't you come with us instead?'

'I can't.' Rhianna swallowed, dismally realising the trouble
she was in.

'I shouldn't even be here. My aunt told me I must stay by
the stables.'

'Your aunt?' the girl asked, and paused. 'Oh, you must be Miss
Trewint's niece,' she went on more slowly, adding doubtfully, 'I
heard Mummy and Daddy talking about you.' There was another
silence, then her face brightened again. 'But you can't hang
round the yard all day with nothing to do. That's silly. Come with
Simon and me. I'll make it all right with Mother and Miss
Trewint, you'll see.'

And somehow, miraculously, she had done exactly that—by
dint, Rhianna thought drily, of smiling seraphically and refusing
to budge. Just like always.

Rhianna, she'd insisted cheerfully, had come to live at Penvarnon
House and therefore they would be friends. End of story.

And start of another, very different narrative, Rhianna
thought. Although none of us knew it at the time. A story of past
secrets, unhappiness and betrayal. And this time there would be
no happy ending.

I should have stayed by the stables, she thought with irony. It
was safer there. I should never have gone down the path to the
cove and spent the afternoon climbing over rocks, peering into
pools, running races along the sand and splashing barefoot in the
freezing shallows of the sea. Discovering childhood again.
Drawing my first breath of happiness in weeks.

She'd assumed that Simon—tall, also blond-haired and blue-
eyed, and clearly older than Carrie by a couple of years or
more—was Carrie's brother, but she had been mistaken.

'My brother? Heavens, no. Both of us are "onlys", like you,'
Carrie had said blithely. 'He's just a grockle—an emmet.' And she'd
dodged, laughing, as Simon lunged at her with a menacing growl.

'What's a—grockle?' Rhianna asked doubtfully.

'An incomer,' Simon informed her, pulling a face. 'A tourist.
Someone who doesn't live in Cornwall but only comes here for

holidays. And an emmet is an ant,' he added, looking darkly at Carrie. 'Because in the summer that's what the tourists are like— all over the place in droves. But we're not either of those things, because we have a house just outside the village and spend half our lives down here.'

'So we have to put up with him for weeks at a time,' Carrie said mournfully. 'What an utter drag.'

But even then, young as they all were, some instinct had told Rhianna that Carrie didn't mean it, and that Simon, the golden, the glorious, was already the centre of her small universe.

Both of them, she'd discovered, would be going back to their respective boarding schools at the end of the Easter holidays, whereas she would be attending the local secondary school at Lanzion.

'But there'll be half-term to look forward to,' Carrie had said eagerly. 'And then we'll have nearly eight weeks in the summer. The sea's really safe down at the cove, so we can swim every day, and have picnics, and if the weather's foul we can use The Cabin.'

She was referring to the large wooden building tucked under the cliff, which, as Rhianna was to discover, not only housed sunbeds and deckchairs, but had a spacious living area with its own tiny galley kitchen, an ancient sagging sofa, and a table big enough to sit round to eat or play games. The late Ben Penarvon, Diaz's father, had even had the place wired for electricity.

'It's going to be great,' Carrie had added, her grin lighting up the world. 'I'm really glad you came to live here.'

And even Aunt Kezia's overt disapproval, and the fact that Moira Seymour, Carrie's mother, had looked right through her on their rare encounters, had not been able to take the edge off Rhianna's growing contentment. The feeling that she could relax and allow herself to feel more settled.

She'd still grieved for her mother—the more so since Aunt Kezia had made it clear that any mention of Grace Carlow's name was taboo. At the same time Rhianna had realised that there was not one photograph of her mother, or any family memen- toes, anywhere in the cheerless little flat. Moreover, her own framed photo of her parents' wedding, which she'd put on the table beside her narrow bed, had been removed and placed in the chest of drawers.

'I have quite enough to do in the house,' Aunt Kezia had returned brusquely when Rhianna, upset, had tried to protest. 'I'm not coming back here and having to dust round your nonsense.'

On the upside, she'd liked her new school, too, and had come home at the end of the summer term excited at being given a part in the school play, which would be rehearsed during the autumn and staged before Christmas.

But, to her shock and disappointment, Aunt Kezia had rounded on her. 'You'll do nothing of the kind,' she declared tight-lipped. 'I won't have you putting yourself forward, giving yourself airs, because it only leads to trouble. And there's been too much of that in the past,' she added with angry bitterness. 'Quite apart from this nonsense with Miss Caroline. And after all I said to you, too.'

She drew a harsh breath. 'Kindly remember that you're only here on sufferance, my girl, and learn to keep in the background more than you have been doing while you're living in Mrs Seymour's house.'

'But it isn't her house,' Rhianna objected. 'Carrie told me it really belongs to her cousin, Diaz, but he's away most of the time, either living on his other estates in South America or travelling all over the world as a mining consultant. So her parents look after it for him. She says when he decides to get married they'll have to find somewhere else to live.'

'Miss Caroline says a deal too much,' her aunt said grimly. 'And I'm still going to have a word with your teacher. Knock this acting nonsense on the head once and for all.'

And, in spite of Rhianna's tearful protests, she'd done exactly that.

'Poor you,' Carrie had said, her forehead wrinkled with concern when Rhianna had eventually told her what had happened. 'She's so hard on you all the time. Has she always been like that?'

Rhianna shook her head. 'I don't know,' she said unhappily. 'I only met her for the first time when she came to Mummy's funeral and told me that she'd been appointed my legal guardian and I had to live with her. Before that I'd never heard from her at all—not even on my birthday or at Christmas. And I could tell she was angry about having to take me.' She sighed. 'I'm not really welcome here either. I just wish someone would tell me what I've done that's so wrong.'

'It's not you,' Carrie said hesitantly. 'I—I'm sure it's not.'

Rhianna bit her lip. 'You said once you'd heard your parents talking about me. Would you tell me what they said?'

Carrie's face was pink with dismay. After a pause, she said, 'It was ages ago, so I'm not sure I remember exactly. Besides, I shouldn't have been listening anyway,' she added glumly. 'And I'm sure it would be better coming from your aunt.'

'She won't talk about it,' Rhianna said bitterly. 'She doesn't talk about anything.' She looked beseechingly at the other girl. 'Oh, please, Carrie. I really need to know why they all seem to hate me so much.'

Carrie sighed. 'Well—I was on the window seat in the drawing room, reading, and my parents came in. They didn't realise I was there, and Mummy was saying, "I can hardly believe that Kezia Trewint would do such a thing. Agree to take in that woman's child—and have the gall to ask to bring her here." Daddy said he supposed she hadn't had much choice in the matter, and he told Mummy not to do anything too hasty, because they'd never find anyone to run the house and cook as well as your aunt.'

She swallowed. 'Then he said, "And it's hardly the child's fault. You can't blame her for things that her mother did years before she was born. And that's how it was, so don't start thinking anything nonsensical." Then Mummy got cross and said that your mother was—not a nice person,' Carrie added in a little embarrassed rush. 'And that the apple never fell far from the tree, and what the hell would Diaz say when he heard? Daddy said, "God only knows," and he thought that everyone should reserve judgement and give you a chance. Then he went off to the golf club.'

She added tearfully, 'I'm so sorry, Rhianna. I should never have listened, but when I met you I was really glad, because you looked so unhappy and lost, and I told myself that Daddy was right. Only now I'm afraid I've made everything a hundred times worse.'

'No,' Rhianna said slowly. 'No, you haven't—I promise. Because I—I really wanted to know.' She flung back her head. 'Besides, none of it's true. Mummy wasn't a bit like that. She was a wonderful person.'

And so beautiful too, she thought, with all that deep, dark auburn hair that Daddy said was the colour of mahogany, and the green eyes that tilted at the corners when she laughed. Whereas my hair is just—red.

She swallowed. 'After Daddy died she got a job as a care worker, and the people she visited really loved her. They all said so. And Mrs Jessop told someone that if Mummy hadn't been so involved with looking after everyone else she might have thought about herself more, and realised there was something wrong. Seen a doctor before it was—too late.' Her voice wobbled. 'So, you see, there must be some mistake. There *has* to be.'

Carrie gave her a comforting pat. 'I'm sure,' she said, but her anxious eyes said that even if her parents had been wrong, that still didn't explain Kezia Trewint's strange, unloving attitude to her only living relative.

Understanding that had still been a long way in the future, Rhianna thought wearily, leaning back in her seat and closing her eyes. In the meantime it had remained on the edge of her life, a cloud no bigger than a man's hand, yet occasionally ominously hinting at the storm to come.

Like the day she'd encountered Diaz Penvarnon for the first time.

It had been, she remembered, one of those burning, windless days in August, when the sun seemed close enough to touch.

They'd been down at the beach all day, slipping in and out of the unruffled sea like seals, Rhianna by then as competent and confident a swimmer as the other two. It had been Simon who'd called a halt, explaining that he needed to get back as his parents had friends coming to dinner.

In spite of the heat, it had always been a matter of honour to see who could get to the top of the cliff path ahead of the others. The girls rarely won against Simon's long legs, but this particular afternoon he had dropped one of his new trainers in the loose sand at the foot of the cliff and halted to retrieve it, so that Carrie and Rhianna had found themselves unexpectedly ahead, flying neck and neck up the stony track.

And when Carrie had stumbled Rhianna had got there first, laughing and breathless, head down as she launched herself towards some invisible finishing tape.

Only to cannon into something tall, solid and all too real, finding, as she had staggered back with a gasp of shock, strong hands grasping her shoulders to steady her, while a man's cool voice had said, 'So—what have we here? A fleeing trespasser? This is private land, you know.'

She looked up dazedly into the face above her, swarthy and lean, with high cheekbones only to see the faint amusement fade from the firm mouth and the grey eyes become as icy as snow clouds in January. He studied her in return, his glance shifting with a kind of incredulity from her unruly cloud of hair to her long-lashed eyes and her startled, parted lips.

She said, 'I'm Rhianna Carlow. I—I live here.'

He drew a swift sharp breath, lifting his hands from her and stepping back in a repudiation that was as instant as it was unmistakable.

He said, half to himself, 'Of course—the child. I'd almost forgotten.'

'Diaz!' Carrie was there, hurling herself at him. 'How truly great! No one said you were coming.'

'It was intended as a surprise,' he said, returning her exuberant hug with more restraint before he looked back at Rhianna. He added unsmilingly, 'It seems to be a day for them.'

And she thought with inexplicable desolation, Someone else who doesn't want me to be here…

Simon's panting arrival provided a momentary diversion, but the greetings were barely over before Moira Seymour came sauntering across the lawn towards them, cool in a blue cotton dress, and fanning herself languidly with a broad-brimmed straw hat.

She said, 'Simon, my pet, your mother's telephoned, asking

where you are. Carrie, darling, get cleaned up for tea, please.'
Her glance flickered dismissively over Rhianna. 'And I'm sure,
young woman, that your aunt can find something for you to do.'

The first direct remark Mrs Seymour had ever made to her,
Rhianna realised. And one that made her inferior position in the
household quite explicit. Turning her back into the intruder. The
trespasser that Diaz Penvarnon had just called her. A name that
might have started as a joke, but was now, suddenly, something
very different.

My first starring role, Rhianna thought bitterly, and one that
will probably haunt me, for so many reasons, as long as I live,
wherever I go, and whatever happens to me.

Diaz—Diaz Penvarnon…

He was a chain, she told herself, linking her with the past,
which must be broken now that he was out of her life for ever.

I've got to start thinking of him as a stranger, she thought,
almost feverishly. I must…

But from that first moment of meeting he'd imprinted himself
indelibly on her consciousness, and Rhianna had found her life
changing once more—and not for the better, either.

Because she had once more been strictly relegated to the flat
over the stables and its immediate vicinity, pretty much reduced
to the status of non-person again, while a protesting Carrie had
simply been whipped away and absorbed into the sudden surge
of activities at the house itself, putting her out of reach for the
duration of the owner's visit.

The owner…

Even at a distance, Rhianna had sensed that the whole place
seemed to have lost its languid, almost melancholy atmosphere
and become—re-energised.

And that had been even without the constant stream of visitors
filling the place at weekends, flocking down to the cove to swim
and sunbathe, or play tennis on the newly marked court at the
side of the house. Not forgetting the dinner parties that went on
into the early hours, with music spilling out through the open
windows into the warm nights, and dancers moving on the terrace.

With Diaz Penarvon at the forefront of it all.

On the few occasions that Rhianna had dared venture further than the stable yard she had seen that. Had recognised that his tall figure seemed to be everywhere, exercising effortless dominion over his surroundings, as if he'd never been absent, with the cool, incisive voice she'd remembered only too well issuing orders that were immediately obeyed.

'And I wonder how Madam likes that?' Rhianna had overheard Mrs Welling, the daily help, comment with a chuckle to Jacky Besant, who worked in the grounds, while they were enjoying a quiet smoke in the yard.

'Not much, I reckon.' Jacky had also seemed amused. 'But she's no need to fret. He'll be gone again soon enough, and then she'll have it easy again.'

Maybe we all will, Rhianna had thought, stifling a sigh.

It had occurred to her that Diaz wasn't a bit as she'd imagined when Carrie had first told her about him.

For one thing she'd assumed he'd be much older. Physically much heavier, too. Not lean, rangy, and possessed of a dynamism she'd been able to recognise even at her immature age.

'He's what they call a babe magnet,' Simon, himself sidelined under the new regime, had commented resentfully when Rhianna, sent on an errand by her aunt, had met him emerging from the village Post Office. 'Tall, dark and mega-rich. My parents say that every female in Cornwall under thirty is trying to have a crack at him.'

'Well, I think he's vile,' Rhianna said vehemently, remembering how those extraordinary eyes—almost silver under their dark fringe of lashes—had frozen her.

Recalling too how she'd seen him in a corner of the terrace one evening, when she'd slipped round to listen to the music. How she'd become aware of a movement in the shadows and realised he was there, entwined with some blonde girl in a way that had made her burn with embarrassment, together with other sensations less easy to define.

And how, as he'd pushed the dress from his companion's shoulders, she'd turned and run back to her own domain, and not ventured out at night again.

Now, she added with renewed emphasis, 'Sick-making.'

Simon grinned faintly. 'Keep thinking that way.' He paused. 'Fancy going down to the harbour for an ice cream or a Coke at Rollo's Café?'

She shook her head. 'I—I have to get back.' It was only partly true. She didn't want to admit that she'd been sent out with the exact money to pay for her aunt's requirements and no more.

'You can be spared for ten minutes, surely?' Simon said reasonably. 'And you need something cool before you bike back to Penvarnon or you'll be roasted.' He paused. 'My treat.'

She flushed with pleasure. Simon the cool and totally gorgeous was actually offering to buy her an ice cream. Normally he didn't take a great deal of notice of her, when Carrie was there. They'd been friends long before she came on the scene, and she'd always accepted that, told herself it was nasty of her to feel even slightly envious.

But now Carrie was occupied, and she had this one blissful chance to spend a little while with Simon on her own. Without, she thought, having to share him. And instantly felt thoroughly ashamed of herself.

Then she saw Simon smiling at her, and drew a small, happy breath. 'I mustn't be too long,' she temporised.

He bought their ice creams, and they sat on the harbour wall in the sunshine, watching the boats and chatting about everything and nothing, until Rhianna said regretfully she really had to get back, and Simon lifted her down from the rough stones.

'Hey,' he said. 'This has been great. We must do it again.'

As she'd cycled back to Penvarnon her heart had been singing. It might only been half an hour, but for Rhianna it had become thirty minutes framed in gold. A pivotal moment for a lonely girl on the verge of adolescence. Heady stuff.

But certainly not enough to provide the foundation for any dreams about the future.

But I didn't know that then, she thought unhappily. And it was long, long in the future before I realised that by the time you're sure of your dream and want it to come true it may be completely beyond your reach.

She was startled out of her reverie by the train manager's voice announcing the express's imminent arrival at her station.

Rhianna rose, reaching for her sunglasses, reluctantly collecting her suitcase and dress carrier as she prepared to alight.

You don't have to do this, an inner voice urged. You could stay right here, extend your ticket to Penzance, and from there catch the next train back to London. Then make the excuse you've been hit by some virus. Summer flu. Anything…

Carrie will be disappointed if you don't show, but that will surely be a minor issue when she has so much else to be happy about.

And if you can't stand the idea of London, then get yourself to the nearest airport. You've got your passport in your bag, plus your credit cards, so buy a flight somewhere—anywhere—and chill out for a while.

And stop—stop agonising over the past. Because there's nothing you can do—not without ruining Carrie's happiness. And that's never been an option.

But she was already caught up in the small stream of people who were also leaving the train. The door in front of her had opened, and she was stepping down into the sunlight.

It was hot, but Rhianna felt the fine hairs on her arms react as if a chill wind had touched them.

She paused, all her senses suddenly alert, and saw him.

He was waiting at the back of the platform, taller and darker than anyone else in the bustling crowd around them. A shadow in the sun. His anger like a raised fist. Waiting for her, as she'd somehow known he would be. As she'd felt him deep in her heart—her bones—even while she was trying to convince herself that he'd be long gone, a thousand miles away, and that she had nothing more to fear.

Then, as their eyes met, Diaz Penvarnon began to walk towards her.

CHAPTER TWO

RETREAT was impossible, of course. There were people behind her, and she was being carried forward by their momentum. Towards him.

And then a voice beside her said, 'It's Rhianna Carlow, isn't it? Lady Ariadne from *Castle Pride*. This is a bit of luck. May I have a quick word?'

Rhianna turned quickly to the newcomer, youngish and thin-faced, his brown hair slicked back, his smile confident, but her relief was short-lived.

'I'm Jason Tully,' he went on. 'From the *Duchy Herald*. May I ask what you're doing so far from London? They're not planning to shift the new *Castle Pride* series down to Cornwall, are they?'

'Not as far as I know.' She could handle this, she thought, making herself smile back, every nerve in her body tinglingly aware that Diaz Penvarnon was standing only a couple of feet away. 'Although that would be lovely, of course. *But* I'm actually here on a private visit.'

She was careful not to mention it was a wedding, in case her presence there was enough for him to rouse the rest of the press pack and bring them homing in on Polkernick Church.

Which would no doubt be interpreted as her deliberate attempt to upstage the bride, she thought bitterly.

'I see.' He signalled to an older stouter man, carrying a camera, then looked past her to the train. 'So, are you travelling alone, Rhianna? You don't have a companion?'

'I'm on my way to see friends,' she returned, not daring to look at Diaz and see his reaction.

'Sure.' Jason Tully grinned again. 'I guess you know it's just been announced that your co-star Rob Winters has split up with his wife? I'm wondering how you feel about that?'

Ah, so that's who you were expecting to see following me off the train, you little weasel.

She suppressed an inward groan.

'No, I hadn't heard that,' she returned steadily, aware that Diaz was absorbing every word of the exchange, brows lifted cynically, that other people were halting to stare—and listen. 'And if it's true I'm—sorry. However, I'm certain that it's a temporary difficulty which will soon be resolved.'

'But you and Rob Winters are pretty close?' he persisted. 'Those were some very torrid love scenes you played in the last series.'

'Yes,' Rhianna said. 'We *played* them. Because we're actors, Mr Tully, and that's what we're paid for.'

And you will never know, she thought, how true that is—for me, anyway.

She added, 'And now—if there's nothing else…?'

'Just a picture, if you don't mind.' He looked at Diaz, standing in silence, his hands on his jean-clad hips. 'And you are?'

'Miss Carlow's driver.' Diaz stepped forward and took the bags from her unresisting hands. All of them, she realised too late, including her handbag, with her money, return ticket and everything else.

'I'll be waiting in the car—madam,' he added, as he turned away, heading for the exit. Leaving her staring after him.

'We only came down here to do a story about the delay in track repairs,' Jason Tully announced jubilantly as Rhianna recovered herself, posing obediently for the camera. 'This is a real bonus.'

Your bonus, she thought. But my can of worms.

'Have a nice visit,' he added as she began to walk away. 'I hope you enjoy yourself with your—friends. When you meet up with them.'

The innuendo was unmistakable, and she rewarded it with

another dazzling smile, wishing that she could knock him down and jump on him.

He'll be on to the nationals as soon as he can get his mobile phone out of his pocket, she thought bitterly as she left the station. I only hope that idiot Rob is staying with his parents in Norfolk, and hasn't chosen to go to ground somewhere, in true dramatic fashion. Or nowhere west of Bristol, anyway.

But she couldn't worry about that now. She had her own problems to deal with. The most major of which was standing beside his Jeep, his face bleak and hostile, his pale eyes brooding as he watched her walk towards him.

Her mouth felt dry, and her hands were clammy. If there had been anywhere to go she'd have turned and run. But that wasn't possible, so she'd have to fall back on sheer technique.

Treat it as stage fright, she thought. Then go on and give a performance. The kind that saves the show.

'Mr Penvarnon,' she said, her voice cool and detached. 'What a surprise. I thought you'd be on the other side of the world.'

'You hoped,' he said, as he opened the passenger door for her. 'Was that why you decided to ignore my advice?'

Her brows lifted. 'Is that what it was?' she asked ironically. She climbed into the vehicle, making a business of smoothing the skirt of her plain *café au lait* linen dress over her knees. 'I thought I was being threatened. And I don't respond well to threats.'

'But you deal very well with inconvenient questions from reporters, I notice,' Diaz said smoothly. 'I'm so glad you didn't use that coy old cliché, We're just good friends, when he was quizzing you about your involvement with Robert Winters.' He paused. 'So, what is he? Your consolation prize for missing out on the man you love?'

Her heart seemed to stop, but she managed to keep her voice level.

'No,' she said. 'Both Rob and his wife are genuinely friends of mine, but Daisy and I are closer because we met at drama school. And the reason they're having problems is that she wants to stop work and have a baby, whereas he sees them as some starry theatrical couple on a smooth and uninterrupted ride to the top. I see no reason to mention that to the press, local or national.'

She paused, drawing a swift breath that she tried to keep steady. 'And I'm telling you this only because I'm sick of the implication that any other woman's man is fair game as far as I'm concerned.'

'Your protest is touching,' he said, as the Jeep moved forward. 'But the evidence is against you.' His mouth twisted. 'Perhaps it's genetic.'

'If you mean like mother, like daughter,' she said. 'Why don't you just say so? I have no objection. Because I know that whatever my mother did it was for love, and that I *am* no different.'

'Slow curtain,' he said sardonically, 'and tumultuous applause. I loved the authentic quiver of sincerity in the voice, sweetheart. You could make a living in straight drama without needing to take your clothes off on television. But perhaps you enjoy it.'

He paused. 'Incidentally, how did this *good friend* of yours react to the sight of you cavorting naked with her husband?'

She shrugged. 'She thought it was funny.'

Even now she could remember being in Daisy's kitchen, the pair of them hooting with uncontrollable laughter as they waited for Rob to come back with their Indian takeaway.

'Do you know how long it took me,' Daisy had asked tearfully, 'to put concealer on his bum because he thought he was getting a spot?'

'He didn't mention that.' Rhianna shook her head, hiccuping. 'He just kept c-complaining about the draught on the set.'

'He does that when we're in bed,' said his loving wife, wiping her eyes. 'Invariably at the wrong moment. He's terrified of catching a cold. Some people have champagne in their fridges. We have gargle, bless him.'

God, but they were so right for each other, Rhianna thought. Rob—his ambition and talent battling his anxieties. Daisy— serenely grounded.

Their love for each other had been unquestioned and unquestioning—until Daisy's biological clock began ticking away.

If they *were* now separated it had to be a glitch, she told herself passionately, because they belonged together in a way she could only observe and admire. And, if she was honest, envy.

'So what are you doing here, Rhianna?' Diaz's voice broke harshly across her thoughts. His hands were gripping the wheel so fiercely that the knuckles stood out. 'God knows there isn't a soul that wants you at Penvarnon—apart, I suppose, from Carrie. In her case, love is indeed blind, or she'd have seen you a long time ago for the treacherous, self-serving little madam you really are.'

'Heavens,' she said. 'What a turn of phrase. If we ever need a scriptwriter for *Castle Pride* I'll recommend you. Unless, of course, you're planning an alternative career as a cabbie?'

'You didn't really think I'd risk Simon coming to meet you from the train?' he said softly. 'Because my poor trusting Carrie would have let him do it if I hadn't stepped in.'

'Dear me,' she said lightly. 'Is he so little to be relied upon?'

'No.' His voice hardened. 'You are. You're the loose cannon around here. The snake in the grass. And don't think I'll let that slip my mind even for a minute.'

They were outside the town by now, and he swung the wheel suddenly and sharply, pulling the Jeep on to the verge at the side of the road and bringing it to an abrupt halt.

'And this isn't more advice,' he went on. 'It's a warning to be taken seriously.'

He drew a deep breath. 'You probably have every red-blooded man in Britain lusting after you, but that's not enough for you—is it? Because you didn't learn your lesson five years ago. You had to make another play for Simon, and this time it worked.'

He paused. 'But, sadly for you, the Rhianna effect didn't last. You can't have been too pleased when the stupid bastard came to his senses just in time, and realised what was genuine and worthwhile in his life, and how easily he could have lost it. After all you're irresistible—according to the television company's publicity machine.'

His voice roughened. 'You betrayed the best, most loyal friend you've ever had in order to bed Simon, just to prove that you could. But on Saturday she's still the one he's going to marry. And you will say nothing and do nothing to jeopardise that in any way. Do I make myself clear?'

'As crystal.' She stared straight ahead of her through the wind-screen. 'Tell me—did Simon receive a similar lecture, or was this fascinating diatribe designed for me alone?'

'I didn't need to have another go at him,' he said. 'Simon is subdued enough already. And he's made it clear that he bitterly regrets the criminal stupidity of putting his entire future on the line, however potent the temptation. I recommend you keep out of his way,' he added grimly.

'No problem,' she said. 'It's not as if we'll be sharing a roof for the next two nights, after all. And if you're concerned about the daylight hours, why not ask the Hendersons if they'll move out of the flat and put me back in the stables—the servants' quarters—where I belong?'

'When,' he said harshly, 'did you ever *belong* anywhere at Penvarnon?'

She should have expected it, but for a moment Rhianna felt her throat close in shock.

But I never wanted to be there. She wanted to say it aloud. Shout it. *Not once. And I left as soon as I could. If it wasn't for Carrie, I wouldn't be here now. And once these next few ghastly days are behind us, you'll never—ever—see me again.*

But she remained silent. Because he would no more believe her now than he'd done in the past, so there was no point in hoping.

She simply had to deal with the present pain, and face the uncertainty of the future. Both of which she would accomplish alone.

Then his hand moved. The engine roared into life and the Jeep moved forward.

Taking them to Penvarnon.

'Alone at last.' Carrie's laughter had an edge to it, and her hug was fierce. 'Oh, Rhianna, I'm so thankful that you're here. Wasn't it ghastly downstairs just now? You must have noticed.'

'You could have cut the atmosphere with a knife,' Rhianna conceded drily as she returned the hug. 'But I attributed that to my arrival.'

'Don't you believe it,' Carrie returned. 'Besides, no one cares about a lot of old nonsense that happened years ago. Not any more.'

Don't they? Oh, God, don't they? What makes you so sure? Because I can think of one person at least who hasn't forgotten a thing. Or forgiven...

She was still shaking inside, she thought, as she had been throughout the remainder of that taut, silent drive to the house. Seated beside him, hands clamped in her lap. Staring at nothing.

Still shaking when she reached for the door handle almost before the car had stopped on the wide sweep in front of the main entrance and swung herself recklessly, desperately, out on to the gravel.

She'd thought—imagined—just for a moment that Diaz had very quietly said her name, and in that instant had been tempted to turn and look at him.

Only to see Carrie, almost dancing with excitement at the top of the shallow stone steps, while Henderson, very correct in dark trousers and a linen jacket, came down to collect her luggage. So she'd walked towards the house instead.

And as they'd moved inside she'd heard the car drive off—fast.

Swallowing, she now applied herself to the task in hand—hanging the dress carrier in the elegant wardrobe and unzipping her travel bag. 'So, what's the problem?'

Carrie sighed. 'Just that the bell seems to have gone for round fifty in the battle of the mothers. Dad says it's like Waterloo—"a damned close-run thing"—then disappears to the golf club. His answer to everything these days,' she added, with an unwonted hint of bitterness.

'Well, you can't expect him to take a passionate interest in hemlines, flower arrangements and tiers on the cake.' Rhianna tried to sound soothing. 'He probably thinks it's his duty just to keep quiet and write the cheques. Besides,' she added, 'knowing that he's going to have to give you away very soon now and watch you disappear to Cape Town must be preying on his mind, too. Maybe he needs time and space to deal with that?'

'It's going to be hard for me too,' Carrie admitted unhappily. 'Oh, Rhianna, Simon and I—we are doing the right thing, aren't we?'

Rhianna's heart lurched. 'In what way?' She tried to sound casual.

'The new job. I sometimes get the feeling that Simon's having second thoughts about it. He's been so quiet over the past few weeks. Yet when I ask him he says everything's fine.'

Rhianna bent over her case, letting a swathe of waving mahogany hair hide her sudden flush. 'Then probably everything is,' she said constrictedly. 'And don't forget that it's only a job, Carrie, not a life sentence. If it doesn't work out, you move on.'

'I suppose so. But Diaz probably wouldn't be too pleased about that.'

'And is the maintenance of his goodwill really so vital?' She tried to speak lightly. 'Or just a habit?'

'Well, he has been incredibly kind,' Carrie said. 'After all my parents could never have afforded a place like this, and Diaz has let us live here all this time.' She sighed. 'Although that's coming to an end quite soon, as I expect he told you.'

'No.' Rhianna straightened. 'No, he didn't mention it. But we're hardly on those terms.'

'Oh.' Carrie looked at her, dismayed. 'I thought maybe things had improved a little in that quarter—especially as he offered to fetch you from the station. Simon volunteered, naturally, but Diaz reminded him he was supposed to be getting his hair cut in Falmouth, and said he'd go instead.'

'Yet another of his many acts of kindness,' Rhianna commented unsmilingly. 'So, what's happening about the house?'

Carrie shrugged. 'Apparently he's coming back here. To settle, would you believe? Mother thought, from something he said in passing, that he might be getting married, but there doesn't seem much sign of it. No announcement, and he certainly isn't bringing anyone to the wedding. In fact he may not even stay for it himself. Not with his new toy to play with.'

'Toy?'

'His boat.' Carrie rolled her eyes. '*Windhover* the Wonder Yacht. Or that's how Dad describes it. Like the best kind of floating hotel suite, but powered by a massive engine and moored down at Polkernick. He brought it round from Falmouth the day before yesterday and he's sleeping on board, which has saved Ma having hysterics over the bedroom arrangements here, because usually it's all change when Diaz comes to stay, and as he wasn't expected there'd have been uproar.'

'Of course,' Rhianna said. 'The master must have the master bedroom—however inconvenient.'

But at least this boat might keep him at a distance, she thought. Maybe that's where he was driving off to just now? I can but hope.

'Well,' Carrie said tolerantly, 'you can hardly blame him for wanting his own space. It is his home, after all, even if he hasn't spent that much time here in the past. And now, to Ma's horror, he wants it back, and she'll have to give up being Lady of the Manor.' She grimaced. 'Which she'll hate.'

But she'll go down fighting, Rhianna thought, remembering Moira Seymour's bleak gaze meeting hers a short while ago, from the sofa in the drawing room where she'd sat, poised and chilly as ever, in a silence that had been almost tangible.

'Ah, Miss Carlow.' The cut-glass voice had not changed either. 'I trust you had a pleasant journey?' She'd added coldly, 'Caroline tells me she has put you in the primrose room.'

All the attics full, are they? Rhianna had asked silently. The oubliette filled in?

However, she'd smiled, and said, with her best Lady Ariadne drawl, 'It sounds delightful, Mrs Seymour. I'm so glad to be here.'

Then she had turned, still smiling, to the woman sitting opposite. 'Mrs Rawlins, how lovely to see you again. You're looking well.'

Not that it was true. Widowhood had put years and weight on Simon's mother, and given her mouth a sour turn.

'I hear you're making a name for yourself on television, Rhianna?' As opposed to soliciting at Kings Cross, her tone suggested. 'I find so few programmes of any substance these days that I tend to watch very rarely, of course.'

'Of course,' Rhianna had echoed gently.

'Tea will be served in half an hour, Caroline,' her mother had said. 'Please bring your guest to join us,' she'd added, after a brief hesitation.

Rhianna had been glad to escape upstairs to the designated 'primrose room', which turned out to be as charming as its name suggested, its creamy wallpaper and curtains patterned with sprigs of the tiny flowers, and the bed covered in a pretty shade of leaf-green.

Moira Seymour might not be her favourite person, but Rhianna couldn't fault her choice of décor.

Now, she said slowly, 'Your mother's bound to find leaving here a wrench. But it's an awfully big house for two people.'

'True,' Carrie agreed. 'But an even bigger one for a determined bachelor like Diaz. Unless, of course, he does intend to bite the bullet and become a family man.' She paused. 'Did you ever see him with anyone in particular? The times you ran across him in London, that is?'

Rhianna stared at her. She said jerkily, 'Did he tell you we'd met there?'

'He mentioned you'd been at some bash together.' Carrie shrugged. 'Something to do with insurance?'

'Apex, the company sponsoring *Castle Pride*.' Rhianna nodded. 'But it was a very crowded room, so I didn't notice if he had a companion.' *My first lie.*

'And you were both at a first night party for a new play, weren't you?'

'Perhaps. I don't recall.' Rhianna was casually dismissive as she put away the last of her things. She looked at her watch. 'Now, I suppose we'd better go down to the promised tea. But you'd better explain to me first why the swords are crossed and the daggers drawn. I thought Margaret Rawlins and your mother were friends?'

Carrie sighed. 'They were never that close,' she admitted. 'You see, the Rawlins' cottage was originally a second home, and Ma doesn't approve of such things. Cornwall for the Cornish and all that—even though she and Aunt Esther were both Londoners. And the fact that Mrs Rawlins has now moved down here permanently hasn't altered a thing.'

'But that can't be all, surely?'

'No.' Carrie pulled a face. 'When we began discussing wedding plans Margaret opted out completely. Said that whatever we decided would be fine with her. So—we went ahead.'

'Except she changed her mind?' Rhianna guessed.

'And how,' Carrie said fervently. She began to tick off on her fingers. 'We agreed on the guest lists ages ago, but each time we put the numbers in to the caterers she came up with someone else who simply must be invited. That's probably why she's here today—with yet another afterthought. And that's not all. She thought the charge for the marquee was extortionate and insisted we get another quote from a firm she knew, with the result that someone else hired the one I really wanted. Then, last week, Margaret asked with a sad smile if "Lead Kindly Light" could be one of the hymns, because it was "my poor Clive's favourite."' She shook her head. 'It's beautiful, I know, but hardly celebratory. Besides which, all the Order of Service booklets were printed ages ago.'

She took a deep breath. 'There—that's off my chest. Until the next instalment, anyway. And I know there's going to be one. I feel it.'

'Oh God.' Rhianna looked at her with fascinated horror. 'Couldn't Simon have a word with her?'

Carrie sighed again. 'I asked, but Simon's very defensive about his mother. Says she's still mourning his father, which I'm sure is true, and that we must make allowances—especially as we'll be moving so far away.' She paused. 'Anyway, as I said, he seems in a world of his own these days.'

'Oh?' Rhianna picked up her brush and stroked it carefully through her hair, meeting her own watchful gaze in the mirror. 'In what way?'

'Like nearly missing today's hair appointment, for one thing,' Carrie said ruefully. 'And a few times lately I've arranged to ring him at his flat, only he hasn't been there. Says he forgot, and has stuff of his own to do, anyway.'

'Probably hung over after his stag night and doesn't want to admit it,' Rhianna said lightly.

Carrie stared at her. 'But his stag party was ages ago. He went to Nassau with a bunch of guys from work. They got this special deal and stayed for a couple of extra days. Surely I told you?'

'Yes,' Rhianna said. 'Yes, of course you did. I'm an idiot.'

How could I forget? How could I possibly forget the trip to Nassau, when it was only a couple of days later that I found out about the baby?

She put down the brush, aware that her colour had risen swiftly, guiltily, again.

'I keep telling myself that it doesn't matter,' Carrie went on. 'That it will all be over soon and Simon and I will be on our own, making a new life for ourselves. That I'll look back and laugh at all these niggles. Only...'

'Only just for now you'd like to punch Mrs Rawlins' lights out,' Rhianna supplied briskly. 'Perfectly understandable—even commendable.'

'Oh, Rhianna.' Smiling, Carrie slipped an arm through hers. 'Thank heavens you're here. Nothing is going to seem as bad from now on.'

Oh, God, Rhianna thought, her stomach churning as they went downstairs. I just hope and pray that's true.

Her uneasiness increased when the first person she saw in the drawing room was Diaz, lounging in a chair by the open French windows, glancing through a magazine. The new toy, apparently, wasn't as compelling as she'd hoped.

As they came in he rose politely and smiled, but his eyes, slanting a glance at Rhianna, were as hard a grey as Cornish granite. She made herself walk calmly past him, choosing a deep easy chair where he'd be out of her sightline.

But not, unfortunately, eliminated from her consciousness. She was still as aware of him, of his silent, forbidding presence, as if he'd come to stand beside her, his hand on her shoulder.

She had also placed herself at a deliberately discreet distance from the sofas, where the two mothers were ensconced opposite each other—tacitly acknowledging her position as the outsider in this family gathering, but not so far away that she didn't notice there was now a large, flat box beside Margaret Rawlins and wonder about it. But not for long.

'Caroline, dear,' Mrs Rawlins said, as her future daughter-in-law obediently took a seat beside her mother. 'I was thinking the

other day of that old rhyme, "Something old, something new…"
and I remembered the very thing. I wore it at my wedding and
kept it ever since—thinking, I suppose, that one day I'd have a
daughter. But that wasn't to be, of course. So I'd like you to carry
on the tradition instead.'

She lifted the lid of the box and carefully extracted from the
folds of tissue paper inside a mass of white tulle, layer after
layer of it, and a headdress shaped like an elaborate coronet, each
of its ornamental stems crowned by a large artificial pearl.

It looked, Rhianna thought dispassionately, like something the
Wicked Queen might wear in a remake of Disney's *Snow White*.
Only not as good.

In the terrible silence that followed, she did not dare look at
Carrie.

Eventually, Carrie said slowly, 'Well, it's a lovely thought, but
I wasn't actually intending to wear a veil, just some fresh flowers
in my hair. Didn't I explain that?'

'Ah, but a bridal outfit is incomplete without a veil,' said Mrs
Rawlins brightly. 'And although I'm sure your dress is very fash-
ionable and modern, I know Simon is quite old-fashioned at
heart, and he will like to see you in something rather more conventional too.'

She paused. 'You'll have to be very careful with the coronet,
of course. It's extremely delicate, and one of the stems is already
a little loose.'

Rhianna found herself looking at Margaret Rawlins with fascination and some bewilderment. She recalled Simon's mother as
a perfectly pleasant woman, a good cook and devoted to her family,
who had joined in all the local activities with open enjoyment.

So how on earth had she come to turn into the Control Monster?

As for her comments about Simon…

Was it 'old-fashioned' and 'conventional' for a bridegroom to
have been sleeping with someone else for the past three months?
Telling that someone else that he loved her? Inventing that special
deal in the Bahamas in order to be with her for a few stolen days?
And eventually committing the overwhelming error of making
her pregnant?

My God, she thought, a tiny bubble of hysteria welling up inside her. What a truly great tradition to uphold.

She glanced at Carrie and saw her looking anguished, while Moira Seymour's mouth was tight with outrage.

And then the door opened, and Mrs Henderson came in pushing a laden trolley. The tension, perforce, subsided—if only temporarily.

It helped that it was a superb tea, with plates of tiny crustless sandwiches, a platter of scones still warm from the oven, accompanied by a large bowl of clotted cream and a dish of homemade strawberry jam, together with a featherlight Victoria sponge and a large, rich fruitcake.

Mrs Rawlins fussed endlessly about getting the veil back into its protective wrappings before any of it was served—much to Rhianna's regret. A well-aimed cup of tea would obviously have solved that particular problem for good.

So she'd have to think of something else.

As she returned her tea things to the trolley, she casually picked up the coronet and carried it over to the French windows, as if to examine it more closely.

'Oh, do be careful.' Mrs Rawlins' voice followed her. 'As I've said, one of the stems is very fragile.'

'So it is, but I'm sure I can fix that,' Rhianna said brightly, as her fingers discovered that the stem in question had actually become partly detached from the base.

Well, I'm already the least favourite guest, she thought, so what have I to lose? And she gave it a sharp and effective tweak, before gasping loudly in dismay and turning contritely back to the owner.

'Oh, heavens, it's come off altogether now.' Her voice quivered in distress. 'I'm terribly sorry, Mrs Rawlins. I can't believe I could be so clumsy.'

'Let me see it at once.' Margaret Rawlins was on her feet, her face furiously and unbecomingly flushed. 'Perhaps it can be repaired.'

'I doubt it very much.' Diaz had risen too, unexpectedly, and was crossing to Rhianna's side, taking the mutilated object from her hand. 'It looks seriously broken to me. But it's probably better for this to happen now instead of during the ceremony. That would have been really embarrassing.' The smile he turned on the agitated Mrs Rawlins was charm personified. 'Don't you agree?'

'I suppose so,' the older woman returned after a pause, lips compressed. 'But I don't know what Simon will say when he hears.'

Rhianna stared down at the carpet, as if abashed, her long lashes veiling the sudden flare of anger in her eyes. Simon, she thought grimly, has other things on his mind to worry about.

Fussily, Mrs Rawlins picked up the box with the veil. 'You had better take this upstairs, Caroline—before there's another accident,' she added, with a fulminating glance at Rhianna.

'Yes,' Carrie said without enthusiasm. 'Yes, of course.' She glanced appealingly at Rhianna, who picked up the cue and immediately followed her.

'You're a star,' Carrie said simply, tossing the box onto the bed in her room. 'But what the hell am I going to do with a thousand yards of dead white tulle when I'm wearing ivory satin? Look.'

The dress was lovely, Rhianna thought instantly as it was removed from its protective cover and displayed. A simple Empire line sheath, needing no other adornment but Carrie's charming figure inside it.

She considered. 'What flowers are you wearing in your hair?'

'Roses,' Carrie said. 'Gold and cream, like my bouquet.' She took the veil from the box and lifted it up. 'But they won't be substantial enough to hold a weight like this.'

'Then we'll just have to make it manageable.' Rhianna paused. 'Got a sharp pair of scissors handy?'

'Oh, God,' said Carrie. 'What are you going to do?'

'Cement my reputation as the arch-vandal of the western world,' Rhianna told her cheerfully. 'Simon's mother will never speak to me again, of course, but that's a small sacrifice to make.'

Besides, she would have far more powerful reasons to hate me—if she knew...

She took the veil from Carrie and placed it on her own head, studying herself in the full-length mirror. 'Heavens, it swamps me—and I'm taller than you. However, if we just use one layer we'll be able to see your hair through the tulle, and the flowers will help too, of course. Besides, if I'm careful, it can all be sewn back together afterwards,' she added, grinning, and gave Carrie an encouraging push towards the door. 'Now—scissors and sewing kit.'

Left alone, she picked up the dress with immense care and held it in front of her to see the whole effect. She'd use the veil's shortest tier, she thought, as it would only reach Carrie's shoulders and therefore wouldn't detract from the lovely simplicity of the dress itself.

At least she hoped so. After all, she'd had enough costumes practically re-made on her to know what worked and what didn't, she thought drily.

Then paused, staring at herself, suddenly stricken, as she asked herself what she was doing. Why was she taking this trouble over a wedding that shouldn't even be happening? How she could be helping her friend marry a man who had already betrayed her so terribly?

Especially when there was no guarantee that it would never occur again, she thought bitterly. That Simon would suddenly become repentant and faithful.

But he was the husband Carrie had always wanted—had set her heart on from young girlhood. Had waited for. And this wedding was going to be the culmination of all her sweetest dreams.

The image in the mirror was suddenly blurred. Rhianna lifted a hand and quickly wiped away her tears before they could fall on the precious satin. Besides, she thought she heard a movement in the passage outside, and she couldn't risk Carrie coming back to catch her weeping.

Nor could she take the dream of her friend's whole life and smash it. She would have to keep the secret. Pretend she had no idea there had been a hidden love affair. No baby so soon and so finally eliminated from the equation.

And no dream for me, either, she told herself, pain twisting inside her as she put the dress gently back on its padded hanger and covered it.

Out of all that had happened, she thought, that was the hardest
thing to bear. Knowing that she had nothing left to hope for.
And having to live with that knowledge for the rest of her life.

CHAPTER THREE

IT OCCURRED to Rhianna that an excuse to stay out of harm's way in her room was exactly what she'd needed, giving her a chance to catch her breath and regain some of her composure.

Working with immense care, she'd reduced the mass of tulle by two thirds, and the discarded lengths, their raw edges neatly hemmed, were back in the box.

Carrie was reluctantly reconciled to the idea of the shortened version, and by the time Simon's mother discovered what had been done it would be too late. Although the fact that the veil could be subsequently reconstituted in all its voluminous glory might mollify her a little.

Whatever, thought Rhianna. Carrie and I will be long gone anyway, so she'll have to fulminate alone.

But now the time was fast approaching for the next ordeal—a quiet dinner at home with the family. Including, of course, the master of the house.

'The big party's tomorrow evening,' Carrie had told her happily. 'At the Polkernick Arms. We've practically taken the place over.'

Her face had clouded slightly. 'But Simon can't be with us tonight. His godfather and his wife are travelling down from Worcestershire a day early, and Margaret's insisted that he spends the evening at home with them.'

Rhianna had given an inward sigh of relief. At some point, sooner or later, she and Simon would have to face each other, of course. But she'd prefer that to be much, much later.

But his absence was not going to make the occasion any easier for her. Because he was not her only problem, she reminded herself unhappily. There was also Diaz to be confronted yet again, and although there might have been a brief moment's complicity between them in the drawing room earlier, it had been no more than that, and she was totally deluding herself if she believed otherwise.

He would still be gunning for her. Watching her. Waiting for her to make one false move.

So she would have to make damned sure that he was disappointed, she told herself grimly.

And she was armoured for the challenge.

She'd showered, and changed into a silky skirt the colour of indigo, stopped with a white Victorian-style blouse, high-necked and pin-tucked. Demureness itself.

She'd drawn her hair back from her face, securing it at the nape of her neck with a silver clasp, and used the lightest of make-up—a coating of mascara to her long lashes and a touch of colour on her mouth. Nothing more.

She'd accentuated the body lotion used after her shower with a drift of the same fragrance on her throat and wrists, and fixed modest silver studs in her ears.

Neat, she thought, scrutinising herself in the mirror, but not gaudy.

She walked over to the window seat to repack Carrie's sewing basket, and stood for a moment staring out of the window at the grassy headland, the blue ripple of the sea beyond.

It was the last time she would see it like this, because first thing tomorrow they were coming to put up the marquee. So she would take a long, final look now at this view, so familiar and yet at the same time so alien.

So many memories too, she thought wryly, and so few of them to be treasured. In fact, she could almost count them on the fingers of one hand. The feel of the short turf, cool beneath her bare feet as she ran. The hot gritty slide of the sand under her burrowing toes down in the cove, and the eventual, blessed shock of the sea against her heated skin. Misty mornings. Blistering afternoons, lying languid in the shade. All pure nostalgia.

But also tears scalding her eyes, like salt in her throat. And a man's voice saying almost gently, 'What's wrong? There must be something…'

She stirred restlessly. That particular recollection had to go. It had no place in her memory. Not any more.

Perhaps this was really why she was here? she thought. To clear her mind of the past and prepare for a future that in so many ways was looking good. The kind of career many actresses her age could only dream of.

Except her dreams were different, and that was something she had to deal with once and for all.

To accept that she'd been crying for the moon all these years, and that the man she wanted had his own obligations, his own priorities, creating a void between them that could never be crossed.

She turned abruptly away from the window. Took several deep, steadying breaths from her diaphragm, as she did before she began an important scene. She opened her door, stepping into the passage—and ran straight into Simon.

'So there you are.' Abruptly he took her arm, propelling her back into her room and following. 'What's going on, Rhianna? I thought you weren't going to be here. That's what you let me believe, anyway.'

'I told you I hadn't made a decision,' she defended, rubbing the arm he'd grabbed, aware that she was quivering inside, and a lot of it was temper. 'What's the matter, Simon? Conscience troubling you at last?'

'Oh, for God's sake.' His voice was harsh, goaded. 'I made a mistake, that's all. I'm not the first man and I won't be the last to get spooked by the thought of marriage and have a fling before the gates finally shut.'

'A fling?' she echoed bitterly. 'Is that what you call it? It's rather more than that when you tell someone you love her. Make her believe in happy ever after, then dump her, leaving her pregnant with a child she thought you wanted too.'

'Is that why you're here?' he said hoarsely. 'To tell me the termination's been cancelled after all? Or to make some other kind of trouble?'

'No,' she said. 'And—no. Does that put your mind at rest? But understand this, Simon. I'm keeping quiet about this whole hideous mess for Carrie's sake, not yours. You don't deserve her, you appalling creep, and you never have. But you're what she wants.'

'Well,' he said softly, 'she isn't the only one—is she, sweetpea?' He lifted his hand and stroked it insolently down her cheek.

Rhianna flinched away as if she'd been burned. 'Just get out of here,' she said harshly. 'And you'd better make Carrie happy, that's all. Don't ruin her life as well, you complete and utter swine.'

'No,' he said, suddenly sober. 'I won't. Because I really do love her. Maybe it took a stupid, meaningless involvement to teach me how much. To make me realise I couldn't bear to lose her. Can you understand that?'

'I'll never understand you, Simon.' Her glance was cold and level. 'Or anything that's happened in the last months. Not if I live to be a thousand.' She paused. 'And my own loss, of course, doesn't matter,' she added bitterly.

'Come off it, Rhianna.' The mockery was back, coupled with a note of triumph. 'How can you lose what you never had? Get real.' He paused. 'And now, sadly, I must tear myself away. But I'll be back tomorrow, so remember that I'm about to marry your best friend and be nice, hmm?' He gave her a valedictory grin, and departed.

Left alone, Rhianna sank down on the edge of the bed, feeling the inner trembling spread through her body, permeating every nerve, every sinew.

Calm down, she told herself. You've seen Simon. Spoken to him. You don't have to do that again. By now he'll be gone. Tomorrow there'll be a mad rush to get everything done, and avoiding him should be pretty easy. The trick is not to make it too obvious, or Carrie will notice and wonder.

Tonight, you'll simply be—pleasant, speaking only when spoken to. You know how to do that. God knows, you've had plenty of practice over the years, right here in this house, where you'll always be the interloper. The unwanted guest.

And when dinner's over you can yawn, say you're tired after the journey. Make that your excuse for an early night.

But above all you will not—*not*—cry. Certainly not now. But not even tonight, when it's dark, and you're lying on your own, thinking of—him. Trying not to want him and failing miserably. Just as you've done for so many nights in the past. As you'll want to do for the rest of your life.

Having composed herself with an effort before venturing downstairs again, it was something of an anti-climax to walk into the drawing room, her head high, and find it empty.

But the rest of the party were clearly expected, because a tray of drinks, including large jugs of Pimms and home-made lemonade, plus a cooler containing white wine, had been set out on a side table.

The French windows were standing open, and the evening sun was pouring into the room like warm gold, accompanied by the faint whisper of the sea like a siren call.

Rhianna took two steps towards the open air, then paused. However pressing her desire to escape, she was hardly dressed for scrambling over rocks and sand, or for paddling through the creaming shallows of the tide, she reminded herself drily. Far better to stand her ground and hope the evening would pass quickly.

She wandered back towards the wide stone fireplace, and stood looking up at the portraits which flanked it of Tamsin Penvarnon and her Spanish husband.

Carrie had told her all about them one afternoon, when they'd been alone because Simon had been dragged unwillingly to Truro, shopping with his mother.

'Several years after the Armada there was a Spanish raid on Cornwall,' she'd said. 'They burnt Mousehole and Newlyn, but as they were getting away in their galleys there was a fight, and one of their marine captains, Jorge Diaz, was wounded and swept overboard. He was washed up in our cove and Tamsin Penvarnon, the family's only daughter, found him there, half drowned. She had him carried up to the house and nursed him until he recovered.'

She gave an impish grin. 'Then Tamsin found she was having a baby. So she and Captain Diaz got married—only the family put it about that he was really her cousin, one of the Black

Penvarnons from near St Just, in case anyone asked awkward questions. He took the family name, but he and Tamsin called one of their sons Diaz, and the tradition has kept going ever since. So when Uncle Ben and Aunt Esther had a boy, everyone knew what he'd be christened.'

She sighed. 'It's a wonderful story—especially as it turned out that Jorge Diaz's father was one of the *conquistadores* who went to South America and won lots of land and masses of gold, which he left to Jorge's elder brother, Juan. But Juan Diaz got fever and died too, so everything came to Jorge and Tamsin, which is how the Penvarnon fortune started. And, to add to it all, they found enormous mineral deposits on their estates in Chile. Which is why my cousin Diaz is a multimillionaire and we're the poor relations,' she added buoyantly. 'Only Mummy doesn't like me to say that.'

Rhianna digested this. 'Is Mrs Penvarnon—your aunt—dead too?'

'Oh, no.' Carrie shook her head. 'She lives abroad. She just—doesn't come back here.'

'Why not—when it's so beautiful?'

Carrie shrugged. 'I asked Daddy once, and he said that though Mummy and Aunt Esther were both Londoners, some people didn't transplant as well as others. Although Jorge Diaz seemed to manage it,' she added. 'He and Tamsin had their portraits painted when they got rich, and she's wearing the Penvarnon necklace, all gold and turquoise, that he had made for her. Their pictures are in the drawing rooms. One day when no one's around I'll show them to you.'

Carrie had been as good as her word, Rhianna recalled, and she'd stood enthralled as she gazed up at the long-ago lovers—he with the kind of saturnine good-looks to die for, and she a red-gold beauty with vivid blue eyes.

Now, as she took another look, the resemblance between Diaz Penvarnon and his Spanish ancestor was truly amazing, she acknowledged with reluctance once again. Shave the black pointed beard, replace the snowy ruff with an open-necked shirt and substitute a mobile phone for the sword Don Jorge's hand was resting on with such stunning authority, and they could be twins.

Both of them adventurers too, she thought. Their eyes looking outward with challenge, seeking new worlds to conquer and fresh fortunes to be made.

Had Tamsin known what she was taking on that day in the cove? she wondered. Or had she ever sighed for a more settled existence?

She moved slightly closer. Tamsin hadn't the expression of a lady who suffered from doubts. Her eyes and faint smile held the same proud certainty as that of her husband. One hand toyed with an elaborate feathered fan, while the other pointed beringed fingers at the dramatic chain of turquoises, set in gold, that surrounded her neck, its single pendant stone, encircled by pearls, nestling enticingly in the valley between her breasts.

'It used to be kept in that display case over there on the table,' Carrie had told her, as they'd stood gazing that first time. 'But there were problems with insurance, so Uncle Ben decided it should live in the bank. Penvarnon brides always wear it on their wedding days, so I suppose we'll have to wait for Diaz to get married before it comes out again.' She'd darted across the room to the table in question. 'But the fan's still here, if you want to have a look.'

I should have stuck at looking, Rhianna recalled ruefully, but the temptation to take the lovely thing from its satin bed and hold it had been too strong.

And as she'd touched it something strange had happened to her, as if the simple action of unfurling a fan and waving it smoothly and languidly had transformed her into a different person—a grown woman, aware of the power of her own beauty. She'd moved slowly across the room, her walk a glide, glancing from left to right under her lashes, as if acknowledging the admiration she aroused.

She'd thought since that that was the moment when she'd known with absolute certainty she would become an actress. That she might be able to hide from her intrinsic loneliness by becoming other people.

At the time, she'd spun round on her toe, laughing almost shamefacedly at her own silly fantasies—only to look past Carrie and see Moira Seymour standing grim-faced in the doorway, with Diaz Penvarnon just behind her.

'How dare you?' The older woman's voice had been molten with anger. 'How dare you touch anything in this house, you little—?'

'It's not her fault,' Carrie broke in staunchly. 'I told her she could.'

'Then you had no right, Caroline.' Her mother turned on her furiously. 'This is a Penvarnon family heirloom, not some cheap toy to be passed around and played with. In future, the case will be locked. And this girl should not be in the house, anyway. I gave strict instructions about that.' She took a step forward, her hand outstretched, her eyes fixed inimically on Rhianna's white face. 'Now, give it back and get out. And believe me—you haven't heard the last of this.'

'I haven't done anything to it.' The words came out all wrong. They sounded sullen when she'd meant them to be apologetic and reassuring. 'I wouldn't.' She glanced up at the portrait. 'I just wanted to hold it because it was hers, and she's so beautiful.'

Diaz Penvarnon said with quiet authority, 'It's all right, Aunt Moira. I'll deal with this.' He moved past Mrs Seymour and took the fan carefully from Rhianna's numb fingers.

He said, 'You might not mean to harm it, but it's very old and consequently extremely fragile.' He looked at Mrs Seymour. 'And, as I said when I was last here, it properly belongs in a good costume museum. I shall see to that.'

There was a silence, then Moira Seymour said, openly reluctant, 'Of course—if that is what you wish.'

'Yes,' he said. 'It is.' He replaced the fan gently in the case and closed the glass lid. 'There,' he added. 'No real harm done. Now, off you go, both of you, and we'll say no more about it.'

He'd been as good as his word, Rhianna thought. The expected tongue-lashing from Aunt Kezia had never materialised. And the glass case and its contents had been removed from the drawing room and taken away in a van a few days later.

'Mummy's in a fearful temper about it,' Carrie had reported dolefully. 'She used to like pointing it out to visitors—our genuine Elizabethan relic. And now she can't. And she got even more cross when Daddy said the fan belonged to Diaz's ancestors, not ours, and he was entitled to dispose of it as he saw fit.'

She paused, then looked more cheerful. 'He also said that barring you from the house was the kind of stupid, unkind rule which was bound to be broken, and he was only surprised it hadn't happened before. He said that Diaz thought so too. So we don't have to worry about that any more.'

Rhianna knew they almost certainly did, but kept quiet about it anyway.

Now, all this long time later, nothing had changed, she admitted with an inward sigh. She allowed herself one long, last look at Tamsin, a woman who had fought for and won the man she loved—but not, she thought wryly, without breaking the rules of her own time. Then she turned away—only to halt with a stifled gasp.

Diaz was standing in the French windows, one shoulder negligently propped against the frame as he watched her silently.

She said unevenly, 'You—you startled me.'

'Not as much as I'd hoped,' he said. 'Or you'd have stayed away.'

Rhianna bit her lip. She said tautly, 'I meant that I didn't know you were there.'

'You were lost in thought,' he said. 'Clearly those portraits fascinate you just as much now as they seemed to when you were a child.'

She shrugged. 'They tell a fascinating story.' She paused. 'And that's an amazing necklace. I wonder why he chose to give her turquoises?'

'The turquoise is said to represent the connection between the sky and the sea,' he said. 'Which makes it an appropriate stone for a Cornishwoman.'

'Ah,' she said. 'Well, I was rather hoping you'd lend it to Carrie for her wedding, so I'd get the chance to see it in reality.'

'I'm sorry,' he said, without a hint of regret. 'It's to be worn by Penvarnon brides only, as a symbol of constancy and faithfulness in marriage.' His brief smile was unamused. 'Which rather puts it out of the running— wouldn't you say?'

'I think Carrie would be a loyal and wonderful wife for any man,' Rhianna said.

'Of course,' he said. 'I was actually referring to the groom, in this instance, as I'm sure you of all people should realise.'

She didn't look at him. 'Whatever. The decision is yours, naturally. And, as I can't see myself on the guest list when you tie the knot, I'll just have to resign myself to admiring the necklace only through oil on canvas.' She paused again. 'I hope the fan found a good home in the end?'

'Ah, yes,' he said. 'With so much else going on I'd almost forgotten about that particular incident. However, I can assure you that it has indeed been well taken care of ever since.'

He walked forward into the room. 'But I'm forgetting my duties as host, and that will never do,' he added courteously. 'May I get you a drink? Some Pimms, perhaps?'

It was the perfect drink for a warm evening, and Rhianna longed to say yes, but common sense warned that she needed to keep her wits about her, unclouded by alcohol.

She said, 'Thank you, but I think I'll stick to lemonade.'

There was an odd pause. He looked at her, his mouth hardening, then said, 'Yes—of course,' turning almost abruptly to the drinks tray.

Ice cubes chinked in the tall glass as he poured the lemonade and brought it to her.

'So, what shall we drink to?' He raised his own glass in a parody of a toast. 'Our happy couple? Or your continued good health? More necessary than ever now, I should imagine.'

Rhianna's brows lifted sharply. 'Why do you say that?'

He shrugged. 'The shooting schedule for your series must be fairly hectic. You couldn't afford a lengthy absence for any reason—especially when there must be dozens of other pretty faces manoeuvring to take your place in front of the camera.'

'Thank you for reminding me. I expect there are hundreds.' The lemonade, cold and tangy without bitterness, soothed the dryness of her mouth. 'But I manage to stay reasonably fit. I won't need a replacement yet awhile.'

'But there's bound to come a time when that will happen,' Diaz countered. 'The viewing public is notoriously fickle in its affections. So, will there be life after *Castle Pride*?'

'I'm touched by your concern,' she said curtly. 'However, I'm not ready for the scrapheap in the foreseeable future. Unless you've bought a controlling share in the production company, of course, and even then you'd have a fight on your hands.'

'No,' he said softly. 'You're not the type to go quietly, Rhianna. You've made that more than clear.'

There was something in his voice that sent all her antennae quivering again. But as she stared at him, questions tumbling around in her head, the door opened and Carrie came in, face flushed and eyes sparkling. But not with happiness.

'I don't believe it,' she burst out furiously. 'I just don't. After everything else—now this!'

'What's happened?' Rhianna moved to her swiftly.

'Mrs Rawlins,' said Carrie, in a voice that managed to combine anger with despair. '*She's* happened—again.'

'Don't tell me,' Rhianna said quickly, trying to coax her to smile. 'She's found out about the veil and she's planning to sue.'

But Carrie was not to be cajoled. 'She informed us before she left that she'd invited Simon's godparents specially early so that they could come out to dinner with us tomorrow—in order to meet everybody. And said how much they were looking forward to it.'

She spread her hands dramatically. 'Mother immediately explained that the Polkernick Arms can only seat so many people, but she said that she was sure if we all squeezed up a little they could accommodate two more. But they can't, and they won't. I know it.'

Rhianna gave her a comforting hug. 'Well, Simon will just have to talk to his mother. Make her see reason.'

'Unlikely,' Carrie said with unusual brusqueness. 'She's already persuaded him that the guest list is heavily loaded in our family's favour. He'll say we have to fit them in, even if it means cancelling the Arms and finding a bigger restaurant. Something that's already been hinted at,' she added on a note of doom. 'But there's nowhere—not at this late stage anyway.'

They were joined by Moira Seymour, looking thoroughly harassed. 'The manageress won't budge.' She addressed Carrie. 'We're already at the maximum the regulations allow, as I tried to tell that impossible woman earlier. What on earth are we going to do? We can't ask other people to drop out to make room for them.'

'No,' Diaz said unexpectedly. 'But in an emergency you can

always find volunteers.' He looked at Rhianna, his mouth smiling coolly. 'Well, Miss Carlow,' he said softly. 'Will you help save the situation for Carrie tomorrow evening by giving up the party and having dinner on your own with me instead? What do you say?'

There was the kind of silence that seemed to last for ever.

Bombshell at the end of Act Two, Rhianna thought, with a kind of detachment. Cast reaction, followed by slow curtain. Old-fashioned, but effective.

For instance, she could see that Carrie's mouth had formed into an 'o' of pure astonishment, while her mother appeared to have turned into an ice sculpture. She found that she herself had become rooted to the spot, bereft of words, but numbingly aware of the mockery in Diaz Penvarnon's grey eyes as he watched her. Waiting for her response.

Moira Seymour found her voice first. 'But that's quite impossible,' she declared. 'It's awfully good of you, of course, Diaz, but you're Carrie's cousin. She's being married from your house. You can't possibly miss the family dinner.'

'If you recall, it was by no means certain that I was even coming to the wedding.' Diaz's tone was dry. 'And I doubt I'll be here for the ceremony even now. But the occasion will still go ahead without me.' He paused. 'And I believe Rhianna was a late entry to the guest list too,' he added gently. 'Which would seem to make us an ideal pairing.'

'Except that it's totally absurd,' Moira Seymour said angrily. 'You can't possibly want…' She paused, as if realising her next comment might be infelicitous. 'I mean, I can't allow you to sacrifice yourself like this, my dear Diaz. Miss Carlow—Rhianna—wouldn't expect it.'

'Please don't regard me as some kind of victim.' He sounded amused. 'Perhaps you don't realise there isn't a man in England who wouldn't jump at the chance of dinner à deux with television's top fantasy woman.'

Isn't there? thought Rhianna. *Isn't there?* Because I can think of one standing only a few feet away right now. So why are you doing this? *Why?*

'Besides, just think of the moral victory you'll score over

Margaret Rawlins,' he went on. 'Arming for a battle and finding it's been cancelled. All the Brownie points for good behaviour to our side, and only at the cost of two new place-cards.'

He turned to Rhianna. 'I know you must be disappointed at missing out, but comfort yourself with the knowledge that you've headed off yet another difficulty at this happy time, and can bask in the bridegroom's undying gratitude.'

He allowed an instant's silence for her to digest this, then smiled at her charmingly. 'So, are you prepared to make this sacrifice, Rhianna—for Simon's sake, if nothing else?'

She met his gaze, hard and metallic, like silver. Read its challenge, which held no charm at all.

'Put like that,' she said coldly and clearly, 'how can I possibly refuse?'

His smile widened. 'Oh, I'm sure we can both think of a number of ways,' he said softly.

He turned to Moira Seymour, whose expression was still set in stone. 'I suggest Rhianna goes with you to the hotel for a token appearance at the pre-dinner drinks, which will thrill the *Castle Pride* fans, and then I'll whisk her away before the management start counting heads. Agreed?'

'I suppose so.' It was Carrie who spoke, her tone reluctant. She walked over to Rhianna and slid an arm through hers. 'Although it's the last thing I'd planned—to have two of my favourite people missing.' She frowned fiercely. 'But it's a solution to a problem that should never have arisen, and I shall tell Simon so.'

'Well, don't be too fierce.' Diaz smiled at her. 'Or he might change his mind and not turn up on Saturday.'

She relaxed, grinning back at him. 'Never in this world,' she said.

While Rhianna, her own face expressionless, drank some lemonade and felt it turn to pure acid in her throat.

CHAPTER FOUR

THE dinner that followed was not the easiest Rhianna had ever sat through, although the watercress soup, the ducklings with kumquats, and the crème brûlée which rounded off the meal were all flawless.

At another time she'd have been irritated by Moira Seymour's faintly fretful monologue about the wedding, and the problems arising from it, all attributable to Margaret Rawlins, a subject from which she refused to be diverted despite her husband and daughter's best efforts.

But Rhianna was simply thankful not to be required either to contribute or even to listen.

On the other hand, she realised tautly, an absorbing conversation on some neutral topic might have proved a distraction from the presence of Diaz, equally silent, on the other side of the table.

When coffee had been drunk he excused himself, pausing briefly beside Rhianna's chair on his way to the door. His brief smile did not reach his eyes. 'Until tomorrow evening, then. At the hotel.'

She made herself look back at him. 'Yes,' she said. 'Of course. Until then.'

And only she was aware that the hand replacing her cup on its saucer was not entirely steady.

'You didn't eat much at dinner,' Carrie commented critically, as the pair of them walked on the headland later, enjoying the cool, moonlit stillness. 'But be warned—you're not allowed to be ill—not just before my big day.'

'I think I'm just a little tense,' Rhianna admitted, trying to inject some lightness into her tone. 'Thinking more about tomorrow night's meal instead.'

'It'll be fine,' Carrie consoled her. 'In fact, though I hate to admit it, you'll probably be far better off elsewhere.' She grimaced. 'This family dinner promises to be tricky in the extreme, accompanied by a strong whiff of burning martyrs. And after all,' she added, 'it's not the first time Diaz has taken you out to dinner à deux.'

Rhianna stared at her, her throat tightening. 'What do you mean?'

'Your birthday treat,' Carrie prompted. 'You can't have forgotten the high note of your early teens? I've never been so jealous in my life.'

'No,' Rhianna said quietly after a pause. 'I—hadn't forgotten.' She looked up at the sky. 'I might walk down to the cove before I turn in. I love seeing the moon on the water. Want to come?'

'Not in these heels,' Carrie demurred. 'And you take care, too,' she added severely. 'I'm not having you hobbling into church with a broken ankle either.'

'All right, Granny,' Rhianna said meekly, and dodged, laughing.

A broken ankle would heal, she thought as she made her way down the track. But what do you do about a breaking heart? And how do you prevent the ache of all the lonely years ahead of you?

Shoes in hand, she walked down the beach until she reached a particular flat rock, and sat down, looking at the sea, smooth as glass in the moonlight.

Nothing to be seen this time. No movement in the water. No dark head, sleek and glossy as a seal's, breaking its surface in the glitter of the late afternoon sun of that long ago day.

Although she'd been too immersed in her own unhappiness to notice anything around her. Or not immediately, anyway.

Her thirteenth birthday, she'd been thinking with desolation. And no one had remembered. She'd received no presents. Not even a card. And Aunt Kezia hadn't even wished her Many happy

returns of the day. While Carrie, who would at least have sung
'Happy Birthday', was away on a school field trip.

She'd waited in vain all day for something—anything. A token
recognition of this milestone in her young life. Disappointment and
hurt had built up inside her as she'd remembered past birthdays.

Her mother had always made them special, she thought.
Magical. Parties for her schoolfriends, including more recently
a theatre matinee, and a hilarious trip to an ice rink. Always a
cake with candles, and the warmth of arms round her. The knowledge that she was loved and treasured.

She'd tried hard to be brave, telling herself it didn't matter that
the day had been ignored this time. That next year it would be
different. Knowing that it probably wouldn't.

Until eventually she'd escaped down to the cove, the place
where she'd been happiest since she arrived at Penvarnon, and
once there, sitting on her favourite rock, had found her eyes
blurring as she was suddenly tipped over some edge into a morass
of loneliness and pain, where tears were the only relief.

And once she'd started to cry it had been impossible to stop,
and she'd lain, hunched and shaking with her sobs, on the hard,
flat surface.

She'd been pushing herself upright again, hiccupping a little
as she tried to drag a strand of drenched hair away from her face,
when she saw him.

Saw Diaz Penvarnon emerging from the sea, completely nude,
the salt drops glistening on his body as he strode through the
shallows to the beach, as unaware of her presence as she'd been
of his. Until then.

The sound she had made, however, a small choking cry of
shock and embarrassment, had brought his head round sharply,
and he'd stared at her, brows snapping together.

He'd said, with a kind of resignation, 'Oh, God,' then walked
to the folded towel waiting on a patch of shingle, winding it
swiftly round his lower body.

Then he'd walked across to her, grim-faced. 'Rhianna
Carlow,' he said. 'What the hell are you doing here?'

'I wanted to be by myself,' she said huskily. Her eyes were

gummed with weeping, and her face was hot with mortification as she pressed her hands to her cheeks. 'I thought all your visitors had gone and you'd left as well.'

'Didn't you see there was someone swimming and figure they might like some privacy too?' he asked harshly, then paused, his attention arrested as he saw her distress. He went on more gently. 'Come on, it's not that bad, surely? You must have seen a man without his clothes before?'

She hadn't, as it happened, but she didn't say so.

'It—it's not that.' She swallowed another sob.

'Then what's wrong?' He was frowning again, but as if he were puzzled rather than angry. 'There must be something.' He sat down beside her, his hand cool and damp on her shoulder through the thin tee shirt. 'Don't cry any more. Tell me.'

She bent her head, her voice catching on the words. 'It's my birthday—I'm thirteen—and no one remembered...'

He said, almost blankly, 'Dear God.' Then he was silent for so long that she glanced at him, wondering, and saw the tanned face hard and set as he stared at the sea.

She felt nervous again, and moved restively, dislodging his hand. She said haltingly, 'I'm sorry. I'm stopping you getting dressed. I—I'll go. My aunt will be looking for me.'

'Doubtful,' he said. 'In the extreme. But don't run away. I've got an idea that might improve matters.' He added drily, 'And my clothes are in The Cabin, so you don't have to worry. I won't be blighting your adolescence a second time.' He sent her a brief, taut smile. 'So, wait here until I'm decent again, and we'll walk back to the house together.'

She had a belated but pretty fair idea of what she must look like, and was tempted to ignore his instructions and bolt while he was in The Cabin getting dressed. But something told her that he, at least, was trying to be kind, so it was only good manners to wait and hear what he had to say.

She did what she could, scrubbing fiercely at her face with her sodden hanky, and combing her hair with her fingers.

When he came out of The Cabin, she joined him, eyes down, and they walked up the track side by side.

He took her straight round to the stable block, where Miss Trewint was cleaning the paintwork on their front entrance.

She checked, her lips thinning. 'Rhianna, where have you been? I hope and pray you haven't been making a nuisance of yourself again.'

'On the contrary,' Diaz said. 'I found her in the cove, like a sea urchin on a rock, and she's been excellent company. So much so that, with your permission, I'd like to take her out to dinner to celebrate her birthday.'

He paused, and the older woman gazed at him open-mouthed, her face warming with undisguised annoyance.

'Unless you have something else planned, of course,' he added smoothly. 'No? I thought not.' He turned to Rhianna, who was also staring at him, dumbfounded and totally lost for words, but with an odd little tendril of disbelieving joy unfurling inside her too.

'Wash your face, sea urchin,' he directed. 'And I'll be back around six-thirty to collect you.'

Kezia Trewint found her voice. 'Mr Penvarnon, this is nonsense. There's absolutely no need for you to go to all this trouble…'

'Now, there we disagree.' His smile held charm, but it was also inexorable, and Rhianna felt a faint shiver between her shoulder-blades. 'So—six-thirty. Don't be late.' And he was gone.

Alone in the moonlight, Rhianna let herself remember…

Aunt Kezia, of course, had not bothered to disguise her anger and bitterness at this turn of events.

'Barely out of childhood, and already throwing yourself at a man.' She chewed at the words and spat them out. 'And a Penvarnon man at that. The shame of it. And he must have taken leave of his senses.'

'I didn't throw myself,' Rhianna protested. 'He felt sorry for me and was kind. That's all.'

'Because you told him the suffering orphan tale, I suppose? All big eyes and no bread in the house.' Miss Trewint scrubbed at the paintwork as if determined to reach the bare wood beneath it. 'And what will Mrs Seymour have to say when she hears? We'll be lucky to keep our place here.'

Rhianna stared at her. 'Mr Penvarnon wouldn't let us be sent away—not for something he'd done,' she protested.

'So you think you know him that well, do you?' Miss Trewint gave a harsh laugh. 'Well—like mother, like daughter. I should have known.' She paused. 'You'd better get ready, if you're going. You can't keep him waiting.'

Rhianna went up to the flat. Whatever Aunt Kezia said, she thought rebelliously, she wasn't going to allow it to spoil the evening ahead—the prospect of being taken out to dinner as if she was grown-up.

But she couldn't entirely dismiss the older woman's unpleasant remarks, especially when she recalled Carrie's reluctant confidences.

She knew in her heart that Grace Carlow had been a good and loving person, and that she couldn't have—wouldn't have—done anything wrong. All the same there was a mystery there, and one day she would get to the bottom of it and clear her mother's name.

But common sense told her that she must wait until she was older for her questions to be taken seriously.

She had a quick bath and washed her hair, being careful not to use too much hot water, while she mused on what to wear.

She would have given anything to have a cupboard full of the kind of clothes her classmates wore outside school, at the weekends and at holiday times, she thought wistfully, but her aunt considered serviceable shorts and tee shirts, with a pair of jeans for cooler days, an adequate wardrobe for her. And she couldn't even contemplate what Kezia Trewint would have said about the make-up and jewellery the other girls took for granted.

Which only left her school uniform dresses, still relatively new, full-skirted and square necked in pale blue.

Sighing, she put one of them on, slipped her feet into her black regulation shoes, brushed her cloud of hair into relative submission and went downstairs to wait for him.

He was a few minutes late, and for a stricken moment she wondered if he'd had second thoughts. Then he came striding across the stable yard with a set look to his mouth which suggested that Moira Seymour might indeed have had something to say about his plan.

But his face relaxed when he saw her, and he said, 'You're looking good, Miss Carlow. Shall we go?'

His car was wonderful, low, sleek and clearly powerful, but he kept its power strictly harnessed as he negotiated the narrow high-hedged lanes leading out of Polkernick with a sure touch.

It wasn't a long journey—just a few miles down the coast to another village built on a steep hill overlooking a harbour. The restaurant was right on the quay, occupying the upper storey of a large wooden building like a boathouse, and reached by an outside staircase.

Inside, it was equally unpretentious, with plain wooden tables and chairs, and the menu and wine list chalked up on blackboards.

There were quite a few people eating already, but a table for two had been reserved by the window with a view of the harbour, and a girl in tee shirt and jeans came to light the little lamp in its glass shade which stood in middle of the table, and take their order for drinks.

A combination of excitement and her crying jag had made Rhianna thirsty, and she asked shyly for water.

'Bring a jug for both of us, please, Bethan. Ice, but no lemon,' Diaz directed. 'And just a half-bottle of the Chablis I had last time.'

He smiled at Rhianna. 'It's a seafood place,' he said. 'I suppose I should have asked if you like fish.'

'I like everything,' she said simply, adding, 'Except tripe.'

'That's not a taste I've acquired either.' He paused. 'Ever had lobster?'

Mutely, she shook her head.

'Then that's what we'll have,' he said.

And so they did—plain and grilled, with a tossed green salad, a bowl of tiny sauté potatoes, and a platter of fresh, crusty bread. It was preceded by a delicate shrimp mousse, and when the wine came Diaz poured a very small amount into another glass and handed it to her.

'To Rhianna,' he said, raising his own glass. 'On her birthday.'

She sipped the wine carefully, and thought it was like tasting sunshine and flowers.

Her pudding was a raspberry tartlet with clotted cream, carried ceremoniously to the table by a stout man with a large apron over his blue check trousers who, Diaz told her, was the owner and chef, Morris Trencro. In the middle was a tiny ornamental holder, with a lighted candle for her to make a wish, then blow out.

'No room for the proper thirteen, maiden,' Mr Trencro said. 'But reckon you won't mind that.'

What was more, he began singing 'Happy Birthday,' in a strong baritone, and at his signal the rest of the customers joined in, turning to smile at this young red-haired girl whose eyes were shining more brightly than any candle flame.

And then they'd driven home, as decorously as they'd come.

There had been a moon that night too, thought Rhianna, and Diaz had put quiet, beautiful music—Debussy, she thought—on the CD player. And what with that, all the gorgeous food and that little drop of wine, she'd had to fight to stay awake, because she didn't want to miss a single moment of her heavenly evening.

Of course, there had been repercussions later, she recalled wryly. Not from Aunt Kezia, oddly enough, although that was probably due to the brief, private interview Diaz had had with her in the sitting room after he'd brought her home.

But Moira Seymour had seemed to develop another layer of ice whenever she saw her.

And worst of all, she thought, was when she'd returned to school in September and found herself the object of unwanted and unwarranted attention from some of the older girls.

'My sister Bethan saw you at the Boathouse in Garzion with Diaz Penvarnon,' Lynn Dellow had announced, looking Rhianna up and down. 'She says he was making a big fuss about your birthday, and pouring wine down you. She says you were wearing your yucky school dress and looked a proper sight.' She giggled. 'I thought Mr Penvarnon liked ladies his own age, not little schoolgirls.'

'That's a disgusting thing to say,' Rhianna told her hotly. 'It wasn't like that. I—I didn't have many birthday presents, and so he gave me a treat, that's all.'

'Did he try and snog you on the way home?' someone else asked eagerly.

'No.' Shocked and upset, Rhianna felt her face turn the colour of a peony. 'No, of course not. That's rubbish. He wouldn't do anything like that.' And suddenly she remembered the night when she'd inadvertently glimpsed him on the terrace, intimately entwined with that girl, and how it had made her feel. How she'd found herself guiltily wondering what it would be like to be kissed—caressed—in that way by a man...

'Bet you wish he had, though,' said Lynn. She sighed gustily. 'Sex on a stick, that one.'

'Well, you're quite wrong.' Rhianna lifted her chin, dismissing the inconvenient jolt to her memory. 'As it happens, Diaz Penvarnon is the last man in the world I'd ever fancy.'

There was some derisive laughter, and a couple of girls looked at her as if she'd grown an extra head.

'Pretty high and mighty for a nobody, aren't we?' Lynn said critically. 'So who's your dream man, Lady Muckcart?'

Rhianna swallowed. She had to say something—name someone—if only to get them to stop talking about Diaz in that horrible way, which made her burn everywhere all over again.

'Simon Rawlins, actually,' she said, adding, 'If you must know.'

After all, she told herself defensively, it wasn't that much of a lie. Who wouldn't want Simon? And hadn't she been secretly hoping she might run into him in the village again some time?

'That tasty blond bit who comes down here every summer?' Lynn stared at her. 'Lives at the top of the village? Thought he hung around with Carrie Seymour.'

'Not all the time,' Rhianna tossed back over her shoulder, as the bell sounded and she walked away.

'That wouldn't stop her,' she heard someone say. 'Takes after her mother, I dare say.' And there was more laughter.

And she hadn't had the courage to turn back and say, What are you talking about? What do you mean?

But even without that her image of Diaz smiling at her across the table had become blurred, as if it had been touched by a hand dipped in slime.

And her precious birthday celebration had been spoiled—tainted, she thought, with a sigh that was almost a sob.

She recovered herself with a start, and slid down from the rock, smoothing her skirt. Bed for you, my girl, she told herself, with a touch of harshness. Before you get maudlin, remembering a time when he could be kind.

Because tomorrow night, when you have dinner with him for the last time, kindness will be the last thing on his mind and you know it.

Ten years on, at least she didn't have the same problems over her wardrobe, she thought wryly, as she viewed herself in the mirror the following evening.

She'd decided to wear the dress she'd originally planned for that night, a wrap-around style in a dark green silky fabric, which accentuated the colour of her eyes. The skirt reached mid-calf, the sleeves were three-quarter length, and its cross-over bodice revealed a discreet plunge.

She'd slept badly the previous night, and she'd been jumpy all day, thankful for all the tiny last-minute tasks that she'd been able to help with, while all the time she was turning her mind by sheer force of will away from the prospect of the evening ahead of her.

But now the time was nearly here. In less than an hour, she thought, glancing at her watch, she'd be setting off for the Polkernick Arms in one of the taxis that had been ordered.

Where Diaz would be waiting…

She drew a deep breath as she fastened her prettiest earrings—small gold hoops studded with tiny emeralds—into her lobes. She still couldn't fathom the actual motive behind his invitation. If she was feeling charitable, she might attribute it to his wish to solve the Seymours' unexpected problem and save them further embarrassment.

But charity isn't the name of the game, she told herself silently. For either of us.

She took one long, final look, checking that the pink polish on her finger and toenails was still immaculate, and that her make-up was understated but effective.

Then she collected the green patent purse that matched her elegant strappy sandals and went downstairs.

There was the usual momentary hush as she entered the drawing room, and she knew that many of the older people in the room would be looking at her and seeing someone else entirely—her mother, Grace Carlow.

Knew too that someone would be saying in an undertone, 'But you must remember—all that appalling scandal. That's why Esther won't be here. She doesn't come near the place. Hasn't done for years now. Poor Moira must be devastated.'

The devastated Moira simply gave her a look and turned away, but Francis Seymour came over to her with a smile. 'Every inch a star, Rhianna,' he told her kindly. He handed her a glass of pale sherry. 'I hope this is to your taste. You look like a *fino* girl to me.'

She laughed. 'You guessed right.' She raised the glass. 'Here's to the family gathering. I hope it goes well.'

He gave her a dry look. 'I would not put money on it, but we shall see.' He sighed suddenly. 'Sometimes I wish that Carrie hadn't been quite so single-minded about her future. That she'd had other serious boyfriends besides Simon. Oh, I've nothing against the boy. But she was so very young—hardly more than a child—when she decided he was the one, as, of course, you know, which is why I can mention it to you.'

'Yes,' she said. She cleared her throat. 'I think—I believe that sometimes it can happen like that. You meet someone—and you know. And that's it—for ever. No questions. No second thoughts.' She stared down at her glass. 'So then you have to hope that he feels the same.'

She took another steadying breath, praying that her voice would not shake. 'And Simon clearly does, which is why there's going to be a wedding tomorrow.'

'And you, Rhianna?' he said gently. 'When are we going to be invited to your wedding?'

She managed another laugh. 'Oh, I'm an impossible case. Married to my career, as they say. On the other hand, I might meet someone at tomorrow's reception. You never know.'

'No,' he said. He gave her a reflective look. 'Although there was a time when I thought I did.' He paused. 'But now I see my wife beckoning, so I must go.'

Rhianna put down the sherry glass untouched. Carrie's father was a shrewd man, she thought, her stomach churning. What had he been trying to say just then? That he'd once seen something—and guessed how she felt…?

No, she thought. Please, no. Let it stay a secret for just a little while longer. Another twenty-four hours and I'll be gone for good. And no one need ever know—anything.

The initial free-for-all at the Polkernick Arms had some of the overtones of the Montagues versus the Capulets, Rhianna thought detachedly, with the Seymours and Penvarnons on one side of the private bar, and Clan Rawlins on the other. It was to be hoped that the knives in the dining room weren't that sharp, or there could be mayhem.

She was keeping strictly to the edge of the room, away from the small charmed circle of well-wishers where Carrie stood, her arm through Simon's.

She hadn't looked at him, or he at her, while they'd murmured their conventional and meaningless greetings to each other.

Would there ever come a time when she could look at him and see simply Carrie's husband? Maybe one day—once time and distance had done their work. Or that was all she could hope.

She knew, of course, the exact moment that Diaz arrived, and for a blinding instant she wished with real savagery that she could turn back the clock and wipe out the past months with their burden of lies, secrets and shame.

That she could turn and see him standing in the doorway and be free to walk to him, smiling, and say in her turn, 'Diaz—it's been a long time.' And offer him her hand, or even her cheek. That she could see the silver eyes warm with surprise—and something more…

That it could be a beginning, and not an end.

Except that it was too late for that. Too much had happened.

Now, she could hear the buzz as he worked his way round the room. Knew when he'd paused to shake hands and hold a brief conversation with another guest, even as she herself listened politely to the elderly woman beside her. As she responded gracefully to what the other was saying about her favourite characters in *Castle Pride*, with Lady Ariadne very clearly not included among them.

Felt her heart quicken and her mouth dry as he reached her.

'Rhianna,' he said silkily. 'You take my breath away. This evening will be a real privilege.'

She watched him looking at her, frankly assimilating the way her dress clung to her breasts and hips. How the sash reduced her waist to a handspan.

'Allow me to return the compliment,' she returned crisply. One swift glance had been enough to inform her of his immaculately cut dark suit, the crisp whiteness of his shirt, and the sombre silk magnificence of his crimson tie.

'I'm sorry I'm a little late. I had some business to attend to.' He paused. 'Is there anyone else you wish to speak to? Or may I steal you away now?'

Rhianna shrugged. 'We're having a duty dinner,' she said. 'It's hardly an elopement.'

'Then let's go,' he said. 'Before we're arrested and charged with criminal damage to a tiara. I saw Mrs Rawlins bristle as I walked in.' He took her hand and smiled at her companion. 'Will you excuse us?'

She looked arch. 'With pleasure,' she said. 'And may I say you make a very handsome couple?'

No, Rhianna wanted to scream. You may say nothing of the kind. In fact you aren't even allowed to think it. And if the ground would open and swallow me, I'd regard it as a blessing.

But the floor remained in its usual robust state as she walked across it to the door, hand in hand with Diaz Penvarnon, acutely aware of the curious stares and whispers following them.

In the foyer, she detached herself coolly and firmly. 'We really don't have to do this,' she said. 'We can part company here and now and no one will be any the wiser.'

'So what's your alternative?' Diaz asked softly. 'Mourning your loss over a solitary scampi and chips at the White Hart?' He shook his head. 'No way, Rhianna. I asked you to have dinner with me, and the invitation stands—however distasteful you may find it.'

She hesitated, then reluctantly followed him out of the hotel. She glanced around her. 'I don't see the Jeep.'

'It was needed elsewhere,' he said. 'Besides, it's a beautiful evening. I thought we'd walk. Will your shoes allow that?'

'Of course.' But where on earth could they be going? she asked herself in bewilderment. The hotel, the pub, Rollo's Café, plus the fish and chip shop in Quay Street constituted Polkernick's entire claim to gourmet fame, as far as she was aware.

It was only when they reached the harbour and she looked out across the water to the sleek, beautiful motor yacht, riding there at anchor, dwarfing everything around it, that she realised.

'Your boat?' Her voice rose as she turned to him. 'You expect me to have dinner on your boat?'

'Why, yes.' He smiled at her. 'It's like a millpond out there, Rhianna. You can't be that poor a sailor. And I have an excellent chef, so what's the problem?'

You are, she thought, and I am. I'd prefer not to be quite so alone with you, but to have other people at other tables around us. And I can't walk on water if I need a quick exit.

As she hesitated, he added, 'It was either *Windhover* or the Boathouse at Garzion again, and I felt that might be a trip too far down memory lane for both of us.'

'How right you were.' Her own smile was forced. 'Well—if this is the deal, let's go. After all, we don't want to keep your chef waiting.'

And felt her heartbeat quicken as she went with him.

CHAPTER FIVE

AT THE harbour wall, she was forced to take his hand again to negotiate the slippery steps down to the waiting dinghy, where a grizzled man helped her aboard, his teeth flashing in a smile that managed to be admiring and respectful at the same time.

'This is Juan,' Diaz said casually. 'He helps me with the boat. His brother Enrique does the cooking.'

An efficient outboard motor propelled them across the calm water to the side of the yacht and a small platform at the foot of a broad steel ladder, leading to the upper deck, where Enrique, dressed in dark trousers and a white coat, waited deferentially to show her to the companionway leading down to the saloon.

Carrie's 'floating hotel suite' didn't even begin to cover it, she thought, looking round her in astonishment at the elegant pale tweed sofas grouped round a large square table, with drawers and cupboards beneath it.

Behind the seating area was a dining table, large enough to seat eight people, but tonight set only for two. And beyond that, judging by the delectable smells, was the galley.

'A drink?' Diaz suggested as Enrique disappeared, presumably to put the finishing touches to their meal. 'I can offer you fresh orange juice, if you're still swearing off alcohol.'

She noticed decanters and glasses waiting on a side table, and said lightly, 'If you can promise that Juan will be there to save me if I fall overboard, then I'll have sherry, please, as dry as possible.'

'If memory serves, you're probably a better swimmer than he

is,' Diaz observed drily. 'But let's say I guarantee that drowning won't be an option.' He handed her the sherry and raised his own glass. '*Salud!*'

She echoed the toast a little shyly, and sipped. She looked at him, her eyes widening. 'That's superb.'

'I'm glad you approve. You're permitted to sit down.'

She complied, and he took the seat opposite. 'I'm still trying to take it all in,' she said frankly. 'It's just amazing. And it—she—really is brand-new.'

'Just out of her trials,' he agreed. 'She's the new version of my previous boat and rather more powerful, giving me a greater range.'

'I—I didn't realise you were interested in boats.'

'How could you?' he said. 'You went off to London when you were eighteen, shaking the Cornish dust off your shoes. I'm sure you haven't forgotten.'

'No.' She didn't look at him, aware that her throat was tightening.

'And we haven't seen a great deal of each other since that time,' he went on slowly. 'Or not until the last few months when we—met again. And once we had met there were always other things to talk about. We never really got around to my leisure interests, if you remember.'

She stared down at her glass. 'I'm hardly likely to forget.'

'Yes,' he said. 'I think that at least is true, if not the whole truth.' He gave a harsh laugh. 'The curse of a good memory.' He paused. 'So, tell me something, Rhianna. Why, in spite of everything, did you come to this bloody wedding?'

'Because I couldn't think of a convincing reason to stay away,' she said. 'I could hardly tell Carrie that I was being pressured by you. She might have asked you for an explanation, and imagine how embarrassing that would have been. What price the whole truth then?' She paused. 'Anyway, I needed to say goodbye.'

The firm mouth curled.

'To Carrie.' She gave him a defiant look. 'And to all the rest of it. Everything. Cutting the last links for good. You should find that reassuring.'

He contemplated the pale liquid in his glass. 'Very little about you reassures me, Rhianna.' He leaned back against the cushions. 'Tell me, have you seen any more of your reporter friend, or hasn't he managed to track you down yet?'

'You clearly have a very broad view of friendship,' she said shortly. 'But the gentleman concerned—another loose term— seems to have returned to the hole he crawled out of. I only hope he stays there.'

'Amen to that.' He was watching her, the silver eyes sombrely intent. 'I did wonder, of course, if you were planning to hand him the scoop of his career. "Lady Ariadne claims another victim in best friend's nightmare." "Bridegroom flees with TV star." Or something of the kind.'

Her fingers tightened round the stem of her glass. 'What a vivid imagination you have,' she remarked. 'And you seem to have captured the gutter jargon perfectly. Maybe you missed your vocation.'

'Then I'm glad at least one of us has fulfilled his or her potential,' he said. 'Tell me something. Did the television company realise at once it was typecasting, or did you actually have to sleep with someone in order to play Ariadne?'

Oh, God. *Oh, God...*

Pain and outrage, which she could not afford to let him see, clawed at her. She leaned back in her turn, smiling at him with a fair bid for insouciance.

'Believe me, you really don't want to know,' she drawled. 'But I can swear that the casting couch was never as comfortable as this one. Does that satisfy your curiosity?'

She saw a sudden flare of colour along the high cheekbones, a glint in his eyes that might have been anger, or something less easy to define, and felt a stab of bitter triumph.

But when he spoke his voice was even. 'That,' he said, 'is something that *you* really don't want to know. And I think Enrique is ready to serve dinner.'

She would have given a great deal to damn him and his dinner to hell and leave. But that, of course, was impossible. She was virtually trapped there.

And if she insisted on being put ashore immediately he

would know that she was not as unaffected by his jibes as she wished to appear.

Besides, Sod's Law was kicking in, reminding her that she'd eaten very little for the past twenty-four hours, and her usual appetite was being forcibly awoken by the enticing aromas of Enrique's cooking.

She rose in silence and followed him to the dining area, realising with chagrin that she would not be facing him from the opposite end of the long table, but had been seated instead at his right-hand side. Almost close enough to touch.

An altogether too cosy, too intimate placing, but presumably done according to his instructions.

But, whatever game Diaz Penvarnon was playing, she would be a match for him, she told herself with determination.

He held the chair for her courteously, and she sank on to it with a murmured word of thanks, sending him a glancing smile.

This was how to play it, she thought, however much it might hurt. So for the next hour or so Diaz would find himself dining with none other than Lady Ariadne—'the Tart without a Heart', as one tabloid had christened her. Television's favourite Bitch Queen, never more dangerous or desirable than when she was planning something.

She would eat and drink whatever she was offered. She would keep up her side of any conversation and be charming. She might even flirt a little, letting her eyes under the long fringe of lashes offer him all kinds of possibilities. Knowing she was unreachable. Untouchable.

And once the meal was over she would yawn prettily, excuse herself, then leave.

Because first thing in the morning, wedding or no wedding, she would be inventing some dire emergency that required her elsewhere immediately, and catching the next available train out.

Which, she told herself, would finally be the end of it. She could not afford to look back. Or to hope. Not again. Not ever.

Although London wouldn't necessarily be her first destination of choice, she thought wearily. It was hardly a sanctuary for her these days. Even now there were going to be issues to be dealt with before she could attempt to get her life back on track.

And there was also Daisy to consider. Daisy, her friend, whose husband had left her, and who would be shocked and frightened, needing all the comfort and support Rhianna could give her.

But at least, she told herself, that would force her to put the sorrow of her own rejection, her own loneliness and fear, to the back of her mind until she was somehow strong enough to deal with them. Whenever that might be.

She stifled a sigh as she shook out her linen table napkin.

In this whole, reeling, unhappy mess, her only certainty was that it would not be soon. That it would take every scrap of courage she possessed even to survive.

And that the campaign was starting here and now, at this table, with this man.

If the circumstances had been different, she would have openly revelled in the food a beaming Enrique brought to them.

The first course was an array of *tapas*, individual little dishes of spicy sausage, olives, prawns, anchovies and marinated peppers. This was followed by a fillet of lamb, pink and tender, served with garlicky roasted vegetables, and the meal concluded with almond creams, all of it served with a flavoursome Rioja.

It was a delicious and leisurely performance, with Diaz suddenly transformed into the perfect host, and Rhianna found, to her own surprise, that she was perceptibly relaxing her guard as the evening went on. Which could be dangerous.

'Goodness,' she said, half-laughing at one point. 'All this, plus Juan and Enrique too. Is this some reversion to your Spanish ancestry?'

He shrugged. 'It's pointless to deny it exists, and just occasionally over the generations it comes roaring back.' He drank some wine. 'We were all pirates at the time of the first Elizabeth, the Spanish and the English alike,' he went on reflectively. 'All raiders and looters, feathering our nests in the name of patriotism. Taking what we wanted when we saw it, and to hell with the consequences. And my many times great-grandfather was certainly no different. Before his ship went down Jorge might even have been the man lighting the torch that fired Penzance. *Quien sabe?* Who knows?'

'And then he met Tamsin and married her,' Rhianna said quietly.

'Met her and seduced her,' he corrected. 'A fairly high-risk initiative in those days. Her father might as easily have slit his throat as said, "Bless you, my children. The wedding's on Thursday."'

'But it worked out well,' she persisted. 'He stayed on in an enemy country so he must have loved her.'

'Perhaps,' he said. 'But don't forget she was an heiress, and he was then a younger son with his way to make in the world. A few lies about his origins, and a crash course in English may not have seemed too high a price at the time. His own good fortune came later.'

'What a cynical point of view,' Rhianna said lightly. 'I prefer the romantic version.'

His mouth hardened. 'With true love triumphant, no doubt? I can see why that would appeal. Unfortunately real life rarely supplies neat endings.'

'So I've discovered.' Her smile was brief and taut. She needed to change the subject, and quickly. She looked down at her empty plate. 'But Enrique is a gem. Surely he can't be content to hang around on your boat simply waiting for you to show up? He must get bored while you're in South America, or doing your global thing. Isn't he ever tempted to spread his wings—open his own restaurant, perhaps?'

'He's never said so.' Diaz refilled their glasses. 'Why not ask him?'

She flushed. 'Don't be absurd. After all, it's none of my business.'

'I think he'd be flattered,' he said. 'But probably not tempted. He likes his life, and so does Juan. Maybe they've found the recipe for happiness, and want to hang on to it.'

'While for the rest of us the search goes on.' She glanced at her watch. 'Heavens, it's nearly midnight. I should be getting back.'

Diaz also consulted the time, brows lifting. 'Why? The party at the hotel surely won't be over yet.'

'Indeed it will,' she said briskly. 'Carrie has to be home by twelve. You've forgotten the old superstition about the groom not seeing his bride on the wedding day until they meet in church.'

'In all the other excitement it must have slipped my mind. Nor am I particularly superstitious, except when it comes to mines.' He paused. 'I can't persuade you to have coffee, then?'

'Thank you, but not this late,' she said. 'It would keep me awake.'

As if there's any chance of sleeping, anyway...

'And naturally you wish to be at your brightest and best tomorrow,' Diaz commented silkily. He paused. 'However, to use a coy euphemism, would you like to freshen up before you go? If so, I'll get Enrique to show you to one of the staterooms.'

'Yes,' she said, reaching for her purse. 'That would be— most kind.'

'*De nada*,' he said. 'Even pirates can have their moments.'

At the door she hesitated, looking back at him for a moment, at ease in his chair, studying the rich colour of the wine in his glass. Knowing that this was probably the last time she would ever see him and that this was the image she would take away with her, imprinted on her mind—the dark, intelligent face, with its high cheekbones and those amazing long-lashed eyes, and the lean, long-legged muscular body.

Another companionway led down to the sleeping accommodation. The stateroom that Enrique showed her with obvious pride made her jaw drop. The fitted wardrobes and dressing table were made of some pale, expensive wood, while the bed, the widest she'd ever seen, was made up with cream linen, a bedspread in vibrant terracotta folded across its foot. The same colour was echoed among the piled-up pillows, and a small sofa, similarly upholstered, stood against one wall.

Or perhaps they were called bulkheads, she thought. She couldn't remember, and it didn't really matter anyway. It wasn't something she'd ever need to know.

The adjoining bathroom was all gleaming white and azure, with a walk-in power shower, a vanitory unit with twin basins, and a bidet as well as a loo.

'The *señorita* approves?' Enrique asked, pointing out the towels stacked on a corner shelf, and satisfying himself that there was soap in the dish between the basins. 'If there is anything else you require, tell me, *por favor*,' he added, turning to leave. 'There is a bell.'

Thoughtful, Rhianna decided with faint amusement, as she waited to hear the outer door close softly. But unnecessary.

Probably Enrique was more accustomed to women guests who spent longer than just one evening on board with his boss, and who shared far more than dinner.

Whereas I, she thought, swallowing, have to go and put the remains of my life back together.

She dried her hands, and dropped the used towel into the laundry basket, then ran a comb through her hair, wondering whether to renew her lipstick and deciding against it.

As she was doing so, she noticed the toiletries grouped together on the tiled top by the mirror, realising they were all her favourite brands—from the moisturiser to the perfumed body lotion, and even the shampoo.

Odd, she thought, and walked back into the other room, where she checked, her eyes narrowing. Because something else had suddenly appeared on the bed. A woman's nightgown, exquisitely fanned out. *Her nightgown...*

Rhianna took a deep breath, telling herself that it was some weird trick of her imagination, or more likely that she'd had too much of that wonderful Rioja.

At the same time, her instinct told her that she was fooling herself. She spun round and went back into the bathroom to check out the toiletries, her stomach muscles clenching as she saw that they'd all been used before, and that the pretty striped bag which had contained them when she left London was now in a cupboard under the basin.

My things, she thought desperately. Here—on his boat.

A glance in the stateroom's fitted cupboards confirmed her worst fears. All the clothing she'd brought to Penvarnon House was there, neatly hung away, or folded in the drawers, while her travel bag and dress carrier were tucked away at the back of a wardrobe. Her handbag was there too, but, she realised, biting her lip, minus her wallet and passport.

And at that moment she became aware of something else— the steady throb of a powerful engine. And she knew, with horror, that *Windhover* was moving. That they'd sailed.

She almost flung herself at the stateroom door, twisting the handle one way then another, tugging it, dragging at it breathlessly, while swearing softly but comprehensively. Refusing to believe that it wasn't going to open, in spite of her best efforts, because it wasn't just stuck in some embarrassing way—but actually locked.

Telling herself that this wasn't—couldn't be happening. Not to her.

He'd implied that he was descended from a Spanish pirate, but this was the twenty-first century, for God's sake, not the sixteenth, and there were strict laws against hijacking on the high seas.

If Polkernick Harbour actually qualified as any kind of high sea, she thought, quelling the bubble of hysteria rising inside her.

She wanted to beat on the closed door with her fists, screaming to be let out, but a small, icy voice in her brain said this was exactly the reaction he'd expect and would allow for. Therefore it would get her nowhere.

She stepped back and considered as she strove for control. For an element of calm.

Enrique had clearly been busy while her back was turned. It wasn't just her nightgown that had been left ready for her. Mineral water and a glass had appeared on one of the shelves fitted to the bedhead, together with a plate of cinnamon biscuits.

Everything for the discerning prisoner, she thought grimly.

Including the aforementioned bell. Which she rang.

And which was answered with admirable promptness by Diaz himself. He'd discarded his jacket and removed his tie, leaving his shirt open at his tanned throat.

Rhianna faced him from the sofa, legs elegantly crossed, hands folded in her lap to hide the fact they were shaking.

Her brows lifted. 'Enrique's busy, trying on his jailer's costume, I suppose?'

'I thought you might be throwing things.' He closed the door behind him and leaned against it. 'And decided I'd rather they hit me.'

'You're all heart,' she said shortly. She paused. 'Just what do you think you're doing?'

'Taking you for a short but romantic cruise,' he said. 'At least I hope it will be romantic. However, the Bay of Biscay may rule against that.'

'I'm on the side of the Bay of Biscay.' She lifted her chin. 'Diaz, you're being ridiculous. You can't behave like this.'

'And just who is going to stop me?' His voice held faint amusement.

'Your own common sense, I hope,' she said coldly. 'We're both supposed to be attending a wedding tomorrow—your cousin, my oldest friend. You think our absence won't be noted? That people won't ask questions and start looking for us?'

'They won't have to,' he said. 'The letter I left for Carrie earlier when I was collecting your stuff from the house makes the situation perfectly clear.'

Her heartbeat seemed to be rattling against her ribcage. 'Then maybe you could offer me equal clarification. If it's not too much trouble.'

'Not at all.' He settled himself more comfortably against the door, hands in his pockets. 'I told her that we'd got together in London earlier this year, but things had gone wrong between us.' He paused. 'I didn't specify what, or how, but I said I felt I had a real chance to put things right if you and I could just be alone together for a while to work things out.

'I mentioned that I knew that you planned to leave straight after the wedding, and once you'd gone any opportunity to get you to myself would probably be blown too, and I couldn't risk it. So I was extending our dinner date into a trip on *Windhover* for a few days. A kind of advance honeymoon. I thought that was the kind of excuse that might appeal, as she's about to embark on a honeymoon of her own.'

He added unsmilingly, 'I also asked her to forgive us both, and wish us luck.'

She said huskily, 'You actually believe that anyone will be deceived by such nonsense? By that—tissue of lies?'

He shrugged. 'Why not? Admittedly my explanation may not go down well in some quarters, and Carrie will indeed be disappointed, but in this case I feel the end justifies the means.'

'But I don't agree,' she said. 'So I'd be glad if you'd turn this floating prison right around and take me back to Polkernick.'

'Not a chance, sweetheart,' he said. 'You're coming with me. You might not be my companion of choice, you understand, but—hey—the time will soon pass. And when we eventually put in somewhere, you'll find yourself on a flight back to London before you know it.'

'Kidnap is a crime,' she said. 'People end up in jail for things like this.'

'For "kidnap" substitute "brief idyllic interlude for two people who fancy each other like crazy".' His smile was cold. 'Quite apart from the note, I think most of the evidence is on my side. Mrs Henderson was delighted to collaborate in my "surprise" and pack your things for Juan to collect after you'd left for the hotel. Everyone saw us leave the party in perfect amity, and knew we were having dinner together. There was no kicking and screaming at the harbour. There were people around who can verify that you came on board without coercion.'

'But that's not how I've stayed,' she said tautly. 'You had me locked in.'

'Did I?' he countered. 'Or have we just experienced some teething troubles with an ill-fitting door, perhaps?'

'No doubt that will be confirmed by Enrique,' she said bitterly. 'But it makes no difference. Because now I want to leave.' She swallowed. 'I don't even have to go back to Polkernick, if that's inconvenient. There are loads of harbours along the coast. You could simply drop me ashore at one of them, and be rid of me. I—I promise I'll make no official complaint.'

'A selfless thought,' he returned. 'And a real temptation. But no chance, my pet. We're sailing off into tomorrow's sunrise. Together.'

'But why are you doing this?' Her voice was a strained whisper. 'Why? I don't understand.'

Diaz straightened, coming away from the door and walking across to her. Standing over her so that in spite of herself she shrank back against the cushions.

His voice bit. 'To make sure that Carrie's wedding, however

ill-advised I may think it, goes ahead, unhindered and unhampered by any dramatic revelations from you, darling.'

His eyes were hard. 'You see, Rhianna, I just don't think you can be trusted. I think you spell trouble in every line of that delectable body that you use to such effect. But what finally tipped the scales against you was when I caught you parading yourself in front of the mirror yesterday—taking advantage of Carrie's momentary absence to see how her wedding dress and veil would look if you were wearing them instead of her.'

Rhianna felt the colour drain from her face. 'So it was you,' she said. 'I thought I heard someone.'

His mouth curled. 'Unfortunately for you—yes. I could hardly believe what I was seeing. Dear God, you'd only been in the house five minutes and already you were pretending to be the bride. Imagining yourself taking her place. And who could guarantee you might be not be tempted to turn your pathetic little fantasy into reality?'

She said hoarsely, 'Diaz—you have to let me explain…'

'Not necessary,' he said. 'You see, I came back a little later to tell you—warn you that I'd seen you—and tell you for the last time to go. Only I discovered that you were otherwise engaged, talking to bloody Simon.'

She said thickly, 'And you listened?'

'Wild horses wouldn't have dragged me away,' he returned harshly. 'It was—most revealing. Everything finally made a kind of sick sense.'

He looked at her with contempt. 'I don't know if being pregnant by the bridegroom is the kind of "just impediment" the Church was thinking of when it wrote the marriage service, but I sure as hell wasn't planning to find out. I couldn't risk you staging some hysterical last-minute confession scene, Rhianna, some touching plea for your unborn child. So I decided it would be better if you were removed—out of harm's way. And, ironically, Simon's ghastly mother supplied me with the means.'

'How fortunate for you,' she said hoarsely. 'And if she hadn't?'

'I'd have found some other way.' He gave her a cynical look. 'And you won't be gone for too long,' he added. 'Not enough to jeopardise your abortion plans anyway. I presume there's an appointment already booked?'

'Yes,' she said. It was difficult to speak evenly. 'As it happens, there is.'

'Good,' he said. 'Always best to keep things neat and tidy. Although even if Simon had been free to marry you I can't imagine you wanting to have the child,' he went on. 'After all, nothing must impede your precious career, and a pregnant Lady Ariadne would never do.'

'Totally out of character, I agree.' She lifted her brows, fighting the pain that raked her. 'I didn't realise you were such a fan.'

'I'm not,' he said. 'I simply found it—instructive. To see what you've become.'

'I've become a highly paid professional actor,' she said stonily. 'I'm not ashamed of that. But my screen persona and my private life are leagues apart, whatever you may want to believe. And forget that garbage about the casting couch too. I don't go in for casual sex. As you would have found out, Mr Penvarnon, dinner is one thing, but I'd have to love a man before I slept with him.'

She saw his jaw muscles clench and braced herself for anger, but when he spoke his voice was cool.

'Then let me put your mind at rest,' he said. 'The term "advance honeymoon" was only a figure of speech. I wouldn't really want Simon Rawlins' leavings.'

'I'm sure,' she said. 'But I still have a problem. As you've already noticed, I'm pretty recognisable, and if we're seen together—in Spain, France, or anywhere else—the obvious conclusions will be drawn.'

'Maybe,' he said. 'But when we resume our totally separate lives they'll have to think again.'

'And I know what they'll think,' she said curtly. 'That I'm your discarded mistress. You talked about potential headlines earlier. Well, I can see these now: "Ariadne dumped." "Millionaire turns down TV's Sex Siren." I don't court bad publicity. I can't afford to. And I shouldn't think you want it either.'

She paused. 'Especially if people start digging around, unearthing old scandals. How long, do you think, before that nasty little man from the *Duchy Herald* is told gloatingly by someone that my mother was your father's mistress? That she betrayed a sick woman who trusted her, and destroyed her marriage, driving her into a nervous breakdown. Which is why Esther Penvarnon lives in widowed exile to this day—because it's too painful for her to return.'

She drew a harsh breath. 'Isn't that still the authorised version of what happened?'

'You, of course, have a different one.'

'I certainly have another perception of my mother. You never knew her.'

'No,' he said. 'And you never knew mine.'

'True. However, I'm sure she wouldn't want those stories rehashed either, or served up as background to your supposed involvement with me.'

'Indeed not,' he said. 'So I shall make damned sure that our "supposed involvement" remains our little secret, and I advise you most strongly to do the same. Unless you think I missed the vague threat in your last remark.'

He paused. 'I'm not planning to parade you through the streets of Barcelona, sweetheart, or sunbathe nude with you by a pool on the Côte d'Azur. The paparazzi can't board this boat, and this is where you'll stay—until the wedding's past and gone and the happy couple far away where you can't touch them.'

He sent her a grim smile as he turned to leave. At the door he hesitated, glancing back at her. 'In retrospect,' he said, 'wouldn't it have been better just to have taken my advice and stayed in London? Think it over, if by some mischance you can't sleep. Goodnight, Rhianna.'

'In retrospect,' she said, 'wouldn't it have been better, in fact, if you and I had never met? You think about that.'

The door closed behind him, and this time she heard the key turn in the lock. For a moment she sat motionless, then she drew a long quivering breath and bent forward, covering her face with her hands.

While in her head a voice whispered over and over again, What can I do? Oh, God, what I can I do? How can I bear this?

But she heard only silence in reply.

CHAPTER SIX

As a confrontation, she thought painfully, it had not gone too well. She might have had the last word, but the upper hand had eluded her completely.

What on earth had possessed her to rake up past history to throw at him? They both knew what had happened, and nothing could change that—a certainty she'd lived with during the whole five years since she'd first learned the truth.

The summer when her life had changed forever.

She'd had her eighteenth birthday, acknowledged as usual by a card from her aunt, and celebrated joyously by a night out in Falmouth with Carrie and some of the girls from school. Her final examinations had been over, and she'd been waiting for the results—although her grades hadn't really been all that important, she reflected unhappily, as Aunt Kezia had refused point-blank to allow her to apply for a university place, unlike Carrie, who'd been hoping to go to Oxford.

'It's time you went out to work, my girl,' Miss Trewint declared harshly. 'Started contributing to your upkeep.'

In the meantime, almost as soon as the school gates closed, she found Rhianna a job for the season at Rollo's Café. The hours were long, it was poorly paid, Mrs Rollo was a witch and by the time her board and lodging had been extracted Rhianna was left with little to show for each week's hard work.

And this, she supposed, was to be her future. Or some dead-end office job, using the computing and word processing course from school, bolstered by weekend and evening work during the summer.

The only bright spot on the horizon was the anticipation of Carrie's eighteenth birthday, which was going to be marked by a major party at Penvarnon House.

And for once Simon was expected to be there.

He'd pretty much faded out of the picture since he'd gone up to Cambridge two years ago. He still came to Polkernick sometimes in the summer, when his parents were there, but they were fleeting visits, and often he was accompanied by friends from university, his time occupied with them. Sometimes, too, the friends were female.

Instinct told Rhianna, suffering her own pangs, how much Carrie must be hurt by this, and by the fact that her regular letters to Simon had been answered so infrequently since he left for university.

'He's frantically busy, of course,' she'd said once, her clear eyes faintly shadowed. 'With work and all the other stuff he's involved in. Because it's a different world. Everyone says so. Three years of complete whirl.' She'd paused. 'Besides, everything changes. We all move on, and I shall too.'

But Rhianna wasn't convinced. And her own dream image of Simon the Golden wasn't quite as perfect as it had been once, its gold just a little tarnished.

She wondered if he was bringing anyone to Carrie's party, and hoped devoutly that he wasn't.

She'd been invited, although naturally she wouldn't be attending the dinner that would precede the dancing. Judging by Carrie's obvious embarrassment, it was clear her mother had vetoed any such idea.

Carrie had the world's loveliest dress, in aquamarine chiffon, and Rhianna couldn't hope to emulate that. However, a charity shop in Truro had yielded a simple black slip of a dress in a silky fabric, cut on the bias with shoestring straps, nearly new, in her size and affordable. They'd even found her a pair of high-heeled sandals to match—which, the helper had confided, had proved too narrow-fitting for most of their customers.

'Might have been made for you, my handsome,' she'd said cheerfully, as she'd wrapped them.

And they did look good, Rhianna thought as she gave herself a last critical once-over before the party. She was just turning from the mirror when her door opened abruptly and her aunt marched in.

'They're going to be a waitress short at the dinner tonight,' she said, her eyes sweeping scornfully over Rhianna's slim figure. 'One of the girls is sick, so I told Mrs Seymour you'd take her place.'

Rhianna gasped helplessly. 'But I can't do that. Carrie's invited me to the dancing as a guest,' she protested. 'You know that. And I bought this dress specially.'

'Yes, and a rare waste of money too. Good job you have it to burn.' Miss Trewint tossed the dark button-through dress and frilled white apron she had over her arm onto Rhianna's bed. 'Well, you won't be parading yourself like a trollop tonight, madam. So get changed and over to the house, and sharp about it. People will be arriving. And tie your hair back.'

The door banged behind her. Throat tight, eyes burning, Rhianna hung the black dress back in the wardrobe and put on the navy uniform. It was a size too big, but she tied the apron more tightly round her waist to give it more shape. She dragged her hair back from her face and plaited it quickly, her fingers shaking, then changed her sandals for the low-heeled pair she wore at the café.

The hired help, she thought bitterly, and looking just as drab as Aunt Kezia could have wished.

Carrie met her with a look of utter consternation. 'I don't believe this,' she said furiously. 'Your aunt—my mother—what the hell are they playing at?'

'Teaching me my place, I think.' Rhianna gave her a swift hug. 'Don't worry about it. We can exchange above and below stairs viewpoints afterwards.' She wanted to add, I really don't mind, but it wasn't true. She minded like blazes.

It was a very long evening. Rhianna carried round trays of drinks, platters of canapés, and later stood at the dinner, helping to serve the poached salmon and carve the turkey.

Mrs Seymour, she thought, surreptitiously easing her aching feet as she watched Moira's lavender-clad figure floating radiantly among the guests, is certainly getting her money's worth. That is if she actually intends to pay me.

One of the first people she'd seen had naturally been Simon.

'Good God.' He'd looked her up and down blankly, then started to grin. 'If it isn't the lovely Rhianna. Bloody hell, I didn't realise this was supposed to be fancy dress.'

The friend accompanying him had roared with laughter, his hot brown eyes assessing Rhianna in a way she didn't like. She'd cared for him even less when she spotted him later, adding the contents of his hip flask to the non-alcoholic punch.

But the next time she'd seen Simon he'd been dancing with Carrie, his lips close to her ear, whispering things that had her blushing, her face radiant with a delight she couldn't have concealed if she'd tried.

And she wasn't trying very hard, Rhianna thought ruefully. So much for moving on.

During the course of the evening she'd also seen Diaz Penvarnon arrive late. She'd assumed he wasn't coming at all. At the sight of him, she'd longed to fade back into the wall, but he hadn't appeared to notice her, so perhaps the waitress gear had made her temporarily invisible.

Although there was no reason why he should care if she was there as friend or servant, she reminded herself.

Whenever he visited Penvarnon House he always spoke to her, but as if, she thought sometimes, he was taking care to be pleasant. Yet, while there'd naturally never been any repeat of that wonderful birthday dinner, he'd invariably remembered to send her a card when the anniversary came round.

It was getting on for midnight when Simon approached her again. 'Going to dance with me?' he asked, bending towards her, his face flushed.

'For goodness' sake, Simon, I can't,' she muttered. 'I'm here to work, and Mrs Seymour's watching me.' She raised her voice a little. 'Is there something I can get you, sir?'

'Absolutely. Dance with me and I'll tell you.' He grinned at her.

'Simon,' she said. 'This isn't funny. Please go away.'

'Poor Cinderella,' he said. 'But they can't keep you slaving all night. You deserve some fun. And you can at least have some champagne to toast Carrie's birthday, like everyone else. She'd want that.' He paused. 'Tell you what—I'll get a bottle, and we'll meet you round by the stables in ten minutes. How would that be?'

She bit her lip. 'Well, OK. But I can only stay a few minutes.'

When he'd gone, Rhianna glanced round her. She probably wouldn't be missed at this stage, she thought. No one wanted any more food, at least not until the eggs and bacon were to be served very much later on. And Aunt Kezia's eagle eye was now super-intending the clearing-up operation in the kitchen. She probably could slip out for a little while. And if she was spotted then she would have Carrie to defend her.

Apart from the moon, there was no light in the yard. It was cooler now, too, after the heat of the house, and Rhianna hugged herself, shivering a little.

She called softly, 'Carrie?'

'Over here.' Simon's voice reached her from one of the disused loose boxes.

He was standing just inside, leaning against the wall, a dark shape among the shadows. As her eyes adjusted Rhianna realised he was alone, his tie loosened, and that he was clasping an open bottle of champagne, which he held out to her.

'So,' he said, his voice slurring a little. 'Here we are at last. Let's party.'

'Where's Carrie?'

'Being the obedient daughter and perfect hostess.' He said it with a laugh that was almost a sneer. 'Where else?'

'Then I should get back to being the perfect waitress,' she said. 'I haven't got time to party—or not without Carrie, anyway.'

'She won't miss you. Come on, Rhianna, loosen up.' Putting down the bottle, he pushed himself away from the wall and came over to her. 'Neither of us is on the A list tonight, so we may as well drown our sorrows.'

Judging by the alcohol on his breath, Simon's troubles were already well submerged. She drew back. 'No, thank you.'

'Oh, come on, sweetheart. What's your problem?' He looked her up and down. 'Don't pretend you don't fancy me. You have done for years. I heard all about it from a girl at your school. Only I didn't feel like following it up—then. But things—and people—change with time.' He paused. 'Who'd have thought it, eh? From scrawny kid to hot totty in one blink of the eye.'

She was getting more uncomfortable by the second. 'Simon, I have to get back—really.' She turned towards the house. 'People will be wondering where I am.'

'But my need,' he said thickly, 'is much greater than theirs—believe me.' He grabbed her arm, pulling her towards him. 'So stay and be nice. You know you want to.'

Caught off balance, Rhianna found herself pinned against him so closely that his state of arousal became embarrassingly evident.

She tried to say, Stop this now—but her words were smothered by the heat of his mouth, and his hands were tugging at the buttons of her dress.

Then from behind them, a man's cool voice said, 'So there you are, Simon. Everyone's looking for you, particularly Carrie. Your friend Jimmy's drunk and behaving rather badly.'

And, to her horror, Rhianna realised that the voice belonged to Diaz Penvarnon. And that he was standing watching them from the doorway of the loose box, dark brows raised, and his eyes like steel.

Simon let her go as if he'd been stung, and swung round defensively. 'What am I supposed to do about it?'

'You brought him.' Diaz sounded bored. 'You deal with him. He can hardly stand up, let alone walk. And go now, please,' he added as Simon seemed prepared to argue. 'Sorry to upset your pleasant interlude, but Carrie's mother is getting upset.' He paused. 'And so is Carrie.'

Simon shrugged almost airily. 'You know how it is, man.' He glanced, grinning, at Rhianna. 'If the offer's on the table, you can hardly turn it down—especially when it comes so nicely packaged.'

He set off across the yard, walking none too steadily himself.

Dazed, Rhianna watched him go, his words beating in her brain. She thought, He's deliberately made it sound as if this was my idea. As if I came out here to be with him—wanting—*this*…

She turned to Diaz, saw the direction of his gaze, and, looking down, realised her dress was unfastened almost to the waist.

'Oh, God,' she said. Dry-mouthed, fingers shaking, she attempted to fumble the buttons back into their holes.

'A little late for modesty, wouldn't you say?' His voice reached her harshly.

'You don't have to watch,' she said. 'I have to get back to work.'

'No,' he said. 'You don't. You're finished for tonight. The only place you're going is home to bed.'

She said tautly, 'Is that an order—sir?'

'Yes,' he said. 'It is.' He paused. 'So what was this? An extra birthday present for Carrie? Having her heart broken? Because if she'd turned up here instead of me that's what would have happened.'

He shook his head. 'You of all people should know how she feels about Simon Rawlins, Rhianna. And, whatever I think of him, I know that falling in love with the right person isn't always a given—at any age. Maybe he's like a virus, and she'll recover eventually, but that time is clearly not yet. So keep your predatory little hands off her precious apple cart—and that's another order.'

His words seemed to pelt her like stones, making her quiver under the onslaught. Because what could she say in her own defence? *It wasn't like that.* How feeble and unconvincing was that?

Besides, when Simon had grabbed her she'd been too stunned to react immediately, so she hadn't even been fighting him off when Diaz had walked in.

Making herself decent was no longer a priority. All that mattered was getting out of there—away from him—away from the icy condemnation in his voice for which she had no answer that he would ever believe.

But as she went past him he caught her arm, halting her.

The silver eyes were sombre. 'Is this how you rate yourself—sex in an empty stable with another girl's man? You disappoint me.'

'And of course we can't have that.' Anger and bitterness were at war inside her, making her reckless. 'But, as it happens, things would never have gone that far.'

'You imagine *you* were the one in control of the situation?'

he asked derisively. 'Not from where I was sitting, sweetheart. And a last-minute change of heart doesn't always work with someone half-cut and looking for mischief. If I hadn't followed you there could have been trouble.'

She stiffened. 'How good of you to take such an interest in an employee's private affairs,' she said. 'But also quite unnecessary. I can take care of myself.'

He said slowly, 'Can you indeed?'

'Yes,' she said. 'Of course.' And tried not to think of Simon's fingers on her flesh. The pressure of his mouth.

Diaz swung her round, pushing her against the outside wall of the stable. He put one hand on the brickwork beside her and leaned towards her, his other hand cupping her chin, his thumb rhythmically stroking the delicate line of her jaw.

He said softly, 'Are you quite sure of that?'

She looked up into his eyes. They were pale as the moonlight itself, the irises very dark. They held an expression she had never encountered before—with anyone. Certainly not with Simon a few minutes ago, she thought, and realised she was frightened and excited at the same time.

He added, 'Prove it.' Then bent his head and put his mouth slowly and carefully on hers, caressing her lips lightly and sensuously.

It was not the frank lust she'd experienced just now. Nor was it passion. Or not yet, anyway. Even in her comparative innocence Rhianna recognised that.

He was simply asking a question. Testing her quite gently, but also inexorably. This time demanding an answer.

She'd been kissed before tonight, of course. Not often, it was true, and certainly not well. The school had thrown a leavers' party with a disco, and several of the lads had tried their luck during the slow dances. She'd accepted those minor advances with good-humoured resignation, if not pleasure. The boys hadn't been strangers, after all, and she hadn't wanted to make a fuss or hurt anyone's feelings. But she'd moved away as soon as the dance was over, making it tacitly plain there'd be no repetition.

But this—*this*—was wholly different. As his kiss deepened,

coaxing her lips to part for him, his hand was tracing the curve of her slender throat, lingering on the leap and flutter of her pulse, then moving down to her loosened dress to stroke the first delicate swell of her breast and linger there.

Her reaction was instant, shocking her with its intensity. Making her aware of explicit sensations—needs—never before imagined, let alone experienced. Enticing her with the scent—the taste of him.

She wanted, she thought as her brain reeled, to answer all his questions. To twine her arms round his neck and feel the warmth, the male hardness of him against her. To return the pressure of his lips and more. To feel his touch on her naked skin and show him she was ready to be a woman. His woman, if he so desired.

But it seemed he did not.

Instead he was lifting his head and stepping back, his expression guarded as he studied her.

He said quietly, 'I think you seriously over-estimate your resistance levels, Rhianna. Just be glad I don't take sweets from babies, or you'd be spending the night in my bed, not your own. Which is a seriously bad idea for a great many reasons.' He added almost harshly, 'Now, run along, and don't go looking for trouble with men. Because you'll surely find it.'

He turned and walked away, and she stayed where she was, leaning against the wall, her legs shaking too much to move.

And at that moment a light came on, illuminating the entire yard—including the tall figure of Diaz Penvarnon crossing to the rear entrance of the house.

Rhianna turned her head, startled, and saw the dark shape of her aunt standing at the window of the flat, looking down. She couldn't see her face, but instinct warned she'd gone from one kind of trouble straight to another.

Reluctantly she moved, walking slowly round the yard to the flat door and going in.

Kezia Trewint was waiting for her in the living room, her face set, her deep-set eyes burning with anger and scorn as she looked at the girl hesitating in the doorway.

'So,' she said. 'You've been with him. Another Carlow woman chasing after a Penvarnon man. Just as I knew you'd be all those years ago.'

Rhianna gasped. 'What—what do you mean?'

'I mean you—up against the stable wall with Mr Diaz. A slut—a dirty little tart—just like your mother before you.' She drew a hoarse breath. 'Didn't she bring enough shame on our family? And *him* of all men?'

'No,' Rhianna managed. 'It—it wasn't like that…'

Oh, God, she thought. This was an entirely different level of misunderstanding. This was terrible.

'You think you weren't seen sneaking off, and him following?' Miss Trewint demanded derisively. 'That Mrs Seymour didn't go after him, and me with her? That we didn't see you with our own eyes? It's what the family have been expecting ever since you came here. Grace Carlow's daughter, and the living image of her. Made him wonder, I dare say, what Ben Penvarnon once had, and fancy a taste of the same.'

Her eyes rested on Rhianna's still unfastened buttons. Her sudden laugh was vicious, grating. 'But that's where it'll end. I promise you that. Because he's not like his father. Not that one. He won't be setting you up in some London flat and paying the bills in return for his pleasures. Now he's used you, he'll forget you. He can't do otherwise. Because *she* might find out, and he can't risk that.'

Rhianna stared at her. She felt very cold. 'I don't understand,' she said. 'What are you talking about. Who is *she*? And what are you saying about my mother?'

'She was Ben Penvarnon's mistress, bought and kept,' Miss Trewint flung at her. 'As everyone knows. And I was the one, God forgive me, who brought her into this house and put temptation in his way, flaunting herself in front of him.

'"Yes, Mr Penvarnon," she mimicked. '"No, Mr Penvarnon." "I think Mrs Esther's a little better today, Mr Penvarnon."' She drew a shuddering breath. 'Playing sweetness and concern for the sick woman she was supposed to be tending, and all the time she was running off to meet with her wedded husband in that hut on the beach or up on the moors. And you're proving yourself no better with his son.'

'That's a lie. And I don't believe what you're saying about my mother either.' Rhianna's chest was so tight it was difficult to breathe. 'She was in love with Daddy. You only had to see them together to know that.'

'What did she ever know about love?' Her aunt glared at her. 'All she knew was having her fun and wheedling all she could out of another woman's husband. And after he was dead, and there were no more pickings to be had, she had to do something. Find some other fool to keep her.'

Her mouth thinned. 'And you'll have to do the same, my lady. Don't think you're staying here after tonight's goings-on. Even if I was prepared to keep you, Mrs Seymour won't have it. Reckons you're an insult to her sister, and that Mr Diaz must have run mad to look twice at you with what he knows.'

'But nothing happened,' Rhianna protested desperately. 'Or not like you think, anyway,' she added. *But it could have done*, said a sly voice in her head. *He was the one who put a stop to it, not you, so no credit to you. And you can't even claim it was his fault—not this time.*

But I can't think about that, she told herself, wincing inwardly. I've got to forget those dark, urgent moments in his arms when nothing mattered but his mouth on mine and the touch of his hand on my skin.

'*A seriously bad idea for a great many reasons.*' That was what he'd said, and now she knew what he'd meant. Why he'd let her go. And why he'd do nothing to prevent her being sent away permanently. Not this time.

'Nor is it going to happen.' Miss Trewint's voice reached her grimly. 'So you can start packing your bags. I knew you were going to be a bad lot from the first, hanging round Mr Diaz whenever he came here. And there you were tonight, supposed to be working, but throwing yourself at any man who'd look at you.' She snorted. 'I should have turned you out two years ago, when you were sixteen, but for that headmistress of yours insisting you should finish your education—get more qualifications.' She shook her head. 'I was a fool to listen. But you'll make no more mischief here. You're going tomorrow, and good riddance too.'

But where am I to go? Rhianna wanted to ask. What can I do? I haven't earned enough to save anything, so what am I going to live on while I find work—somewhere to live? And although I never wanted to come here, and the last six years of my life haven't been that happy, at the same time they've been centred exclusively on this house. I've grown accustomed to it. I don't know anywhere else.

But she said none of those things aloud. She wouldn't argue, she thought. Nor would she beg.

I can take care of myself. Her own words, she thought. And if they'd been an empty boast a little while ago, she would have to live up to them now.

She was putting the last of her things in her only suitcase the next morning when Carrie put a cautious head round her bedroom door.

'It's all right,' she said. 'Your aunt's supervising the cleaning-up operation, stalking round like Medusa on a bad day.' She saw the open case and her eyes widened in distress. 'Oh, God, it's true. You're really leaving. I heard Mum and Dad rowing in the study when I came down, and apparently there was another huge row earlier, between Diaz and my mother, and he slammed out of the house and drove off somewhere. I thought he might simply be peeved about the state of the house,' she added glumly. 'Wine and food spilled all over the place, half the crockery and stuff abandoned on the lawn, and Simon, among others, getting totally wasted with his ghastly friend Jimmy, who was sick everywhere.' She groaned. 'Thank God I'll only be eighteen once. I couldn't go through all that again.'

She paused. 'But Mum was saying you had to go, and Dad was trying to reason with her, so what's happened?'

Rhianna bit her lip. 'Your cousin Diaz kissed me goodnight.' She tried to sound nonchalant. 'Your mother and my aunt both saw it, and as a consequence all hell has broken loose.'

Carrie gaped at her. 'But it wouldn't have meant anything,' she protested. 'Not from Diaz. He probably realised you were rightly miffed about the waitressing business and was just being kind again.' She sat on the edge of the bed. 'Face it, love,' she said gently. 'You're far too young for him. He dates the kind of women who go to first nights at the opera and have their photographs taken in the Royal Enclosure at Ascot. Mum knows that perfectly well.'

'Yes,' Rhianna said, trying to ignore the sudden bleak feeling in the pit of her stomach. 'But she also knows that my mother had a serious affair with your uncle Ben, and, however unlikely it may be, she doesn't want history to repeat itself.'

If she hadn't been so het-up she might have found the expression of blank shock on Carrie's face almost funny.

'I was going to say you must be joking,' she said at last. 'But clearly you're not. When did you find out about this?'

'Just before my sentence of banishment was pronounced last night.' Rhianna tried to speak lightly. 'In a way, it was a relief to know there is a reason for my having been the resident leper all these years. But it wasn't the most welcome news I've ever had either.' She looked at Carrie. 'You never knew—never guessed?'

The other shook her head. 'Never—cross my heart. But a lot of stuff finally makes sense,' she added soberly. 'Like being told I was too young to understand when I used to ask why Aunt Esther never came back here, even to visit.'

Her tone became brisker. 'But this isn't your fault, love. And Uncle Ben must have died at least four years before you were born, so there can't possibly be any connection there.'

She paused. 'Mind you, I remember Mrs Welling saying once that he'd always been a devil for the women—before and after he married Aunt Esther. So perhaps your mother wasn't really to blame either.' She pulled a face. 'Maybe it was one of those squire and village maiden things.'

'I don't think so.' Rhianna grimaced too. 'Apparently your aunt was ill and my mother was nursing her when it started. Which somehow makes it even worse—if it's true, of course.' She sighed. 'I can't believe anyone as warm and kind as my mother would have taken advantage of a sick woman by stealing her husband.'

She tucked her small make-up purse down the side of the case. 'What was wrong with Esther Penvarnon. Do you know?'

'Not really,' Carrie said, frowning. 'According to my mother she had a bad time when Diaz was born, and was never well afterwards. It might have been one of those virus things, like ME, because according to the Welling information service Aunt Esther spent a lot of time in a wheelchair.'

She frowned. 'Although I have to say Mrs W also claimed she could walk perfectly well if she wanted. She reckoned, and I quote, that my aunt should have "got up and got on with being Mr Penvarnon's missus," thus saving a heap of trouble all round.'

She paused. 'Especially for you. Talk about the sins of the mothers...' Her face acquired the stubborn look that Rhianna remembered from the first days of their friendship. 'However, you can't simply be thrown out on to the streets with nowhere to go.'

'But that isn't the case any longer. I *do* have a place to stay— back in London.' Rhianna forced a smile. 'Remember the Jessops, who looked after me after my mother died? Well, we've always stayed in touch, and over the years they've kept asking me to visit them—but I never could because Aunt Kezia said the fare was too expensive. Well, I phoned them this morning, and as soon as I tell them what train I'm catching they're going to meet me at Paddington. I can live with them again until I've found a job and got settled.'

'Well, thank God for that at least,' Carrie said roundly. 'But you've still been treated very badly by our family—Diaz included. If he wanted to kiss someone, why didn't he pick Janie Trevellin? After all, they were seeing each other when he was over last year, and Mother thought at one point they might even get engaged.'

She shrugged. 'Some hopes. One day he threw his stuff in the car, as usual, and went.' She gave a reluctant grin. 'According to Welling wisdom, Penvarnon men have always been restless. Never in one place, wanting to be somewhere else. "Hard to tie down, and impossible to keep tied after".'

Rhianna made herself speak evenly. 'Then maybe Janie Trevellin had a lucky escape.'

'I bet she doesn't think so.' Carrie watched Rhianna fasten her case. 'Look, are you quite sure about this? Perhaps things were said in the heat of the moment last night, and everyone will have calmed down by now?'

'Not my aunt,' Rhianna said briefly. 'Besides, I never planned to stay here for ever, so maybe being pushed into action now is actually a blessing in disguise.'

'Like the pigs currently flying over the roof,' Carrie retorted. 'You've got my mobile number haven't you. Let me know you're safe and sound, and keep in touch with all your new contact details. Oxford's much nearer London, so, fingers crossed, we can go on seeing each other quite easily.'

Rhianna took a deep breath. 'I'm sure you won't just be seeing me.'

'Well, no.' She flushed a little, her smile tender. 'Simon came over a little while ago, to grovel about Jimmy and a lot of other things besides. He said going to university, getting away from the family and finding his freedom, knocked him sideways for a while, but he's back on track now. And he wants to see me again—seriously this time.'

'Then last night clearly wasn't all bad.' Smiling was an effort, but Rhianna managed it. 'If he's truly the one, Carrie, go for it.' *But, please God, don't let it be true. Let her find someone else.*

'Don't worry,' Carrie assured her. 'I shall.' She paused again. 'How are you getting to the station? You can't possibly walk.'

'No choice. I certainly can't afford a taxi.'

'I shall take you,' Carrie said firmly. 'In Mother's car. And I shall ask her for the wages you're owed for last night, too.'

Rhianna stared into her shoulder bag on the pretext of checking its contents, aware that her face had reddened.

'Please don't,' she said constrictedly. 'I think that's best forgotten. Besides, I don't want anything from her. From anyone.'

But later, at the station, Carrie produced a roll of notes and handed them to her. 'For you,' she said. 'From my father, wishing you all the best.'

Rhianna stared at it in disbelief. 'But it's five hundred pounds,' she said. 'I couldn't possibly take it.'

'He says you have to.' Carrie looked awkward. 'It seems Uncle Ben left your mother some money in his will, but she refused to accept it. By comparison, this is a pittance, but Dad says it will make him feel much better, knowing that you're not penniless.'

'How lovely of him.' Rhianna felt perilously close to tears.

Francis Seymour was such a contrast, she thought, to her aunt, who'd said curtly, 'So you're off, then? No doubt you'll fall on your feet. Your sort always does.'

And Rhianna's brief but carefully prepared speech of thanks for the home she'd been given for the past six years had died in her throat.

And that, she thought now, was the last time I saw her.

The last time I believed I would see any of them.

And, oh, God, it would have been so much better that way.

CHAPTER SEVEN

HER face was wet again now, Rhianna realised, raising her head at last.

Stress, she told herself. A natural reaction to finding herself in this totally unnatural situation. Certainly not an appropriate time to start remembering the unhappiness of the past.

Especially when she should be concentrating all her energies strictly on the present—getting out of this mess.

And yet the past five years had certainly not been all bad. On the contrary. There'd been good things to treasure as well, she thought. The unfailing kindness of the Jessops, who'd treated her as if she'd never been away. Her continued friendship with Carrie, who'd secured her Oxford place with ease, and had only been sorry that Rhianna wasn't there with her.

And the wonderful Marika Fenton, the retired actress running drama classes at a local evening institute, who'd used jealously guarded contacts to get her star student into stage school, and chivvied the board of trustees into granting whatever bursaries might be going.

She'd written regularly to Aunt Kezia, but had never received a reply. Then her aunt had died very suddenly of a heart attack, before receiving the letter in which Rhianna told her she'd just won a leading role in a brand-new drama series called *Castle Pride*.

A clearly embarrassed communication from Francis Seymour had told her that Miss Trewint had given strict instructions that Rhianna was not to attend her funeral service or cremation, that her possessions should be sold and any money raised, together with her meagre savings, donated to the RSPCA.

Rhianna had accepted those harsh final wishes without protest.

The following day she'd begun to rehearse the role of Lady Ariadne. And the rest, as they said, was history.

She stood up, stretching. And history it had to remain. She had to deal with the here and now. Get through the pain of the next few days as efficiently as possible.

And to start with it seemed pointless to spend all night on this sofa when there was a perfectly good bed waiting, she told herself.

If she had to be miserable, then it might as well be in comfort.

So, having changed into her nightgown, performed her simple beauty routine, cleaned her teeth and brushed her hair, Rhianna slipped under the covers.

But sleep proved elusive. However much her mind might twist and turn, she could see no easy way out of this present disaster, she thought. Diaz had set a trap, and she'd walked blindly, insanely, into it.

And the old anodyne about things looking better in the morning didn't seem to apply in the current situation.

Unless she woke to find herself back in the primrose room, recovering from a particularly bad nightmare, she thought wryly. And how likely was that?

Eventually, however, the comfort of the mattress beneath her was too enticing, and the pillows too soft to resist, so that the next time she opened her eyes it was broad daylight.

She lay still for a moment. It's here, she thought. It's today. Carrie's marrying Simon and I'm not there. God help me, I'm in the middle of the ocean with Diaz Penvarnon. No bad dream. It's really happening.

There'd been some troubling moments in the night, she remembered painfully. Her mind had been invaded by disturbing images of weeping, unhappy girls, Carrie and Daisy among them, their faces blotched and swollen with emotion. And another, her expression haggard, the velvet dark of her pansy-brown eyes red-rimmed with tears.

That one most of all, she thought, moving restively.

Her reverie was interrupted by a tap on the door, and Enrique came in with a tray holding a cafetière, cup and saucer, and a cream jug.

'*Buenos dias, señorita,*' he greeted her respectfully, just as if he hadn't had to unlock her door to gain entry. 'It is fine today, with much sun, and the sea is calm. The *señor* hopes that you will join him for breakfast presently.'

A number of responses occurred to Rhianna, most of them occupying a position between fury and obscenity, but she reminded herself that Enrique was only obeying orders, and managed to confine herself to a quiet, 'Thank you.'

Alone again, she leaned back against her pillows and considered. A fine day, she thought. Wasn't there a saying about "Happy is the bride that the sun shines on"?

Oh, let it be true, she begged silently and passionately. Let Carrie's happiness be unclouded, and maybe that will justify this whole hideous business.

In a few hours' time the wedding would be over, anyway, and if there had ever been a time for intervention it was long past.

She could only hope and pray that Simon had been sincere when he'd claimed Carrie was the one he really wanted all along. But his straying could hardly be dismissed as a temporary aberration when it had left such misery in its wake.

Cape Town should be far enough away to give the pair of them a totally fresh start. No chance of embarrassing or agonised encounters in the street or at parties there. No startled recognition in theatre bars or restaurants.

London's a village, she thought. Sooner or later you bump into everyone. As she knew to her cost…

Stop thinking like that, she adjured herself fiercely. Today's going to be quite tricky enough, and you need to be on top of your game, so stop right now.

She turned determinedly to the coffee, which was hot, strong and aromatic, and she could almost feel it putting new life into her.

A shower helped too, even if the limitations of her wardrobe became all too apparent immediately afterwards.

With a mental shrug, she picked out the white cut-offs and the green and white striped shirt she worn on the beach at Penvarnon the previous day, and slid her feet into espadrilles.

She brushed her hair back from her face with unwonted severity, securing it at the nape of her neck with an elastic band which had begun its life round the folder containing her train ticket and seat reservation.

The return portion would now remain unused, of course, she thought. wondering ironically if the train company would deem being kidnapped as a valid excuse for a refund.

Another item, she told herself, to be added to the cost of my stupidity.

Biting her lip, she walked to the door. When she tried it this time, however, it opened easily, and, drawing a long, deep breath, she went out and up the companionway to join her captor.

She found Diaz on the sun deck, where a table and two folding chairs had been placed. He was casual, in shabby cream shorts and a faded dark red polo shirt, his eyes hidden behind sunglasses as he studied some very small item of hand-held technical gadgetry, which probably contained, she reflected, his bank statements, his address book and details of his business commitments for the next ten years.

And she thought how much she'd like to throw it overboard.

At her approach, however, he switched it off and rose courteously to his feet.

'Good morning,' he said. 'I hope you slept well.'

'No,' she said. 'But that was hardly likely—under the circumstances.'

His brows lifted quizzically. 'Because you've been under a certain amount of tension lately? Is that what you're saying?'

She thought of the anguished phone calls, the bitter outbursts, the threats of self-harm, and all those other truly sleepless nights, punctuated by harsh, heart-rending sobbing. All culminating in the final acknowledgement that Simon had gone, and all hope had gone with him.

She looked past him. 'You don't know the half of it.'

'One of those situations where ignorance is definitely bliss.'

His tone bit. 'But you're a really splendid actress, my sweet,' he went on, after a pause. 'Because when I came in to check on you, just after dawn, I'd have sworn you were flat out. I thought I even detected a little snore. How wrong can anyone be?'

She shrugged. 'I'd say the field was wide open.' She sat down, determined not to show her inner disturbance at the thought of him watching her sleeping, and unfolded her table napkin. 'But you seem to have insomnia problems too, if you were lurking around in the small hours.' She gave him a small, flat smile. 'Conscience troubling you, perhaps?'

'Not at all,' he said. 'These are busy waters. I had no wish for a moment's inattention to result in our being mown down by a tanker.'

The arrival of the attentive Enrique, with glasses of freshly squeezed orange juice and a basket of warm rolls, followed almost at once by scrambled eggs with chorizo and another large pot of coffee, saved her having to find a reply.

'I hope the sea air has given you an appetite,' Diaz remarked, offering her the pepper mill.

'I wouldn't know,' Rhianna said icily, aware, to her everlasting shame, that her mouth was watering in response to the aroma from her plate. 'Being shut up in that five-star cell you condemned me to, I didn't know it existed. After all, I could hardly open a window to check the ozone levels.'

'Well, your freedom has been now fully restored, and you can breathe again.' He indicated a powerful-looking pair of binoculars lying on the table beside him. 'Are you interested in birdwatching? It could be a good day for it, now we've left the sea mist off Brest behind us.'

'I'm afraid your plans for my shipboard entertainment are doomed,' she returned, doing her damnedest not to eat too fast, even though these were the best scrambled eggs she'd ever tasted. She added untruthfully, 'I really wouldn't know a canary from a robin.'

'I think Biscay goes in more for shearwaters and arctic terns,' he said. 'But maybe you prefer mammals. We can usually offer a selection of dolphins in good weather, or, if you're lucky, you might even spot a whale.'

'If I was lucky,' she said stonily, concealing a flash of delight, 'I wouldn't be here in the first place. And why would I want to see a whale anyway?'

'Because they're rare and beautiful creatures,' Diaz said quietly. 'I thought like might call to like.'

Rhianna looked down at her empty plate, her throat tightening as he paused.

'Besides,' he went on, 'you might get cast one day in another remake of *Moby Dick*, with the advantage of being already acquainted with the main character.'

'Unlikely,' she said, forbidding herself even a marginal smile. 'Female roles are pretty thin in that particular epic.'

'I'm sure they'd adapt it to accommodate you,' he said, pouring more coffee. 'A girl stowaway on the *Pequod* who slowly wins the heart of Captain Ahab and turns him from his revenge to joint ownership of a seafood restaurant on Nantucket.'

She shuddered. 'Oh, God, don't even suggest it. Someone might hear.'

'But if not that,' he said, 'there'll be other roles to play eventually.'

'I hope so,' Rhianna said slowly. 'I wouldn't like to think that Lady Ariadne would be all I'd be remembered for.' She bit her lip. 'But at the moment I'm not looking beyond the next series.'

'And what would have happened to that,' he enquired levelly, 'if Simon had asked you to marry him after all? If he'd wanted you to keep the baby? What price Lady Ariadne then?'

Be careful, said the voice in her head. *Be very careful. You can't give anything away.*

She shrugged again. 'That was never going to happen,' she said. 'I knew it. Simon certainly knew it. And we both made our choices long before you decided to interfere. Whatever you may have seen or heard, or think you know, the wedding was never in any danger from me.'

She sent him a cool smile. 'So now you'll have to live with the knowledge that it's all been a total waste of time. That you've carried me off for nothing, Mr Penvarnon.' She lifted her chin.

'Therefore, why don't you admit defeat, turn this expensive piece of equipment right around, and take me back to England?'

He pushed his chair back and rose. 'Because it's far too late for that, Rhianna,' he said softly. 'It always has been. And if you don't know that, sweetheart, then you're lying not just to me but to yourself as well.'

And he walked away, leaving her staring after him, her mouth suddenly dry and her pulses pounding.

In spite of the breeze, it was still hot enough for Rhianna to be thankful for the awning above the sun deck, where she lay on a cushioned lounger. But even in its shade her clothes were sticking to her.

I didn't bring a bikini on this trip, she thought wryly, because it never occurred to me I'd have time to sunbathe. Besides, I knew I could always borrow a costume from Carrie if I fancied a quick swim in between pre-wedding chores.

But maybe a bikini, or any kind of swimwear, would not be a good choice for these particular circumstances. Being fully dressed might not be comfortable, but it seemed altogether the safer option.

In view of his parting shot, she'd been half tempted to go to her stateroom and stay there, not venturing back on deck at all. But that might suggest she was disturbed by what he'd said, and she couldn't afford that. She had to appear indifferent, even relaxed, if that was possible.

So she'd simply collected her sunglasses, and the book she'd intended for the journey back to Paddington, and she was now struggling to lose herself in it. The reviews had been good, and it was by an author she liked, but the story was failing to hold her.

Real life seems to keep intruding, she told herself, endeavouring not to glance at the bridge, where Diaz, his shirt discarded, was seated at the controls, and thankful for the designer shades concealing the direction of her gaze.

What's wrong with me? she demanded silently. I've seen plenty of men in less than he's wearing. Come to that, I've seen him in far less too, only I was too young to appreciate it. Even if I've never been able to forget... But would the image of him emerging from the water like some dark sea god be the one she would take with her into the approaching wilderness?

Or would their encounters of a few months ago prove more potent in the end? Become the ones to be treasured?

Like the moment when she'd glanced across the crowded room at the sponsors' party and seen him there, unchanged and unmistakable after nearly five years, chatting to the Apex chairman and his wife.

She'd never really expected to see him again, so the shock of it had held her breathless, motionless for a moment, captive to all kinds of contradictory emotions. Then, obeying an imperative she'd barely understood but had known she might regret, she'd murmured an excuse to the group around her and begun to make her way towards him.

Halfway across the room, she had almost turned back.

I don't know what to say, she'd thought. Or even how I should behave. Surprised—that goes without saying. But should I be pleased to see him, or strictly casual? Just stopping for a quick word in passing on my way out to find a cab?

She had still been undecided when Sir John Blenkinsop had noticed her approach.

'Ah, delightful,' he said heartily. 'Diaz, you must allow me to introduce you to our star—the lovely girl who keeps the ratings for *Castle Pride* sky-high. Rhianna, my dear, this is Diaz Penvarnon, a valued client of Apex Insurance.'

There was an instant's silence, then Diaz said pleasantly, 'Actually, Sir John, Miss Carlow and I have already met. And delightful is certainly the word.' His eyes skimmed her, taking in the white brocade coat-dress, knee-length, its lapels designed to show a definite but discreet amount of cleavage. Then he took her nerveless hand in his and bent to kiss her cheek, his lips warm and firm as they brushed her face.

'Rhianna,' he said as he straightened. 'It's been a long time.'

Say something—anything...

'It has indeed. Too long.' Her numb lips managed to return his smile. 'I suppose this is one of your flying visits to the UK? Is it business or pleasure this time?'

'The usual mix,' he said. 'And my plans are fluid at the moment.' He paused. 'I've just come back from Polkernick.'

'Of course,' she said over-brightly, as guilt kicked in, reminding her of all the reasons she had to avoid him, and why she should have resisted this and every other temptation he represented to her. 'How—how is everyone?'

His grin was rueful. 'Wedding fever has risen to epidemic proportions,' he returned. 'If ever I tie the knot it's going to be at a register office very early in the morning. Guest list limited to two witnesses.'

'Oh, your bride will soon change your mind about that,' said Sir John. 'Women like these full-dress affairs, you know.'

Diaz said gently, 'Then I shall just have to persuade her.' He indicated the empty glass Rhianna was holding. 'May I get you another drink?'

'Yes, you look after her, my boy.' Sir John turned to his wife. 'Marjorie, my dear, I see Clement Jackson has arrived. He's bound to want a word, so shall we leave these two to catch up with each other?'

Rhianna stood, clawed by a mixture of excitement and uncertainty, as she waited for Diaz to return with the dry white wine she'd requested. I shouldn't be doing this, she whispered inwardly. I should be making an excuse and easing myself out. But I can't—I can't…

'Apparently Lord Byron said he woke up one morning and found himself famous,' Diaz remarked, as he handed her the glass. 'Was it like that for you?'

'Far from it,' she said. 'Although it's got trickier since. You become public property. People see me in their living rooms and think they know me.'

'How very optimistic of them,' Diaz said silkily. 'But it's good that you've prospered, Rhianna, after your precipitate exit from Polkernick. I was afraid the sight of me might put you to flight again.'

But I didn't jump—I was pushed…

Aloud, she said coolly, 'I think I'm a little more resilient these days.'

Am I? she thought. Am I—when the memory of you saying 'I don't take sweets from babies' still has the power to tear me apart? When just by standing here like this I know I could be setting up such trouble for myself?

She swallowed. 'I think Sir John's trying to attract your attention. He has someone he wants you to meet.' She sent him a brilliant smile. 'Enjoy your time in London.'

She walked away and didn't look back, her heart hammering painfully against her ribcage.

I've met him, she thought. I've spoken to him. And that's the end of it. There's no point in hoping, or wishing things could be different. Because that's never been possible.

She was halfway down the wide sweep of marble stairs that led to Apex Insurance's main foyer and the street, when she heard him speak her name.

She paused, her hand clenched painfully on the polished brass rail, then turned reluctantly.

He said evenly, 'Clearly we don't share the same definition of resilience, Rhianna, because here you are—running away again.'

'Not at all.' She lifted her chin. 'This evening was work, not social. So I've made my token appearance, kept the sponsors happy, and now I'm going home as planned. Job done.'

'Then change the plan,' he said softly. 'Have dinner with me instead.'

Her heart seemed to stop. 'Heavens,' she said lightly. 'What is this—some bridge-building exercise?'

'It's a man asking a beautiful woman to spend a couple of hours in his company,' Diaz returned. 'Do we really need to analyse it so closely or so soon? Why not simply see where it takes us.'

To disaster, she thought. There can be nothing else. So just utter a few polite words of regret and keep going. That's the wise—the sensible course. The only one possible.

She said, 'But you're clearly the guest of honour for Sir John. Won't he be upset if you disappear?'

'No,' he said. 'Nor surprised either. So will you be *my* guest of honour instead?'

And she heard herself say, unbelievably, 'Yes—I—I'd like that.'

Knowing, with mingled dread and anticipation, that she was speaking no more than the truth. That wisdom and common sense had counted for nothing the moment she'd seen him again. And that she was lost.

'I saw you as soon as I walked in tonight,' he said, as they faced each other across the candlelit table of the small Italian *trattoria*. 'There's only one head of hair like that in the entire universe. As soon as I'd finished being polite to my host I was going to come over to you.'

Rhianna put up a self-conscious hand. 'It's become almost a trademark,' she said, grimacing. 'I'm expected to wear it loose when I'm on show, like tonight. And my contract forbids me to cut it.'

'Of course,' he said. 'It would be a crime against humanity.' And his smile touched her like a caress.

She couldn't remember to this day what they'd eaten, although she was sure it had been delicious. She'd simply yielded herself completely to the luxury of being with him, just for that brief time.

Much later, outside, as he'd signalled to a cab, she'd said huskily, knowing she was a fool and worse than a fool, yet unwilling, in spite of herself, to let him go, 'Would you like some more coffee—a nightcap?'

And he said very quietly, 'Thank you. That would be—good.'

People were just coming out of the theatres, so the streets and pavements were crowded. As the taxi nosed its way along, Rhianna sat beside him in silence, hands clenched in her lap. Waiting and wondering.

She did not have to wait for long. And when Diaz took her in his arms she yielded instantly, her lips parting under the urgency of his kiss, her body pressed against his.

As she clung to him, she rejoiced secretly that her erstwhile lodger was no longer with her, and her flat was her own again. That she would be alone with him there. Then remembered that her precious privacy had come at a price.

She thought, If Diaz ever finds out about Simon...

Then, as his kiss deepened, she stopped thinking altogether,

her whole being possessed by the shock of desire. Because nothing mattered but the fact that she was with him—and the prospect, at last, of long-delayed surrender.

And she ignored the small warning voice in her mind that said, *This is so dangerous*, and allowed herself to be completely and passionately happy.

'*Señorita—señorita*—you come here quickly, please.' It was Juan, grinning with delight. 'Now, *señorita*.'

Startled back into the present, Rhianna got up from the lounger and followed him to the side of the boat, where Diaz was waiting.

'What's wrong?' She spoke curtly, her memories having left her unnerved and uncomfortable. But at least he was wearing his shirt again.

'Nothing at all.' He glanced at her with faint surprise. 'Look over there.'

Rhianna looked and gasped as a long silver body rose from the waves with a joyous twist, then disappeared again with a smack of its tail fin, to be followed by several more, their faces all set in that unmistakable half-moon smile as they jumped and soared.

'Oh, how wonderful.' She could not pretend sophisticated boredom when this amazing show was being performed as if for her exclusive benefit. She leaned on the rail, her face alight with pleasure, watching the dolphins cavort. 'Have you ever seen anything so beautiful?'

'Not often,' Diaz said quietly. 'Except in my dreams.' And she realised with shock that he was looking at her.

Her throat closed. *Oh, God, how can you say such things after everything that's happened? What do you want from me? Haven't I suffered enough?*

She stared at the gleaming, leaping bodies until they blurred, then with one last triumphant 'thwack' they were gone, and there was only the faint glimmer of them through the water as they sped away.

'The cabaret seems to be over,' Diaz commented. 'Conveniently, just in time for lunch.'

'More food?' Back in command of herself, she sent him a challenging look. 'I shall need a week at a health farm after this.'

'After this,' he said, 'the choice will be all yours.'

'Tell me something,' she said as they sat down. 'How much longer will it take to get where we're going?'

His brows rose. 'Is it so important to get somewhere?'

'Of course,' she said coldly. 'Because the faster we arrive, the sooner I can put this nonsense behind me and go home. Only we don't seem to be travelling very fast at all.'

She pointed to a large vessel in the distance that was steadily overhauling them. 'What's that, for instance?'

'The *Queen of Castile*,' Diaz said. 'Sailing between Plymouth and Santander.'

'Don't you find it faintly humiliating when you have all this power, purchased no doubt at vast expense, to be beaten for speed by a car ferry?'

'Not at all,' he said. 'This is a pleasure cruise, not a race. Anyway, I prefer to conserve fuel and have a comfortable passage.' He paused. 'But we should arrive at Puerto Caravejo in the early hours of tomorrow morning.'

'I've never heard of it,' she said shortly. 'Does it have an airport?'

'No,' he said. 'Just a pleasant marina, with some good restaurants. But you can fly to Gatwick from Oviedo. So, now that I've set your mind at rest, shall we eat?'

She wanted to say she wasn't hungry, because under the circumstances it should have been true, but once more Enrique's offerings proved irresistible.

The first course was a creamy vegetable risotto, studded with asparagus tips, tiny peas and young broad beans, and that was followed by grilled fish, served with crisp sauté potatoes, with fresh fruit for dessert.

Diaz consulted his watch. 'By my reckoning they'll be back from the church now,' he remarked. 'And just settling down to lunch in the marquee, with all its attendant rituals. So shall we drink a toast of our own?'

'To the happy couple?' Rhianna asked with irony. She shook her head. 'I don't think so.'

He was silent for a moment, and she saw his mouth harden. 'Naturally I can see that might not appeal,' he said, and picked up his glass of white wine. 'So let's just say—to matrimony.' And he drank.

'Forgive me,' she said, 'if I don't join in that either.'

He said with sudden harshness, 'He's gone, Rhianna. You've lost him. Accept it.'

Diaz paused. 'Coffee?'

'No, thank you.' Rhianna rose to her feet. 'I think I'll go below where it's cooler for a while.'

And where I don't have the nerve-racking disturbance of being in your company with all the attendant memories I can so well do without...

She added, 'Actually, I might start packing my things, ready for going ashore.'

'There's no great rush.' He sounded faintly amused. 'But— just as you wish.' He paused. 'Although I can recommend the old Spanish custom of *siesta*.'

She said unsmilingly, 'You're too kind. But I think I've already experienced enough old Spanish customs to last me a lifetime.'

Downstairs, the air-conditioning was as efficient as she'd hoped, and her stateroom was pleasantly dim too as someone— Enrique, she supposed—had closed the blinds.

Her refuge, she thought, as she sank down on the sofa. But, as she soon discovered, only a fragile sanctuary at best. Because, as she stared in front of her with eyes that saw nothing, she found there was no escape from her inner images of the past.

Or, she realised with anguish, their pain.

CHAPTER EIGHT

HER flat was on the first floor, and she and Diaz had run up the stairs, she remembered, laughing and breathless, hand in hand. Outside her door they'd paused to kiss again, all restraint gone. When they'd fallen apart, Rhianna's fingers had been shaking so much she'd hardly been able to fit the key in the lock, and Diaz, an arm clamped round her, his lips nuzzling her neck, had done it for her.

In the hallway they'd reached hungrily for each other again. His mouth pushing aside the loosened brocade lapels, seeking the curve of her breast. Her hands inside his unbuttoned shirt, spread against the hard, heated wall of his chest, registering the thunder of his heart.

He'd said her name hoarsely, and then, like a small uncertain echo, she'd heard 'Rhianna' spoken by a different voice, coming from an entirely different direction.

Her life had stopped. She'd turned sharply in disbelief and seen the small, slender figure standing, fragile and woebegone, in the doorway of the sitting room. Seen the dishevelled hair, the trembling mouth and the eyes swollen with tears.

'Donna?' She swallowed. 'What are you doing here?'

'I had to come back. I had nowhere else to go.' The other woman gave a little sob. 'Oh, Rhianna, I'm so sorry. Please try to understand…'

She looked past her at Diaz, a hand straying to her mouth. 'I— I thought you'd be alone. I didn't realise…'

'Don't worry about it.' Someone was speaking in her voice, Rhianna thought. Someone who sounded controlled and capable. Who wasn't dying inside, of disappointment and so many other things besides.

She said levelly, 'Donna, may I introduce Diaz Penvarnon? A cousin of my friend Caroline Seymour, whom I've mentioned to you.' And paused. 'Diaz, this is Donna Winston, a fellow cast member from *Castle Pride*. She was my flatmate until a short while ago, when she found—somewhere else.'

'Which clearly hasn't worked out,' Diaz said quietly. He didn't have to add, Exactly like tonight. But the words were there, all the same, hanging in the air between them, in all their regret and frustration. He said, 'I'd better go. May I call you tomorrow? Are you in the book?'

She wasn't, so she gave him her number hurriedly, watching as he logged it into his mobile phone.

Donna said with a catch in her voice, 'I'll make some coffee,' and trailed off to the kitchen.

Diaz took Rhianna in his arms, smiling ruefully down at her. 'I see the drama continues off-screen sometimes.' He paused. 'Man trouble?'

'It seems so.' *I know so.* She shook her head. 'Oh, God, I'm so sorry…'

'So am I.' His lips were gentle on hers. 'But we'll have our time, Rhianna. That's a promise.'

And even then, when it had all started to fall apart, she'd believed him.

He'd rung the next day. 'How's the friend in need?'

'Still needy,' she'd admitted, worn out after a night of tears, recrimination and seriously bad news, but feeling her heart lift when she heard his voice.

'And clearly around for the foreseeable future?' He sounded amused and resigned. 'I shall just have to be patient.' He paused. 'All the same, may I see you this evening? A film, maybe?'

'Yes,' she said, smiling foolishly into space. 'That would be lovely.'

Donna, having slept late, mooned tearfully round the flat most of the day. In the late afternoon she said she was going to see her agent, and departed.

Rhianna, sighing with relief, could only pray that she'd also visit a company arranging flat rentals.

Because she cannot stay here, she told herself, sinking gratefully into a deep hot bath. Not again, and not now. Things have gone too far, and she knows that.

She was still in her robe when the door buzzer went, and she looked at her watch and laughed, because he was nearly forty minutes early.

She was still smiling when she opened the door.

'Hello, Rhianna,' said Simon, and walked past her without waiting for an invitation. 'Are you alone? Good. Because it's time for a serious chat, I think.'

'Not now,' she said quickly. 'It—it's really not convenient. I'm expecting someone.' *The last person in the world who should find you here...*

'Tough.' He went into the sitting room, straight to the corner cupboard, and found the Scotch, pouring himself a generous measure.

When he turned, there was brooding anger in his face.

'I suppose she's told you?'

'Yes,' she said. 'Also that you've dumped her, accused her of getting pregnant deliberately in order to trap you, and ordered her to have an abortion. Nice work, Simon.'

'Of course you're on *her* side,' he said. 'All sisters together against the male oppressor. I know how it works. But don't be taken in by the innocent big brown eyes. She didn't need much persuading—as you must have noticed when you walked in on us that night.'

She hadn't forgotten. One of her rare migraines had threatened, sending her home early from a supper party. She'd heard noises from the sitting room and pushed open the door, to see Donna and Simon, naked and entwined on the rug in front of the fireplace, engrossed in vigorous and uninhibited sex.

Donna had seen her first and screamed. Simon had flung himself off his partner's body with more haste than finesse.

Rhianna had retreated to her room, sitting on the edge of the bed, fighting incipient nausea as the implications of what she'd interrupted came home to her.

She took a breath. 'Believe me, I'm on no one's side,' she said bitterly. 'But do you realise she was actually threatening suicide last night?'

'That's just ridiculous talk,' he said flatly. 'Ignore it.' He added, 'You do realise, I hope, that this baby simply cannot be born? I'm not going to lose all I want out of life just for one bloody stupid mistake.'

'Don't you mean a whole series of them?' She faced him, chin up, angry herself as she wondered defeatedly what had happened to the Simon she'd once known and whom, briefly and long ago, she'd thought she wanted.

I used to envy Carrie so much I was ashamed to look at her, she thought. Now I'm just ashamed.

She added fiercely, 'This is hardly a unilateral decision by you. A termination is incredibly serious for a woman.'

'And my future is equally serious,' he retorted, taking a gulp of whisky. 'For God's sake, Rhianna. You know what this would do to Carrie if she found out. That can't be allowed to happen. Admit it, damn you.'

'Yes,' she said bitterly. 'I know. And I swear she won't find out from me.'

'Good. Then you'll do whatever's necessary? Donna trusts you, and you can persuade her to do the right thing—if not for my sake, then for Carrie's.' He finished the Scotch and put the glass down. 'You're a great girl, Rhianna,' he went on more slowly. 'And you look bloody amazing in that robe. I'd bet good money you're not wearing anything underneath it. Care to prove it—for old times' sake?'

'There are no "old times"'. She looked at him with steady contempt. 'There never were. Now get out of here at once.'

He whistled. 'Hard words, but you're still going to help me, aren't you? Because you don't really have a choice.' He paused at the front door she'd thrown open. 'I'm relying on you, remember,' he added. 'So don't let me down.'

He turned to go, and she saw his face change. Looking past him, she realised that Diaz had indeed arrived ahead of time, and was standing motionless at the top of the stairs, his brows drawn together as he watched them.

'So this is the expected admirer,' Simon said mockingly. 'Well, well, you are a dark horse, Rhianna. I'll give your love to Carrie—shall I? Hello and goodbye, Diaz. Have a pleasant evening. I guarantee you will.' He winked at Rhianna and went, the sound of his footsteps clattering down the stairs.

Rhianna stood dry-mouthed as Diaz, still frowning, walked towards her, knowing that he would ask questions she would not be able to answer.

And felt the last remnants of hope shrivel and die inside her, as she had always somehow known they must.

As the flat door closed behind them, Diaz said abruptly, 'Does he make a habit of calling here?'

I don't want to lie to him. Please don't make me lie to him...
She said, 'He's around from time to time.'

'Carrie didn't say you were seeing each other.'

'She probably didn't think it worth mentioning.' Rhianna forced herself to play along and shrug lightly. 'After all, we're hardly strangers, he and I.'

'No,' he said slowly. 'I hadn't forgotten.' He paused. 'Is that how you usually receive him—dressed—or undressed—like that?'

'Of course not.' Her indignation at least could be genuine. 'And I certainly wasn't expecting him this evening, if that's what you think.'

'Frankly,' he said, 'I don't know what to think. After all, it was hardly the welcome I was anticipating.'

She looked away. 'Nor the one I'd planned, believe me.' Her voice was bleak.

He glanced around. 'So, where's the weeping willow?'

Rhianna bit her lip. 'That's neither kind nor fair.'

'Perhaps I'm not feeling particularly charitable. And you didn't answer my question.'

'She's gone out,' Rhianna said.

His brows rose. 'Good news at last,' he said softly. 'So, why don't we forget about the cinema and stay here?'

If she took two steps forward, she thought, she'd be in his arms, all questions silenced. He wanted her. She wanted him. Simple.

Except it was nothing of the kind. Because she knew, none better, the dangers of sex without any kind of commitment. She'd heard them being paraded only a little while ago, in this very room.

She was aware of her own feelings, but not his. Diaz was still an enigma to her. He'd spoken of her running away five years before, but he'd made no attempt to follow. He'd let her leave Penvarnon alone and, as far as he knew, friendless. It had been Francis Seymour and Carrie who'd stood by her, not him.

And he was here with her now only because of this nameless, inexplicable thing between them that had burst into life that night in the stable yard, subjecting her to the torments of the damned ever since.

Something apparently that he'd not been able to forget either, even as he lived his life, made his money and slept with other women.

An appetite in him that she'd aroused and he wished to satisfy. And when he'd taken all she had to give and he was no longer hungry—what then? What was to prevent him just walking away, leaving her used up and discarded? Like Donna?

And all on the strength of one short-lived and disastrous encounter when she was eighteen years old.

I'm worth, she thought, far more than that.

Aloud she said, 'Because Donna will be back very soon. So it appears that it's the cinema or nothing.' She added coolly, 'And in your present mood, Diaz, I have to say the second option seems preferable.'

'I could make you change your mind.'

Yes, but not my heart...

'Why, Mr Penvarnon,' she said mockingly, just as if she wasn't weeping inside, 'how very uncool.'

The look he sent her was long and totally deliberate, stripping away the concealing robe in order to create her nakedness in his imagination. And knowing what he was doing, and why, made it no easier to bear.

She stood, her body burning, hardly able to breathe, until at last he turned away, and she heard the outside door close behind him.

Then she sat down and covered her face with her hands.

She'd thought at the time that it was the nadir—the depths— the worst that could happen.

But I was wrong about that too, she told herself now.

She got up from the sofa, pushing her hair back from her face. She'd come down here to pack, she thought, not indulge in useless introspection. Therefore pack she would.

Be positive, she adjured herself. After all, there could hardly be more than another twenty-four hours for her to endure in his company. And if there was still a measure of physical attraction between them, then it could not be allowed to count. She didn't need it, and nor did he. *Finis.*

She opened the wardrobe and gave the selection of clothes there a jaundiced look.

She'd keep out her coffee linen dress, she decided, pulling a face, and stow the rest in her travel bag. But as she dragged it from the back of the cupboard it toppled over, and a medium-sized brown envelope slid out of the front pocket.

Rhianna picked it up, frowning. It was addressed to her, in handwriting she didn't recognise, she thought as she weighed it speculatively in her hand. Who on earth? And what on earth?

She wasn't in the mood for mysteries, but she couldn't help being curious all the same as she ran a finger under the flap. Inside she found a folder of photographs and a note.

She sat down on the bed, switched on the lamp, and read the note first.

Dear Miss Carlow,
We found this when we had the bedroom unit in the flat taken out. It must have fallen down behind it. We could see it belonged to your late aunt, and thought you might want to have it, so I put it with your things. I hope I did right.
M. Henderson.

So, Rhianna thought with a grimace, I seem to have a legacy from Aunt Kezia after all. How very weird.

She opened the folder and tipped out the handful of snapshots it contained.

It was an odd collection, all apparently taken round Penvarnon House and its grounds. None of the local views she might have expected. Just people. And clearly not posing. No one was smiling or saying 'cheese' because they'd glanced up and seen a camera on them.

And Aunt Kezia had been no photographer either. The angles were odd, capturing her subjects' back views, and the shots were hurried and blurred because the subjects were moving.

She studied them more closely, recognising Francis Seymour in several of them. But mainly they featured another man entirely, and for a bewildered moment she thought, It's Diaz. Why did she take all these pictures of Diaz?

Then she looked again, and realised that this was Diaz as he would be in ten or twenty years time—broader, heavier and greyer. But the resemblance was almost eerily strong, and she said, under her breath, 'Of course—it's his father. It's Ben Penvarnon.'

The next one showed a woman seated on the terrace at the house, her head bent, her body slumped, and it was only when Rhianna looked more closely that she realised she was sitting in a wheelchair.

How cruel, she thought, of Aunt Kezia to take a photograph of Esther Penvarnon, her employer, like this, and how unnecessary.

The rest all seemed to be of Moira Seymour, taken invariably from a distance and only just recognisable. In one she was standing near the top of the path down to the cove, glancing back over her shoulder, as if she knew there was a camera trained on her. In others she was emerging from the shrubbery, pushing the bushes aside, her face white and formless, or standing under the shadow of a tree with her husband.

There was something strange, even furtive about the photographs, Rhianna thought with distaste as she shuffled them together to replace them in the wallet. Then paused, because there was something else there. A slip of folded paper.

A cheque, she realised, for twenty-three pounds, made out to K. Trewint, and bearing the signature Benjamin Penvarnon. It was over twenty-five years out of date, and had clearly never been presented.

Rhianna stared at it in utter astonishment. How could her aunt possibly have overlooked such a thing? She'd have backed her to pay it into her account the same day—even if it had only been for twenty-three pence. So how could she have forgotten?

She refolded it and put it back in the wallet with the snaps, aware that her breathing had quickened. She felt as she'd done once when she was very young, when she'd turned over a stone in the garden only to release a host of creeping things that had scuttled everywhere. She'd screamed, knowing that if one of them ran over her sandal she wouldn't be able to bear it, and that she'd be sick or worse.

Now, she just felt—grubby in some odd way, wishing very much the bedroom unit at the stable flat had stayed where it was, with its secret intact.

Her instinct told her to destroy the entire folder, but she could hardly throw it overboard. It didn't seem fair to the dolphins. So she'd have to take it back to London with her and get rid of it there, she decided, tossing it back in her bag.

And now what she needed most in the world was a shower, she thought with a sudden shiver.

In the bathroom, she stripped and walked into the cubicle, rubbing handfuls of her favourite gel into every inch of her skin as if she were taking part in some essential decontamination process. Then she stood, head thrown back and eyes closed, allowing the cool, refreshing torrent to pour over her until every last trace of foam had gone.

She turned off the shower at last, with a sigh of relief and pleasure. Twisting her hair into a thick mahogany rope in order to squeeze out the excess water, she stepped back into the bathroom.

She'd heard no sound above the rush of the shower. Had felt no prickle of awareness. Yet he was there, standing in the doorway, watching her. Waiting for her.

She halted, hands still raised, totally, sublimely exposed, as a slow, quivering heat suffused her body under his silver gaze. As she acknowledged that it was much too late for even a token attempt to cover herself.

Nor was there any point in asking what the hell he thought he was doing there, because she already knew. But she had to say something—if only to break this taut and terrible silence stretching between them.

Her voice a husky whisper, she pleaded, 'Diaz—no…'

'You are so beautiful.' The words seemed torn from him. He moved, lithe as a panther, walking over to the pile of towels to take one and envelop her in it before, without haste, blotting the moisture from her skin.

'How can you do this?' she protested again, her voice shaking. The slow movement of his hands on her body through the layer of towelling was already an unbearable, shameful incitement. He was shirtless again, and the clean, sun-warmed scent of his skin filled her nose and mouth, turning her dizzy. 'Feeling as you do—despising me?'

'Because this is unfinished business between us, Rhianna, and you know it.' He spoke calmly. 'And whatever you've been to Simon Rawlins, it hasn't stopped me wanting you, although God knows I've tried.'

A fist seemed to clench inside her, and she knew she needed to stop him urgently, tell him everything before it was too late.

'Please,' she said, rapidly. 'Please, Diaz—you must listen. You don't understand…'

'No,' he said. 'You're the one who doesn't understand.'

He lifted her into his arms, stifling any further protest with the hard pressure of his mouth, and carried her into the other room. The coverlet on the bed had been turned back in readiness, and he put her down on the snowy sheet, followed her down.

Kneeling over her, he unwrapped the towel from her body and tossed it on to the floor. Stripped off his shorts and sent them to follow the towel, before stretching himself, naked, beside her.

'I need to erase him,' he told her quietly, almost conversationally, looking down into her widening scared eyes. 'To wipe him from your mind and memory for ever. To prove to you that you can't live in the past, Rhianna, and set you free. To show you that there's a present, and there can be a future.'

'No,' she said hoarsely. 'You're so wrong. There never will be—not without the man I love.'

He smiled with faint bitterness. 'You may be right,' he said. 'But at least I can try.'

He put his hand on her stomach, smoothing the damp skin with almost exquisite care, and she felt the pleasure of it shiver through every nerve-ending in her body.

'And you don't have to worry,' he added softly. 'I swear I'll be gentle.'

'Oh, God.' Her voice sounded stifled, caught as she was between terror and desire, as she realised what he meant. Remembered what he believed. 'Diaz—no. There's something I must say. Please let me go.'

'Yes,' he said. 'I will. As I promised. But not yet. We'll talk later. Afterwards.'

He leaned down and kissed her again, his lips moving on hers this time in a slow and seductive quest, coaxing them apart, preparing her for the heated, silken invasion of his tongue, carrying her, as some reeling corner of her mind acknowledged, beyond denial. But not beyond shame.

When at last he raised his head she was breathless, wordless, her pulses playing all kinds of tricks as she stared up at him through the veil of her lashes.

'I should have made love to you weeks ago,' he told her huskily. 'That night at your flat when I found him there. But I was too angry then. You were right to send me away. Before that you wanted me, and I knew it. Later, when I realised you were still sleeping with him, I told myself that it was too late—that I could never come near you—never bear to touch you again—not after—him.'

His mouth twisted. 'Yet here I am. Needing you so badly that I'm prepared to forget decency and reason, along with everything else that should be keeping us apart. I no longer have a choice.'

His stroking hand moved slowly upwards, over her midriff and ribcage, to cup the soft swell of her breast, his thumb grazing her nipple and awakening it to hot, aching life.

'We could even treat it as a pact,' he whispered. 'I'll release you from Simon and you, my lovely Rhianna, you can release me—from you. And maybe we'll both have some peace at last. Show me what you like.'

He bent, taking her tumescent rosy peak in his mouth, caressing it with the sweet agony of his tongue, making her gasp, her body arching involuntarily towards him.

She had only instinct to guide her. No prior knowledge of what the responses of her flesh might be to his hands and lips, or what he, in turn, might expect from her.

All those love scenes, taunted the only rational part of her brain still functioning. All that simulated ecstasy. And now that you're faced with reality instead of play-acting you haven't got a bloody clue...

And yet this is what you've longed for in all those long, empty years since you were eighteen—for Diaz Penvarnon to take you in his arms again and make love to you. To bring you to fulfilment as a woman.

No guilt. No shadows from the past. Just two people on a bed, together, just for a while.

And even if it is happening for all the wrong reasons, it's probably all you'll ever have of him—your one chance of happiness—so give him the only gift you have to offer and be thankful.

As if he'd picked up some unspoken cue, she heard him say, on a soft breath of amusement, 'This is usually a duet, sweetheart, not a solo. Aren't you going to touch me too? Let yourself remember how you once enjoyed being in my arms?'

She reached up to his shoulders, stroking the taut skin, feeling the strength of bone and the play of muscle under her shyly exploring fingers.

With a murmur of satisfaction Diaz drew her closer into his

arms, kissing her mouth again, while his own hands slowly traced the length of her long, supple spine, moulding the rounded curves of her buttocks.

She moved against him deliberately, the breath catching in her throat as she felt the answering pressure of his aroused hardness against her belly. She reached down, her fingers shyly seeking a more intimate acquaintance with all that iron male strength, but Diaz forestalled her, his hand on her wrist.

'Easy, my love,' he whispered, dropping light kisses on her eyelids, his lips tugging softly at her long lashes. 'I've waited far too long for this to be in any hurry, but God knows I'm only human, and I'm not sure how much of that particular delight I can bear right now. So let's—take our time.'

He began to caress her body, his fingertips brushing the creamy satin of her skin, and Rhianna lay, sighing through parted lips, her entire being subsumed in this glory of sensual pleasure he was creating for her.

And where his hands lingered his mouth followed, tasting the hollows at the base of her throat, the inside curve of her arms, the indentation of her navel, the faint swell of her hips and the slender length of her thighs.

She was moving restlessly beneath his touch, her flesh burning, eager for more. When his mouth took hers again she clung to him, her passionate response lacking all inhibition.

His lips returned to her breasts, suckling on their hard, aroused peaks, making her moan aloud, while his hand slid down to the shadowed cleft between her thighs and paused there.

He lifted his head and looked down at her, at the fever-bright eyes, the storm of excited colour along the high cheekbones, and the swollen, reddened mouth.

He said harshly, 'Do you still want me to stop? To let you go?'

'No.' Her voice was a shadow of itself. 'Oh, God—please—no…'

He began to touch her *there*, in the hot, secret centre of her, and she offered herself unequivocally to the intimacy of this new exploration, the mastery of his subtle fingers irresistibly enticing.

She'd never believed it could be possible to feel with such intensity, she thought as her breathing splintered, her mind and body focussed almost painfully on the sensuous stroke of his hand as he sought her tiny sheltered nub of sensitive flesh and brought it to aching delicious life.

Don't stop. The words were a silent scream in her head. *Never stop…*

Her body awash with fluid, scalding excitement, she heard him say hoarsely, 'Darling *now.*'

As he moved over her, above her, Rhianna obeyed instantly, clasping the rigid silken shaft of his virility with shaking fingers and guiding him into her with a little sob of anticipation.

Then, between one heartbeat and the next, everything changed. Because the last thing she'd expected was that it would hurt. That his physical possession of her would cause actual pain. The kind that made her flinch and tense into resistance, crying out before she could stop yourself.

Because that notion of virginity as a barrier to be breached was surely a myth belonging to past generations?

Yet here she was, with beads of perspiration on her forehead, sinking her teeth into her lower lip.

Diaz was suddenly very still. He said urgently, his breathing harsh and ragged, 'What is it? What's wrong? Darling, tell me…'

Then as he looked down at her, looked into her shocked, scared eyes, she saw realisation dawn—and a kind of horror.

He whispered, 'Oh, my God,' and lifted himself out of her—away from her—in one swift movement of utter finality, flinging himself on his side, his back to her, his breathing hoarse and ragged.

She lay staring at the ceiling, trying to say something—his name, perhaps, out of a throat tight with tears.

But eventually it was Diaz who broke the silence. 'You've never done this before.' It was a statement, not a question He turned back slowly to face her, pulling up the sheet to cover the lower part of his body and propping himself on an elbow. 'Simon Rawlins was never your lover, and you're not having his child. Because until a few moments ago you were *virgo intacta.*'

'I'm sorry,' was all she could manage. 'I'm so sorry.'

'Yet, knowing that,' Diaz went on, as if she hadn't spoken, 'you encouraged me to—violate you. Why?'

She said, 'Because I wanted you.' *Because I love you. I always have and always will.*

Those unsayable words he would not want to hear. Therefore they went unsaid.

She took a deep breath. 'I decided long ago that my first time was going to be with someone I'd always really fancied, who knew what he was doing. You fitted the template perfectly—and created the opportunity too. You can hardly deny that. So it was never a—a violation. I truly wanted it, and you must believe that.'

She added unevenly, 'I thought being a virgin was simply a state of mind. I never dreamed there'd be—consequences.'

'Apart, you mean,' he said with chilling irony, 'from the dangers of unprotected sex? You didn't take those into consideration? The fact that there might be a real baby to be disposed of this time?'

She winced. 'Don't!'

Do you really imagine I'm capable of that? Especially if it's your child involved? I'd rather die...

'What the hell did you think you were doing?' he demanded. 'Taking part in some episode from that damned series? Making life up as you went along? Why in God's name didn't you tell me the truth about Simon Rawlins? Why did you let me think you were having an affair with him?'

For the first time she turned away from him, sheltering her naked body with the protection of her arms.

She said tonelessly, 'Because it was what you wanted to think. My mother took your father away from your mother. I had to be the one to take Simon away from Carrie. History repeating itself. Another ideal template.'

'No,' he said. Then, more forcefully, 'No, Rhianna, that makes no sense. You stood there and let me accuse you of being Simon's secret mistress without one word in your own defence. How do you explain that?'

He paused. 'You say you've always wanted me, but you went to great lengths to ensure we wouldn't be together.'

'No,' she said. 'Our joint family history did that. Because if it had ever become known we were lovers, all the old stories about my mother would have been dragged out for another airing. Her memory doesn't deserve that, whatever you believe.' She paused. 'Nor does your own mother, who is still around to be hurt. How would she feel if she knew you were sleeping with Grace Trewint's daughter?'

She stared sightlessly ahead of her. 'Maybe, unconsciously, when you started accusing me of being Simon's mistress I saw it as a convenient get-out clause—a means of escape from an impossible situation. And, perhaps what happened just now is fate's way of telling us that wanting each other still doesn't make it right.'

She bit down on her already torn lip. 'Would you go now, please? I—I'd rather be alone.'

'Tough,' Diaz said succinctly. 'Because I'm going nowhere.' He drew her back into his arms, swearing softly when he saw the expression of mute apprehension on her face. 'No, darling, I'm not planning to try and have sex with you again. I just need to hold you.' His mouth twisted. 'You look as if you need that too.'

It was suddenly all too much—the misery and disappointment, the knowledge that inevitably there'd be more questions to come, more blame assigned. The certainty that any remaining flicker of hope was gone for ever. Yet now, almost from nowhere, this unexpected kindness.

Rhianna turned her face into his shoulder and could taste the salt of his sweat on her trembling lips as she wept softly and bitterly in the arms of the man who could never be her lover.

CHAPTER NINE

As SHE cried, she was aware of his hand smoothing her damp, tumbled hair, and his voice murmuring to her in a language she dimly recognised as Spanish.

And in some strange way both seemed equally comforting.

At last he lifted her and put her back against the pillows.

He said, 'I'm going to get you some water.'

'I'm not thirsty.'

'No,' he said. 'But you've bled a little.'

Her face burned. 'Oh, God, I'm so sorry,' she muttered, totally humiliated.

'Why?' Diaz dropped a kiss on the top of her head. *The kind of caress you'd offer a child.* 'I'm the one who feels like the biggest bastard in the known world.'

He reached for his shorts and zipped himself into them with a kind of finality.

When he returned from the bathroom she'd retrieved the towel from the floor and shrouded herself in it. She held out her hand for the cloth he'd brought, blushing again. 'Please—I'll do it.'

His hesitation was momentary, then he shrugged. 'If that's what you wish.' He added levelly, 'I assume it's also another way of asking me to give you some privacy?'

She looked away, nodding jerkily, and thought she heard him sigh.

'Then I'll go,' he said, and paused. 'But it's not over yet, Rhianna. We still have matters to discuss, you and I. You said so yourself.'

'But that was—before. I—I don't see what else you need to know,' she protested.

'Something quite simple really,' he drawled. 'It's known as the truth.'

He walked to the door and halted, looking back at her, his mouth twisting in a faint smile. 'Until later,' he promised, and went, leaving her staring after him, her eyes stricken.

Once alone, she sponged the tell-tale spots of blood from the sheet, then took another quick shower. Half an hour later, her hair dry, her face made-up, buttoned into the coffee linen dress, she was curled into the corner of the sofa, considering her options.

Which were few, she admitted wryly, and singularly unappealing.

Diaz wanted the truth. But what good could it possibly do—especially now that the marriage had taken place exactly as planned?

And particularly since he knew beyond all doubt that she'd never been Simon's mistress, or pregnant with his child. Why couldn't that be enough for him? Why did he need more?

Because nothing had changed. There was still a bitter, devastated girl out there who needed her support, no matter how tired she herself might be of the entire situation. How angry and sick at heart.

'Donna,' she whispered under her breath. 'Donna Winston. Oh, God, I wish I'd never met her. Never known of her existence.'

At the time, of course, it had all made perfect sense. The young actress had just won the role of governess Martha Webb in *Castle Pride*, and had wanted to move out of the noisy, overcrowded flat she shared with three other girls. Rhianna had had a spare room, which she'd offered as a temporary solution, while Donna looked around for a place of her own.

And at first it had gone reasonably well. Donna was also an only child, and they'd been careful to respect each other's space, although Rhianna had worked out fairly soon that the other girl, a year younger than herself, would probably never be a close friend. She was altogether too dependent, complaining constantly of being homesick, and spending a lot of time on the telephone to her parents in Ipswich.

One evening, after a hard day's rehearsal, they'd dropped into a local pizza place, too tired to face cooking at the flat. They'd finished their meal and were about to order coffee when a man's voice had said, 'Good God, Rhianna, fancy seeing you here.' She'd looked up to see Simon smiling at her.

It was far from the encounter of choice. She'd seen him several times when she'd been to Oxford, visiting Carrie, and had learned reluctantly to accept that they were very much an item again.

'Isn't this terrific?' Carrie had said happily one weekend when the three of them had been picnicking by the river. 'Just like old times.'

And Rhianna had seen Simon's eyes rest on her with a faint sneer, as if he was remembering that night in the stable yard and daring her to do the same. After which she'd made a conscious effort to time her visits when he was elsewhere.

A policy she'd pursued with reasonable success ever since. And the main reason she'd backed away from being a bridesmaid at the wedding, when Carrie had asked her months before.

'Simon—hi.' She tried to sound pleasant, but not unduly welcoming. 'Didn't Carrie tell me you were in Glasgow?'

'A temporary secondment,' he said. 'I came back a week ago.' He looked at Donna, assessing the heart-shaped face and enormous brown eyes, and his smile widened. 'Won't you introduce me?

She did the honours briefly, then signalled to the waitress to bring the bill.

'It seems we're having coffee at home,' Donna said with faint disappointment, then brightened, her eyes shining. 'I know— why don't you join us, as you and Rhianna are such old friends? Then you can catch up with each other's news.'

'I'd love to.' He turned to Rhianna, brows lifting. 'No objections, have you, sweet pea?'

Enough to fill a telephone directory, thought Rhianna.

'Of course not,' she said briskly. 'Although it will have to be a flying visit, I'm afraid. Donna and I have an early start tomorrow.'

'Well,' Simon said softly, 'instant coffee will be fine.'

She'd supposed afterwards that they must have swapped contact numbers while she was in the kitchen, because it had been within the following week that Donna's unaccountable absences had first begun.

But even then the penny hadn't dropped, Rhianna thought, because she'd seen Donna lunching in the canteen more than once with one of the assistant producers on the show, who was known to be something of a Lothario, and drawn her own conclusions.

I'm not her Mother Superior, she'd told herself, shrugging. If she wants to stay out all night with Hugh the Rover, she's entitled. She just doesn't seem the type, that's all.

She might have remained in the dark indefinitely, their unwitting and witless accomplice, but for that opportune headache.

She'd waited in her room that night until she heard the door slam behind Simon, then she'd gone in search of Donna. She'd found her crouching in a corner of the sofa, her dressing gown thrown round her, clutching a damp ball of a handkerchief in one hand. She'd looked at Rhianna with drowned eyes.

'I'm so—so sorry,' she gulped.

'Sorry?' Rhianna repeated incredulously. 'For God's sake, Donna, Simon's engaged to my best friend. The wedding's only a couple of months away. You know that perfectly well. The invitation's right there on the mantelpiece.'

Donna swallowed convulsively. 'Yes, I know. And Simon's told me all about it—how they were childhood sweethearts. But he's not going to go through with the wedding,' she added defiantly. 'He can't. Because he's fallen in love with me.'

'No,' Rhianna said bluntly. 'You're fooling yourself. Simon may be enjoying a bit on the side, that's probably the way he is, but he won't let Carrie go—not when push comes to shove. I can guarantee that. So stop this now, before you, and other people get hurt.'

'You're just jealous.' Donna rounded on her tearfully. 'You wanted Simon yourself years ago, and you made a really heavy pass at him. But you were found out, and as a result you got turned out of your own home by your aunt. He's told me all about it.'

'Then he's lied,' Rhianna told her icily. 'Not that it matters. You disgust me, the pair of you.' She took a deep breath. 'You'll have to move out, Donna. I can't let you stay after this.'

'So what are you going to do?' Donna demanded sullenly. 'Spill the beans to your little friend, I suppose?'

'On the contrary,' Rhianna returned curtly. 'I'm simply going to wait for Simon to come to his senses.'

Donna flounced past her to the door. She was gone within the hour—presumably to Simon. Rhianna didn't ask, and could only look forward to when the final episode of the current series was finished, and they didn't have to encounter each other on set any more.

Even so, she had to listen to the girl bragging about her gorgeous, sexy boyfriend, and how he was paying for her to meet up with him in Nassau.

Was Donna aware that she was simply an add-on to Simon's stag party in the Bahamas? Rhianna wondered wearily. And if so, did she care?

And then, several weeks later, Donna made that sudden unwanted reappearance back at the flat, confessing in floods of hysterical tears that she was pregnant, and that Simon had done a total and brutal about-face, telling her the affair was over and that she had to get rid of the baby.

'You were right about him,' she sobbed to Rhianna when they were alone. 'You said he'd marry her in the end. But I still love him. I can't bear to think of life without him. And how can he tell me not to have our child?'

Quite easily, Rhianna thought, when he'd never seriously considered relinquishing his commitment to Carrie. For him the baby was just a temporary inconvenience, to be dealt with swiftly and expediently.

The last thing she'd expected was to find herself dragged unwillingly into Simon's battle with Donna over the proposed termination, or to face its damning effect on her relationship with Diaz.

After the evening when he'd found her with Simon and walked out, she'd heard nothing from him for nearly two aching, unhappy weeks.

Then she'd gone to an opening night party for a friend from drama school in her first West End role, and Diaz, to her amazement, had been the first person she saw as she entered the room.

'What are you doing here?' she asked, her heart jolting painfully as he reached her side.

'I got a journalist friend to speak to your PR company,' he admitted ruefully. 'They said you'd be here, so I wangled an invitation.'

She looked at him uncertainly. 'Wouldn't it have been easier just to telephone me?'

'I tried that,' he said grimly. 'And I spoke to your flatmate who was doing her ongoing impression of a watering can. Something told me you might not get my message, so I decided to find a different way to make contact with you.'

Rhianna hesitated. 'Donna's not living with me,' she said. 'She comes round to see me because she's not—very happy.'

Not happy? She's totally hysterical most of the time, still threatening to harm herself. Sometimes I dare not let her be by herself…

'You amaze me,' he said. 'God preserve me from ever being in the vicinity when she's totally miserable.'

I wish I could tell you about it, she thought passionately. I wish I could go into your arms and unload the whole, horrible sordid mess and ask you to deal with it, because it's getting beyond me.

Yet I can't—I dare not. For Carrie's sake. Because even if you didn't half-kill Simon, you'd certainly do everything possible to stop the wedding, which would break her heart.

And it's still just possible that something can be saved from the wreckage, if I can just persuade Donna that Simon really isn't coming back. That even if the baby doesn't wreck her career, being a single mother in a chancy profession like acting isn't a sensible option. And besides, as she's said herself through floods of tears, it would destroy her mother.

Simon doesn't deserve Carrie, but maybe marriage will change him. Who am I to say that it won't? Maybe this thing with Donna has given him the scare he so badly needs, and he really will behave himself from now on?

I have to try and believe that, anyway.

She looked away from Diaz's intent gaze, afraid he would read the uncertainty and trouble in her eyes. 'Did you have something in particular that you wanted to say to me?'

'Yes,' he said. 'I need to apologise for my total overreaction the other night. I have no excuse except that Simon Rawlins has never been my favourite person.' His mouth twisted. 'Frankly, I find it hard to trust him.'

Her heart skipped a beat. *Oh, God, if you knew. If you only knew...*

She said in a low voice, 'Perhaps trusting isn't that big a deal where you're concerned?'

'I'd deny that,' he returned, unfazed. 'And so, I think, would the majority of my loyal and devoted staff around the world.' He paused. 'On the other hand they'd also tell you I don't cope well with being thwarted, although I appreciate that's no excuse for behaving like a bear with a sore head.'

She studied his waistcoat buttons with minute attention. 'Is that what you were? Thwarted?'

'Yes,' he said, his eyes lingering on her mouth. 'As you know perfectly well, my sweet, so don't play games.'

She shook her head. 'I—I don't think I know very much about you at all.'

'Well,' he said slowly, 'with your co-operation, I'm hoping to change all that.'

She looked back at him then, her eyes wide and candid. 'Do you think that's wise—given past history?'

'I wasn't considering wisdom,' he said. 'I had sheer necessity in mind. I thought you felt that too.' He allowed her an instant to digest that, then added more roughly, 'I'm not pretending it's going to be easy, Rhianna, but we'd be crazy not to try.'

'Or die in the attempt?' She tried to smile.

'I'd much prefer to live,' he said quietly. 'And with you.' He paused, glancing round. 'But there are a lot of people who also want to talk to you looking daggers at me, so don't answer me now. But soon—please.'

He reached for her hand and kissed it, his lips grazing the softness of her palm, making her whole body shiver.

She wanted to say, 'Take me with you. Take me—now.' But he was already turning away, and she could see an influential director bearing purposefully down on her, so realised she must wait for the glimpse of paradise that Diaz had offered her. The dream of joy, secretly nurtured for so long, and now astonishingly, incredibly, within her reach once more.

And she greeted the director with a smile so radiant that he almost jumped back in surprise.

She'd assumed that Diaz would stick around until they could leave together, and her heart sank when she suddenly realised that he'd already gone. Slipped away into the night at some point while she was talking to Helen, the euphoric lead in an undoubted hit.

As soon as she could she made her own excuses and left too. Sitting in the back of a cab, she let herself think about Diaz—how he'd looked, what he'd said, and the way his lightest touch could make her feel—until she tingled all over, wondering how soon she would see him again. Praying she would not have to wait too long. Teasing herself that she ought to be ashamed of her eagerness. Hoping that he would not be too disappointed when he realised she didn't have the experience he expected.

All the lights in the flat seemed to be on when she let herself in, and she halted abruptly, brows lifting, when she saw the dining table laid for two with her nicest lace placemats and crystal, and tall ivory candles already lit in their ceramic holders.

As Donna came in, carrying the salt and pepper shakers, Rhianna turned on her. 'Just what is going on here?'

'Simon's coming over.' The other girl's face had a sharp, intense look. 'He rang earlier, sounding completely different, and said he wanted to talk.'

'And you're cooking him dinner—here—in my flat?' Rhianna fought the sheer rage welling up inside her. 'Knowing how I feel about all that's happened—about him?' She punched a clenched fist at the ceiling. 'How dare you?'

She took a deep breath. 'Well, that's the end, Donna. From now on you're on your own. You can give me back the key you've been using and go.'

'Rhianna, please—let me stay—just one last time. Simon and I can't talk properly, not in that shoe box I live in, and I simply have to see him—don't you understand?' Donna's voice trembled. 'Something's changed with him. I know it has. And I have a really good feeling about it.'

'Which makes one of us.' Rhianna walked to the mantelpiece and took the embossed invitation wedged behind the clock. 'Recognise this?' She flung it on the table. 'The wedding is still going ahead, whatever you may think.'

She saw the other woman flinch, and, remembering her charged emotional state, made herself speak more gently. 'He's messing you around, Donna. Playing with your head. He won't give up Carrie and he wants you to go ahead with the termination, as agreed. In your heart you must know that.'

'Heart!' Donna spat the word. 'What would you know about hearts?'

'More than you think, perhaps.' Rhianna stalked to the bedroom, pulled out an overnight bag and began to fill it, swiftly and economically.

'What are you doing?'

'Getting out of here and going to a hotel. I can't throw you out physically, though I'd like to, but I'm damned if I'm going to hang around as if it's all right when it's all wrong.' Rhianna zipped her bag and swung it off the bed, giving Donna the look with which Lady Ariadne regularly curdled men's blood—and never to better effect.

'As it is,' she went on, 'you'll kindly get both of yourselves out of here when you've eaten. I'll be back by seven a.m. tomorrow, and I'd better not find you here.'

The hotel she went to had only a suite available, but as Rhianna slapped down her credit card she told herself it was worth every penny.

In the end she waited until gone nine o'clock the following morning before staging her return, to find the flat deserted and her bed ominously stripped.

She would consider the implications of that later, she told herself, drawing a deep breath.

The dinner table, however, had not been cleared, and although Rhianna wrinkled her nose at the used plates and cutlery, the crumbs and dribbles of wine, and the candle wax that had been allowed to spill down the holders, at least it was a mess she could deal with. Besides, it seemed a small price to pay in order to be rid of that precious pair and their squalid affair.

But don't rejoice too soon, she thought with sudden grimness. If Simon has changed his mind and they really are together permanently, how am I going to cope with the fallout? And how can I possibly explain my part in it all to Carrie? Come to that, what the hell will she do?

She went into the bathroom and began to run water into the tub.

'Survive,' she said aloud. 'That's what women do when they're dumped by the only men who'll ever matter to them. When they're torn and bleeding and stumbling around. They survive. Somehow.'

But please—please don't let it come to that...

She was clean, dry, scented and in her robe, making coffee in the kitchen, when the buzzer sounded.

Donna? she wondered ironically as she went to answer the door. Come back to lend a hand with the washing up, or offering to take the sheets to the launderette?

But it was Diaz who was waiting outside.

Diaz as she had never seen him before—heavy-eyed, unshaven, and still in the clothes he'd been wearing the previous night, minus the silk tie, and with his waistcoat and shirt unbuttoned.

'My God, what's happened?' She took a pace towards him and he stepped back, flinging up both hands as if to ward her off.

'Don't touch me,' he grated. 'Or I might do something we'll both regret for the rest of our lives.'

'I don't understand.' She stared at him. 'What's wrong?'

'You are,' he said. 'My sweet, treacherous Rhianna. Stringing me along. Encouraging me to make a total fool of myself. You're what's wrong. You—and Rawlins, of course.'

'You—you must be mad.' Her mouth was dry, her heartbeat quickening into panic. *He knows—but what does he know?*

'I was,' he said. 'But fortunately my sight wasn't affected. I saw him arrive last night, and let himself in with his own key. A very convenient and intimate arrangement.'

A key? Donna actually gave him his own key?

His eyes were on her face. He said harshly, 'It's all right, Rhianna, don't look so shocked. I know he's not here now, because I also saw him leave just after dawn. I was sitting in my car across the street, so I was able to time his visit to the minute.'

He threw back his head. 'And now I'm back again, to take a long look at you in daylight. No lamps, no candles, no moon, and no shadows for you to hide in.'

She could feel the anger radiating from him, hot and danger-ous. She tried to say his name, but no sound would come.

He walked past her into the flat, into the living room, his mouth curling in distaste as he surveyed the debris on the table.

'A cosy dinner,' he observed flatly. He walked across to her bedroom, glancing at the unmade bed. 'Followed no doubt by an ecstatic end to a perfect day? I do hope, Rhianna, that you weren't also planning to share that bed with me?'

She found words. 'It's not what you think…' Oh, God, couldn't she have come up with something better than that hack-neyed formula, usually employed when someone had been caught bang to rights? As he assumed she had.

'Did you tell him I wanted you too, Rhianna? Did you share that with him during pillow talk, or were you too preoccupied?' He shook his head. 'You should have dumped him for me, darling. I'm a very rich man and I'd have paid a great deal for the pleasure of you. Actresses, even with bodies as lovely as yours, are two a penny. You could have made a small fortune allowing me access to that treacherous, delectable little body of yours. Used it as your pension fund when your other work even-tually dried up.'

He added mercilessly, 'You've used me. Just as your mother used my father, years ago.' He gave a short mirthless laugh. '"Past history", you said. The pair of you, mother and daughter, unable to keep your greedy, selfish hands off other women's men, and I wouldn't let myself see it.'

He drew a breath. 'All this time—cheating on Carrie. Pre-tending to be her friend when you were out to steal her fiancé. I should have remembered that you're an actress, trained to de-ceive. You're even better in real life than you are on television.'

Last night's receipted hotel bill, she thought, showing the hot chocolate she'd ordered last thing from Room Service and this morning's breakfast, was in her bag. She only had to show it to him to throw his accusations back in his face.

Except that it wouldn't stop there, she realised just in time. Because if *she* hadn't been with Simon last night, then someone else clearly had. And he would want to know who that was.

She swallowed. 'Are you going to—tell Carrie?'

It was all she could ask. She'd been drawn into this disaster by the need to shield her friend from the knowledge that Simon had enjoyed a blatant and cynical affair only weeks before their wedding. She still needed to do that. Now she had to discover the terms.

'No,' he said. 'How can I? I hold no brief for Rawlins, but it's the fact that he cheated on Carrie with you that sticks in my gullet. Although I can't blame him, or any other man, for being tempted. I haven't exactly been immune myself,' he added curtly. 'I've seen the way you move, the shape of your mouth. Those eyes a man could drown in. Who wouldn't want to get you into bed?'

He shook his head. 'But you were supposed to love her, Rhianna. You should have said no. I can't bear her to know how you've betrayed her.'

She said quietly, 'No, I can see that. Thank you.'

She saw him look past her and realised that the wedding invitation was still lying on the table, where she'd tossed it earlier. Diaz picked it up and tore it into small fragments, which he dropped on to a dirty plate.

'You will not come to the wedding,' he said, his eyes cold steel. 'Do you understand me? You'll make some excuse. I don't care what it is. But you'll bloody stay away—from my home and my family. And especially from Carrie, before and after her marriage. That friendship ends now. Because I don't trust you, Rhianna. This might have been a casual fling for Rawlins, but you're still sleeping with him, which makes me suspicious that you might have your own agenda where he's concerned. Not on my watch. You keep your distance, and your mouth shut, Rhianna, or you'll be sorry. Don't say you weren't warned.'

He walked to the door. 'I've decided to return to South America tomorrow,' he said. 'So with luck we won't meet again.' His smile made her shiver. 'Just pray that we don't.'

And he went out, leaving her standing in the ruin of her life, her arms wrapped defensively round her shaking body.

And now they had met again, and it seemed that she was going to have all the opportunities for regret that could possibly be crammed into one lifetime.

Circumstantial evidence had amazing power, she thought bleakly. Seemingly incontrovertible facts, piling up against her like great stones. Crushing her and silencing her.

Her only—her ultimate—defence had turned out to be the physical innocence she'd surrendered to him on that bed. Ironically, when it no longer mattered.

But the fact that she'd been a virgin did not mean there'd suddenly be bluebirds flying over the rainbow.

Because all the old problems between them hadn't gone away. In fact they'd probably been compounded by her abject failure to keep him at arm's length.

And they still had no future.

Sighing, she got to her feet. She couldn't stay down here for ever, as if she was too shy or too scared to face him. Once she'd seen to her delayed packing she would go up on deck and do her best to seem calm and collected, as if the events of the past two hours had never occurred. Or were somehow no big deal.

Smoke and mirrors, she thought. Playing a part she would never have chosen in a million years. So that soon, maybe within a day or two, she could walk away from him for ever, without looking back or letting him see how high a price she was paying for her departure.

Diaz was sitting at the table under the awning, looking out to sea, but at her approach he rose politely. He'd changed too, she saw, into close-fitting chinos and a dark blue shirt, open at the neck, sleeves turned back.

Realised too that just the sight of him was enough to send her spinning into some infinity of pain mingled with a desire that was no longer just a figment of her imagination but a recently experienced reality.

God help her, she could still taste his mouth on hers, feel the warm arousal of his hands on her breasts and thighs. Could recall in every detail the sheer impetus of need that had driven her to surrender such a short time ago.

It took all the courage she possessed to walk forward and join him now, wryly aware as she was that her swollen nipples were chafing against the confines of her bra, and that a soft languorous ache was coming to slow life deep within her all over again.

As she sat, he indicated a jug filled with deep red liquid, clinking with ice cubes and afloat with lemon slices, that stood in front of him.

'Enrique concocts a lethal sangria,' he remarked. 'Are you prepared to risk it?'

She shrugged. 'Why not?'

It would make as good an anaesthetic as any other, and she needed all the help she could get, not just for the next few hours, but for the remainder of whatever time she had to spend in his company.

I wish I could fall asleep, she thought, and wake up in London with all of this behind me, so that I could begin to put myself together again. Rebuild my life and plan for some kind of future. Find another dream—if that's possible…

In the meantime… 'Any more dolphin sightings?' she asked brightly, trying not to gasp as the sangria hit home.

'Sadly, no, but they may be waiting to catch another glimpse of you.' He paused. 'I like your dress.'

'You've seen it before.'

'Ah,' he said lightly, 'but perhaps I wasn't in the mood to appreciate it at the time.'

There seemed no answer to that, so she took another cautious sip of sangria.

'Be careful,' he warned lazily. 'I don't want you to pass out on me.'

And there was definitely no answer to that, Rhianna decided, staring resolutely down at the table. She needed a neutral topic of conversation, and quickly.

'What happens in the morning?' she said. 'When we get to Puerto Caravejo?'

'We may have to wait for a flight,' he said, after a pause. 'So I thought I'd show you my house.'

'Goodness,' she said. 'You have a castle in Spain as well?'

'Is that what you're expecting?' His tone was dry. 'Then you'll be disappointed. It's little more than a farmhouse which, unlike the rest of our family estate in the Asturias, managed to survive the Civil War. It's been extended since then, but it's still more comfortable than luxurious.'

She digested that. 'Do you spend a lot of time there?'

'Not as much as I could wish,' he said. 'But all that will change when I finish disposing of our assets in South America.'

She put down her glass. 'But I thought that was where your real home was? Where you spent most of the year?'

'It has been,' he said. 'But I decided some time ago that my life needed to be simplified. Racing from one side of the globe to the other isn't much fun any more. And nor is being saddled with an armed guard much of the time,' he added with a touch of grimness. 'Besides, the mineral workings are coming to the end of their natural span anyway, and the land can be used for other purposes.'

'But you'll miss the travelling, surely?'

He shrugged. 'The consultancy is growing each year, and although I have a great team I'm still actively involved, so that should take care of any lingering wanderlust. For the rest of the time I plan to put something back into my land in Spain. Plant more apple orchards, maybe some vines. A friend of mine made the Rioja we drank the other night, and he offered a while back to teach me the wine business. So in many ways I'm going to be busier than ever.' He paused. 'Then there's the reclamation project at Penvarnon.'

'You're going to rebuild it?' she asked uncertainly.

'Not with bricks and mortar,' he said. 'I intend to—take it back. Spend much more time there. Make it mine. I've only allowed the present situation to drag on like this because it's suited my convenience. My uncle's always understood that, and he'll be relieved to go. He's never been happy there.'

She said without thinking, 'It's never been a happy house.'

'No,' Diaz said, after a pause. 'Which is something else I mean to change.' He leaned back in his chair. 'And, while we're enjoying this full and frank exchange of information, my sweet, you can start telling me about your tearful little friend Donna Winston. In particular how long she and Simon Rawlins have been sleeping together and why you kept quiet about it. Because that's something I really need to know.'

CHAPTER TEN

FOR a long moment Rhianna was silent, then she said quietly, 'How did you know it was Donna?'

'I realised a little while ago,' he said. 'When I was in the shower. Great places, showers, for clearing your head and getting you to think straight.' His mouth twisted. 'So, I used the time-honoured method of adding two and two, and arrived, for once, at the correct answer.'

He shook his head. 'God in heaven, how could I have been so dumb? "Man trouble". I said it myself, the night I met her.' He looked at her unsmilingly. 'And you said, "It seems so." Only you *knew*, Rhianna. You knew exactly what was going on, yet you said nothing. You even condoned the affair by letting them meet at your flat.'

'Never.' She looked back at him, her eyes fierce. 'And I didn't know—not at first. We bumped into Simon in a pizza place one night, quite by accident, and he deliberately inveigled an invitation back for coffee—the last thing I wanted, as he very well knew. Relations between us had been cool for a long time, and I'd have crossed busy streets to avoid him. I was probably too damned annoyed at being manipulated like that to pick up any other nuances.'

She paused. 'Then I just happened to walk in on them one night—and caught them *in flagrante*. After he left there was a confrontation between me and Donna. She claimed they were in love. I advised her to think again, and told her to go. But later I started feeling almost sorry for her—because I'd introduced them, after all, and she probably thought Simon was a friend of mine who could be trusted. Or maybe she'd turned him into some romantic golden-haired hero—the way you do when you're young and silly.' She bit her lip. 'I can hardly blame her for that. There was a time when I thought he was wonderful too.'

'That,' he said, 'had not escaped my attention.'

She said swiftly, 'If you're thinking of Carrie's birthday party, then you're so wrong. I was over him long, long before that.'

'Then why go to meet him?'

'Because he said—he made me think Carrie would be there too. I'd never have gone otherwise.' She bent her head. 'I know how it must have looked.'

He said, 'I didn't give you much chance to explain. But why didn't you tell me what was going on that evening when I arrived at the flat and found him with you?'

She sighed. 'Because I could have been opening Pandora's box. The consequences might have been awful. Besides, Simon kept insisting it was all over between them, that he'd learned his lesson and it was only Carrie that he wanted. And I—I wanted so badly to believe that. Because I couldn't convince myself that she'd be happier without him. Better off, maybe—probably—but not happier. So,' she added unhappily, 'I took the coward's way out and hoped it would all simply go away—that no one else need ever know.'

His brows rose. 'So you were trying to keep the peace? Is that it?'

'No,' she said. 'I can't even claim that.' She took a breath. 'The fact is—I was frightened. I can make all the excuses in the world, but that's what it comes down to in the end. I told myself that if I said nothing I'd be protecting Carrie, saving her from this terrible hurt, when all the time I didn't want to be the one to tell her.'

She looked down at the table. 'In the old days they used to kill messengers who brought bad news, and I was scared that I'd lose her too—lose our precious friendship. For so long it was all I had, and I was afraid that she'd never forgive me if I was the one to destroy her illusions about Simon and break her heart.'

He said, 'That's not such a bad reason. Except, of course, it didn't all go away.'

'No,' she said. 'Donna had come back that night to tell me she was pregnant, and Simon wanted her to have an abortion. She was going to pieces right there in front of me, so I could hardly throw her out. She had her own place, but she virtually moved back in with me, just weeping hysterically and refusing to eat or get dressed half the time. She kept her key too, and must have had it copied for Simon—though I didn't realise that until too late.'

She added flatly, 'I don't think they ever really stopped seeing each other. Not even when he was accusing her of deliberately getting pregnant because she knew he was going to finish with her, and she was threatening to take an overdose or cut her wrists if anyone mentioned termination. Eventually she calmed down enough to make an appointment at a clinic, but she told Simon she'd only go through with it if I went with her. He's been hassling me over that ever since. Or until yesterday, anyway.'

She frowned. 'I haven't actually seen Donna since the night Simon stayed at the flat, so I don't know her current stance. And in spite of everything I haven't been able to lose all sympathy with her.'

He said, 'Then you must have the patience of a saint.'

'No.' She looked out to sea. 'It—it's not—it can't be easy to accept that you're never going to have the one man who means everything to you. And I think she did fall for him very badly, and believed that he loved her too.'

'A little naïve,' he commented.

'Yes.' Rhianna was silent for a moment. She added reluctantly, 'Although Simon did claim originally that *she'd* targeted *him*, and made all the running.'

'Hardly a reliable authority,' he said unsmilingly.

'No, but plausible—and it made me wonder. Because Rob, who's usually kindness itself to newcomers on the cast, avoided her like the plague. And when he heard she was moving into the flat he told me that she was a damned sight older than her age, and infinitely more streetwise, and warned me to be careful.'

'What I still need to know,' Diaz said slowly, 'is why you let me think you were the one involved with that two-timing bastard?'

'Because it seemed the one way to guarantee you wouldn't tell Carrie either.' She met his gaze. 'I couldn't believe you'd cause her more suffering by letting her know she'd been betrayed not just by Simon but by her best friend too. I was certain that her peace of mind would be far more important to you than your contempt for me. It was more important to me too.'

'But you stood there,' he said, 'and you let me say those foul, unforgivable things to you.'

'Because I was involved in it.' She spread her hands almost helplessly. 'I couldn't deny that. And I hadn't been able to do a thing to stop it. I couldn't even pretend that it was just one of those things that happens when people have had too much to drink.'

He lifted a hand and smoothed a strand of hair back from her face. 'About which you know so much, of course,' he said, his voice caught between tenderness and amusement.

'I don't think I know very much at all,' she said, as her pulses leapt in unbidden, dangerous delight. 'About anyone or anything. I'm better with someone else's script.' She paused. 'Would you have kept quiet—to spare her feelings—if I'd told you the truth? I felt I couldn't take the risk—especially when you were so angry.'

'No,' he said quietly. 'Probably not.'

'Well, then,' she said. 'Maybe it's all turned out for the best.'

'I wish I shared your optimism,' he returned drily. 'Whatever, it's too late now. They'll be off on their honeymoon.'

He reached across, and took her hand, playing gently with her fingers. 'So—do you forgive me?'

'For saying what you did?' She was embarrassed to hear the sudden quiver in her voice that his touch had engendered. 'Of course. In some ways I deserved it.'

Diaz shook his head, smiling faintly. 'Not just that.'

'Oh,' she said, trying to ignore the dismaying fact that she was also blushing. 'You mean *that*.'

'Indeed I do,' he agreed.

Rhianna tried unsuccessfully to free her hand. 'Couldn't we simply forget it ever happened?'

'Not a chance,' he said. 'Because I don't want to forget.' He added drily, 'Nor do I wish you to have that as your abiding memory of me as a lover.'

She was trembling inside. 'Please don't say things like that.'

'That sounds ominous.' He sent her a searching look, then raised her hand to his lips, kissing her fingertips very gently. 'Has our recent encounter put you off for life? I do hope not.'

'No. I mean—I don't know.' She was stumbling now, and Lady Ariadne's glamorous self-possession had never seemed further away. 'But I—I must have been a terrible disappointment.'

'No, my sweet,' Diaz said, and smiled at her. 'Believe me, that couldn't be further from the truth. My sole regret is that I didn't know it was your first time, or I would have dealt with the matter rather differently.'

'Oh,' she said, wondering how, and knowing she could never ask.

She rallied. 'Anyway, it's all over now, and in a few hours we'll be in Spain and I'll be leaving. So maybe what happened is all for the best too.'

His smile widened into a reluctant grin. 'Not from my point of view, darling. Nor, I'd have said, from yours. However,' he went on, more gently, 'if you give me the chance, I think I can guarantee you more enjoyment next time.'

Hunger for him—for the intimate riches he was offering—clenched like a fist inside her.

But at the same time she knew it would be infinitely safer to starve. Because all he was proposing was a consummation—the satisfaction of a mutual desire.

And she wanted all of him. For ever. It was that simple. And that impossible.

Was this how Donna wanted Simon? she wondered, and realised why, in spite of everything, she'd found herself pitying the girl who'd given everything to a man she adored and watched him take it and walk away.

Because Diaz would be no different, she told herself. He had no choice in the matter. They were who they were. His father's son, her mother's daughter. Nothing could alter that.

But at least he'd been honourable enough not to pretend, or to make promises he wasn't prepared to keep.

He might want me, she thought, but he's never mentioned love.

He said he wanted to wipe Simon from my mind for ever and erase his own need for me at the same time. And maybe he can do that. But I—I can't. I might not have known it then, when I was in his arms, but I do now.

And when I told myself it was enough—that I would make it enough—I was lying. I can't let myself be chained to him for the rest of my life by the memory of a night's pleasure.

I need to save myself. Somehow.

She released her hand from his clasp and sat back. 'I don't think so,' she said, her answering smile polite, even faintly regretful. 'But thank you, anyway. Because you've helped me to achieve what I wanted. Some uncommitted experience, without any untidy emotions in the way.'

She paused. 'So please don't feel guilty that you didn't make the earth move. After all, it was hardly likely under the circumstances. And now my curiosity's been satisfied, at least, so I'll know what to expect in future—what the possibilities could be. I'd much prefer to settle for that—for the time being.'

She shrugged gracefully. 'Everything else can wait until I fall in love.'

There was a silence, then Diaz said expressionlessly, 'How neat. How tidy.'

She looked away. 'Maybe the events of the past few months make order and decency in my life seem strangely attractive.' She added abruptly, 'I'm sorry.'

'Don't be.' It was his turn to shrug. 'It's your decision, and I can't argue with that—much as I'd like to. Because I suspect that with you, Rhianna, those possibilities you mention could be endless.'

He paused. 'But I hope at least you'll allow me to kiss you goodbye when the time comes?'

'Why not?' She drank some more sangria, praying she'd never be obliged to touch it again as long as she lived, because it would always—always—bring this moment back.

The time I did the right thing, she thought, and felt myself die inside.

She added, 'I know we probably won't see each other again
after this, but I'd like us to part friends. If we can.'

'A nice thought,' he said silkily. 'But hardly feasible. Under
the circumstances.'

He emptied his glass, pushed his chair back and rose. 'Dinner
will be early this evening, and I suggest you get some rest after
it. You won't get much sleep once we reach port.'

He hesitated, looking down at her. 'And if you're speaking from
someone else's script, you need more rehearsal. Because right now
it doesn't work. Not for me, and probably not for you either.'

He added flatly, 'I'll see you later,' and walked away to the
bridge.

Dinner was paella, produced by Enrique with a delighted
flourish, and Rhianna smiled and said, 'How wonderful,' and ate
her share, even asked for more—although every mouthful tasted
like cardboard, and her stomach was twisted in knots anyway.

She'd expected it would be a quiet meal. That after her rejection of him Diaz would not have a great deal to say to her, but
she was wrong. Clearly his male pride hadn't been dented too
badly, she told herself wryly, as he chatted lightly, amusingly, and
above all impersonally, keeping the topics of conversation
general, and making it easy for her to pick up a similar tone.

While in between, very carefully, ensuring that his attention
was safely on his food, she watched him from under her lashes
with passionate concentration, etching every line of his dark,
mobile face into her consciousness, then closing it away in some
secret compartment in her mind which she could unlock sometimes. Not every day, she promised herself. Just when the loneliness and the need became too much to bear.

'Tell me something,' he said suddenly, when the coffee had
been placed on the table and Enrique had returned to the galley.
'What made you choose acting as a career?'

'It was something I'd always loved to do,' Rhianna said, after
a startled pause to register that they'd moved from impersonal
to personal again. 'But my aunt had different views, so I didn't
have much opportunity until I went back to London. There were

evening drama classes at one of the education centres, and I went along.'

She shrugged. 'My teacher thought I had something, and arranged for me to audition at stage school. I got a place, plus a bursary I never knew existed. And the people I was living with—the Jessops—were absolutely wonderful, and refused to take a penny from me while I was training.'

She bent her head. 'I can't help imagining sometimes how different my life would have been if they'd been allowed to foster me when my mother died. They wanted to, but Aunt Kezia insisted on taking me away. I never understood why, because she never wanted me or even liked me. She made that quite clear. And she inflicted me on a place where she knew I'd be unwelcome, when there was no actual need.'

She sighed. 'I've never been able to figure it.'

He said quietly, 'She was certainly a strange woman.'

'Stranger than you know.' Rhianna paused. 'Apparently she used to take these really terrible, pointless photographs of people, as if she was deliberately catching them off-guard.'

His brows lifted. 'What people?'

'Your aunt and uncle,' she said, adding reluctantly, 'And your father. There are lots of your father.' *And your mother in a wheelchair, but I'm not mentioning that. Or the cheque. In fact I wish I'd said nothing about them at all.*

'You have these photographs?'

'The Hendersons found them at the flat and passed them on to me.' Her mouth twisted. 'My sole Trewint legacy.'

'Not quite,' he said. 'You have that amazing hair, like some beautiful dark red cloud. That's an inheritance to treasure.'

Which was altogether too personal, Rhianna decided. She finished her coffee and rose.

She said politely, 'If you'll excuse me? I think I'll take your advice and get some sleep.' And turned away, only to find him beside her at the companionway.

She said crisply, 'I know my own way, thanks.'

'Of course,' Diaz said, and smiled at her. 'But you seem to have forgotten you promised me a kiss.'

Her heart thudded. 'When we said goodbye,' she returned. 'That was my understanding of the agreement.'

'But there's always such hassle at airports,' he said softly as they reached her door. 'Let's make it goodnight instead.'

She hesitated uneasily. 'Well—if you insist.'

It's a kiss. That's all. Don't make a big deal about it, or let him see it matters. Just get it over with.

'Well, yes,' he said, faint amusement in his voice. 'I think I do.' He reached for the handle and opened her door.

She gave him a startled glance. 'But there's no necessity for that. Right here and now will be fine.'

'Except that I prefer privacy,' he said. He picked her up and carried her into the stateroom, kicking the door shut behind him. 'And comfort,' he added, putting her down on the bed and coming to lie beside her.

'You said *a kiss*,' she reminded him, her voice shaking.

'Did I specify a number?' He drew her to him. 'I don't think so.' He lifted a strand of scented hair and carried it to his mouth. He said gently, 'You are loveliness itself.'

He began to kiss her without haste, his mouth touching her forehead, her eyes, her cheekbones, the soft vulnerability below her ears, and the trembling corners of her mouth.

His lips were warm as they parted hers, and infinitely beguiling. His tongue began a lingering silken quest of the inner contours of her mouth, and her breath sighed with his. He gathered her closer, holding her against the hard length of his body, letting the kiss deepen slowly, endlessly.

When she could speak, she whispered brokenly, 'Diaz—this isn't fair.'

'I'll spare us both the obvious cliché.' He put his mouth against her throat as his fingers began to release the long row of buttons at the front of her dress. 'If this is all I'm to have of you, Rhianna, then I intend to make the most of it. And I'm still only kissing you,' he added huskily. 'Even if it's not how—or where—you expected.'

As the edges of her unfastened dress fell apart, Diaz looked down at her for a long moment, then bent, his lips brushing the creamy swell of her breasts as they rose from their lacy confinement.

Lifting her slightly, he freed her from her dress, tossing it to the end of the bed, then dealt with the hook of her bra, taking the tiny garment from her body and sending it to follow her dress.

He began to kiss her breasts, circling her nipples with the tip of his tongue, bringing them to hot, aching life, before taking each soft, scented mound into his mouth and laving their tumescent peaks with slow, voluptuous strokes that made her moan aloud.

His lips moved down her body, leaving a trail of fire over her ribcage and the flat plane of her stomach, his tongue teasing the whorls of her navel, while his hands deftly removed her remaining covering of silk and lace as if brushing aside a cobweb.

It was only then that Rhianna realised where this downward path was leading, and as his mouth reached the silky triangle at junction of her thighs she stiffened in panic, her fingers tangling in his hair as she tried to push his head away.

'No!' She choked the word. 'God—no...'

Effortlessly Diaz captured her wrists, holding them at either side of her shocked body, before he bent to her again, kissing the smooth length of her thighs, and their soft inner flesh, every brush of his lips a silent enticement, coaxing them to part for him, until she could resist no longer and sank, sighing, into the promise of this new and startling intimacy.

His mouth took possession of her with a gentleness that was almost reverent, kissing the secret woman's flesh she had yielded to him, then slowly and sensuously deepening the caress into explicit exploration.

His tongue was a quiet flame flickering against her, at one moment probing delicately into her innermost self, at the next seeking out her tiny hidden bud and urging it to swollen, delicious arousal.

Offering her with patience, tenderness and untiring, unhurried grace, a glimpse of an unknown, undreamed-of world of pleasure.

Time was suspended. There was only this endless—exquisite—torment. This intolerable, unceasing delight. She was consumed by sensation, conscious of it building inside her with all the irresistible force of a giant wave. Aware that each lingering, sensual stroke of his tongue was carrying her away, sweeping her inexorably, helplessly, towards some trembling, anguished pinnacle.

And when the wave broke, and she was flung out into some shimmering, shattering void, she heard herself cry out in sobbing triumph at the glory of her first sexual release.

Diaz wrapped her in his arms, his hand cradling her head, until she stopped shaking and her body began to relax into peace.

When she could speak, she said, 'Is—is it always like that?'

'I don't know,' he returned softly. 'I'm not a woman. But I hope so.'

She remained still, her lips against the column of his throat, her hand pressed to the wall of his chest, feeling the thud of his heartbeat through his shirt, thinking dreamily she'd be content to stay where she was for ever.

Yet at the same time it occurred to her that there was an incongruity about being naked in his arms when he was still fully dressed that made her feel almost shy. And how ridiculous was that, considering what had just taken place?

She reached up and began to unfasten his shirt, but he halted her.

'Not now, my sweet.'

'But don't you want…?'

'Yes,' he said. 'But later. When we have all the time we need.' He kissed her eyes and, gently, her lips. 'Get some sleep now, and I'll wake you when it's time to go ashore.'

He lifted himself off the bed and covered her with the sheet, stroking her damp hair back from her forehead.

He said again, 'Later,' the promise repeated in his smile, and went.

CHAPTER ELEVEN

THE first thing Rhianna noticed when she opened her eyes was that the light was different. The next that the room wasn't moving. The third that she was in a much bigger bed than the one on *Windhover*.

She was also alone, although the crumpled pillow beside her and the thrown-back covers demonstrated that this had not always been so.

She sat up, yawning, and considered her new environment.

Her actual arrival in Spain remained something of a blur. She could recall there'd been certain formalities to undergo before they'd been free to make their way to the car waiting on the quayside. The driver, an undeniably handsome lad, called Felipe with smouldering eyes and a sulky mouth, had stared at Rhianna with undisguised admiration until a quiet word from Diaz had recalled him to his duties.

It had been too dark to form any impression of the countryside they'd travelled through, and eventually, supported by the comfort of Diaz's shoulder, she'd dozed again.

She hadn't absorbed much about the house either, apart from being greeted by a stout woman with greying hair, who'd watched with an expression of faint disapproval when Diaz had swung her off her feet and carried her upstairs to this room.

She had a dim memory of him sliding into bed beside her at some point, and of turning into his arms with a murmur of pleasure. But after that—nothing.

And now here she was, all by herself.

For a moment a cold hand seemed to brush her skin, but she shook the feeling away. It was too late for regrets—for wishing that last night had not happened. No point in telling herself it had been a matter of male pride to show her that after pain there could be pleasure. Or that he'd tricked her.

She was out of her depth and drowning with all she felt for him, and she'd change nothing—apart from wishing he'd been with her when she woke.

She lay back against the pillows again, and looked around her with growing pleasure. It was a large room, its pale walls the colour of aquamarine, which appeared even more spacious because of the few items of furniture it contained. Apart from the bed there was only a large wardrobe and a tall chest of drawers, elaborately carved in some dark wood, and two smaller matching tables flanking the bed.

The shutters at the long windows were slightly open, and a bright shaft of sunlight was spilling across the tiled floor, while the drapes of unbleached linen stirred in the faint breeze.

Opposite the bed was a door leading to a bathroom, judging by the glimpse of azure tiles and creamy marble beyond.

What she couldn't see anywhere was her luggage. Even the things she'd been wearing last night had disappeared.

But perhaps they were in that enormous wardrobe.

She got out of bed and, for want of anything better, took the sheet with her, winding it round her body in case the woman with pursed lips, whose name she recalled was Pilar, should suddenly reappear.

But the wardrobe and drawers contained only male attire, proving that this lovely room belonged to Diaz.

She padded into the bathroom, which was equally pleasing. As well as the powerful shower in its glass-walled cubicle, there was a deep bathtub, and twin handbasins set side by side in a marble-topped unit.

Indicating, she thought, swallowing, that she wasn't the first to share his room. But she wouldn't think about that—nor about the other women before her who must have sobbed their rapture into his shoulder. Or those who would follow her into his bed.

Particularly not those, she thought, fighting a sudden twist of pain as she headed back to the bedroom. Because that way lay madness.

'Rehearsing for *Julius Caesar*?'

At the sound of his voice Rhianna turned, almost tripping on her trailing sheet. He was lounging in the doorway, his mouth curved in amusement, the towel draped round his hips his only apparent covering.

'Auditioning for *Tarzan*?' she retorted.

'No chance,' he said. 'All that swinging through trees is far too strenuous. I'd have saved my strength for Jane.' He paused. 'You were sleeping like a baby, so I thought I'd go for a swim. But now,' he added softly, 'I'm back, and you're awake. How very nice.'

'I was looking for my clothes.' She gestured helplessly. 'Do you know where they've gone?'

'Pilar, my housekeeper, has them. They'll be returned to you later, beautifully laundered.' His smile widened. 'And speaking of later…'

He dropped the towel, walked across to her, and picked her up, carrying her back to the bed.

'We can't,' she protested breathlessly as he took her in his arms. 'Do you realise what the time is?'

'Better than you, darling. But no one is looking for us. At least, no one here present,' he added with a touch of wryness. 'Pilar has shepherded her family off to Sunday Mass, and she's left salad and stuff for our lunch—if we ever get round to eating it. She'll be back to cook dinner this evening, but until then we have the house to ourselves.'

He bent over her. 'And I have you,' he whispered.

At the first touch of his mouth on hers she was drawn instantly, eagerly, into the world of the senses she'd discovered last night.

She kissed him back without reserve, her hands stroking their way over his cool skin, marvelling at the strength of bone and muscle, learning him through her fingertips.

Felt her own body respond with joy to his touch, to the caress of his hands and mouth, now suddenly as necessary to her as the air she breathed.

Knew too that she was melting, hot with desire for the final consummation of their lovemaking. The moment when she would belong to him completely.

Diaz took her with immense care, his body gentling its way into hers, his eyes watching her face intently for any hint of discomfort.

But Rhianna was aware of nothing but a sense of completion, as if a missing piece of her life had been found at last.

He said hoarsely, 'Do you know—do you have the least idea what total heaven you are?'

'And I,' she whispered, 'was thinking the same about you.'

As she moved with him, joined to him, she felt like a bird soaring, her only song one sweet, uncontrollable cry of pleasure as her body splintered into the fierce rapture of climax.

Afterwards they lay quietly entwined, exchanging kisses, murmuring nonsense to each other.

'It's just occurred to me,' he said, twining some of her hair round his fingers and breathing its fragrance. 'I'm now potentially the most hated man in Britain.'

'Then it's just as well you're in Spain.' She nestled closer. 'But why?'

'The ultimate fantasy,' he said. 'I'm in bed with Lady Ariadne.'

'No,' she said quickly. 'Don't say that, Diaz. Never say that. She doesn't exist, and you know it.'

'Sweetheart, I was joking.' His tone was remorseful as he tipped up her chin and studied her. 'But I admit I'm curious how you ever got cast in a part like that.'

'Good audition,' she returned frankly. 'Something told me the series was going to be a smash, and I wanted it—even though Ariadne wasn't a leading character originally. But when we went into rehearsal they suddenly realised her potential and began changing the scripts.'

She sighed. 'Now she's seen off two husbands, a lover, and the heir to the estate—the Victorian equivalent of Lucrezia Borgia. Some fantasy.'

'At the same time,' he said, 'stunningly beautiful and incredibly sexy.' He paused. 'In spite of your astonishing state of innocence, my love, you can't tell me that your co-star, however good a friend he may be, wasn't turned on even marginally in his love scenes with you.'

A gurgle of laughter escaped her. 'Rob's an actor,' she said. 'His main concern when we were in bed was ensuring the camera got his best side.'

He stared at her. 'You have to be joking.'

'Not a bit of it,' she said, still giggling. 'Ask the director. Ask anyone. For Rob, love scenes are just work, and he takes that extremely seriously. Besides,' she added more soberly. 'He doesn't play around. He's a one-woman man, which is why I'm sure that he and Daisy will get together again. She's the other half of him.'

There was a silence, then he said quietly, 'Let's hope you're right, and it works out for them.' And began to make love to her again.

And as her body lifted to his touch, the words, *Because it never can for us* seemed to hover unspoken in the ether.

They were still there in the back of her mind, impossible to shake off, when they eventually ate lunch, sitting on a terrace at the rear of the house overlooking the swimming pool, with Rhianna wearing one of his shirts.

'I really wish we'd arrived in daylight,' she said, drawing a deep breath. 'I've only just realised there are mountains.' She shaded her eyes, studying the range of jagged grey peaks towering towards the sky that filled the distance. 'They're spectacular. And is that actually snow I see?'

'It's usually there somewhere on the *cordillera*,' Diaz agreed. 'So are bears, although I admit I've yet to see one.'

She shuddered. 'Just as well, I imagine.' She paused. 'And everything's so *green*. I didn't expect that.'

'We get a fair amount of rain here,' he said, adding laconically, 'Don't confuse Asturias with Andalusia.'

'Here— the mountains. In Cornwall—the sea. You seem to have picked the best of both worlds.' She managed to keep a wistful note out of her voice.

He shrugged. 'I have roots in both. After all, this is where Jorge Diaz was born, even if the original house no longer exists.'

Seen in daylight, the farmhouse itself wasn't particularly beautiful, just a large rambling structure with white walls and a roof of faded terracotta tiles, but it fitted solidly and reassuringly into its landscape.

Like Penvarnon, she thought, it had all the makings of a home.

It suddenly seemed necessary to change the subject.

She waved a fork at the clustering trees beyond the garden's perimeter fence. 'Is that your apple orchard?'

'Part of it.' He offered her some tomato salad.

'My God, she said. 'What happens to all the fruit? I didn't know the Spanish were big on apple pie.'

'These apples make cider,' he explained. 'They drink a great deal of it here in the north. But it's quite mild, unlike scrumpy.'

'And your pool.' She raised an eyebrow. 'After what you said about the house, do you reckon that's a comfort rather than a luxury?'

'I'd say both. You can try it after we've eaten, and give me your opinion.' He smiled at her. 'It's also pretty much a necessity. Asturias has always been a big coal mining area, and most of the rivers are still polluted, so not much swimming there.'

'Can't something be done about that?'

'Yes, but it all takes time.'

My cue, she thought. Aloud, she said lightly, 'Which reminds me—my time here is running out fast. I really need to find out about flights to London.'

'Dressed like that?' His grin teased and warmed at the same time. 'You'll be a sensation.'

She forced a shrug. 'I get my clothes back tonight. I can leave tomorrow.'

There was a brief silence, then he said, 'Of course. I'll see what I can arrange.'

Making her realise just how much she'd hoped he would say, Don't go. Not yet. Stay with me.

Which proves he's far more of a realist than I am, she told herself ironically. A man with roots and his future planned. A future that could never seriously include the girl whose mother wrecked his parents' marriage.

Whereas I—I'm the twenty-first century equivalent of a strolling player, a rogue and a vagabond who performs and moves on.

Had their time together achieved the desired effect? she wondered, pain stabbing at her. Had it cleared her from his mind and appeased his body? When she left, would he finally be rid of her, even if it hadn't happened as he'd expected?

'What are you thinking?' His question cut abruptly across her reverie.

She pulled a rueful face. 'Oh—just that I'm probably going to have some explaining to do when I get back.'

His mouth tightened. 'The questions are already being asked, it seems,' he commented. 'Pilar tells me there were four telephone calls from my aunt yesterday, all bordering on the hysterical.'

Rhianna gasped. 'Even while the wedding was still going on?' She paused. 'Have you called her back?'

'No,' he said. 'She may be my mother's sister, but she has no jurisdiction over my life.'

Rhianna said awkwardly, 'Perhaps she's just being protective—thinking how your—how Mrs Penvarnon would feel if she knew about us.'

'They're hardly close,' he returned drily. 'It suits my aunt to play lady of the manor at Polkernick, while my mother lives in St Jean de Luz, but there are no family visits—not even for this wedding, as you may have noticed.'

'Maybe that's why Mrs Seymour's so upset?' Rhianna suggested. 'Because you weren't there either?'

'I made it totally clear to her that could happen,' he said. His eyes met hers. 'I was there for one reason only, if you remember, and it wasn't to see Carrie throw her life away on that waste of space.'

'And then you found there wasn't really a reason after all.' She tried to smile. 'It's a pity that virgins can't be issued with some kind of barcode. Think of the problems that would have saved you.'

He pushed his chair back with such force that it fell over with a clatter, then came round the table to her, pulling her to her feet.

'Don't say that,' he muttered roughly. 'Don't even think it. Dear God, Rhianna, this may not have been what I intended, but it was what I wanted. You were what I wanted, and I need you still—for whatever time we have left.'

And she went trembling into his arms, closing her mind to everything but the passion of his kiss.

They spent a quiet afternoon by the pool. Rhianna ventured into the water once, but found it cold, much to Diaz's amusement, and retreated back to the padded sun mattress under the huge striped umbrella.

She turned her head, beginning to smile as she watched him emerge from the water.

'For a moment,' she said, 'I thought I was a teenager in the cove at Penvarnon again.'

'My God,' Diaz said, as he towelled down before stretching out with a sigh of pleasure on the adjoining mattress. 'One of my life's most difficult moments, and you still remember it.'

'Of course,' she said. 'You were the first naked man I'd ever seen.'

He grinned at her. 'I thought you didn't look.'

'I certainly tried not to,' she said demurely.

'I see.' He paused. 'And has your attitude undergone any significant change since then?'

She propped herself on one elbow, her eyes openly caressing him, while her free hand began to stray, taking whatever liberties it chose.

'Now,' she said softly, 'now I could look at you for ever.'

'Take all the time you need,' he said lazily, his eyes half closed, magnificently unselfconscious as his body quickened and hardened at her touch, before pulling her to him and making slow, sweet love to her in the drowsy afternoon.

But as they lay together afterwards Rhianna became aware that the breeze had freshened, and shivered suddenly.

Diaz sat up, looking at the sky. 'The weather's changing,' he said. 'See the clouds gathering above the mountains? It's going to rain.' He sighed. 'We'd better go in anyway. I think I heard the car, so Pilar will be back.'

It was, she thought, the end of an idyll...

And the end of everything.

'I hate to think what she'll say if she sees me wearing your shirt.' She kept her tone light.

'Well, she's unlikely to say it to you.' His mouth twisted in amusement. 'I'm the one who gets the full force of her disapproval. She loves me, but she thinks I'm a bad influence on her menfolk.' He added wryly, 'Juan and Enrique are her cousins, and Felipe is her grandson, so she takes their moral welfare very seriously.'

He shook his head. 'She's always said that I'll—' He stopped abruptly.

'That you'll—what?' she queried, then realised. She said hesitantly, 'That you'll break your mother's heart?'

His mouth tightened. 'Something of the sort.' He zipped himself into his shorts, then held the shirt for her to put on.

Pilar was indeed back. They did not see her, but her voice could be heard in the distance, shrilly upbraiding someone.

'Felipe, no doubt,' Diaz muttered as they escaped upstairs. 'He wants to go south to Marbella, to earn lots of money and have fun with foreign girls. Pilar, as you can imagine, is against the idea. War is intermittent, but fierce.'

The first thing Rhianna saw in the bedroom was her clothing, fresh, clean, and laid neatly across the bed.

'Why the hell didn't she put it away in the wardrobe?' Diaz said, frowning.

'Too intimate, perhaps.' She smiled valiantly. 'Also too suggestive of permanence. You'd better reassure her that her fears are unnecessary.'

He turned away. 'I'd better say something, certainly.' He looked down at the dresses on the bed, and picked up the green one she'd worn that first evening on the boat. 'Wear this for me tonight, Rhianna. Please?'

Her heart seemed to twist. 'If—that's what you want.'

'It's what I have to settle for, anyway,' he said, and walked into the bathroom.

Presently she heard the shower running, and realised he had not invited her to join him as he'd done earlier that day, when her attempt to wash his back had turned into something very different. When, with both of them drenched and laughing, she'd found herself lifted on to his loins and brought to a swift and tumultuous climax which had left her clinging to him, her legs too shaky to bear her weight.

She sank down on the edge of the bed, the dress draped across her lap and thought, He's starting to say goodbye.

She dressed with extra care that evening. Diaz had gone by the time she emerged from the bathroom in her turn. Outside, the sky looked like granite, and she could hear the first heavy drops of rain thudding on to the balcony. Everything, she thought, was changing.

She put on her favourite underwear, silk embroidered with little silver roses, and made up her face with a light touch. She brushed her hair to the lustre of satin, then slipped into the green dress, winding the sash tightly round her slender waist.

She even chose the same earrings. Then, after touching scent to her pulse points, she went downstairs.

Diaz was waiting for her in the salon, a long, low-ceilinged room, with creamy walls and the same slightly old-fashioned furnishings that she'd noticed elsewhere, which seemed so much in keeping with the house. The enormous fireplace at one end of the room didn't seem out of place either, she thought, listening to the splash of the rain.

But it was the portrait hanging over the fireplace that brought her to a surprised halt. For an instant she thought she was looking at Moira Seymour, only a frailer, more shadowy version, and then she realised who it must really be.

She said uncertainly, 'Your mother?'

'Yes,' he said. 'Painted not long after I was born. It was meant to hang at Penvarnon, but I had it shipped over here.'

Rhianna looked again. No, she thought. That could never be Moira Seymour. There was a quietness about the seated figure, a softness to the mouth that bore no resemblance to her sister's glossy self-confidence. And Esther Penvarnon looked sad, too. Not at all like someone who'd just given birth to a much wanted child.

She hesitated. 'Will you tell me about her—and your father? After all, it can't make any difference now.'

He stared down into his glass, his brows drawn together. 'I was away at school from the time I was seven,' he said. 'But even before that I knew somehow that they weren't happy. My father was a big man, larger than life and full of energy. He taught me to swim and row a boat, and to bowl at cricket. He made life special, and I pretty much worshipped him. I saw much less of my mother. She suffered constantly from this terrible debilitating virus that left her with hardly the strength to move. I was always being told as a child to be quiet because she was asleep, or keep out of her room because she was resting.'

He added expressionlessly, 'Looking back as an adult, I can see that it probably hadn't been a real marriage for a very long time. There was my mother in a wheelchair, with my father still young, virile, and attractive to women. A recipe for the usual disaster.'

He shook his head. 'I suppose there must always have been other women. Certainly he spent less and less time at Penvarnon, and I began to stay away too, discovering family life in other people's houses.'

She said, 'But your aunt and uncle…?'

'Were there principally for my mother.' His mouth twisted. 'My father thought it would be good for her to have her sister's companionship. The reality, I think, was very different. Eventually someone from the village was employed to care for her—your aunt.'

Rhianna looked at him gravely. 'I would hardly mention Aunt Kezia and caring in the same breath.'

'Yet she was devoted to my mother, apparently,' he said. 'Then, when she was promoted to housekeeper, her place was taken by her younger sister, Grace, who was planning to become a nurse.'

He moved restlessly to the fireplace and stood looking up at the portrait.

'Apparently he fell in love with her at first sight,' he said abruptly. 'So it can't have been easy for him to be married yet not have a wife in any meaningful sense. So maybe there was some excuse for him finding consolation elsewhere.'

He drew a harsh breath. 'But he came back to Penvarnon, Rhianna, and had a blatant affair with a girl almost young enough to be his daughter, totally humiliating and distressing my mother in the cruellest way. Then, when Grace Trewint was dismissed, he followed her to London and lived with her in a Knightsbridge flat he bought for them both. He never came back to Cornwall. We lost him. I—lost him.'

She said, 'But if they loved each other—'

'What kind of love is that?' he returned harshly. 'When so many people get hurt by it? My mother ended up in a nursing home, for God's sake. She was there for almost a year, but gradually she put her life back together. Her health improved, and she even learned to walk again.'

He shook his head. 'But she wouldn't return to Penvarnon— and, with its memories, who could blame her? At first she bought a house in Brittany, then she moved south. But not here. Still not to Penvarnon property.' He paused. 'And she remains—fragile.'

He turned slowly and looked at her, his eyes haunted, anguished. 'Rhianna…'

She went to him, putting her forefinger gently on his lips to silence him. 'You don't have to say anything,' she told him huskily. 'Truly, you don't. Because I—understand.'

We love each other, she thought. But we can never say so. Because he's right. What kind of love deliberately causes more hurt to someone who's suffered enough?

She moved away and sat down. 'Did she never think of divorce?' she asked tentatively.

'That's one of the few things I've felt able to ask her.' Diaz walked to the windows and stood looking out at the rain. 'All she said was, "It wouldn't have been right."'

She said with difficulty, 'She must have loved him very much.' She paused. 'Did you ever see your father again?'

'Yes,' he said. 'When your mother eventually left him he went back to South America, and I spent a lot of time with him there. But he wasn't the same. He looked old and tired, long before his final heart attack. And I blamed her for that too.' He saw her flinch and took a step towards her. 'Darling...'

'It's all right.' She held up a hand, smiling resolutely. 'It's just that I still can't equate the woman I knew with this—this heartless home-wrecker.'

She took a deep breath. 'Which is perhaps the moment to change the subject. Did you manage to find me a flight back to Britain tomorrow?'

'Yes,' he said. 'At five p.m. from Oviedo. The ticket will be at the Transoria desk.'

'Thank you.' She looked down at her glass. 'There's one more thing. Tonight—may I—is it possible for me to sleep in another room?'

Diaz turned back to the window. 'Yes, of course,' he said quietly. 'I should have suggested it myself.' He paused. 'I'll tell Pilar to transfer your things.'

She said, too brightly, 'Another victory for morality. She'll be delighted—especially when she finds I'm leaving tomorrow.'

'Then at least one cloud has a silver lining.' He drained his glass. His smile skimmed her. 'Shall we go into dinner?'

It was a wretched meal, eaten mainly in silence, although the food was superb. There was a delicate almond soup, followed by thin slices of tender beef cooked in wine and green olives, and to finish *crème* Catalan, flavoured with lemon.

She said, 'I didn't think anything could better the food on your boat, but now I'm not so sure.'

His smile was abstracted. 'Hardly surprising. Pilar taught Enrique all he knows.' He rose. 'Would you excuse me for a little while? I have some correspondence I should attend to.'

She said swiftly, 'And, once again, I have to pack.' She paused. 'So, I'll see you tomorrow.'

Her new room was just across the passage from the one she'd shared with Diaz the previous night. Everything had been prepared for her. The shutters had been closed and the lamp lit. The ceiling fan was whirring softly and her nightgown waited on the turned-down bed.

And on the night table was the photograph wallet, which Pilar must have found when she'd been unpacking for her.

Rhianna sat down on the bed and looked at the contents again. The pictures of Ben Penvarnon were the least terrible in the selection, so maybe she should offer them to Diaz, who might like them as a memento of his father.

But she couldn't imagine he'd want the awful ones of Moira Seymour, skulking about in the bushes, she thought critically as she riffled through them. What on earth had Aunt Kezia been thinking of?

I'll sort them out in the morning, she told herself, and began to get ready for bed.

She felt unutterably weary as she lay in the darkness, listening to the splash of the rain, but her mind wouldn't let her rest, imprisoning her on an emotional treadmill of regret and longing.

Images of Diaz smiling into her eyes jostled with the bleakness in his face as he'd talked of his parents' marriage. He'd been a lonely child, she thought, and his initial kindness to her had been prompted when he'd recognised the same sadness in herself.

But now the trap of loneliness was closing round them again, and although she'd tried to armour herself against it by spending tonight apart from him it hadn't worked. She was just wasting precious hours when they could have been creating a last beloved memory together.

Besides, after what they had shared, how could they part in this coldness? It just wasn't possible.

She slipped out of bed and went to the door, quiet as a ghost in her white nightgown.

He might be asleep, she thought as she crossed the passage. Or, worse, he might decide things were better as they were and reject her.

It was a thought that halted her, but even as she hesitated his door opened suddenly, and Diaz confronted her, wearing a black silk robe.

For a moment there was silence, then he said her name very softly, and took her hand.

Colour stormed into her face. 'I couldn't sleep.'

'Neither could I,' he said huskily. 'I was just coming to your room. I thought—I hoped that perhaps you might let me hold you. I wouldn't ask for anything else.'

She said, 'Then I'll simply have to plead for both of us,' and went into his arms.

CHAPTER TWELVE

SHE awoke just before dawn and lay for a moment watching him sleep, before easing herself to the edge of the bed, careful not to disturb him.

He deserved his rest, she thought with tenderness, remembering how he'd exerted all his self-control in order to pull himself back from some edge of desperation when he'd first begun to touch her, and the lingering, exquisite arousal to the aching passion of mutual fulfilment which had followed.

However, Pilar also deserved her illusions, she told herself, rescuing her torn nightdress from the floor and slipping noiselessly back to her room.

So it would be as well to pretend they'd spent the whole night apart.

She dropped the nightgown into her waiting travel bag, and then, her body still glowing with remembered pleasure, slid back into bed.

The rain had stopped, and a grey light was filtering into the room through the shutters. Somewhere in the garden a bird sang.

Another memory, she thought, to be recalled when she was far away, and she turned, burying her face in the pillow.

She hadn't planned on sleeping, but when she eventually stirred the floor was slatted with brilliant sunlight, and a glance at her watch told her it was nearly mid-morning.

She scrambled almost guiltily out of bed and headed for the bathroom. Why had no one woken her? she asked herself, as she stood under the shower. It seemed to her that at some point someone had touched her hair, but that was probably just a dream.

Half an hour later, dressed and with most of her packing done, she ventured downstairs. As she stood hesitantly in the entrance hall, Pilar appeared from the *salon*, according her the beginnings of a smile.

'*Buenos dias, señorita.* You come—eat?'

'Thank you.' Rhianna paused awkwardly. 'I'm sorry I'm so late.'

The housekeeper shrugged. '*No importa.* Señor Diaz say leave to sleep. So I leave.'

A place had been set for her on the rear terrace. Coffee was brought in a tall pot, followed by hot rolls, a dish of honey, and a bowl of fresh fruit. And finally Pilar put a platter in front of her, with a vast omelette filled with smoked bacon, tomatoes, peppers, potatoes and cheese.

'Heavens.' Rhianna surveyed its proportions with faint dismay. 'Just for me?'

'*Por supuesto,*' Pilar returned. 'Of course.'

'The *señor* has had his breakfast?' Rhianna ventured as she poured her coffee.

'Many hours ago.' Pilar gave her an astonished look. 'Then he work on computer, on telephone. Much busy. Now he go to Puerto Caravejo—to boat.'

'Oh.' Rhianna's brow wrinkled as she calculated the distance. 'Do you know how long that will take? It's just that I have to get to the airport...'

'No worry. He say he be here. He will come.' Pilar allowed her another judicious smile and departed.

To her own surprise Rhianna demolished every scrap of the omelette, and ate two rolls with honey after it.

After all, she reasoned, she might not eat again until she was back in England.

She was up in her room when she heard the sound of the car. Her lift to the airport, she told herself. She picked up her bags, took a last look around to make sure she'd forgotten nothing, then started for the stairs.

She would greet him smiling, she told herself. And not a word or a gesture would betray how much their separation would cost her.

As she turned the corner a bright light flashed in front of her, and she halted, blinking. In the same instant she realised that it was not Diaz waiting in the hall below but two men, one of whom was just lowering a camera.

The other was the reporter from the *Duchy Herald*, Jason Tully.

'Hello, Rhianna.' His smile was triumphant. 'I just knew we'd meet up again.' He looked at the luggage she was carrying. 'Going somewhere?'

'Yes, back to England.' She spoke calmly and continued her descent, putting the bags down at the foot of the stairs. But under her surface composure she felt sick, and her heart was going like a trip-hammer.

'But not back to Cornwall, I hope? You're *persona non grata* down there, as I imagine you know.' He paused. 'I suppose you *have* read my exclusive in the *Sunday Echo*? No?' He took a folded newspaper from his pocket and handed it to her. 'Be my guest. And you might want to sit down.'

Something warned her to do as he said, and she seated herself on the bottom step. As she opened the paper, the strapline above the front page leapt out at her.

Castle Pride star's wedding shock: 'He's mine,' says tearful Donna.

Oh, no, she whispered silently. Oh, God, please, no.
The story, with pictures filled the whole of page three.

Wedding guests at a picturesque Cornish church were left stunned yesterday when Donna Winston, rising star of hit TV series *Castle Pride*, halted the ceremony, claiming, 'I'm having the bridegroom's baby!'

Donna, twenty-two, told the shocked congregation that she and Simon Rawlins, scheduled to marry childhood sweetheart Caroline Seymour, had been involved in a passionate three month affair, which had left her pregnant.

Standing at the altar rail, just minutes before the arrival of the bride, Donna turned weeping to the blond, six-foot groom and declared, 'You're my baby's father, Simon. You belong to me, and I won't let you go.'

Ushers hustled the distraught Donna out of the church amid the murmurs of horrified onlookers. Standing in the sunshine, she declared defiantly, 'Simon's been living a lie. But it has to stop. He has responsibilities.'

She also revealed that she met twenty-six-year-old Simon through her former flatmate, Rhianna Carlow, and that many of their passionate love trysts had actually taken place at the *Castle Pride* star's Walburgh Square pad.

'Rhianna knew exactly what was going on,' she said. 'Even though she's supposed to be the bride's lifelong friend. But she must have had a recent attack of guilty conscience, as she's been trying to bully me into having an abortion. I wouldn't do it, because I know Simon loves me, and our baby is part of that love.'

Meanwhile, inside the church, the Vicar of Polkernick, the Rev. Alan Braithwaite, announced that both the ceremony and the lavish reception for two hundred guests would be indefinitely postponed.

As disappointed friends and family left the church, the bridegroom and best man departed by a side door, refusing to comment.

Also unavailable was Rhianna Carlow, who allegedly aided and abetted the secret affair, and whose portrayal of scheming, immoral Lady Ariadne in *Castle Pride* has raised eyebrows all around the world.

According to local reports she has not been seen since she left a prenuptial party hand in hand with glamorous multimillionaire Diaz Penvarnon, whose gracious home, Penvarnon House, was due to host the cancelled reception.

It is believed the couple decided to boycott the wedding for a love tryst of their own aboard the millionaire's luxury yacht, which sailed from Polkernick Harbour on Friday evening for an unknown destination.

Meanwhile the betrayed bride, pretty twenty-three-year-old Caroline Seymour, is being comforted by her family, with callers barred from the Penvarnon mansion.

Rhianna drew a deep breath and looked at Jason Tully. 'Not such an unknown destination after all, it seems.' She tapped the paper with a contemptuous finger. 'Well, you've already done your worst, Mr Tully, and earned yourself a national by-line. So why are you here?'

'To confirm a few things and make some more money.' He looked around. '*Very* cosy. But where's the boyfriend? Still sleeping off the Ariadne effect?' His smile was a lecherous insult. 'Hasn't lasted, though, your grand passion, has it? Maybe it occurred to him that having Grace Trewint's daughter as his mistress was a bit too close to home.

'Oh, yes,' he added softly, as Rhianna gave an involuntary gasp. 'People couldn't wait to fill me in on the old scandal—not when they heard what you'd done to Miss Seymour. Your name's dirt in Polkernick. And lucky me has another exclusive. I gather the wronged wife lives just over the French border,' he went on. 'What will she say, I wonder, when she hears that her son's been following so closely in his father's footsteps? Will she be impressed? I don't think so.'

Rhianna said calmly, 'The most you'll get is "no comment". I can promise you that. Anyway, why involve her when you have me? I'll give you what you want to know.'

She got up, smoothing her dress and smiling. 'As you've guessed, it was just a brief fling.' She slowed her voice to a drawl. 'One of those things that happen when you've both had too much to drink, alas. I threw myself at him, and he caught me. Something that seemed like a good idea at the time, but wasn't. And now it's over, and I'm out of here.' Her smile widened. 'If you're heading for the airport I'd be glad of a lift.'

For a moment Jason Tully looked almost nonplussed. 'You have no plans to meet him again?'

'Absolutely none,' she said. 'We agreed on just one thing—enough is definitely enough.'

'Right,' he said slowly. 'And what are you planning to say to Caroline Seymour next time you see her?'

How was it possible to stand and talk and function with some semblance of normality when you were hurting so much? When all you wanted to do was sink to your knees and howl?

She shrugged. 'I have no idea, but I'm sure I'll think of something.'

'And how do you react to rumours that your *Castle Pride* contract may be cancelled after the next series has been shown?'

She certainly hadn't been expecting that, she thought, flinching inwardly. Who said there was no such thing as bad publicity?

She said lightly, 'Merely that all good things come to an end.'

She was braced for another question, but at that moment Pilar suddenly erupted on to the scene from the back of the house, her voice rising in a crescendo of fierce Spanish as she flourished a threatening broom at the startled Tully and his companion.

'Hey!' he shouted as the bristles grazed his shoulder. He turned on Rhianna. 'You tell her that's assault, and I'll have the law on her.'

'I think she'll tell you this is trespass,' Rhianna returned evenly. 'Also this is her country, and her boss is a respected figure locally, so don't count on the police being on your side. I'd just leave, if I were you.'

She didn't expect her advice to be taken, but with a lot of muttering they went, and she heard the car drive away.

It was only when she felt Pilar's hand on her shoulder, and the older woman's voice urging her to be calm, that she realised she had sunk back on to the bottom stair and was sitting with her face in her hands.

She said shakily, 'Pilar, I have to go now. This minute. I must get back to England. Get an earlier flight if I can. Could Felipe drive me to Oviedo?'

'Felipe is disgrace,' Pilar said icily. 'He let in men—strangers—to the house of Señor Diaz. Take money. Bring dishonour on family.' She paused. 'Better you wait for the *señor*.'

'No!' Rhianna grasped her hand. 'I can't—not after this.' *I can't face him. Not after what's happened—and what I've said.*

She went on, 'Whatever Felipe's done, I really need him to drive the car. Please, Pilar. Tell him to take me to the airport, *por favor*.'

There was a silence, then Pilar nodded reluctantly.

'*Ay de mi*.' She raised clenched fists. 'What I say to the señor when he comes? What I tell him of men in house?'

Rhianna handed her the crumpled newspaper. 'Just give him this,' she said quietly. 'It will explain everything. And now will you get Felipe, please? Because I really have to go.'

'You're not serious.' Daisy stared at Rhianna open-mouthed. 'You're coming out of *Castle Pride* because of this nonsense? Darling, you don't mean it.'

'Yes,' Rhianna said steadily, 'I do. I've realised I simply can't do it any longer.' She pushed the tabloid newspaper she'd brought with her across the kitchen table. 'This decided me.'

She pointed at a large picture of Diaz walking along a street, his face cold and fierce with anger as he realised the presence of the camera, and at the screaming headline which accompanied it: 'He laid Ariadne and lived! Millionaire's drunken sex romp!'

She shook her head. 'Oh, God, how vile and sordid is that? Diaz is the last man in the world to want his private life gloated over in this ghastly way. Especially now that the papers have all picked up the story about my mother and his father being lovers.'

She attempted a smile. 'My attempt at a diversionary tactic has just made things a thousand times worse. I've failed everyone, including myself. But I've been well punished for my failure. Diaz must really hate me after all this.'

Daisy picked up the coffee pot and refilled their cups. 'Well,' she pointed out reasonably, 'as you've sworn you're never going to see him again that hardly matters. Nor are you responsible for something that happened long before you were born.' She paused. 'Besides, *you* didn't drag Diaz Penvarnon on board a yacht and sail off with him into the wide blue yonder. That was all his own idea, and if it's backfired—tough. It's certainly no reason to jeopardise your entire career.'

She gave Rhianna a long look. 'What on earth did your agent say?'

Rhianna bit her lip. 'Plenty.'

'I bet,' said Daisy. 'And the production company probably said even more.'

'I haven't had their reaction yet,' Rhianna returned. 'Although I've reason to believe they won't be too upset. Not that it will make any difference.' She leaned forward. 'Don't you see? In everyone's minds I've turned into Lady Ariadne—this monstrous creature. She's become the reality instead of me. And I can't handle that any more. When I started playing her it all seemed quite harmless, but it isn't any more. And I—I need to get away from it all. To get away from *her*.'

I've also realised I don't want to take off any of my clothes again in front of anyone but the man I love, she thought with sudden anguish.

'Just don't be too hasty.' Daisy put a comforting hand on her arm. 'Because it won't always be like that. This Donna Winston rubbish will soon be forgotten.'

'Not,' Rhianna said bitterly, 'by me. Or by many other people while she's on every daytime TV chat show, banging on about her fight for love and the safety of her unborn child. Making me into the real-life villainess of the piece.'

'Whereas, of course, the actual villain has got off scot-free.' Daisy wrinkled her nose in distaste. 'According to one story I read, he's vanished to South Africa—and good riddance.' She hesitated. 'Have you managed to contact your friend in Cornwall yet?'

'No,' Rhianna admitted dejectedly. 'I've tried phoning the house, but they won't let me speak to her.' She stared into her cup. 'And last time, when her mother answered, she called me a treacherous bitch.'

'And why wouldn't she?' Daisy said robustly. 'You've said yourself she's always hated you. She needs someone to blame, that's all.'

'She and a million others,' Rhianna said unhappily. 'I feel I'm a step away from being stoned in the streets. I came here this morning in a wig and a pair of sunglasses so no one on the Tube would recognise me. And though the Jessops have been wonderful, as always, letting me stay with them while the press are camped out at my flat, it can't be a permanent arrangement.'

She sighed. 'I feel I need to go and hide somewhere that no one will ever find me.'

'As long as you come out of hiding in six months' time,' Daisy said agreeably. 'Because you're going to be wanted as a godmother.'

'A *godmother*?' Rhianna sat up sharply, her own woes temporarily on hold. 'Truly? Oh, Daisy, my love, that's so wonderful.' She hesitated. 'Is that why Rob…?'

'Went into panic mode and ran?' Daisy supplied, brows raised. 'Absolutely. My beloved idiot suddenly saw a future where all the work had dried up and he had a wife and child he couldn't support. He got all the way to his parents in Norfolk, realised he was insane, and came back.'

She began to smile. 'Now he's given up the idea of being theatrical knight and his lady in favour of being a patriarch, with his family and their golden retriever in the garden of their palatial country home.'

There was a silence, then Rhianna collapsed in the first fit of genuine laughter she'd experienced since her return from Spain over a week before. Daisy joined her.

'God bless our boy,' Rhianna managed weakly at last, wiping her eyes. 'Incorrigible, or what?'

She was still smiling to herself as she made her way back to the quiet road where the Jessops lived.

Mrs Jessop met her in the hall, her kind face concerned. 'You've got a visitor, dear. A lady. She's in the front room.'

Carrie, Rhianna thought as she pushed open the door and went in. Oh, please, let it be Carrie.

Instead, she saw a tall woman with silvered blonde hair, dressed in immaculate grey trousers, with a matching silk blouse, and a coral linen jacket hanging from her shoulders.

For the first startled instant, as her visitor turned from the window to face her, Rhianna thought that it was Moira Seymour, and braced herself for the inevitable onslaught. But this woman was smiling at her. Diffidently, perhaps, but quite definitely smiling.

'So.' It was a soft, clear voice. 'Grace's daughter. We meet at last.'

Oh, God, thought Rhianna, panic tightening her throat as she recognised the face from the portrait. It's Diaz's mother.

She said uncertainly, 'Mrs—Penvarnon? I—I wasn't expecting this. What are you doing here—and how did you find me? I don't understand.'

'To be frank, I hoped you'd never be obliged to,' the older woman returned wryly. 'But when Diaz sent me the photographs he'd found in your room and demanded an explanation, I knew I no longer had a choice.'

'The photographs?' Rhianna stared at her. As soon as she'd got back to London she'd realised they'd gone. That they'd somehow been missing from her bedside table when she cleared her room. 'You mean Diaz had them?' She added with constraint, 'But why would he send them to you when they were mainly shots of his father?'

'Mostly,' Esther Penvarnon corrected her quietly. 'But not all. There were—others.'

'Well, yes,' Rhianna agreed, still puzzled. 'There were several of Mrs Seymour, plus a few taken with her husband. But I don't see…'

'No,' the older woman said. 'It wasn't Moira with her husband. Those photographs were of me—with my lover.'

'You?' Rhianna looked at her, stunned. '*You* were having an affair?'

'Yes.' The reply was steady. 'An affair with my brother-in-law, Francis Seymour. He and Moira had come to live at Penvarnon when I'd first become ill, to provide me with company and run things when Ben was away. He used to sit with me in the evenings and read to me, or we'd listen to the radio together. Gradually our relationship—changed.'

'It wasn't a trivial thing,' she added with emphasis. 'We were both unhappily married and we fell deeply in love. Although I realise that is no excuse for the damage that was done.'

'But you were in a wheelchair,' Rhianna protested.

'I had been, certainly,' Esther Penvarnon returned. 'But my health had been slowly improving for many months. However,

I chose for my own reasons to maintain the fiction that I was helpless.' She paused. 'May we sit down? It might make what I have to say a little easier for me.'

Rhianna drew a deep breath. 'I think that's a good idea.'

Esther Penvarnon seated herself in the armchair on one side of the fireplace, and Rhianna occupied the opposite one.

'Firstly,' Mrs Penvarnon began, 'my husband did not leave me because of some illicit passion for your mother. Grace Trewint was only ever resident housekeeper at his London flat—and a much needed friend. Ben told me so in a letter he wrote to me not long before his death, and I believe him. He left Cornwall, and the home he loved, because he too had been shown photographs, far more damaging ones than those Diaz saw, proving that I was being unfaithful to him, and he was devastated.

'Your mother wasn't dismissed because of any wrongdoing, either. She'd left of her own accord weeks before, because she suspected the truth and wouldn't lend herself to such gross deception of a good man. And Ben Penvarnon *was* a good man, Miss Carlow. He was also very rich, dynamic, and extremely handsome, and he attracted women like wasps round honey. He was just—not for me.

'I'd always been the quiet one, you see, living in my sister's shadow. So I was flattered—dazzled—when Ben fell in love with me, not her, and I somehow managed to convince myself that I must love him too.' She stared into space, as if she was contemplating an image too terrible to bear. 'However, the realities of married life soon taught me differently. I felt—nothing for him. Eventually I became sick with dread whenever he came near me.'

Rhianna moved restively. 'Mrs Penvarnon, I don't think you should be telling me these things. They can't matter any more.'

'Ah, but they do. Because they're my sole excuse for the continued pretence that I was ill. I was cheating the kind, considerate, generous husband who loved me for a long time before Francis and I became involved. And I think that was what he could not forgive—the lengths I went to in order to avoid being a wife to him.

'Once he'd gone, the three of us that were left went to even greater lengths to make sure the truth didn't get out. Moira was too fond of being lady of the manor to contemplate divorce. And I—I was shattered, and wanted only to get away. So when Kezia Trewint began to spread her tissue of lies we denied nothing.'

'But she took the photographs,' Rhianna said slowly. 'Took them, then showed them to your husband. Why did she turn on him?'

'Because she was in love with him—obsessed by him.' The older woman shrugged wryly. 'She believed, poor creature, that he'd be grateful to her, and much more besides. But he left by himself, and when she learned that Grace was working for him all that hidden passion turned sour, and she deliberately twisted their relationship into dirt.

'And I let her,' she added sombrely. 'Even after Ben's letter I said nothing. I told myself there was nothing to be gained by the truth. That Moira and Francis had patched up their marriage, and by this time even had a child. Best, I told myself, to let sleeping dogs lie. To go along with the myth of the betrayed wife.'

Esther Penvarnon paused. 'But none of us bargained for you—Grace's double—reawakening all the old resentment and all the guilt.' She added quietly, 'And I didn't allow for the possibility, my dear, that my son might love you so much that he would insist the record be set straight and your faith in your mother vindicated at last.

'So I'm here to ask if you can forgive me. If some good can finally come out of the sorrow and bitterness of the past, and there can be healing.'

There was a silence, then Rhianna said slowly, 'Perhaps—if it was just the past. But it isn't.' She lifted her chin. 'I'm grateful that my belief in my mother has been justified, but I can't go any further than that. You see, Mrs Penvarnon, nothing's changed for me. My whole life is a mess. A disaster I was drawn against my will into a totally unacceptable situation where I was also forced to keep other people's secrets. As a result I've been vilified in the tabloids and on television.'

She got to her feet, her legs shaking under her. 'My career, such as it was, is finished. My attempt to protect the happiness of my best friend has been a disaster. Her life is ruined, and she'll probably never speak to me again. And my relationship with Diaz, which began for all the wrong reasons anyway, has been dragged through the gutter press and distorted beyond recognition. You've seen the papers. How could he ever want to know me again—even if his sense of honour has demanded that the truth must be told?'

She drew a trembling breath. 'I got everything so terribly wrong—even with the best possible motives. All in all, I've caused more trouble than my Aunt Kezia ever dreamed of. Yes, I can forgive what happened in the past, if that's what you want to hear. That's the easy part. After all, the people most affected by it are no longer with us to be hurt any more. But this is the present, and I've had my own conspiracy of silence to contend against, and lost.

'I'm alive, Mrs Penvarnon, but who is there in this entire world who will ever forgive me? And how can I possibly bear it?'

From the doorway, Diaz said gently, 'With me beside you, my dearest love. We'll get through it together.'

Rhianna swung round, staring across the room at him with a kind of anguish. 'How did you know where to find me?'

'I've always known,' he said. 'Did you really think I'd let you leave Penvarnon five years ago without reassuring myself that you were safe and being cared for? When I found the press camped outside your flat, I guessed where you'd be.'

'But you can't stay here. You have to go—go now.' And she turned away, covering her face with trembling fingers.

In the silence that followed she heard the door close, and for a moment she thought he had really left her. Then his hands descended firmly on her shoulders, pulling her round to face him, and she realised that it was Esther Penvarnon who had departed, leaving them alone together.

He said quietly, 'Darling, without you, I'm going nowhere. You're the other half of me, and I refuse to live without you. So get used to the idea.'

'How can I?' She looked up at him with desperation, her clenched fists pushing at his chest. 'If the reporters trace you here, they'll crucify you all over again.'

'For what? Another drink-crazed orgy?' He grinned at her. 'It sounded terrific. I only wish I could remember it. Could you arrange an action replay some time?'

'It's not funny.' Her voice was almost a wail. 'I told that revolting Tully man that we'd just had a brief fling to try and get rid of him. He was threatening to talk to your mother—to tell her about us—and I couldn't let him do that.'

'It would have got him nowhere. She already knew.'

She stared up at him. 'She did? But how?'

'I told her myself, much earlier that same day. Not long after I woke up and found myself in bed alone, and realised I might be doing that for evermore unless I took positive action. I'd spent the better part of my life avoiding my family's no-go areas, but with my entire future happiness in jeopardy it was time to call a halt.

'So I rang my mother, told her we were lovers, and that I intended to bring you down to St Jean de Luz that day on *Windhover* to meet her. I was half expecting tears, accusations and hysterics, but instead there was the oddest silence, before she said very calmly that it might be best, as there were things that must be said, and that she would see us later.

'I went to your room to tell you, but you were deeply asleep and I didn't want to disturb you. However, I saw the photographs beside your bed and decided to have a look at them. And then I was the one to be disturbed,' he added drily. 'All this time I'd just accepted what I'd been told about my parents' marriage. I never questioned it—even when I knew I was falling in love with you. Suddenly my whole perspective underwent a radical change, and I realised what my mother might be waiting to say. So I sent the photographs to her via my computer, and gradually the whole miserable story came out.'

Rhianna shook her head. She said in a low voice, 'It must have cost her a great deal to tell you—and to come here today.'

'She says it's been a relief to speak the truth at last, and not have all that deception hanging over her any longer. She admitted she was always terrified that if I found out I might not be able to forgive her. After all, my father wasn't the only one to be kept at a distance by her supposed ill-health. But I think she's been punished enough.

'So, I told her that I was more concerned with how the whole sorry story had affected you. That I couldn't forget the lonely, unhappy child who'd come to Penvarnon to live under her mother's supposed shadow. Or that, with the exception of Carrie, we'd all treated you pretty badly. And I was one of the worst,' he added sombrely. 'Especially when I realised what I'd begun to feel for you and tried to end it.

'Only I never could, Rhianna. In all those five years I couldn't put you out of my mind, no matter how I tried.' He grimaced. 'And I did try. I didn't want to be torn apart between my need for you and my family's potential outrage. I still believed, you see, that my mother was too emotionally fragile to cope with the notion of my spending my life with you. My aunt Moira hinted that any nervous strain could lead to another breakdown.

'When you'd gone, I tried to tell myself I was suffering from a simple case of sexual frustration. That if I'd taken you to bed I'd have got you out of my system. However, eventually watching you as Lady Ariadne didn't help one bit. And when I saw you again I knew that wanting you physically was only part of what I felt for you. That somehow you were still the scared, isolated girl I yearned to love and protect for ever.

'And I was going to tell you so—only finding you with Rawlins stopped me in my tracks. The night I spent outside your flat, imagining you with him, was the lowest point in my whole existence. Yet even then I still ached for you. So when I learned you were defying me and coming to the wedding I made my plans accordingly. I tried to tell myself that I was taking you away for Carrie's sake, but that was sheer hypocrisy.

'Only then I found myself in bed—not with the practised seductress I'd expected, but the innocent girl I'd longed for and believed I'd lost for ever.' He gave an unsteady laugh. 'Dear God, I didn't know whether to turn a cartwheel or slash my wrists. What I had to do—and quickly—was rethink all my assumptions and win you round to the idea of being my wife. And no past scandals could be allowed to interfere.'

'But we still have the present ones to contend with,' Rhianna reminded him unhappily. 'And it's Carrie we have to think of now.' She bent her head. 'I was trying to protect her, and I've made everything a thousand times worse. And Donna Winston keeps adding fuel to the flames every day.'

'Well, the inventive Miss Winston's fire is about to go out,' Diaz said with distaste. 'It seems, my darling, that Rawlins wasn't the only one to give her money for the proposed termination. A guy she'd been seeing in Ipswich also paid for the same privilege. He kept quiet when the story first broke, because he was trying to salvage his marriage, but his wife has now left him so he's spilled the beans. The news will be in all the tabloids tomorrow. I think a lot of attitudes will change very quickly.'

'But that won't make things any better for Carrie.' Rhianna tried unavailingly to release herself from his arms. 'And how can I let myself begin to think of being with you when she's so wretched—and hating me? The Seymours are your family, Diaz, and we can't pretend they don't matter. That they won't do everything they can to stop us being together. You didn't hear how Carrie's mother spoke to me.'

'I can imagine,' Diaz said calmly. 'But I'd be surprised if that had much to do with her daughter's feelings. She's far more concerned about the past resurfacing so inconveniently, and losing her status as mistress of Penvarnon House to you, sweetheart. It seems she married Uncle Francis mainly so that she could stay in Cornwall and live at Penvarnon, maybe making my father realise, at the same time, that he'd chosen the wrong sister.'

His mouth twisted. 'But she was the mistaken one. He let her run the house for him, but that was all. Sadly for him, he loved my mother, and I believe he did so until the day he died.'

He paused. 'And don't worry too much about Carrie, my darling. Yes, she's still shocked and hurt, but she's had a lucky escape, and I think she's starting to recognise it. We went for a long walk together a couple of days ago, and she admitted she'd sensed there was something wrong in the weeks before the wedding. That Simon had changed so much there seemed to be little left of the boy she'd fallen in love with all those years ago. She'd even begun to wonder if she was doing the right thing, although she managed to convince herself it was bridal nerves.

'And she certainly doesn't hate you, whatever her mother may imply. She says she knew that you'd been wary of Simon for years, and avoided him as much as possible. So you'd hardly have played Cupid between him and your flatmate.'

He bent his head and kissed her gently on the lips. 'She'll be fine, my love. Just give her time.'

She moved closer, resting her cheek against his chest, her whole body warming to his nearness. 'But it may not be the same between us,' she said, with a touch of sadness.

''No,' he said softly. 'But how could it be, darling? Because you're going to be my wife, and that's bound to change things anyway.'

He picked her up in his arms and carried her over to the armchair, settling her on his knee. 'Now, can we just think about ourselves for one minute?' He reached into an inside pocket and produced a flat leather case. 'I have a present for you.'

From their satin bed, Tamsin Penvarnon's turquoises gleamed up at her.

'Even if I can persuade you to marry me incredibly quickly,' he went on, as Rhianna gasped, 'these have to be part of the ceremony.' He kissed her again, slowly and sensuously. 'And we'll take them on honeymoon with us,' he whispered. 'I want to see you wearing them and nothing else on our wedding night.'

There would still be gossip, and even more newspaper head-lines before they'd be allowed to live in peace with each other. But with Diaz beside her Rhianna knew beyond all doubt that she could face anything life brought her. That their love would guard them always.

'It will be my pleasure,' she answered softly, and slid her arms round his neck to draw him down to her in promise and trust.

THE MULTI-MILLIONAIRE'S VIRGIN MISTRESS

BY
CATHY WILLIAMS

Cathy Williams was born in the West Indies and has been writing Mills & Boon® romances for more than fifteen years. She is a great believer in the power of perseverance, as she had never written anything before (apart from school essays a lifetime ago!), and from the starting point of zero has now fulfilled her ambition to pursue this most enjoyable of careers. She would encourage any would-be writer to have faith and go for it!

She lives in the beautiful Warwickshire countryside with her husband and three children, Charlotte, Olivia and Emma. When not writing she is hard-pressed to find a moment's free time between the millions of household chores, not to mention being a one-woman taxi service for her daughters' never-ending social lives.

She derives inspiration from the hot, lazy, tropical island of Trinidad (where she was born), from the peaceful countryside of middle England and, of course, from her many friends, who are a rich source of plots and are particularly garrulous when it comes to describing Mills & Boon® heroes. It would seem from their complaints that tall, dark and charismatic men are way too few and far between! Her hope is to continue writing romance fiction and providing those eternal tales of love for which, she feels, we all strive.

PROLOGUE

'WHAT the hell did you think you were playing at?'

Alessandro had stormed into the bedroom. There was no other way to put it. He had stormed into the bedroom. The beautiful, angular lines of his face were tight with anger and Megan didn't know why. Well, she sort of knew why. She just couldn't quite understand the depth of his fury.

'Playing at?' she asked weakly, hands clasped behind her back as she leant against the wall.

Having been practically shoved into the bedroom an hour before, like a stray bug that had inadvertently wandered into his bedsit, necessitating immediate quarantine, she had been on the verge of dozing off when the sound of his footsteps heading towards the room had seen her springing off the bed and virtually standing to attention by the window. Of course she had known that he wouldn't be sunshine and light, not after his reaction to her perfectly innocent and well-intentioned birthday surprise. She just hadn't reckoned on this backlash of anger.

'You heard me! That ridiculous stunt of yours!'

The voice that could make her weak with love and longing, that could drive her mad with desire, was cold and cutting.

'It wasn't a ridiculous stunt. It was a birthday surprise. I thought you'd *like* it.'

'*Like* you barging in unannounced and bursting out of a *birthday cake*? When I'm in the process of having a meeting with people who could change the direction of my life?'

Megan chewed her lip and stared at him. God, he was so beautiful. Even now, when he looked as though he would happily throttle her given half a chance, he was still sinfully sexy. Six foot two inches of gorgeous, head-turning masculinity, and all she wanted to do was coax him out of this black humour—because it *was* his birthday, after all, even if he had no desire to celebrate it.

She risked a little smile. 'You have no idea how strenuous it is being a birthday cake! I have the scars to prove it!' No exaggeration there, she thought. Her amazing plan had involved her friend Charlotte rigging up two boxes into something that resembled a cake—a piece of engineering which, Megan had been assured, would work like clockwork. One spring, and *bingo*! She would be revealed in all her glory! Her blonde curls had been tamed into a Marilyn Monroe format of soft waves, a mole had been perfectly positioned on one cheekbone, her full lips had been primed to scarlet, pouting perfection.

Needless to say they had not bargained on the full hour it had taken to be delivered in rush-hour traffic. Nor had they foreseen the possibility that the cunning contraption might prove to have a mind of its own, refusing to oblige a swift and easy exit, so that once in Alessandro's poky front room she had found herself having to do battle with masking tape when her legs were numb and her blood circulation virtually non-existent.

It had all added up to an inglorious, fairly shambolic situation, which had seen her crawling out of the box amidst a mass of screwed-up tape and crunched-up pink tissue paper—at which point she had been confronted by the embarrassing sight of three men in pinstriped suits and one very, very angry boyfriend.

'I was supposed to be Marilyn Monroe,' she expanded, when her smile failed to make headway.

She gestured to her outfit, which had started off in much better condition. Three hours before it had been a glamorous black swimsuit, revealing a tantalising amount of cleavage. She also wore high, black shoes, long black gloves and fishnet stockings. The swimsuit was still intact, but one glove was currently residing somewhere in said birthday cake, the shoes had been kicked off, and the fishnet tights now sported a long, unattractive rip down one leg. Not so much Marilyn-of-the-Happy-Birthday-Song as Marilyn-on-Tour-of-War-duty.

'I thought you'd be pleased.' Her voice was growing less confident by the second. 'Or at least find it funny.'

'Megan…' Alessandro sighed. 'We need to…to talk…'

She relaxed a little. Yes, she could do talking. He was the most fascinating man she had ever met, and she could talk to him until the cows came home—especially now, when he was no longer glaring at her with eyes that were like chips of dark, glacial ice.

'I guess we could…' she said, taking a couple steps towards him. 'Talk. Although…' a few more steps and she was standing directly in front of him, looking up at him '…I can think of more interesting things to do…' She splayed her hand across his chest, loving the feel of its rippling hardness. 'I prefer it when you wear shirts, Alessandro. I like unbuttoning them. Have I ever told you that? Tee shirts just aren't the same. Not that this black tee shirt doesn't look very nice on you.' It did. It wasn't baggy and shapeless, but clung in a very masculine way.

Alessandro reached out and caught her wandering hand in his. 'I said talk, Megan. And we can't *talk* in here.'

'Have your friends gone?'

'They weren't my *friends*.'

He dropped her hand and turned away, walking out of the bedroom so that she was obliged to follow him. He couldn't think straight when Megan was anywhere near the vicinity of a bed—especially when she was wearing an outfit that revealed every single curve of her fabulous, sexy little body.

'And put something on,' he commanded, without looking round.

'Oh, right. They're the people who are going to change the direction of your life.'

En route, she grabbed one of his shirts. He only wore white shirts, which she had told him was a very boring trait indeed. She had tried to even the balance by buying him a garishly coloured Hawaiian shirt, with a pattern of lurid coconut trees against a brilliant blue background, but he had yet to wear it. She suspected that it had been shoved at the bottom of his wardrobe somewhere.

She sensed him stiffen at her throwaway remark, but he didn't say anything. Just flung himself on the sofa that occupied one side of the space in his modest student accommodation, which only someone massively optimistic could call a *sitting room*.

It was literally a poky box, as he had told her on more than one occasion. But he had worked like a slave, he said, to put himself through university, and his destiny was to become master. Master of all he surveyed. Once he left, he would never look back

Megan didn't like to think too hard about where all of this mastery and conquering of the universe stuff was going to take him. Out of her life, she guessed. But who knew? Eternally optimistic, and madly in love for the very first time in her life, she was happy to put any thoughts about an uncertain future on hold. She was nineteen. She had her own college life to think about. She didn't want to foresee a day when her life wasn't going to be joined up with his.

'So who were they, anyway?' she asked now, settling on the sofa next to him and tucking her legs underneath her. She had to stop herself from reaching out and touching his face.

It still surprised and delighted her that she had been lucky enough to fall in love for the very first time with a man so absolutely perfect in every way. Her friends all led chaotic love-lives, constantly euphoric or depressed, or else hanging on the end of the line waiting for some guy to call. Alessandro had never done that. He had taken her virginity and cherished the gift she had given him, never taking her for granted or making promises he had no intention of fulfilling.

'They were…some fairly important people, Megan.'

He turned to look at her. Her hair was all over the place— soft, blonde hair, the colour of vanilla. Her cheeks were flushed, because he had obviously surprised her dozing. Only Megan could fall asleep in the space of seconds. Whilst wearing a ridiculous outfit. And after having made a complete fool of herself.

'Sorry,' she said in a contrite voice. Then, because she just couldn't help herself, she leaned towards him and stroked the side of his face with the back of his hand. 'I can understand why you were a bit put out when I appeared unannounced. Or should I say when I was brought in? Would have given anyone a shock. Especially an old man like you, Alessandro. Twenty-five years old! Practically over the hill! Do you realise it's just a matter of time before you're collecting your pension?'

She laughed, a rich, warm laugh which he had found infectious from the very first minute he had heard it across a crowded room, in a club to which he had been dragged by one of his colleagues at university who'd seemed to think he needed a break from his books. Every time he heard that laugh, which was often, he wanted to smile. Not, however, now.

'Here's how it was supposed to go. In an ideal world I would have made a dramatic entrance…or at least the cake would have made a dramatic entrance…and I would have leapt out of it, like the Marilyn Monroe equivalent of a Jack in the Box, stunning you with my wonderful outfit. Then I would have sung you 'Happy Birthday', even though I'll be the first to admit that my voice is pretty average…'

'Unfortunately…' He edged away and looked at her with a shuttered expression. 'Unfortunately you couldn't have chosen a worse moment for your little surprise.'

'No, well…' Always so comfortable in his presence, Megan could feel stirrings of unease nibbling away inside her, even though really he no longer looked angry. 'You never told me that you were expecting guests. You said that you would be working, and I just thought that it would be kind of nice to be surprised. You work too hard.'

'I do what I have to do, Megan. How many times have I told you that?'

'Yes, I know. You hate this place, and you work hard so that you can get out of it and do something with your life.'

'I intend to do more than just *something* with my life.'

His father had done just *something* with his life. He had left poverty in Italy, hoping to find that the streets of London would be paved with gold. In the event they had been paved with tarmac and cement, just like everywhere else, and his father's talents, his tremendous mathematical brain which had so enchanted Alessandro as a young boy, had become lost in the mindless boredom of manual work—because he had not been qualified to do anything else, and provincial little England had not been kind to a man whose grasp of English was broken. Never mind that his wife was English. An English rose with as few qualifications as her Italian husband. An English rose whose hands had been prematurely old from the cleaning jobs she had held down so that they could afford a small holiday once a year by the cold British seaside.

Alessandro didn't like to think of the mother he had only known for the first ten years of his life. He liked even less to think of his father, loyally working for a haulage firm for twenty-five years, only to be made redundant at a time when he had been too old to get another job.

To his dying breath he had continued to tell his son what a wonderful life he had led.

To Alessandro's way of thinking his father's talents had been wasted, by lack of opportunity and the cruelty of a world that judged a man's worth by bits of paper. He would, he had determined from an early age, get those bits of paper, and he would control the world so that it could never control him the way it had his father.

'Those three men,' he said, keeping that unaccustomed drift of memory to himself, 'who were treated to your impromptu performance, are instrumental in my plan for the future.'

'You mean, the pinstriped crew?'

He paused. 'You need to grow up, Megan.'

That one statement, delivered with a coldness she had never heard before, was shocking. Yes, they were total opposites. They had laughed about that a million times. But he had always indulged her. She'd drag him away from his books with homemade picnics in the park and he would laugh at the sausage rolls and packets of biscuits and cheap wine. She would make a fool of herself singing karaoke, and he would shake his head in good-natured wonder and tell her never to consider a career in singing. He had never told her to grow up—and certainly never in that tone of voice.

'It was just meant to be a bit of fun, Alessandro. How was

I to know that the instruments of your plan would be here? And why do you have a plan, anyway? Really? Life's not a chessboard, you know.'

'That's exactly what it is, Megan. A chessboard. The life we end up getting depends entirely on the moves we make.'

'I know you want to do stuff with your life, Alessandro, but…' Megan shot him a look of bemusement. This wasn't quite the sort of talk she had been expecting, but it was certainly revealing. 'You can't plan *everything*. I mean, I really hope that I end up being a good teacher…'

'In a small country school somewhere…'

'What's wrong with that?'

'There's nothing wrong with it,' Alessandro told her patiently.

He looked at her expressive, open face and felt like a monster, but this was a conversation that had to be undertaken. His future had unexpectedly come rushing towards him like a freight train, leaving him no choice.

'Did you ever think about qualifying and going to teach somewhere else?'

'Somewhere else? Why should I? You know that St Nicks have offered me a post for after I qualify.'

Her face softened as she thought of the pleasing prospect of teaching the children there. She was nothing like the high-flier that Alessandro was, and her future might not be so ruthlessly controlled as his appeared to be, but it was still looking pretty rosy from where she was sitting.

'Where else should I be going to teach?'

'What about an inner-city school?'

'Why are we having this conversation? Is it because you're still mad at me—because I embarrassed you in front of those people? Don't be…You wait right here, and I'm going to get us both something to drink. Some wine…'

She didn't give him time to answer, or to follow up with

some more heavy-duty remarks about life choices. Instead, she stood up and did a little sexy shimmy, throwing him a seductive look over one shoulder, before heading for the kitchen and pouring them a large glass of wine each.

She'd kind of hoped that he would be undressed when she returned, because he was always, but *always*, predictable when it came to being turned on by her, but he wasn't. In fact, he was standing up, and he had an awkward look on his face that promised more *talking*.

Whatever those guys had said to him had obviously made him a little too thoughtful, and it was her duty, she told herself mischievously, to take his mind off matters. And at the back of her mind she knew she really didn't want to hear what Alessandro wanted to say….

A very good place to start would be with his shirt. She placed the glasses on the small, beaten-up round table by the window and pulled off the white shirt, which she casually tossed over a chair.

'Megan…' Alessandro turned away and leaned heavily against the wall. 'This isn't a good time for this.' He tensed as he heard her walk towards him. He could picture the teasing smile on her face.

'Don't tell me you're getting too old for sex,' she said to his averted back. 'You're only a year older!' She wrapped her arms around his torso and then slipped her hands under the tee shirt, gently rubbing his flattened brown nipples with the tips of her fingers.

Alessandro shuddered, furious with himself for not being able to push her away when he knew that he had to. For both their sakes.

He felt the push of her breasts against him and turned round with a stifled moan, his big body arching back in denial of the primitive instincts he seemed unable to control.

He closed his eyes and shuddered again.

Nine months of seeing her, practically living with her, even though her college was over twenty miles away. Out towards the country because, she had told him often enough, big cities gave her a headache. Something about her was irresistible.

She took his hand and guided it to the strap of the black swimsuit which she was still wearing.

'At least the cake wasn't real,' Megan murmured, already wet and hot for him. 'Can you imagine if I'd emerged covered in Victoria sponge?'

She stood on tiptoe so that she could kiss his neck, and even though he wasn't, as he usually was, devouring her with his hunger, he *was* responding. She could feel it in the tension of his muscles—and... She put her hand on him and shivered with pleasure at the very big, very hard indication of just how much he wanted her—even if, for some weird reason, he *was* trying to fight it.

'Mind you,' she said thoughtfully, 'you would have had to lick it all off...'

The image was too powerful for Alessandro. He looked at her, at the deep cleavage inviting him to touch, promising him physical satisfaction of the kind he had never known in his life before.

I am, he thought with a strange feeling of helplessness, *only a man, dammit*!

He hooked his fingers under the straps of the swimsuit and ran them up and down against her smooth skin.

'A man could lose himself in the thought of that,' he said roughly, and all thoughts of *talk* vanished as he pulled down the straps and gazed at her breasts, large in comparison to her small frame, and perfectly formed. Milky-white and succulently heavy, with rose-pink nipples like discs, pouting provocatively at him.

He pulled her shakily towards the sofa and then, kicking

off his shoes, lay down. He figured he had damn near found heaven as she moved on top of him, sitting just in the right spot, so that he could feel the friction of his hardness against her through his trousers. She leant forwards, letting her breasts dangle temptingly above his mouth, and with a groan of utter abandonment Alessandro took one of the proffered nipples into his mouth, losing himself in the sensation of tasting her. He suckled on it, then when he was finished lavished the same attention on the other.

He wanted her completely naked. With fierce, driven movements he rid her of the swimsuit, stopping her when she tried to pull the tee shirt over his head.

'But I want to see you...' Megan whimpered.

He didn't answer. Instead, he pushed her back, spreading her legs in one deft motion, and her protest died on her lips as she felt his tongue invade her, sliding and exploring her depths until she was squirming, turned on to the point where thinking became an impossibility.

'Alessandro!' She curled her fingers into his dark hair and tugged him up. She was breathing heavily, her eyes closed, and she felt him undo the zipper of his trousers so that he could free himself.

She wasn't even entirely sure that he had removed his trousers before driving deep into her, his thrusting urgent, taking her by surprise.

It was quick, fierce lovemaking, and afterwards they were both breathless and spent. Alessandro was unusually quiet as he pushed himself away from her, so that he could get back into his jeans and then fetch a bottle of water from the fridge, which he proceeded to drink in one long swallow.

'You need to get dressed, Megan, and then we'll talk.'

Megan felt a chill of fear race up and down her spine, obliterating everything in its path.

Talk about what? she was desperate to ask, but his shut-tered expression kept that question reined in, and she silently went to the bedroom and rescued the only items of clothing she kept at his place: a pair of jeans and a sweater.

When she returned, it was to find that he had taken up position by the table, so that when she sat down, facing him, it felt like an awkward interview.

'If it's about my cake surprise, you have my word I won't do anything like that again. It'll take more than one shampoo before my hair recovers from the masking tape. In fact, I'm going to have to sack my production manager.'

Alessandro didn't return her grin. This was going to be a difficult conversation, made all the worse by the fact that they should never have made love. He had allowed himself a selfish luxury, one which he deeply regretted.

'This isn't about your cake surprise, Megan. This is about those three men who were here. I've been head-hunted.' It had come as no great surprise to Alessandro. He was good. He had been head-hunted before, and had turned down all offers. With or without intervention, he was going to go places— although this particular intervention would be helpful in the near future.

'Wow, Alessandro! That's fantastic! We should cele-brate…' But it wasn't a celebrating atmosphere. 'You don't look overjoyed.'

Alessandro shrugged. 'Little do they realise it, but they will discover that they need me more than I need them.'

Megan laughed. 'Well, no one could ever accuse you of not having a healthy ego, Alessandro.'

That wonderful laugh stirred something inside him which he chose to ignore.

'I've been offered a job.' He stood up, distancing himself from her. 'In London.'

Those two words stilled the easy smile on her lips, replacing it with the cold hand of dread. 'London? But you can't go to London.' *What about us?* 'What about your Masters?'

'It will have to take a back seat. I can finish it in my own time, but for the moment my future calls.'

She was trembling. She had banked on having him around for a few more months, at which point she would be able to cross the inevitable bridge. That bridge was now staring her in the face. Maybe, she thought, desperately salvaging the best possible take on the situation, they could carry on a long-distance relationship? It wouldn't be ideal, but it could work. A few hours on the train every other weekend, and then there were the holidays…

'When?'

'Immediately.' Alessandro allowed the finality of that word to settle between them like a rock sinking into deep, uncharted waters. It hurt to look at her distraught expression.

'Immediately…as in *immediately*…?'

'Just time to pack up my belongings—what little I have—and put my past behind me for good.'

'It's not that bad,' she whispered. Thoughts and fears were whizzing around in her head and she was beginning to feel sick. 'What…what about us…?'

Alessandro didn't answer, and the silence stretched between them until she could almost hear it vibrating in the air.

'We…we can still carry on seeing each other, can't we? I mean, I know London's a long way away, but loads of people have long-distance relationships. It might be romantic! Who knows? We could…um…meet up every so often…' Her babbling trailed off into silence. More silence.

'It wouldn't work,' Alessandro said flatly.

'Why not? Wouldn't you even be willing to *give it a try*?' Desperation had crept into her voice, and she searched his face for the smallest sign of comfort. But she was looking at a stranger. His expression was closed and hard.

'There's no point, Megan.'

'No point? *No point?* How can you say that, Alessandro? We've practically *lived together* for the better part of a year! How can you say that there's *no point* in trying to stay together? I...we...Alessandro, *I love you.* I really do. You're the guy I gave myself to...you *know* how much that meant to me...'

Alessandro flushed darkly. 'And I cherish that gift.'

He said it as though their relationship had already been consigned to the memory box.

'Then tell me that you won't walk away.'

'I...I can't say that, Megan.' He embraced the room in one sweeping gesture with a look of distaste. 'This...this was a chapter in my life, Megan, and it's time for me to move on with the book.'

'What you're saying is that *I'm* a chapter in your life. You had your fun but all good things come to an end.'

'All things *do* come to an end. And your life is here, Megan. Here with your family, with your teaching job out in the country. You know you hate the city. You've always said that. You told me that the only reason you ever ventured into Edinburgh in the first place was because your cousin had dragged you there, and that the only reason you kept coming back was to see me... If you think Edinburgh's city living, then London is in a league of its own.'

'You're twisting everything I said to you! My life could be *anywhere* with you!'

'No.'

He almost wished that she would cry. A crying female he could deal with, because crying females had always irritated the hell out of him. But she wasn't a crier.

'You're a country girl at heart, Megan, and you would be

miscrable if I—or anyone else, for that matter—removed you from the open fields you enjoy. That aside…' He paused, because he wanted to be completely honest with her. That much she deserved. 'This step of my journey I must take alone. I'm about to devote myself to my career. I literally wouldn't have time to spend…'

'…taking care of a hopeless country bumpkin like me?' Megan finished for him.

She stared down at her bare feet. The bright red nail polish she had applied to her toes earlier in the day was already beginning to flake. She would have to get rid of it. She actually hated bright red nail polish anyway. She had only put it on because it matched the Marilyn image she had wanted for her stupid, childish surprise cake gimmick.

'Taking care of *any woman*.' But maybe, he thought, there was some truth in her statement. Falling out of a box in front of three of the country's top finance gurus might seem a bit of a joke to her, but this was going to be his life, and falling out of boxes just wasn't going to cut it.

'I don't believe you.' Megan held her ground stubbornly, determined to wade through every inch of pain until the picture was totally clear in her head. 'You just don't think that I'm good enough for you now you're about to embark on this wonderful jet-setting career of yours. If I had been an… accountant, or…an economist, or someone *more serious*, then you wouldn't be standing there, airbrushing me out of your life as though I'd never existed!'

'What do you want me to say, Megan?' He finally snapped, furious that she was making this already difficult situation even more difficult by demanding answers to hypothetical speculations. 'That I can't see myself in a permanent situation with someone who will probably still be fooling around and singing karaoke when she's thirty-five?'

If he had extracted a whip from his back pocket and slashed it across her face it couldn't have hurt more, and she stared at him mutely.

'I apologise,' he said brusquely. 'That remark was entirely uncalled for. Why can't you just accept that there are limitations to this relationship and always have been?'

'You never mentioned anything about limitations before. You let me give you my undivided love and you never said a word about me not fitting the bill.'

'Nor did I ever speak to you about a future for us.'

'No,' Megan agreed quietly. 'No, you never did, did you?'

Alessandro steeled himself against the accusatory look in her big blue eyes. 'I assumed you were aware of the differences between us as well as I was—assumed you knew that my intention was never to remain in Scotland, playing happy families in a cottage somewhere in the middle of nowhere.'

'I assumed you cared about me.'

'We had fun, Megan.' He spun round and stared out of the grimy window to the uninspiring view two floors down. In the rapidly gathering dark the strip of shops opposite promised fish and chips, an all-you-can-eat Indian buffet every lunchtime, a newsagent and that was about it—because the other three shops were boarded up.

'Fun?'

Alessandro ignored the bitterness that had crept into her voice. When he had first made love to her, had discovered that she was a virgin, he had felt a twinge of discomfort. In retrospect, maybe he should have walked away at that point, rather than allowing her to invest everything into him, but he had been weak and—face it—unable to resist her. He was now paying the price for that weakness.

'You're better off without me,' he said roughly, as he continued to stare outside. 'You have all you need right here.

You'll teach at that school of yours, only a short distance away from all your family, and in due course you'll find a guy who will be content with the future you have mapped out.'

Megan had thought that the future she had mapped out for herself had *included him*!

'Yes,' she said dully. He wasn't even looking at her. He had already written her out of his life and was ready to move on. 'Why did you make love with me just now if you intended to get rid of me?' she asked. 'Was it a one-last-time session for poor old Megan before you sent her on her way?'

Alessandro spun round, but he didn't make a move towards her. 'It was…a…mistake…' And never again would he allow his emotions to control his behaviour.

He gripped the window sill against which he was leaning and reminded himself that, however much she was hurting now, she was still a kid and would bounce back in no time at all. She would even thank him eventually for walking away from her—would realise in time to come that they were worlds apart and whatever they had had would never have stayed the course of time. It was a reassuring thought.

Megan couldn't bear to look at him. She stood up, staring at the ground as though searching for divine inspiration.

'I think I'm going to leave now,' she said, addressing her feet. 'I'll just check the bedroom. See if there's anything of mine that I should take with me.'

He didn't try to stop her rooting through his stuff. The lack of anything belonging to her now seemed ominous proof of her impermanence in his life. He had never encouraged her to leave any of her things at his place. Sure, she's forgotten odd bits and pieces now and again, like the clothes she was currently standing in, but he'd always returned them.

The only things she had insisted on leaving were some of her CDs. She was voracious when it came to modern music, whereas he preferred more chilled sounds. *Easy listening to the point of coma*, she had teased him. Yet another example of those differences between them, which she had stupidly failed to spot but which he had probably noted and lodged away in his mind somewhere, to be brought out later and used in evidence against her.

Without looking in his direction, she quietly gathered her CDs and stuffed them in a plastic bag.

'I think that's about everything.' Some CDs, a toothbrush, some moisture cream, some underwear. Precious little. 'Good luck with the new job and the new life, Alessandro. I really hope it lives up to expectations and I'm sorry about the mess from the cake. You'll have to get rid of that yourself.'

Alessandro nodded. He didn't say anything because there was nothing left to say, and for the first time in his life he didn't trust himself to speak.

Megan turned away, and was half-disappointed, half-relieved when he didn't follow her. There was an emptiness growing inside her, and her throat felt horribly dry and tight, but there would be time enough to cry. Once she was back in her little room at college. Just one last look, though. Before she left for good. But when she turned around, it was to find that he was staring out of the window with his back to her.

CHAPTER ONE

MEGAN stooped down so that she was on the same level as the six-year-old, brown-haired, blue-eyed boy in front of her. Face of an angel, but spoiled rotten. She had seen many versions of this child over the past two years, since she had been working in London. It seemed to be particularly predominant at private schools, where children were lavished with all that money could buy but often starved of the things that money couldn't.

'Okay, Dominic. Here's the deal. The show's about to start, the mummies and daddies are all out there waiting, and the Nativity play just isn't going to be the same without you in it.'

'I don't want to be a tree! I hate the costume, Miss Reynolds, and if you force me then I'm going to tell my mummy, and you'll be in *big* trouble. My mummy's a lawyer, and she can put people into prison!' he ended, with folded arms and a note of irrefutable triumph in his voice.

Megan clung to her patience with immense difficulty. It had been a mad week. Getting six-year-old children to learn and memorise their lines had proved to be a Herculean feat, and the last thing she needed on the day before school broke up was a badly behaved brat refusing to be a tree.

'You're a very important tree,' she said gently. '*Very* im-

portant. The manger wouldn't be a manger without a very important tree next to it!' She looked at her watch and mentally
tried to calculate how much time she had to convince this tree
to take his leading role on stage—a role which involved
nothing more strenuous than waving his arms and swaying.
She had only been at this particular school for a term, but she
had already sussed the difficult ones, and had cleverly steered
them away from any roles that involved speech.

'I want my mummy. *She'll* tell you that I can be whatever
I want to be! And I want to be *a donkey*.'

'Lucy's the donkey, darling.'

'*I want to be a donkey!*'

Tree; donkey; donkey; tree. Right now, Megan was heartily
wishing that she had listened to her friend Charlotte, when she
had decided to leave St Margaret's and opted for another
private school. Somewhere a little more normal. She could
deal with *normal* fractious children. She had spent three years
dealing with them at St Nick's in Scotland, after she had
qualified as a teacher. None of *them* had ever threatened her
with prison.

'Okay. How about if we fetch your mummy and *she* can
tell you how important it is for you to play your part? Remember, Dominic! It's all about teamwork and not letting
other people down!'

'Donkey,' was his response to her bracing statement, and
Megan sighed and looked across to where the head of the
junior department was shaking her head sympathetically.

'Happened last year,' she confided, as Megan stood up.
'He's not one of our easier pupils, and fetching his mum is
going to be tricky. I've had a look outside and there's no sign
of her.' Jessica Ambles sighed.

'What about the father?'

'Divorced.'

'Poor kid,' Megan said sympathetically, and the other teacher grinned.

'You wouldn't be saying that if you had witnessed him throwing his egg at Ellie Maycock last Sports Day.'

'Final offer.' Megan stooped back down and held both Dominic's hands. 'You play the tree, and I'll ask your mummy if you can come and watch me play football over the vacation if you have time.'

Forty-five minutes later and she could say with utter conviction that she had won. Dominic Park had played a very convincing tree and had behaved immaculately. He had swayed to command, doing no damage whatsoever, either accidental or intentional, to the doll or the crib.

There was just the small matter of the promised football game, but she was pretty sure that Chelsea mummies, even the ones without daddies, were not going to be spending their Christmas vacation at home. Cold? Wet? Grey? Somehow she didn't think so.

Not that she had any problem with six-year-old Dominic watching her play football. She didn't. She just didn't see the point of extending herself beyond her normal working hours. She wasn't sure what exactly the school policy was on pupils watching their teachers play football, and she wasn't going to risk taking any chances. Not if she could help it. She was enjoying her job and she deserved to. Hadn't it taken her long enough to wake up in the morning and look forward to what the day ahead held in store for her?

From behind the curtain she could hear the sound of applause. Throughout the performance cameras and video recorders had been going mad. Absentee parents had shown up for the one day in the year they could spare for parental duty, and they were all determined to have some proof of their devotion.

Megan smiled to herself, knowing that she was being a little unfair, but teaching the children of the rich and famous took a little getting used to.

In a minute everyone would start filtering out of the hall, and she would do her duty and present a smiling face to the proud parents. To the very well-entertained parents—because, aside from the play, they would be treated to substantial snacks, including *crudités*, delicate salmon-wrapped filo pastries, miniature meatballs and sushi for the more discerning palate. Megan had gaped at the extravaganza of canapés. She still hadn't quite got to grips with cooking, and marvelled at anyone who could produce anything edible that actually resembled food.

Out of nowhere came the memory of Alessandro, of how he'd used to laugh at her attempts at cooking. When it came to recipe books she was, she had told him, severely dyslexic.

It was weird, but seven years down the road she still thought of him. Not in the obsessive, heartbroken, every-second-of-every-minute-of-every-waking-hour way that she once had, but randomly. Just little memories, leaping out at her from nowhere that would make her catch her breath until she blinked them away, and then things would return to normal.

'Duty calls!'

Megan snapped back to the present, to see Jessica Ambles grinning at her.

'All the parents are waiting outside for us to tell them what absolute darlings their poppets have been all term!'

'Most of them *have* been. Although I can think of a few...'

'With Dominic Park taking first prize in that category?'

Megan laughed. 'But at least he waved his arms tonight without knocking anyone over. Although I *did* notice that Lucy the donkey kept her distance. Amazing what a spot of blackmail can do. I told him he could watch my next football match.' She linked her arm through her colleague's and together they headed out to the main hall, leaving behind a backstage disaster zone of discarded props and costumes, all to be cleared away the following afternoon, when the school would be empty.

The main hall was a majestic space that was used for all the school's theatrical performances and for full assemblies. A magnificent Christmas tree, donated by one of the parents, stood in the corner, brightly lit with twinkling lights and festooned with decorations—many from the school reserves but a fair few also donated by parents. Elsewhere, along one side, were tables groaning with the delicacies and also bottles of wine—red and white.

The place was buzzing with parents and their offspring, who had changed back into their school gear, and numerous doting relatives. In between the teachers mingled, and enjoyed the thought that term was over and they would be having a three-week break from the little darlings.

Megan was not returning to Scotland for the holidays. Her parents had decided to take themselves off to the sunshine, and her sisters were vanishing to the in-laws'. Playing the abandonment card had been a source of great family mirth, but really she was quite pleased to be staying put in London. There was a lot going on, and Charlotte would be staying down as well. They had already put up their tree in the little house they shared in Shepherd's Bush, and had great plans for a Christmas lunch to which the dispossessed had been cordially invited. Provided they arrived bearing food or drink.

A surprising number of people had seemed happy to be included in the 'dispossessed' category, and so far the numbers were up to fifteen—which would be a logistical nightmare, because the sitting room was small—but a crush of bodies had never fazed Megan. The more the merrier, as far as she was concerned.

She heard Dominic before she actually spotted him. As was often the case with him, he was stridently informing one of his classmates what Father Christmas was bringing him. He seemed utterly convinced that the requested shed-load of presents would all be delivered, and Megan wondered whether he had threatened the poor guy with a prison sentence should his demands not be met.

She was smiling when she approached his mother, curious to see what she looked like. Matching parents to kids was an interesting game played by most teachers, and this time the mental picture connected perfectly with the real thing.

Dominic Park's mother *looked* like a lawyer. She was tall, even wearing smart, black patent leather flats, with a regal bearing. Dark hair was pulled back into an elegant chignon, and her blue eyes were clever and cool. Despite the informality of the occasion, she was wearing an immaculate dove-grey suit, with a pashmina loosely draped around her shoulders.

She was introduced via Dominic, who announced, without preamble, that this was Miss Reynolds and she had promised she would take him to watch her play football.

'You must be Dominic's mum.' Megan's smile was met with an expression that attempted to appear friendly and interested but somehow didn't quite manage to make it. This was a woman, Megan thought, who probably distributed her smiles like gold dust—or maybe she had forgotten how to smile at all, because it wasn't called for in a career that saw her putting people into prison, if her son was to be believed.

'Correct, Miss Reynolds, and I must say that I was very disappointed when Nanny told me today that Dominic would be playing a tree. Not terribly challenging, is it?'

She had an amazing accent that matched her regal bearing perfectly.

'We like to think of the Nativity Play as a fun production, Mrs

Park, rather than a competition.' She smiled down at Dominic, who was scowling at some sushi in a napkin. She took it from him. 'And you made a marvellous tree. Very convincing.'

'When will you be playing football?' he demanded.

'Ah... Timetable still to be set!'

'But you won't forget, will you?' he insisted. 'Because my mummy's a—'

'Yes, yes, yes... I think I've got the message on that one, Dominic.' Megan smiled at his mother. 'I've been told that I shall be flung into prison without a Get Out Of Jail Free card if I don't let him watch one of my matches....'

'Silly boy. I've told him a hundred times that I'm a corporate lawyer! And we shall have to discuss Dominic watching your football match, I'm afraid. We're very busy over the Christmas period, and Nanny won't be around for three days, so I shall be hard-pressed to spare the time to take him anywhere.'

Megan was busy feeling sorry for poor Nanny, who had clearly been inconsiderate enough to ask for time off over Christmas, when she was aware that they had been joined by someone. The elegant lawyer had stopped in mid-flow, and there actually was something of a smile on her face now as she looked past Megan to whoever was standing behind her.

'Alessandro, darling. So good of you. I'm absolutely *parched.*'

Alessandro!

The name alone was sufficient to send Megan into a tail-spin. Of course there was more than one Alessandro in the world! It was a common Italian name! It was just disconcerting to hear that name when she had been thinking about him only minutes earlier.

She turned around, and the unexpected rushed towards her like a freight train at full speed, taking her breath away. Because there he was. Alessandro Caretti. *Her* Alessandro.

Standing in front of her. A spectre from the past. Seven years separated memory from reality, but he had remained the same. Still lean, still muscular, still staggeringly good-looking. Yes, a little older now, and his face was harsher, more forbidding, but this was the man who had haunted her dreams for so long and still cropped up in her thoughts like a virus lying dormant in her bloodstream—controlled, but never really going away.

She had never seen him in a suit before. Seven years ago he had worn jeans and sweatshirts. He was wearing a suit now, a charcoal-grey suit, and, yes, a white shirt—so some things must not have changed.

Megan could feel the blood rushing into her face, and it was a job to keep steady, to hold out her hand politely and wonder if he would even recognise her. Her hair was shorter now, but still as uncontrollable as it always had been. Everything else was the same.

She was shaking when she felt the brief touch of his hand as she was introduced.

What was he doing here? Was he Dominic's *father*? But, no. From next to her she could hear that cut-glass accent saying something about her fiancé. He was engaged! Wearing a suit and engaged to the perfect woman he had foreseen all those years ago when he had broken up with her.

He didn't appear to recognise her as he held out the glass of wine to his fiancée, eliminating her from the scene by half turning his back on her.

On the verge of flight, she was stopped by Dominic announcing yet again—this time to Alessandro—that Miss Reynolds would be taking him to a football match. At this, Alessandro focused his fabulous dark eyes on her and said, unsmilingly, 'Isn't that beyond the call of duty, Miss Reynolds?'

How can you not even recognise me? Megan wanted to yell. Had she been so *forgettable*? Didn't he even recognise *her name*? Maybe he had met so many women over the years that faces and names had all become one great big blur.

'It seemed the only way to persuade Dominic to be a tree.' It was a miracle that her vocal cords managed to remain intact when everything else inside was going haywire. 'And it's not taking him to a football match. It would be to watch me playing football.'

'You play football?'

His dark, sexy voice wrapped itself around her, threatening to strangle her ability to breathe.

'One of my hobbies,' Megan said, taking one protective step back. She dragged her eyes away from that mesmerising face and addressed his fiancée. 'I hope you have a lovely Christmas, Mrs Park.' She realised that she was still clutching the discarded sushi, which had seeped through the napkin and was now gluey against the tightly closed palm of her hand.

'You'll have to give my mother your phone number, Miss Reynolds, and your address. For the football match? You promised!'

Two steps further back and a brief nod. 'Sure. I'll leave it on a piece of paper on the front desk. Now, I really must dash…meet some of the other parents… Very nice to meet you…'

Her eyes flickered across to Alessandro, then away. He wasn't even looking at her. He was sipping his wine, his eyes drifting in boredom across the room, indifferent to her babbling. An insignificant teacher. Why should he be interested in anything she had to say? He didn't even remember who she was!

For the next hour Megan kept her distance from them, but time and again she found herself seeking him out in the crowd. He was always easy to spot. He dominated the room—and not just with his powerful physical presence. He looked as though he owned the space around him and only the special chosen few were invited in.

She should really have stayed to the end, until after all the parents had departed, because a few of the teachers were planning on going out for a drink, but with her nervous system in total meltdown she fetched her coat, scribbled the wretched phone number and address on a piece of paper, which she left on the front desk, and headed for the underground.

It was a sturdy walk from the school, away from the chaos of expensive cars bearing the little darlings back home. After a few minutes there was only the sound of her boots on the pavement and the usual delightful London noises. The distant thrum of traffic, the occasional high-pitched whine of a police siren, the muted voices of people passing her.

Hunched into her coat and with her head down, braced against the freezing wind, Megan only became aware of the car after it had stopped right in front of her—and she only became aware of it then because she nearly crashed into the passenger door, which had been flung open.

Two words. 'Get in!'

Megan bent and peered into the car. She knew the driver of the car. Of course she did. She would have recognised that voice anywhere.

'Drop dead.' She slammed the door shut with such ferocity that she was surprised it didn't fall off its hinges.

The cool walk had restored some of her sanity, and she had figured out *why* he hadn't seen fit to say that they had met before. He was a successful city gent now, engaged to be married to his female counterpart. Why spoil the rosy picture by announcing any connection to a lowly teacher? Even *before* he had become successful—which he undoubtedly was, if the suit and the car were anything to go by—he had ditched her because she had been *inappropriate* to his long-term plans. How much more *inappropriate* would she be now?

The car cruised alongside her, its window now rolled down,

and she heard him say with lazy intent, 'You can either get in, or else I'll pay you a little visit at your house. Your choice.'

Megan looked through the window. 'What are you doing, Alessandro? I thought you didn't recognise me.'

'Naturally I recognised you. I just didn't see fit to launch into an explanation of how our paths had crossed. Wrong time, wrong place.'

The baldness of that statement only skimmed the surface of the shock he had felt on seeing her. To have your past leap out at you and grab you by the throat... He had felt driven to do this—to follow her on her way home—although now that he had Alessandro was beginning to wonder what would be achieved. Curiosity had got the better of him—maybe that had been it?

Somewhere in his seven-year meteoric rise to power, curiosity had become a rare luxury. His gift for money-making in the complex world of derivatives had engineered a swift rise to giddy, powerful heights. It had also provided him with more than sufficient disposable cash to move effortlessly into acquisitions. Alessandro had everything that money could buy, but the ease with which he had made millions had left him with a jaded palette. After his initial shock on seeing Megan, his curiosity to find out what she had been up to in the past seven years had been overpowering and irresistible, and—face it—he could indulge his curiosity. He could indulge anything he wanted to.

'What do you want?'

'Get in the car, Megan. It's been a long time. It would be bizarre not to play a little catch-up game, don't you think?'

'I think it's bizarre that you left your fiancée so that you could follow me.'

'Old friends meeting up. Victoria would have no problem with that. Thankfully she's not a possessive woman. I'll drop you home. It's a ridiculous night to be...doing what? Catching a bus? Taking a tube somewhere?'

'Go away.'

'Not still playing childish games, are you, Megan? You know you're as curious to find out about me as I am to find out about you, so why fight it?'

Megan got in. For one thing the wind was whipping her coat all over the place. For another the tube would be packed and uncomfortable, and quite possibly not running to schedule. And, yes, she *was* curious. He had been an important piece of her past, and maybe catching up, hearing all about his bright, shiny new life, would provide her with the tools for closure.

'Nice car.' She took in the walnut dashboard and the plush leather seats. 'I don't know much about cars, but I'm thinking that you climbed up that ladder without taking too many knocks on the way up, Alessandro.' She couldn't prevent the note of bitterness that had crept into her voice—a leftover from the hurt all that time ago.

'Did you ever think that I wouldn't?' He wasn't looking at her. His concentration was entirely on the road and on the illuminated map on his dashboard, detailing directions to her house. He had got the address from the scrap of paper she had left at the front desk, and had punched it into his navigation system as soon as he had got into his car, having safely seen Victoria and Dominic to a taxi.

Not looking at her, but still seeing her in his head, he thought she looked exactly as she had all those years ago. Curly blonde hair, big blue eyes, full mouth that always looked on the verge of laughing. He had had no choice but to follow her.

'Arrogance isn't a very nice trait.'

'Who's being arrogant? I'm being realistic. And *nice* isn't a trait that gets anyone very far in the business world. What are you doing in London, anyway?'

'Oh, I forgot. I was supposed to be a little country girl who was destined to stay in the country.'

'You're bitter.'

'Can you blame me?'

'I did what was necessary. For both of us. In life, we all do.'

His casual dismissal of her feelings was as hurtful as if he had taken a knife and twisted it into her. 'So…you live in London? Have you made a name for yourself? I know that was top of your list of things to do. Oh, along with making lots of money.'

'Yes, to your first question—and as far as making money, let's just say that I'm not living hand-to-mouth.'

'You mean, you're rich?'

'Filthy rich,' he agreed easily.

'You must feel very pleased with yourself that your plan worked out, Alessandro.' And the very suitable lawyer with her posh voice was obviously part two of his plan. He had dumped all handicaps and moved on, with the same relentless focus that she had seen in him years ago. 'And how did you meet…Dominic's mother?' she asked, twisting the knife herself now.

'Work,' Alessandro said abruptly.

'She tells me that she's a corporate lawyer.'

'The top of her field.'

'Guess she ticks all the boxes, then.' Megan thought of all the boxes *she* had failed to tick—but wasn't it stupid to still be bitter after all this time? He had moved on with his life and so, really, had she. Of course, he was getting married, which rated a lot higher on the *Moving On With Life* scale than having had a couple of boyfriends, neither of whom had lasted more than seven months, but she wasn't going to dwell on that.

'All the boxes,' Alessandro agreed smoothly.

'You've even managed to land yourself a ready-made family!'

'Dominic has his own father. I'm not required to play happy families with my fiancée's offspring.' In actual fact, Alessandro had met Dominic all of three times, even though he had now been seeing Victoria for six months. Their schedules were both ridiculously packed, and meetings had to be carefully orchestrated—usually dinner somewhere, or the theatre, or supper at his Kensington place. With his own personal chef, eating in was as convenient as dining out. Family outings, therefore, had not been on the agenda—something for which Alessandro was somewhat relieved.

'Charming,' Megan said brightly. 'I always thought that when you married someone you hitched up to *all* their baggage, including any offspring from a previous marriage. Crazy old me.'

'I don't remember you being sarcastic.'

'We're both older.' She shrugged and gave him the final directions to her house, which was only a few streets away. 'We've both changed. I don't remember *you* as being cold and arrogant.' Not that that didn't work for her. It did, because she disliked this new, rich Alessandro, with his perfect life and his ruthless face. 'You can drop me off here. It's been great catching up, and thanks for the lift.'

About to open the car door, she felt his hand circle her wrist. It was like being zapped by a powerful bolt of electricity.

'But we haven't finished catching up.' He killed the engine, but remained sitting in the dark car. 'You still have to tell me about yourself.'

Megan looked at him. 'Do you mind releasing me?'

'Why don't you invite me in for a cup of coffee?'

'I share a house. My housemate will be there.'

'Housemate?'

'Charlotte. Do you remember her, Alessandro? Or have

you wiped her out of your memory bank along with the rest of your past?'

'Of course I remember her,' Alessandro said irritably. Hell, here he was, being perfectly nice, perfectly interested, and what was he getting? She'd used to be so damned compliant, always smiling, always laughing, always keen to hear what he had to say, no sharp edges. 'And I have a very vivid recollection of my past. I just have no wish to revisit it.'

He had released her, but her whole body was still tingling from that brief physical contact.

'You can come in for a cup of coffee,' she told him. 'But I don't want you hanging around. You might think that it's all jolly good fun, taking a trip down memory lane, but—speaking as the person you dumped—I have zero interest in reliving old times.'

She opened the car door and walked towards the house, leaving him to decide what he wanted to do. She felt his presence behind her as she rustled in her bag for her keys, but she pointedly didn't look round at him as she slotted the key into the lock.

'The kitchen's through there,' she said, nodding towards the back of the house. 'I'm going to change.'

She took the stairs two at a time, her heart beating like a hammer. She couldn't believe that this was happening, that some quirk of fate had brought her past catapulting into her present. She also couldn't believe that seeing him could have such a huge impact on her. She had sometimes imagined what it would be like to see him again, never believing in a million years that it would actually happen. In her head she had been cool, contained, mildly interested in what he had to say, but with one eye on her watch—a busy young thing with a hectic life to lead, which didn't involve some guy who had dumped her because she didn't match up to the high standards he had wanted. In other words, a woman of twenty-six who was *totally over the creep*.

Now look at her! A nervous wreck.

She glanced at her reflection in the mirror and saw a flushed face and over-bright eyes. Charlotte, who would have given her a stiff pep talk on bastards and how they should be treated, was, of course, conspicuous by her absence. Where were friends when you needed them? Living it up with work colleagues somewhere in central London, instead of staying put just in case an urgent pep talk was required.

She was only marginally calmer when she headed downstairs fifteen minutes later, in a pair of faded jeans, an old sweatshirt, and her fluffy rabbit bedroom slippers—because, hey, why should she put herself out to dress up for a man whose taste now ran to sophisticated brunette lawyer-types with cut-glass accents?

He was waiting obediently in the kitchen, a graceful, powerful panther who seemed to dwarf the small confines of the room. He had removed his black coat, which lay over the back of one of the kitchen chairs, and was sitting at the table, his long legs extended to one side and elegantly crossed at the ankles.

'So…tell me what you've been up to these past few years,' he said, watching her as she turned her back on him to fill the kettle.

This, more than the woman in the black skirt and neat burgundy shirt, was the Megan he remembered. Casual in jeans and an oversized jumper and, as always when pottering inside her flat, wearing the most ridiculous bedroom slippers. Aside from kids, he'd always figured her to be the only person in the country who wore gimmicky bedroom slippers. His eyes drifted up her body, along her legs to her breasts, and he felt as though the room had suddenly become airless.

'I got my teacher training qualifications,' she said, stirring coffee into the boiling water and finally turning round to hand him a mug. 'Then I taught at St Nicks for three years. I moved down to London because Charlotte was working here and I thought it would make a change. I spent a year or so at St Margaret's, and I started working at Dominic's school in September.'

'That's a very dry, factual account. Why London? The last time I looked there were remarkably few open fields or running brooks, or little cottages with white picket fences.'

'I decided that I fancied a change from open fields, Alessandro. Maybe you were a little too quick to shove me into the role of the country bumpkin.' She wasn't going to tell him how claustrophobic her life had suddenly seemed the second he had walked out of it, how the excitement of teaching in a rural school had been tarnished with the uncomfortable feeling that outside her tiny world lay excitement and adventure. He didn't deserve to know anything about her.

'Look, I could embellish it with all the fun things I've done in between, Alessandro, but they would mean nothing to you.'

'Try me.'

'I'd rather not. I'm tired, and I don't have the energy.' Acutely conscious of those dark, fabulous, watchful eyes on her face, Megan took a sip of coffee and stared down at the table.

'I see you're still buying those ridiculous bedroom slippers.'

'Christmas present last year from one of my pupils,' she said crisply, tucking her feet beneath the table. 'It's one of the perks of the job. Lots of bath stuff, candles, picture frames and, in this case, gimmicky slippers.'

'How long have you lived here?'

'Since I moved to London.'

'Is this going to be a question and answer session?' Alessandro drawled. 'I ask the questions and you use as few words as humanly possible to answer?'

'You wanted to find out what I'd been up to and I'm tell ing you. My life is probably not nearly as fascinating as yours has been, but I love what I do and I'm very happy.' She drained her cup, then looked at him. 'How long have you known... Dominic's mum?'

'Roughly six months.'

Roughly six months! Less time than he'd been with *her*. It hurt to think that he must have been bowled over to have moved from dating to engagement in such a brief period of time.

'Not long. A whirlwind romance?' She forced a smile. 'It must be the icing on the cake, Alessandro. I'm very happy for you.'

Alessandro hadn't thought about it as a *whirlwind romance*. He had met Victoria when she had been working with her firm of lawyers on one of his deals. He'd liked her, admired her intelligence, and appreciated her ability to respect his ferocious working agenda. Was that *romance*? It had certainly been enough for him to take the next step forward, but he had to admit that it was at least partly fuelled by the fact that he wasn't getting any younger.

Unlike a lot of his city colleagues—men in their thirties, climbing the ladder to success—Alessandro had no intention of remaining a bachelor because of a preference for playing the field. Nor was he going to hang around until he was too old to enjoy playing with his kids. Sure, he had had women, but some restless, dissatisfied urge had always held him back from commitment.

Victoria, he recognised, was undemanding. She had her own high-powered job, and therefore did not look to him for constant companionship. Nor did she nag for assurances about love or any such thing. She worked for him and he, he suspected, worked for her. It was a mutually gratifying situation.

'Icing on the cake?' he mused. 'Yes, I suppose it is....'

CHAPTER TWO

IT HAD not been a satisfying meeting with Megan.

Alessandro stared out of his floor-to-ceiling office window at the busy, grey London streets five storeys below. Wet pavements were illuminated by lights, and everyone seemed to be laden down with shopping. The usual splurge of money-spending on presents—at least half of which would inevitably be returned to the shops on the first working day after Christmas because they didn't fit the bill. He had already bought something for Victoria—a diamond necklace which had cost the earth and which he had dispatched his personal assistant to source with the guiding words that it should be classy and very expensive. His personal assistant was extremely efficient.

Thinking about Christmas presents made him think about the one and only Christmas present he had ever bought for Megan. A pair of tickets for a concert by a band she had been crazy about. A dark, intimate venue where the noise had made the walls vibrate. They hadn't been able to stop grinning.

The memory surfaced seemingly from nowhere, and Alessandro frowned and thought back to his unsatisfactory meeting with Megan. He didn't know what he had been expecting, but the conversation had been awkward, forced, and the more awkward and forced it had become, the keener he had been to go beyond her polite responses and get the real flavour of the person sitting so stiffly opposite him.

He had left the house forty-five minutes after he had arrived, with the very clear impression that he had only been invited for a cup of coffee because she had found herself between a rock and a hard place, and that, having invited him in, she had been utterly uninterested in talking to him. Every word had been squeezed out of her, and each word had been less informative than the one before.

The woman hated him and couldn't be bothered to hide the fact.

Having enemies was part and parcel of Alessandro's life. Every successful man had his fair share. But his enemies would never have dared show their faces—and he had never known any woman to be less than madly in love with him! He knew that Megan had good reason. Just as he knew that breaking up with her at the time had been for her own good, whether she accepted that fact or not. There had been an innocence about her approach to life that would have been damaged had he dragged her along in his wake. He had made an attempt to tell her that, but she had listened to him politely, head cocked to one side, and then had said in a cool little voice, 'Whatever.'

Nor had he been able to get her to talk about her private life. Was she seeing someone? He couldn't imagine Megan making such a long-haul transfer, leaving behind her family, unless a man was involved. But when he had asked—out of *genuine interest*—all he had got was the same polite smile and, 'That's really none of your business, is it, Alessandro?'

Victoria's call interrupted his frowning contemplation telling him that she and Dominic were in Reception.

Family outing number one—and Alessandro hadn't ob-

jected because the outing in question was to the promised
football game, which Dominic had followed up on with unexpected tenacity for a six-year-old kid. Football games didn't
usually feature high on Dominic's agenda. His father lived in
New York and only assumed a parental role once a year, for
a fortnight when he came to London. And Alessandro certainly couldn't see Victoria slashing her work commitments
to take him to a football match, or even for that matter, arranging football lessons for him. She wouldn't be able to commit
to picking him up from them.

The vague feeling of dissatisfaction that had sat on his
shoulders ever since he had bumped into Megan three days
previously was dispelled slightly by a mental tallying of all
the things he had in common with his fiancée—first and
foremost their overriding work ethic.

It was all well and good for Megan to sit there with icy hostility stamped all over her face, as though he had single-
handedly been responsible for coining the word *bastard*. What
she didn't realise was that long-term relationships were built
on more than just fun and romance. In fact, when it came to
marriage, it was far more likely to succeed as a business
proposition.

It frustrated him that he hadn't been able to convey that
message to her three days ago. He might not now be scowling as he slung on his coat and headed for the elevator had
he done so.

No one enjoyed being vilified for a crime they hadn't committed, and Alessandro was no exception.

In fact, he decided, as the elevator doors pinged open and
he spotted Victoria and her son sitting on the low olive-green
and chrome sofa in the reception area, it was almost a *good*
thing that he would be seeing Megan again. If he had a chance
to have a word with her—he certainly wouldn't be *engineer-*

ing any such thing, but if the situation arose—then he would tell her, politely but firmly, that they had both been kids when they had broken up. That it had been for the best. That it was ridiculous for her to be carrying a grudge after seven years.

He was barely aware of Dominic fidgeting next to him in the back seat of his Bentley, which his chauffeur was driving, and he only vaguely tuned in and out of Victoria's conversation— which he would have to get back to later, because it involved an offshore deal he was working on at the moment.

In fact, he was finding that he was actively anticipating seeing Megan's face when she realised that he had shown up to her football game. Trust Megan to have a hobby most normal women would steer clear of. He tried to picture Victoria in a football kit, running around on a field somewhere, but his imagination couldn't stretch to it. She was impeccably well bred, impeccably dressed and utterly uninterested in sport— both playing and watching.

He reached behind Dominic and absent-mindedly caressed her neck, just as the car pulled up to the school grounds.

Caught up in a tackle, Megan briefly registered Dominic's arrival before refocusing on the game.

She had known he would be coming because his mother had got her secretary to call her. She assumed the unfortunate nanny had been manoeuvred into this particular duty, and then forgot all about it for the remainder of the game—which was a very muddy, very physical, very invigorating one.

An hour later she walked across to three people barely visible because it was now so dark. She would have a two-minute chat with Dominic and maybe try and interest him in some football lessons—a plan which she had already mentioned to Robbie, the guy who coached at the school. In fact, coached at various schools.

'You tell me his mother's a hard-nosed lawyer?' Robbie had slung his arm around her shoulder. 'Just my type. Sure I'll take the kid on.'

'A hard-nosed *engaged* lawyer.' Megan had laughed. 'Who won't be at the match anyway. Just try and get Dominic interested in some lessons. I think it would do him good.'

An absentee father who lived in New York, as she had discovered from Jessica at school, and a soon-to-be stepfather who didn't see parenting someone else's child as part of his job description. It was a lose-lose situation for the poor kid, and a little outdoor fun wouldn't hurt him.

She was trying to untangle her hair from the elastic band which had started off the evening in place but seemed to have travelled in the wrong direction during the game, when she looked at bit more carefully at the three figures taking shape in front of her.

There was Dominic in the middle, huddled in a dark coat, and on either side of him…

Megan felt the colour surge into her face. His mother—surprisingly—and Alessandro.

She had thought to have seen the last of him after their horrible little *catch-up chat*, which had been more painful for her than Chinese water torture. Seeing him again out of the blue had stirred up a hornets' nest in her head. Now here he was, larger than life and playing happy families.

'You scored a goal, Miss Reynolds! And you're covered in mud!' Dominic sounded delighted at this revelation.

'If you're not careful, I shall put some on you!' She was caked in mud from head to foot, while Alessandro stood there watching her in his city suit and his beautiful coat and his very, *very* clean handmade Italian leather shoes. And Dominic's mother looked even more impeccable. How on earth could anyone watch a football match in high-heeled shoes?

'Dominic has had a super time. Thank you so much for asking him along to watch you, Miss Reynolds.'

'No problem.' She made sure not to look at Alessandro. 'I…er…I actually wanted to talk to you about maybe letting Dominic have football lessons, Mrs Park…'

'I'm afraid that's quite out of the question, Miss Reynolds.'

She hadn't finished the sentence before Dominic was jumping up and down in a state of high excitement.

'He might take you to court if you don't agree,' Megan said lightly, and the other woman managed to crack a smile at that. Depressingly, Megan found that it was hard to dislike her, because somewhere under that hard-edged, business-like surface she sensed a nice person.

'I'll leave you to think about it, anyway. I'm going to make my escape and get cleaned up. Have a brilliant Christmas!'

She still hadn't looked in Alessandro's direction, but she could feel his eyes on her. Even more depressing than the fact that she couldn't hate his fiancée was the fact that she was still mortifyingly aware of *him*. Two miserable seconds in his company and he was back in her thoughts as though it was yesterday.

She fled towards the changing rooms—angry with him for rubbing his jolly, settled, oh-I've-found-the-perfect-woman life in her face, and angry with herself because he still got to her and it wasn't fair.

She was flinging all her dirty kit into her bag when something made her look up—to find the object of her thoughts lounging by the door to the changing room, arms folded, watching her.

'What are you doing here? This is the women's changing room, in case you hadn't noticed!'

'The only woman in here is you. I waited outside, expecting to see you emerge with the rest of them, but after fifteen minutes I thought I'd come in. Make sure you hadn't collapsed.'

'Well, I haven't, so you can leave now.' She had showered, washed her hair and blowdried it, and put it into two stubby plaits. She had changed into jeans and a jumper and her thick waterproof anorak, which was a fashion disaster but could withstand anything the weather could throw at it.

'You played a good game out there. Football. Hmm... Wonder why I'm not surprised?' Covered in patches of mud, she had looked like an urchin. A very cute, very willful little urchin.

'What are you still doing here, Alessandro?' She snatched up her kit bag and drew in a deep breath before walking to the door. 'I haven't collapsed, and your fiancée will be waiting outside for you.'

'Victoria's been swept off her feet by your coach chap, who's taken her and Dominic to some coffee bar round the corner to discuss football lessons.'

'Robbie?' Megan paused, and then burst out laughing.

'What's so funny?' Alessandro said with a tight smile, feeling as though he was standing on the edge of some private inner joke. Did she laugh that laugh with *him*, the blond, athletic football coach who had managed to persuade Victoria out of her tightly allotted timetable?

'You wouldn't get it.' Megan brushed past him, still amused at her rogue of a coach, who had obviously charmed the very proper Mrs Park into breaking with tradition and taking time out.

'I haven't lost my sense of humour,' Alessandro told her with irritation.

'I'm sorry,' Megan apologised insincerely. 'Is that what you thought? No, I was just thinking about Robbie, that's all. He always manages to put a smile on my face.'

'Does he, now?'

'I'm not sure where *you're* going, but I'm heading for the bus stop. You're more than welcome to stand in the biting cold and wait with me, but I don't suppose you do public transport these days?'

'Give me five minutes.'

'Give you five minutes to do *what*?'

'To explain to Victoria that I'm going to see you home, and to tell my driver to wait for both of them.'

'No!' Megan stood with her hands on her hips, her football kit dumped on the ground next to her. 'This isn't going to do, Alessandro.'

Her heart was thumping inside her. He was so tall, so dominant, and her head was so full of memories that made her weak and vulnerable. But she was going to stand her ground—because what gave him the right to swan into her life after seven years and turn it upside down?

'We've had our little chat. I don't know how much clearer I can be when I tell you that I don't want you in my life. I made a fool of myself over you seven years ago, but I'm a different person now. We have nothing in common and nothing to talk about! You're not my friend, and quite honestly…' she crossed her fingers behind her back '…I have no idea what I ever saw in you in the first place.'

'Don't you? Well, the sex was pretty good.'

Megan flinched as though she had been struck, and Alessandro raked restless, frustrated fingers through his hair. He hadn't intended to say that. In fact, even harking back to the sex they had had made him feel as though he had crashed through an invisible barrier that should have remained intact.

'Forget I said that. Like everything else between us, that is history. I'm here because I didn't like the way things were left between us.'

'Not my problem.'

She began walking towards the bus stop—sports bag in one hand, rucksack slung over one shoulder, and yet another bag, over the other shoulder. She felt him take the sports bag out of her hand and she spun round, glaring.

'What do you think you're doing?'

'Don't you want to go and see what your boyfriend is up to?' He dangled the bag over his head and watched as she simmered impotently in front of him. God knew, but hearing her say that she regretted ever going out with him had touched a raw nerve— and who the hell was this Robbie character to her, anyway?

Momentarily distracted by his misconception that Robbie was her boyfriend, Megan laughed again—that rich, warm laugh that could still find some crazy crack in his armour that he hadn't been aware even existed.

'Maybe I should…' She trailed the words out, as if giving them a lot of thought. 'Do you think he might need protecting from your fiancée?'

'You really *have* changed, Megan. I remember when we used to go out you couldn't even tolerate the thought of me *looking* at another woman, never mind having a cup of coffee with one.'

'Yes, I remember. It was a very unhealthy place to be, had I but known it at the time.' Why did this feel so dangerous? she wondered. How could these unpleasant, unproductive exchanges make the hairs at the back of her neck stand on end and give her the giddy sensation that she was walking a tightrope?

'Maybe I *will* go and see what Robbie's up to,' she said, just in case he really did decide to get on the bus with her. 'Although I think you should be the one to worry. Little tip here, Alessandro. Robbie could charm the birds from the trees if he put his mind to it. And, since you're so intent on playing the gentleman that you're not…' she dumped all her bags at his feet '…you can carry the lot.'

She eased her tired shoulders and looked at him, wondering if he would reconsider his decision to hound her and tell her to carry her own bags. He didn't. He effortlessly picked up all her bags, and seemed to have little concern for the welfare of his expensive clothes.

'So you think I should be worried about your football coach, do you?' Alessandro's voice was threaded with amusement.

'It's not all about money,' Megan snapped, walking towards the only coffee shop in the vicinity—the same one they all used after football games.

'Do you really think that Victoria is interested in my money? More to the point, do you really think that *I* would give the time of day to *any* woman if I thought she *was* after my money?' He laughed shortly. 'Victoria wouldn't look twice at a man who wasn't as driven as she is.'

'What an exciting life the two of you must lead. Do you spend hours talking about work, and how wonderful it is that neither of you has any fun?'

'Whoever said that we don't have fun, Megan?'

That low, silky voice sent a nervous tremor rippling through her—made her think about all the things he and his fiancée might do for fun. She thought about him sharing his nights with the other woman, waking up to her, congratulating himself on the perfect match they made.

'I can't say that I'm interested one way or the other, actually.'

'No, you made that perfectly clear the last time I tried to engage you in conversation.'

'Which reminds me—have you told Dominic's mother that we know one another?'

'Naturally.' Alessandro shrugged. As he had predicted, Victoria had been surprised, but not alarmed.

'And she didn't mind?'

'That I dropped you home? Why should she? It's hardly as though there's anything between us now.'

He thought of her in her jeans and jumper, wearing her ridiculous slippers which he imagined had been some kind of protest vote at him being under her roof. She hadn't been wearing a bra, and he didn't know how he had known that. Maybe the swing of her full breasts under the cloth as she had reached over to hand him his mug of coffee, or maybe he just *knew*, because her body had once been his and the familiarity of a woman you possessed never quite left you.

'She has her own ex boyfriends,' Alessandro commented neutrally. 'In fact, she regularly sees one of them—an investment banker who works in the city. It's no big deal.'

'I can't believe you're so...*civilised*...about your fiancée having a relationship with an ex, Alessandro. My, my, my...what's happened to all that Italian possessiveness? *I* may have been jealous, but let's not forget that *you* blew a fuse every time you saw me talking to one of my male friends from university.'

'Like you said, Megan, an unhealthy place. How long have you known this football-coach character, anyway? Was he the reason you decided to move down to London? I suspected that a man must have been involved.'

'I would never let a man influence any of my decisions,' Megan told him scornfully. If he wanted to think that she and Robbie were involved, then why not let him? 'I met Robbie after I came to London and he's a great guy.'

'A football coach?'

'He's more than just a football coach, Alessandro, and there's no need to play the snob card. You weren't always rich—in case you had forgotten!'

'Ah, but I always knew I would be. There's a difference between a man with ambition and a man who enjoys doing nothing with his life. Here's a piece of advice for you, Megan—your football coach will age into an overweight ex-athlete; ask yourself whether you'll find his lack of drive such a bundle of laughs then. Are you going to be happy serving him up his food on a tray in front of the television in the two-bedroom house you've stretched yourselves to buy? With a couple of kids squawking in the background?'

Alessandro didn't know why he felt compelled to pour cold water on her relationship. He supposed that it sprang from the remnants of the feelings he'd once had for her, and a certain amount of guilty awareness that he had been, just maybe, a little harsh when he had dispatched her.

She didn't answer, and her lack of response was like a red rag to a bull.

Couldn't the woman see that he was being *kind* in pointing out the obvious?

'What I choose to do with my life isn't your concern, Alessandro. There's the café. I can't believe Robbie managed to persuade your fiancée to have a coffee in a place that serves bacon and eggs all day to lorry drivers and cabbies.'

Ahead of them, the café was bursting at the rafters. Once upon a time this would have been the kind of crowd he regularly mingled with, sitting in some half-baked café, ploughing into a bargain fry-up. Outside, a group of youths were larking around, wearing hoodies. It was like looking through a glass window at his past, and for a few mad seconds Alessandro felt the kick of nostalgia. He reached out and yanked Megan back.

'The guy's a loser,' he said abruptly. 'And I'm telling you this for your own good, Megan.'

'You've never done anything *for my own good*, Alessandro!'

'You wouldn't last a minute with the kind of people I mix with.'

'Would that be because I'm a loser as well?'

'Dammit!' He released her and raked frustrated fingers

through his hair. He would have to stop doing this—touching her. 'You know what I'm saying!'

'Yes. I know you're insulting me.'

They looked at each other, their eyes tangling in the darkness, and Alessandro drew his breath in sharply. Those lips—he wanted to crush their softness under his, wanted to sweep his hands under her jumper and lose himself in her glorious body. He pulled back, breathing thickly.

'Not that it's any of your business, but Robbie only does football coaching on the side! He's studying for a law degree.'

Alessandro found that he preferred to think of the man as a loser. 'Bit old for that, wouldn't you say?'

'Not everyone knows what they want to be from the age of ten! Robbie knows what he wants to be now, and he's working bloody hard to get there! He's going to get his law qualifications and work to help the little people. Those people who don't have a voice, because they don't have loads of money to employ lawyers who charge the earth.'

'A do-gooder, in other words…' His voice was laced with disdain, but he was sickeningly aware that that was just the sort of guy Megan *would* lose her head over.

'Call it what you like.'

'Are you in love with him?'

Megan didn't answer that. Telling an outright lie was beyond her. She was deeply fond of Robbie, and admired his drive and his idealism, but they had never had that kind of relationship. And who the hell was Alessandro to even *ask* her that question? Did he think that he had a right to *feel sorry for her*? Because he had moved on? Found everything that he had been looking for? The right life with the right woman?

'I really hope Robbie's managed to convince your fiancée that Dominic should do some football out of school. Don't you?' Her voice was cool and tight. 'It must be hard for him.

I think that boys need a father figure—a role model they can look up to.'

'Is that some kind of veiled criticism?'

Because he had moved beyond criticism. That had been a lifetime ago, if it had ever existed at all. Now he occupied that sacred realm of men who were surrounded by sycophants, telling them everything they wanted to hear. He had buried the demons of his past and created a life of unsurpassed ease—a life he controlled. He had become untouchable. If only his parents could see him now—could see what riches could be born out of hardship.

'No, it's not. Dominic is a superbright boy, but being superbright can be as much a curse as a blessing. He's prone to boredom, and boredom makes him destructive. Football would enable him to expend all his energy.'

'And your boyfriend's just the guy to help him do that?'

'Stop calling him my *boyfriend*!'

'Okay, then. What about *lover*?'

'To answer your question—yes, Robbie would be just the guy to take Dominic in hand. He's great with kids.'

As far as answers went, that wasn't what Alessandro had been looking for, but they were already entering the café, and continuing the conversation was impossible.

There was a smile on Megan's face as she spotted the three of them sitting at the far end—two in front of mugs of coffee and Dominic with his chin cupped in his hand, staring in fascination at the blond-haired, blue-eyed do-gooder, who was smiling and talking with a lot of hand gestures and body language.

Just her type, Alessandro thought dismissively. She had said that he could charm the birds from the trees, and Victoria certainly seemed to be in a good mood, cutting an elegant figure among the crowd in the café like a…like a…

He couldn't help it. His eyes were drawn to the small blonde with her back to him as she strolled across to her boyfriend, who was now grinning at her.

Like a rose among thorns, he thought, hastily refocusing on Victoria.

'Have you been sold on the football lessons?' he asked, breaking up the trio at the table as he walked across.

'All sorted.'

Mother and son smiled at one another. Alessandro hadn't been around the two of them together much, but he was sensing that this was something of a rare occurrence, and he forced himself to smile at the man who was now standing up, reaching out with an open, good-natured expression, asking him if he wanted anything to eat and then joking about the quality of the coffee while telling him that the egg and chips were second to none.

He was ruffling Megan's pigtails, yanking them playfully, abstractedly, as though the gesture was a familiar one.

And Dominic was still staring at him, his mouth half open and his eyes wide.

From ruffling Megan's hair, he moved to ruffle Dominic's.

'So,' he said, still grinning, 'it's a date, then, is it? You? Me? The next Chelsea football match?' He turned to Victoria, now rising to her feet too, after, it would seem, eating *egg and chips*. 'You'll have to come too, of course. All of us should go together—have a bit of an evening out!'

Frankly, Alessandro couldn't think of anything worse, but he was very much aware that the loser was drawing Megan against him, and that both of them were laughing and saying something about the Chelsea football team. He wasn't sure what.

'See you before then, anyway!'

'How's that?' Alessandro looked at Robbie with a cool frown.

'Christmas? Christmas Day?'

'What are you talking about, Robbie?' Megan asked. She was thrilled to see her little tyrannical pupil hanging on to every word Robbie was saying. She suspected that a humble football might well be finding its way to his Christmas list, as a last-minute request.

'Hope you don't mind…' Robbie gave her waist an affectionate little squeeze, and Megan just *knew* that she wasn't going to like what was coming next. 'I've asked this disreputable rabble to come along on Christmas morning for a drink, if they're not doing anything special!'

'Come along *for a drink*?'

'You know our dispossessed little crowd…!' He winked at Dominic's mother. 'Nanny, I gather, is missing in action on Christmas Day…tut, tut, tut…and so Vicky here has pretty much promised that she would like nothing better than to fling a turkey in the oven and head to where it's all happening! *Your* house!'

'But…' Megan smiled apologetically, and swore to herself that she would do untold damage to Robbie just as soon as they were in private somewhere.

'Of course.' Alessandro looked at her, one hand in his trouser pocket, the other slung round his fiancée's shoulder. 'Why not?' He kissed Victoria on her temple. 'What do you say? My chef is on duty twenty-four-seven. He can get our lunch prepared and we can head to…*where it's all happening…*'

'It's a very small house…!' Megan glanced at Dominic, because the one thing kids hated was to be confronted by their teachers out of school hours. Unfortunately he didn't appear to be conforming to the stereotype. 'It'll be very crowded…' she stammered. 'You wouldn't believe the amount of people who seem to have nothing going on on Christmas Day… I'm sure you'll be all wrapped up with… opening presents…and stuff…'

'Of course we wouldn't dream of intruding,' Dominic's mother said, her exquisite good manners coming to the fore.

Megan smiled weakly. 'No—you wouldn't be, Mrs Park. It's open house…as Robbie said…just drop in, if and when you get the chance!'

'And please do stop calling me *Mrs Park*…' This time the smile was real, and it didn't look as though it had required lots of effort. 'I realise that it's not exactly protocol, but do call me Victoria.'

'Victoria…right…'

What a tableau they must make. She, Robbie, a kid who seemed to be undergoing a severe case of sudden hero-worship syndrome, and a man and a woman who might have stepped straight out of the pages of a magazine—although she was slightly gratified to notice that Alessandro's pristine suit was no longer in quite the same condition as it had been an hour before.

'And of course I'm Megan.' She winked at Dominic, and tried a friendly, teacher-like chuckle, but he was still staring at Robbie. There was ketchup smeared round his mouth and he was clutching a chip as though it was a once-a-year treat that might just vanish at any moment. 'And, yes…please… feel free to join us on Christmas Day!' Her laugh sounded a tad hysterical. 'The more the merrier!'

CHAPTER THREE

THINGS were under control. In support of the three vegetarian guests coming, and in frank and open acknowledgement of the fact that neither she nor Charlotte were any good in the kitchen—particularly when the meal involved handling raw meat—turkey was off the menu. Instead they had gone for loads of salads and a poached salmon, which their local fish-monger had kindly supplied, cut-rate, for his two pretty customers. In return they had given him a Christmas present of a ceramic vase—made by Charlotte, materials provided by Megan—which he solemnly promised would take pride of place on his mantelpiece.

Drinks were in liberal supply. Homemade punch, which was lethally strong, several bottles of wine, and some beer for the guys.

It had left a satisfying amount of time for Megan to take her time getting ready, and she was going all out. They had decided on a colour theme for the guests. Green and red. Christmas colours. Accordingly, Megan had found the perfect red dress. It clung like a second skin to mid-thigh, and was offset by some lacy tights in an interesting shade of bright green. Megan was pretty sure she looked like a deranged elf, but nevertheless she was pretty pleased with the result.

Being a teacher was in danger of turning her into a conformist. She felt that she should be allowed to be ridiculous for one day in the year.

Some might say that the red hair was taking things a bit too far, but it was a wash-in, wash-out colour, so that was all right.

She looked critically at her reflection in the mirror, not sure whether red hair really suited her, but it made a change from being blonde. Made her look wild. Especially with the clingfilm dress, the fluorescent tights and the fabulous red shoes. She was sure she would never be able to walk properly in them.

It had turned out in the end that Alessandro and entourage *weren't* coming. Robbie, who seemed to have developed a cordial relationship with Victoria over the very short space of a week, had reliably informed Megan that she would be too busy in the morning, doing 'Christmas stuff'.

'Fiancé's chef will need some supervision,' he had said, shaking his head. 'No nanny and a chef unfamiliar with the territory. Never let it be said that life in the fast lane can't be tough.'

'I know,' Megan had replied, relieved that she wouldn't have to face the ordeal of feeling persecuted in her own house on the one day when she was owed relaxation. 'Much easier to just scrap the Christmas meal altogether and head for the salad counter. Somewhere in the country there'll be a turkey thanking us.'

She was feeling very relaxed as she put the finishing touches to her outfit. Some bright red lipstick and matching nail polish. On her bed was an assortment of Christmas presents. From her parents, much-needed cash and a necklace. From her sisters, clothes and make-up, and a very jolly Christmas card that cracked a supercorny joke when opened. From her friends, presents largely of the ridiculous nature. Right now she was wearing some earrings in the shape of Christmas trees. Fabulous.

And she wasn't going to think about Alessandro at all today. She had spent way too much time thinking about him, ever since he had resurfaced in her life like a bad dream she'd thought she had finally put to rest. Today she was going to relax and have fun.

An hour later and the punch was helping with her mission. She and Charlotte had put it together, making up the recipe as they went along. They hadn't been entirely sure of the ingredients, but had figured that, if in doubt, better too much alcohol than too little. It was consequently very potent and now almost finished, thanks to a houseful of nearly twenty people, all of whom had come bearing an interesting array of food. The kitchen table and counters were groaning under the weight of a nut loaf, a lentil loaf, several quiches, cold ham, sausages, and salads of every description. There was even a huge pot of curried chicken, courtesy of Amrita, one of Charlotte's friends from work.

Somewhere along the line someone had stuck a silver cardboard crown on Megan's head, which was tilting precariously to one side. The music was blaring and there was Robbie, more sober than might have been expected, taking on the role of host. He was decked out in a pair of red surfer shorts—the only red item of clothing he'd been able to rustle up from his wardrobe, he had told them—and an outrageously green shirt which he had bought from a charity shop especially for the occasion. Megan had to admit that he looked pretty good, with his blonde hair and blue eyes and muscular body. She grinned and waved, and he weaved over towards her.

'Your crown's slipping,' he said, righting it and then standing back to inspect his handiwork. 'You're in danger of your people revolting if they think you're no longer in charge of the throne, Your Majesty.'

Megan had to smile. 'You seem to have been getting along

like a house on fire with Dominic's mum,' she remarked. She had been meaning to prise a few more details about *that* from him, and had had no chance thus far.

'She's a very nice lady,' he said, before waxing lyrical about the importance of sport for young kids and Dominic's enthusiasm to join a football club.

'You're beginning to sound like a spokesperson for the Ministry of Health.'

Megan was still laughing, one hand on her crown, the other wrapped around her second plastic cup of punch—which must be her last drink, at least until something solid went into her stomach—when Robbie whipped out a piece of mistletoe from his pocket and dangled it over her head.

It was so sudden and so unexpected that at first Megan wasn't quite sure what he was doing, waving a leaf above her. But it clicked when his hand went to her waist and he pulled her towards him. With an audience of eighteen people, hooting with laughter, he delivered a kiss worthy of any theatrical performance.

She was tilted backwards at the waist, and it flashed through her mind that it wasn't a very dignified position when wearing the short scarlet dress. One shoe went flying, and as she regained a vertical position, still laughing, with her arm slung around Robbie's neck for balance, she froze at the sight of Alessandro and Victoria standing at the doorway—late arrivals.

What the heck were they doing here?

'We have unexpected company,' she groaned in a mortified undertone.

Robbie followed the direction of her glance and she might have had a little too much to drink, but why did she get the impression that the appearance of Alessandro and his fiancée was not entirely shocking for him?

'Didn't think they would make it,' he murmured, settling

his hand around her waist. He was smiling, leading her towards the door, while the rest of their assembled audience got on with the business of having fun.

Megan wanted the ground to open and swallow her up. This had all the hallmarks of the birthday-cake fiasco, which had been forever branded in her mind as the day romance died. Of course it was a silly notion, because as she now knew, for Alessandro, she had always been an interlude, but it had often seemed easier to pin her misery on that one isolated incident.

And now here she was, in a ridiculous situation all over again, as though she still made a habit of being wild.

She could feel Alessandro's eyes pinned coldly on her face as she paused to stagger into the mislaid red shoe.

And Victoria?

Megan groaned mentally. Great image of the responsible teacher! She was certainly looking a little gimlet-eyed and upset. Probably considering her son's options for changing schools even as she walked towards her.

'You're here!' Megan trilled, plastering a delighted smile on her face. 'Robbie said…' she slapped his hand away from her waist '…you probably wouldn't be able to make it… No nanny…chef having to work in someone else's kitchen… Is Dominic…here…?'

'My mother's joining us for lunch,' Victoria said stiffly, sidestepping Robbie to present Megan with an exquisite box of chocolates. 'I thought it best to leave Dominic at home with her, playing with his toys, and of course, she can supervise Alessandro's chef in the kitchen. We won't stay long.'

'But long enough for a drink, I hope!' Robbie reinserted himself into the picture.

Victoria shook her head and looked at him coolly. 'I don't think so. We really are just popping in, and I wouldn't want to…'

'Don't…' Robbie told her, linking his arm through hers

'...be such a crashing bore. There's some punch lurking somewhere in the kitchen. You're going to have a glass—or should I say a plastic cup...?' He winked at Megan. 'And why don't *you* take care of our other guest, Megan? He looks as though he could do with a bit of loosening up....'

'Quite an outfit.' Alessandro skimmed his eyes lazily over her scantily clad body.

Not only was the dress ludicrously short and ludicrously red, it was also ludicrously revealing. Why was she bothering to wear it at all? he wondered. Unless it was to invite the male eye to follow the generous cleft of her cleavage down to the point where only someone with a stupendous lack of imagination wouldn't be fantasising about what wasn't on show.

'And nice hair.' He reached up and briefly twirled a few red strands between his fingers, so that she jerked back, out of reach. 'Are you supposed to be a scarlet woman?'

'Fancy dress. Of sorts. It's just some cheap hair colour. Tomorrow I shall go back to being blonde. I didn't expect to see you here.'

'I think I'm going to need a drink to handle this...party....'

'Sure. What would you like? There's the usual stuff in the kitchen...' She looked around desperately, to see if she could catch Robbie's eye, but having played perfect host for the past two hours, he had now inconveniently disappeared. 'I'll fetch you something and introduce you round.' She tugged the hem of her dress, as though by doing so she might lengthen it a couple of crucial inches.

'This is just like your university parties, Megan,' Alessandro said, following her towards the kitchen, his hands shoved into the pockets of his casually elegant and totally incongruous dark trousers. 'Cheap booze, loud music...'

'Are you telling me that I haven't grown up?' She spun round and glowered at him.

'If the cap fits…'

'You used to rather enjoy those university parties!' She thrust a cup of punch into his hands and looked at him.

It was a clear, cold morning, and some of the guests had spilled out into the tiny garden, where they had put a rented patio heater in anticipation. Out of the corner of her eye she could see Robbie talking expansively to Victoria, who seemed to have made inroads into the drink she'd claimed she wouldn't be having.

'There's a time and a place for everything.' God, he realised he sounded a bore, but the sight of her literally being swept off her feet by a football coach in a pair of shorts had unsettled him. And he didn't understand why. 'Sure, getting drunk in cheap digs was fine seven years ago—but time moves on.'

'These *digs* are far from cheap, let me tell you, and I am *not* drunk.'

'You could have fooled me. Unless you just enjoy making a spectacle of yourself?'

Megan began doing something with paper plates and cutlery. 'I don't know why you came here, Alessandro. You think I'm immature and silly, and you think Robbie's a loser.' She turned to face him, balancing on both hands as she leant against the kitchen counter. 'Why didn't you go for champagne cocktails and canapés at one of your business colleagues' houses? Where you could have had a civilised drink and talked about the world economy and politics, or the shocking price of houses in London and this year's City bonuses?'

'Because you wouldn't have been there.' Alessandro said it without thinking, and in the tight, ensuing silence he downed his drink, angry with himself for having spoken without thought. In fact, he hadn't even realised that he had been *thinking* that until the words were out of his mouth and it had been too late to take them back.

'You came here…because you *wanted to see me*?' She could feel the slow, treacherous thud of her heart. 'Oh, I'm getting it. You came because you weren't finished preaching to me about how I should live my life. Hence the crack about me being a scarlet woman?'

Relieved to have been let off the hook, Alessandro crumpled the paper cup in one hand and tossed it into a black bin bag which had been thoughtfully hooked over two handles of one of the kitchen doors and was already getting full.

'Well, as a matter of fact, Robbie was only kissing me because he whipped out a piece of mistletoe from his pocket…' She smiled. 'He can't resist being the centre of attention.'

'So I gathered. And he seems to be fine tuning the talent with my fiancée.'

So he *was* still a jealous sort of guy—maybe just better at hiding it now that he was older. The realisation was a let-down.

'Do you mind?'

'Victoria can take care of herself. You…I'm not too sure.'

'*Me?* What does this have to do with *me*, and what gives you the right to gatecrash our party and then start preaching to me about my life choices?' Here, in the small-cluttered kitchen, she could feel his presence crowding her.

'First of all, I did not gatecrash your party.' He needed another drink. There was a bottle of white wine on the counter and he helped himself to another cup. 'Secondly, I recognise that we parted seven years ago on a fairly hostile note—'

'*Fairly hostile?* You tossed me aside like an old shoe that you'd grown sick of. Did you think I was going to smile and be sunshine and light as I conveniently vanished over the horizon? Did you think that I would meet up with you after seven years and welcome you with open arms?' Megan took a deep breath, counted to ten and remembered that this was supposed to be a jolly, relaxing, stress-free day. 'I think we should get back to the party now. There's no point arguing and going over old ground. What happened, happened. We've both moved on with our lives and…'

Alessandro moved towards her, dark, powerful and intimidating without even trying, and Megan watched him jumpily—the way she might have watched a predator circling her, waiting for an opportune moment to pounce.

Which, she berated herself, was a stupid thought, because he happened to be in *her* house, which gave her the right to chuck him out any time she felt like it.

'Have you, though?' he asked in a silky, lazy drawl. 'Really?' He looked at her carefully, aware that this was hardly the right place for a private conversation. At any given moment someone would be sure to barge into the kitchen, on a quest for more drink or food, or just lost because they all seemed to be pretty far gone. 'Because…and here's the thing…I always wondered how you were faring after we broke up….'

'That was very thoughtful of you, Alessandro.' Inside, she was thinking that that was pretty rich, considering she had practically begged to hang on to their relationship at the time.

'Don't you think so?' As he'd expected, she bristled angrily at his glib agreement with her statement. 'Now, having met you again, I worry that you haven't actually moved on as much you keep telling me you have.'

Megan's mouth dropped open at the sheer audacity of that remark, and she did the first thing that came to her head. She picked up a half-full cup of wine that was on the table next to her and flung its contents over his smug face.

He was upon her before she could blink, his hand curled mercilessly around her wrist, his breath warm on her face, sending shivers of apprehension and *horrible, sickening, unwanted, forbidden excitement* racing through her.

'I'm not about to apologise,' she said breathlessly, fixated by his mesmerising eyes.

'Why should you?' Alessandro grated. 'You're angry, and the reason that you're angry is because you know that I speak the truth. You're going out with a guy who's no good for you. He's a flirt, and who knows what he does behind your back?'

'How dare you?'

'I dare because once we were lovers.'

'That's no excuse for you to think you have the right to have an opinion on my life!' Her body, she knew, with anger and frustration, was betraying every sensible protest she was making. Her breasts felt tender, her nipples aching and sensitive in the lacy low-cut bra she was wearing, and there was a heat inside her that was shameful. 'And just because Robbie laughs easily and flirts it doesn't mean that he's running around behind my back, having affairs!' *Why was she still pretending that she and Robbie were an item?* 'He's a great guy....'

'Is he the only man you've had since we broke up?'

'Is Victoria the only woman *you've* had since we broke up?'

She matched his burning gaze with one of her own. This was dangerous territory they were treading. For him it was just a heated exchange, one he felt he had the right to indulge. For her this was a release of passion that threatened to tip over into something else—something for which she would never forgive herself.

'Oh, for goodness' sake! I'm not going out with Robbie,' she confessed unsteadily. 'Okay? I'm not going out with him and never was. We've only ever been good friends.'

'Then why the pretence?' Alessandro released her and stepped back, shaken by what he had felt just then. 'Did you feel that you had to prove something to me?'

Megan was rubbing her wrist, glad of the small distance

he had put between them. At least now her breathing stood a chance of returning to normal.

'Of course I didn't feel that I had to prove anything to you!' She drew in a shaky breath. 'Okay, maybe there was a bit of that. Can you blame me? You suddenly show up and you've got the perfect life—the life you always wanted. You've made your money, and I'm guessing you have a fan club of admirers and people who would bend over backwards to do whatever you want them to do… The past is just some horrible, dusty old memory you've stuck away in a box somewhere… And to top it off you've found the woman of your dreams and you're marrying her… When, by the way? I never asked… When is the wedding set for?'

'We haven't set a date yet.' Alessandro wondered how it was that his perfect life was beginning to feel so damned complicated and *imperfect*. Hadn't he achieved everything he had ever wanted?

'So…' Megan shrugged, and then grinned ruefully— because what was the point getting all worked up when there were people out there having fun?

Perhaps the punch had lowered her defences, making her think that if, now and again, she still had that old familiar pull towards him, then it wasn't that surprising, was it? Everyone carried a certain weakness for their first love.

'Can you blame me if it suited me for you to think that I had a boyfriend? Truth is, I *have* had boyfriends—but not Robbie.' And just in case he took that small confession as a sign that she was somehow still hankering for *him*, she added, 'But as far as not moving on with my life, you couldn't be further from the truth—and it's not just that I've done what I always wanted to do career wise. I learnt a big lesson from you. I really learnt what sort of man I *should* be attracted to… The guys I've gone out with have been kind, funny, smart, caring…'

'Kind, funny, smart, caring… Hmm… Yet the relationships haven't lasted, I take it? Or else one of these wonder men would still be somewhere on the scene…helping little old ladies across roads…making you laugh as he whipped up a soufflé for dinner… having a serious, in-depth conversation about the joys of being broke…'

Megan didn't like where she thought that innocuous remark was heading—and she liked his sarcastic tone of voice even less. 'Sometimes things don't work out. It's no big deal. I mean, I'd rather kiss a thousand frogs on the way to finding my prince.'

'*Kiss a thousand frogs? Find a prince?* What planet are you living on, Megan? That's the sort of cliché an adolescent with starry eyes might come out with! Not that unfailing optimism isn't a heart-warming trait, but haven't you realised by now that life isn't about finding the ideal—it's about learning how to compromise?'

'Is that what you're doing with Victoria, Alessandro? Compromising?'

'I'm using my head, Megan. In life, it's what people do if they are to succeed.'

'Does she know that you're just *compromising*?' Megan found that she preferred the word *compromise* to the phrase *using his head*. *Compromise*, in her eyes, meant that she could remove him from that pedestal of total achievement which he had been so smugly pleased to show her that he occupied. *Compromise* was all about *making do*. No one *compromised* because they wanted to; they *compromised* because they couldn't work out another option.

'Well…' for the first time since she had seen him again after all this time, Megan decided that she could safely occupy the high ground. 'I may be an eternal optimist, but I refuse to *compromise* my emotional life because it *makes sense*. And if I were going out with a man, I'd hate to think that he was only marrying me because it was the *practical* thing to do. As if,' she continued, getting into the swing of things, 'your personal life, the way you feel, can be worked out on a piece of paper like…like a budget!'

Her eyes gleamed with triumph. She was hardly aware that there was a party happening outside—that *her* party was happening outside. She had been vaguely aware of a couple of people entering and leaving the kitchen, but they hadn't interrupted them. An earthquake couldn't have interrupted them.

It was just like when she was young—when sharing the same space as him could hold every fibre of her being captive. She was fixated by the dark, dangerous charisma in his glittering eyes.

It was strange to think that she could just reach out and touch his chest. Accordingly, she had her arms resolutely folded, and her knuckles were white from the pressure of her fingers biting into the soft flesh of her upper arms.

'Well…maybe you're right,' Alessandro drawled softly. 'Maybe the wise thing is to hold out until the search for the perfect mate is successful. Of course, there's always the chance that a person could grow old waiting….'

'It's a risk,' Megan told him airily.

'A risk you're willing to take?'

Megan had a moment of discomfort as she pictured herself getting older and older in the pursuit of Mr Right, until she was a shrivelled up old woman, living on her own, with only a cat for company. She came from a close family unit and had never doubted that she would marry, be happy, have kids— just like her sisters and her parents.

'If it means never settling for second best…'

'And what went wrong with those guys, Megan? The witty, thoughtful ones? Why did *they* fail to measure up? Maybe your standards were a little too high. Do you think that was it?' He smiled slowly. 'Or maybe I set an impossible benchmark....'

'You...*you* are the most *conceited, arrogant*...'

'Yes, yes, yes—but you still haven't answered me....'

Victoria was probably looking at her watch, her eyes darting round in search of him as she tried to avoid the ministrations of the pushy football coach. But Alessandro was hostage to this intense, disquieting conversation. Megan's eyes were blazingly angry, but that didn't faze him. In fact, he wondered how he could have forgotten how passionate and vibrant she was by nature.

'What's there to say? Your benchmark was an upwardly mobile, soon-to-be-a-multi-millionaire guy without a conscience. Fair to say that it's a definite plus if I meet a man who doesn't live up to *that* sterling example.'

'Upwardly mobile?'

'What would you prefer, Alessandro? Ambitious to the point of ruthless?'

'Better.'

'You really mean that, don't you?'

'There's nothing wrong with ambition, Megan, and you knew that about me when we were going out. Don't tell me that you saw me sitting in front of books, chasing a Masters degree for the sheer hell of it?'

'No, but at least you were more fun then. Did you get your Masters in the end?'

Alessandro's face was taut with displeasure. It had been a long time since anyone had dared be so outspoken with him. In fact, he thought grimly, he couldn't think of anyone else who had *ever* dared be so outspoken with him—even before he had made his millions and attained his position of invincibility.

'Well?' Megan recklessly flirted with danger, every pore of her being alive to his presence and the heady effect of those glittering dark eyes. 'Are you still in there? Don't tell me that magnificent brain of yours has suddenly decided to hibernate…'

There was a part of her that was very much aware of the quicksand on which she was leaping up and down, but it was a very small part compared to the part that was relishing the feeling of subjecting him to a little criticism on *his* life choices, considering he had been so blasé about criticising *hers*.

He'd hate to be thought a bore. It had always been his most incisive put-down—the one word by which he would casually dismiss someone, out of his sphere. In the past, any lecturer referred to by him as *a bore* had stood the uncomfortable risk of being subjected to Alessandro's verbal wordplay—and Alessandro had never lost even then, even as a young man in his twenties. And now any colleague he considered *a bore* simply became invisible.

'You are getting out of your depth with this conversation, Megan,' Alessandro gritted. His eyes flickered to her, to the cup she was still holding. 'Maybe it's time you called it a day.'

'I've had two cups of punch! I don't think I'll be keeling over any time soon.'

'Two cups too many, judging from your wild antics with the football coach who may not be your lover but might be within your sights. *Is* he?' Alessandro gripped her arm and jerked her towards him.

'Is he what?'

'In waiting for the role of Prince Charming?'

'Of course not! And you're hurting me!'

Alessandro let her go immediately and stepped back, suddenly aware of the build-up of emotion that was flowing between them like a live charge of electricity.

'This isn't what it's about, you know,' he told her, unerringly going for the soft spot in her defences. 'Relationships. Men don't *want* a woman who screams and provokes attack.'

'I get the message,' Megan said, her face burning as she saw herself through his eyes. Punch-drunk, or so he might think. She knew that she wasn't even close to being out of control. Even though he'd seen her being kissed in front of an audience by a man she claimed she had no interest in, aside from a platonic one.

'You might believe in the value of melodrama, but has it occurred to you that for every one man who enjoys that sort of stuff there are a hundred who don't?'

'I wasn't being *melodramatic*. I was just having a bit of fun.' But the fight had gone out of her. She felt like a Cinderella who hadn't quite managed to make it to midnight at the ball.

'I think it's time Victoria and I left now.' Alessandro turned away and headed for the door.

He couldn't believe that he had been totally unaware of the steady thump of music outside, the shouts of laughter emanating from the sitting room and out in the small hallway.

It was a small house, but he still had to hunt down his fiancée, who seemed to be having great fun playing some sort of drinking game with a group of people—including, naturally, the football coach, towards whom Alessandro was beginning to nurture some fairly healthy feelings of hostility.

A regular one-man cabaret show, he thought, grabbing his coat and slinging it on. When he wasn't slobbering over women, he was holding court with a can of beer in one hand and a cup of punch in the other.

He didn't know whether Megan was still in the kitchen or not. He hadn't looked over his shoulder when he had walked out. He would get back to the sanity of Victoria's Chelsea house, enjoy what would be a predictably superb lunch, and then head back to his own place, where he would usefully be able to catch up with some correspondence.

He would not spend the night at Victoria's. He never did. She had made noises about Dominic not being old enough to understand the situation until it was more formalised, and Alessandro was fine with that decision. She occasionally stayed the night at his place, though rarely, and that, too, suited him.

He was congratulating himself on the sanity of his life, on the easy preordained lines along which it ran, when the flicker of red caught his eye.

Even at a distance, and amongst a crowd of colourful people, Megan still managed to stand out. She always had. He shook his head, resigned to polite goodbyes, and walked towards her, his hand resting lightly on the back of Victoria's neck.

'Water!' Megan said, pointedly lifting the paper cup she held. She had had time to gather herself, and wasn't about to let her confrontation with Alessandro wreck her day. People only got under your skin if you allowed them to. She looked at Victoria and laughed. 'I'm afraid your fiancé thinks I'm a disreputable woman, because I've had two cups of punch today.'

This surely wasn't the same uptight, rigid, painfully polite woman she had met at the Nativity Play at school. Her cheeks were flushed and her eyes were sparkling. Maybe *she* had been a little over-indulgent on the punch as well, Megan thought. Poor thing. She'd be in for a stiff lecture on the demon drink.

'I never realised you disapproved of alcohol.' Victoria looked at Alessandro with surprise.

'I don't,' Alessandro said through gritted teeth, 'disapprove of alcohol.'

'Only the effects of it.' Megan smiled sweetly at him and piously sipped some of her water.

'Well…' Victoria laughed—a proper, warm laugh. 'Everyone needs to let their hair down now and again. Now, darling, shall we leave?' She turned to Alessandro, brushing aside his hand in the process and smoothing her hair. 'It was so good of you both to invite us here for a drink. Super party! But my mother will be tearing her hair out if we stay much longer, and I can't imagine what havoc Dominic's been wreaking in my absence! He begged Santa for a football,' she confided.

'And let me guess… Santa obliged…?'

'More than that! Santa managed to get one signed by the captain of the Chelsea team—and of course, Robbie… Mr Chance…' She pinkened. 'His new hero, it would appear….'

'Robbie *can* have that effect on people.' Megan broke with tradition and gave the other woman a quick, warm hug. 'Have a wonderful Christmas lunch…' She sneaked a look at Alessandro, following the movement of his hand as he rested it lightly on Victoria's shoulder, and felt a stab of pure, unattractive, inappropriate *jealousy*. She pulled back as though she had been stung, her face hot. 'Tell Dominic happy Christmas from me. It's been nice…' she smiled stiffly at Alessandro '…catching up. In case I don't see you again, take care!'

And there was no chance then to prolong the farewells, as food was calling. In the sudden confusion of people heading to the kitchen, she was only aware of Alessandro, as he disappeared behind Victoria through the front door and off to his perfect, refined Christmas lunch.

CHAPTER FOUR

FOR Megan and Charlotte, Christmas lunch was not so much refined as chaotic, noisy and lively. The last guest reluctantly left at a little after seven, and by eight-thirty most of the detritus had been cleared away—or at least channelled into the kitchen to await further action. At which point Charlotte announced that she would be spending the night at her boyfriend's.

Megan was relieved. She was tired, and she wasn't in the mood for a post mortem of the day which would inevitably include lots of questions about Alessandro which Charlotte had been itching to ask ever since he had walked through their front door with Victoria hanging on his arm. She had managed to ask quite a few during the clear-up but Megan knew her friend better than most, and knew that given a few minutes' peace over a cup of coffee in their sitting room, she would move in for the kill.

She had picked up the pieces seven years ago, and had a lot to say on the subject of Alessandro the rat. Hence why Megan had decided to tactfully omit mentioning their initial meeting. The only wonder was that Charlotte had managed to be reasonably polite to him earlier, and that was probably because she had been too busy rushing around.

By nine, then, Megan had the house to herself, and the full weight of her thoughts settled on her shoulders like a burden of lead.

It shouldn't hurt, but seeing Alessandro with Victoria did. It had been one thing to contemplate over the years the sort of life he might have been having, the sort of women he might have been seeing, but to have the reality of his happiness thrust upon her was a bitter pill to swallow.

Worse than that was the fact that he felt sorry for her. And *even worse* than that was the sickening suspicion that she still had feelings for him—that she was still attracted to him even though he had derailed her life once before and ticked none of the boxes in what she considered her mental file of suitable men. He was arrogant, egotistical and driven. She liked shy, genuine and easygoing. But just thinking about him made her feel hot under the collar, and her nervous system seemed to go haywire the minute she was within spitting distance of him.

She wondered what the point of lessons was if you didn't actually learn from them. Alessandro had dispatched her years ago, because he had been moving up and she wasn't suitable to make the journey with him. She had spent a long time hating him, an even longer time trying to rid her system of his memory, and longer still allowing men to re-enter her life— men who were good for her, who boosted her confidence, who never implied, not *once*, that she wasn't good enough.

The two guys she had gone out with had not been earth-shattering affairs, but they *had* been good for her. They had made her realise that there was life beyond the high-octane, high-intensity, high *everything* passion that had consumed her when she had been with Alessandro.

She had managed to reach a vantage point of inner strength. Or so she had imagined. One accidental meeting and here she was, back to emotional free fall.

It seemed ridiculous to still be wearing the small red dress, even though the high-heeled shoes had been dispatched to the black bin liner in the kitchen, along with the green tights. She had a quick shower, changed into track pants, and was doing a last-minute check to find anything that might be lurking behind doors, under sofas or wedged beneath cushions that might reasonably begin to smell unless immediately removed, when she spotted the jacket.

It had probably begun life on the coat hooks by the front door, but the situation with the coats had been a bit of a disaster. Too many of them and not enough hooks. Not enough space altogether by the front door, so some had been removed to one of the bedrooms upstairs, others to the little utility room at the back of the kitchen, and a few hung over the banister. This stray had obviously slipped through and ended up wedged behind the tall earthernware contraption which they used as an umbrella stand.

She shook it out, frowning. A man's jacket, and an expensive one. She could tell immediately from how the fabric felt in her fingers, even with dust covering it. Charcoal-grey, with a deep navy silk lining.

Of course she knew who it belonged to. She knew even before she reached into an outside pocket and extracted one of the business cards with Alessandro's name on it. His name, the name of his company and the various telephone numbers on which he could be reached.

Just looking at his name in elegant black print made her feel shaky.

At a little before ten in the evening there was a high chance that he would be at his fiancée's house. She could, she supposed, always wait until morning, because not even a high-powered, self-motivated, money-making tycoon such as he was needed a jacket at ten in the evening, but she dreaded making the call and would have a sleepless night if she knew that it would be awaiting her in the morning.

She strolled into the sitting room with the business card in her hand, and before she could start convincing herself that she would be better off pretending never to have found the damned jacket, she dialled his mobile number and waited.

The man must have had his phone glued to his ear, because he answered on the second ring, his voice reaching her as though he was standing next to her in the room.

'I have your jacket.' Megan decided straight away that there was no point with pleasantries. 'It's Megan, by the way,' she added.

'I know who it is.' Alessandro pushed back the chair in his office and extended his long legs to rest them on the desk.

He had had an enjoyable Christmas lunch. The food, as expected, had been superb, but the atmosphere had seemed limp after Megan's drinks party. He had met Victoria's mother once before, and she had been as charming as he remembered, but he had found it difficult to concentrate on her conversation, and matters hadn't been helped by Dominic, who had insisted on listing all of the football coach's outstanding qualities, which largely consisted of a willingness to spend limitless time explaining the rules of football to him. He had also offered to take him to a *proper* match, which apparently constituted reasons for immediate sainthood.

The signed football had even accompanied them to lunch, and had been placed reverently on the table next to Dominic, as though expecting to be served turkey with all the trimmings.

Every time Alessandro had looked at it, which had been often because it had been impossible to miss, he'd thought of the man kissing Megan. And every time he'd thought of that, he'd wondered whether she was considering taking him as her lover.

All in all, he had been relieved when, at six, he'd been able to make his excuses and leave.

Victoria had given him a wallet, and he had made all the right noises, but it now lay forgotten in his coat pocket. He would put it in his drawer in the morning, but doubted he would ever use it. He was attached to the one he used, which harked back to his university days. His Megan days.

He hadn't remembered the jacket until now. He had worn his coat over the jacket, and had been in such a hurry to leave that the lack of the jacket hadn't been noticed.

'Where was it?' The computer in front of him was reminding him of the report he had been in the middle of writing, and he swivelled it away from him.

'It must have fallen. I'm afraid it's a bit dirty, because it got stuck behind our umbrella stand.'

'Have your guests all gone?'

'Of course they have, Alessandro. Have you seen the time? Anyway, I won't keep you from your Christmas Day. I just wanted to tell you that I have your jacket, and you can collect it whenever you want.'

'Now might be an appropriate time.'

'*Now?*' What, Megan wondered, could be so important about a jacket that he would want it right at this very second?

'I don't like putting things off. You know that.' He also knew that he had at least twenty other jackets hanging in his wardrobe, hand-tailored, silk-lined, mega-expensive and totally disposable. 'My driver isn't available at the moment, but I will send a taxi to pick you up. You and my jacket.'

'No, Alessandro. For starters, I don't see why *I* have to be the one to bring you your jacket. It's *your* jacket; *you* can come and fetch it yourself—and anyway, it's too late now. I've spent the past two hours clearing up this house and I'm tired. I want to go to bed.'

She fingered the business card, rolling her thumb over the indented letters of his printed name. She had told herself that she never wanted to lay eyes on him again, that she wouldn't let him ruin her peace of mind, but now, hearing his voice, she was once again reduced to helplessness.

'Fine. I'll be over first thing in the morning to collect it— just in case you have plans for Boxing Day.'

Did she? Victoria would be going to her family in Gloucester for three days, an invitation which he had declined due to his workload. Naturally she had understood perfectly, because she, herself, could hardly spare the time for the short break, but her own absence, she had told him, would be un-forgiveable. He had a selection of parties from which he could choose, but he didn't relish any of them. Champagne cock-tails, smoked salmon and lots of City talk. Just the kind of thing that Megan had scornfully told him he should have gone to today, instead of imposing his presence on her fun-loving crowd of friends.

No, he would fetch his jacket and then have a quiet day in the company of his computer.

Or rather he would send a taxi to bring Megan and his jacket to him. He found that that was a much more satisfying option.

'No plans to speak of,' Megan was now telling him slowly. 'I shall probably go to the pub with Charlotte and her boy-friend for lunch.' She yawned. 'Anyway…'

Her voice trailed off and he took the hint. He said goodbye and hung up, but even though she had gritted her teeth and spoken to him on the phone, she still wasn't rewarded with a peaceful night's sleep.

She awoke the following morning with a groggy head and an urgent feeling that she had to get ready as quickly as possible, so that she would be ready and waiting at the door with the jacket.

Every time she saw Alessandro she could feel her peace of mind being chipped away—a gradual erosion that frightened her and made her hark back to the days when all he'd had to do was snap his fingers to have her running to him. She would make sure that she was standing at the door when he arrived, with the jacket in one hand and the doorknob in the other, just so that he didn't get any ideas of a pleasant cup of coffee and some more of his killer chit-chat before he headed off. It was a measure of how much he had forgotten her that he could look at her and talk to her and try to set her straight on the facts of life with the polite detachment of a well-meaning but essentially indifferent ex-boyfriend.

Alessandro. Indifference. Was there anything more hurtful than indifference? And was there anything more infuriating than *trying* to be indifferent and failing?

Megan bolted down a very quick breakfast of some left-over quiche washed down with a cup of tea, and was ready, as planned, when the doorbell went at a little after nine.

She strolled to the front door, opened it, and had a polite smile pinned to her face. She was wrong-footed to find a taxi driver grinning back at her.

'Sorry.' Megan dropped the polite smile and frowned. 'I was expecting someone else.'

'I've been asked to collect you and a jacket, I believe, miss?'

'Here's the jacket.'

'My instructions were to bring you as well.'

'Sorry. No can do.'

'Can't return without you, miss. But you can take as long as you like making your mind up 'cos the meter's running. I would really appreciate it if you came, miss, as I'm promised a very generous tip—enough for me to get back home to my family and not be out here on Boxing Day trying to pull fares.'

Megan clicked her tongue in disgust. Alessandro was either

too busy or too lazy to run this boring errand himself, and too suspicious to entrust his measly jacket to a taxi driver, even a black cab driver, a notoriously honest species. No, he would see nothing wrong in dragging her out of her house on Boxing Day, just so that she could chaperon a jacket to his fiancée's house and save him the effort.

'Give me ten minutes,' she said in a seething voice.

She was still seething fifteen minutes later as she sat in the back of the cab with the precious jacket on her lap, bitterly regretting her decision to phone him when she should have just stuffed it back in its cubbyhole and waited for Charlotte to make the discovery. Which she would have. In due course. Possibly after a month or two.

London was a different place when the roads were clear and the pavements relatively free of pedestrians. In an hour or so when some of the big stores opened, people would once more venture out of their houses in search of early sales bargains, but at the moment it was possible to appreciate the graceful symmetry of the buildings as the taxi took her away from Shepherd's Bush and towards Chelsea.

She had no idea where Victoria and Dominic lived, but she wasn't surprised when the cab pulled up outside a tall, redbrick house with neat black railings outside. The value of the property could be guessed by the quality of the cars parked on the street outside, and the peaceful, oasis-like feel of the area. This might not be a rural idyll, but it was London life at its most elegant.

She followed the cab driver up to the regal black front door with its gleaming brass knocker and banged it twice. It was opened almost immediately—and not by Victoria.

'Ah. You've brought my jacket.'

Megan looked at Alessandro and scowled.

'You could have come and fetched it yourself,' she told him, holding up the precious cargo.

He didn't answer as he paid the taxi driver, and from the exchange of notes, Megan wasn't at all surprised that the cab driver had been anxious for her to accompany him with the jacket. The tip looked sufficient to fund a two-week family holiday somewhere hot.

'Here you are.' She stuck her hand out. In return, Alessandro stood aside and motioned her in. Megan stayed put. 'Thanks, but I have to go.'

'How did I know that you would say that?' He began walking inside, and knew she had followed him by the slam of the front door. 'You've become very predictable,' he threw over his shoulder.

'Where's Victoria?' Megan demanded, stopping short by the door and looking past his retreating back for other signs of life.

The hallway was airy and gracious, with gleaming wooden flooring complementing the gleaming wooden banisters that led up the stairs. It was an old house that had obviously been renovated to the highest possible modern standard. Suspiciously, there was no sign of a Christmas tree anywhere. Nor were there any signs of toys, which she would have expected to have seen lying around in the wake of a small, over-indulged boy on Boxing Day.

'At her own house, I would imagine.' Alessandro turned to look at where she was still hovering by the front door, clutching the jacket which, six months ago, had been so reverently handled by his tailor in the City.

'Where am I?'

'At my house, of course. Where else did you imagine I would be?'

'What are you doing here?'

'I live here.'

'I *thought* I would be delivering this to Victoria's house!'

'Did you? Maybe I should explain.' He walked towards her,

reached out and relieved her of the jacket. 'I don't do nights at Victoria's house. She's of the opinion that Dominic wouldn't understand the concept of a live-in lover.'

'Why have you brought me here?'

It was a very good question, and one which Alessandro struggled to answer. Why would he choose to jeopardise his orderly life by courting conversation with a woman who had made it clear that she didn't want to converse with him? Their recent meetings had been tense and unproductive, but it was as though something bigger than him was driving him on to see her.

He didn't know whether it was because the guilt he had felt seven years ago when they had broken up had never really left him—was, in fact, resurfacing, forcing him to try and put things right between them—or whether, having once possessed her so fully that she would have jumped through hoops for him, he couldn't deal with the fact that she now hated his guts. Maybe he needed to convince her that he wasn't the bad guy she thought he was. Although he couldn't work out why it should matter. When had he ever cared about anybody else's opinions? Even an ex-girlfriend's?

Victoria had no problems with him seeing Megan. In fact, she had been positively encouraging on the subject. But how long before she picked up on the strange electricity that still seemed to connect them? How long before that became a problem?

'I don't want you to have a problem with me,' Alessandro told her bluntly. 'Yes, I know you think I'm a bastard who dumped you, but, face it, there'll be times when we bump into one another. You teach Dominic; I am involved with his mother. Therefore I will see you occasionally at school. Presumably.'

He frowned, and wondered why he was having trouble imagining any routine of domesticity with Victoria and her son. He had had no such problem when he had mooted his marriage proposal to her three months previously. At that time he had been comfortable with the notion of settling down with an undemanding, highly motivated wife who would complement his lifestyle, and allow it to carry on with seamless ease.

'It is ridiculous that we clash every time we meet—and please don't tell me that it is unavoidable. You're choosing to make things difficult between us, and I want us to iron out the creases.'

Megan had figured out why he wanted to 'iron out the creases'. A smooth relationship between them would mean, for him, an easy conscience—and he was right. They probably *would* bump into one another from time to time as he became absorbed into the routine of family life with Dominic and his mother. The school was very hot on parental involvement, and sooner or later their paths would cross. An atmosphere between them could create all kinds of gossip.

She could jack in her job and look for another one, but that thought lasted all of one second. There was no way she was going to alter her life because she couldn't handle seeing him.

'And that's why you dragged me over here? So that you could try and *iron out creases*?'

'Stop fighting me!'

'Is that an order? Have you become so accustomed to obedience, Alessandro, that you can't stand the thought of anyone refusing to bow, and scrape, and do exactly as you say?'

'You never obeyed me, Megan.' He gave her a crooked smile, remembering the way she had been able to tease him out of studying, had laughed when he had frowned at some of her micro-mini skirts, and coaxed him into going to gigs with her even though he had hated most of the bands.

Megan wanted to ask him whether that was why he had seen no future in their relationship—because he hadn't imagined her in the role of obedient wife. But then she thought that there had probably been a hundred reasons why he had seen no future in their relationship, and asking for a breakdown of them would just be taking yet another stupid step into a past that was best left behind.

In the end he was right when he said that she was fighting him. What he didn't realise was that she was also fighting herself, for still having misplaced feelings towards him.

Right now, for instance, even though he had dragged her from the comfort of her own house at his bidding, she still felt achingly *aware* of the stark dynamism of his personality, the sexy, lean magnetism of his hard-boned face and muscular body. He was wearing a pair of black running pants and a black tee shirt. It had always been his uniform for relaxation, and he looked as much at ease wearing them now, in the expensive splendour of his Chelsea home, as he had in the squalor of his one-bedroom rented studio flat.

She wondered how long it would take him to realise that her prickly reaction to him was as much to do with her as it was to do with him. He had almost hit the bullseye when he had told her, mockingly, that maybe the memory of him had prevented her from finding a replacement, but he hadn't pursued that line of thought.

She shuddered to think how he would react if he ever realised how close he'd been to the truth.

'You're right.' She gave him a wry smile—an olive-branch smile. 'I think the word you used to use was *stubborn*.'

'Like a mule,' Alessandro agreed.

'Not one of life's most attractive animals.'

Alessandro couldn't recall having had a problem with finding her as sexy as hell, whatever stubborn traits she had had. In fact, he *still* found her as sexy as hell. In a purely objective way, he told himself. The red had been washed out of her hair, which was now back to pure pale blonde, and was doing what it had always done: refusing to buckle under the control of clips and a hair tie.

'Stay for coffee?'

'Maybe a quick one. You have a fabulous house, Alessandro. How…um…how long have you lived here?'

He couldn't resist teasing her. 'Um…four years….'

'I was just being polite!' She told herself not to bristle, but when he looked around at her, he was grinning. When he chose to bring it out, he had a smile that could knock anyone sideways. He was bringing it out now. 'How was your Christmas Day?' she asked, retreating to the least offensive topic she could think of.

'Well…' Alessandro's kitchen was a marvel of black granite and chrome. He reached into a cupboard for a couple of mugs and began making them a pot of coffee. 'I went to a very good drinks party in the morning….'

'Oh, really? And what would you describe as *very good*?' There were three stools tucked under one of the kitchen counters and Megan perched on one, swivelling it around so that she could look at him as he poured boiling water into mugs. Even the kettle looked like something out of a spaceship. Very high-tech. 'Do you mean that there was caviar and champagne? Smoked salmon on brown bread? Stuff like that?'

'I can tell you don't move in wealthy circles, Megan.' He handed her a mug and pulled out the stool next to hers. 'And before you jump down my throat, all I'm saying is that smoked salmon and caviar are a bit old hat now.'

'I'm disappointed. I've always wanted to chance my luck with a bit of caviar. Guess I missed the boat. So, what was this fabulous drinks party like, then?'

'Very…energetic. The hostess, unfortunately, didn't appreciate my presence.' He took a sip of coffee and looked at her over the rim of his mug. 'Or if she did, she wasn't showing it.'

God, he was beautiful. Long, thick eyelashes…sexy eyes…the curve of his mouth…

She snapped out of it and remembered that this was what being friendly was all about. It was conversing without edginess, and without dredging up past hurts and recriminations.

She also reminded herself that he was engaged to be married.

'She was probably just a little startled to see you there. Did you have a delicious Christmas lunch?' she asked.

Alessandro shrugged. 'One superb meal tastes much like another.' Just like making the last million was much like making another. Only the first ever really counted. He looked at the heart-shaped face, the big, blue, almond-shaped eyes looking back at him, the full, kissable mouth.

'Oh, to be able to say that!' She felt a slight shift in the atmosphere and awkwardly edged her way off the stool. 'I really should be going now.'

Caught up in the meanderings of his own thoughts, Alessandro frowned.

He didn't want her to go.

What the hell did *that* mean?

Cutting through all the reasons he had given himself for his inexplicable urge to keep seeing her in the face of her obvious reluctance to see *him*—the guilt factor…the altruistic concern for her welfare…the practicality of having a civilised relationship because they would meet up occasionally as a matter of course—cutting through all that, like a dark undercurrent under the placid surface of a lake, lay the disturbing realisation that he still found her attractive, still found his eyes drifting along her body, remembering the exquisite sexual pleasure she had once afforded him.

Where did that leave Victoria?

He would have to talk to her. He owed it to both of them. But it was just as well that Megan was going.

When, as she approached the front door, she turned around and said politely that, at the risk of repeating herself, she probably *wouldn't* be seeing him any time soon, and to take care and *have a good life*—whatever the hell that meant—he inclined his head in agreement.

That brief window of easy companionship was fading fast. She could see it in his eyes. She wasn't sure what she had interrupted—work, probably—but he was eager to have her gone now, so that he could get back to whatever he had been doing.

She had wondered whether she had never been obedient enough. Now she suspected that she had just been tiresome. Suddenly she wanted to get away as fast as her legs could take her.

She gabbled something about his jacket needing dry cleaning.

'No need. I will call a taxi for you.'

'No! Thank you. Public transport…'

'Don't be ridiculous! The bus and tube service today will be extremely limited.'

He picked up the jacket and there it was—that tiny weight nestling in the concealed pocket on the inside. He could feel it because it was where he often kept his own cellphone, and it was where he had stashed Victoria's yesterday. He had completely forgotten about it—even when, over Christmas lunch, she had asked him, frowning, whether he knew where she had left it.

It just went to prove how much seeing Megan again had made him take his eye off the ball.

'I have a phone here….'

He flipped the lid and stared at five messages, opened them, read them, and continued staring at the innocent little metal object in the palm of his hand.

'What's up?'

Reminded of her presence, Alessandro looked at her distractedly

'The taxi…?' Megan prodded nervously, because he was now staring at her in a really odd way and she figured that the egg timer that measured his patience levels was beginning to run perilously low. She would imprint this memory in her brain for ever, she told herself fiercely. It would do her well to remember, should she ever start going down the nostalgia road again, that she could outstay her welcome in a very short space of time.

She backed towards the door, but she doubted he even really noticed. He looked as though he were a million miles away.

'Yes. The taxi.' Alessandro snapped shut the phone and shoved it in the pocket of his sweats. 'Might be quicker if I walk out with you and hail one.'

'Are you sure you're okay, Alessandro?'

'What? Yes,' he told her irritably. 'Why? Are you planning on getting your Florence Nightingale hat on if I'm not?'

'There's no need to jump down my throat,' Megan snapped back, pulling on her coat. 'I only asked.'

'Because underneath that thin veneer of hating my guts you still really care about my well-being, right?' He clenched his fist round Victoria's cellphone, burning a hole in his pocket, and willed his legendary self-control back into place. 'I'm being rude. Apologies. You did me a favour bringing my jacket, and for that I thank you.'

'No problem,' Megan said coolly. They were out in the street now and there was no sign of him feeling the cold, even though the wind was brisk and the skies promised freezing rain later.

She had to half run to keep pace with him as he headed towards the Kings Road — which, predictably, was already crowded with restless shoppers, who were clearly bored with enforced inactivity.

Tellingly, he wasn't even glancing in her direction. She might almost have not existed at all. So much for the friendly truce. Once established, he obviously saw no need to prolong it.

He managed to hail a taxi with the efficiency of a magician pulling a rabbit out of a hat, and Megan couldn't dash towards it fast enough.

'How much?' Alessandro reached for his wallet and Megan looked at him with freezing disdain.

'I can pay for this myself,' she told him flatly. 'Teachers may not be the highest-paid workers in the city of London, but we can still run to the occasional taxi fare.'

'Be quiet, Megan, and get in the cab. This is a journey you undertook for my benefit, so don't waste your time arguing about something as pitiful as the cost of a cab ride to Shepherd's Bush.'

He was already fishing out the amount quoted, and handed it over while Megan glared at him, confused and stung by his abrupt change of mood.

She sat back and stared straight ahead in total silence, half expecting him to say something. *Anything.*

He didn't. He pushed himself away from the taxi, and as she turned her head she saw him quickly disappearing as he half-jogged back to his house.

It had been a learning curve, she told herself brightly as the cab driver pulled away. Learning curves were very important, and this particular learning curve had come at a very opportune moment. Because he had catapulted back into her life and shattered her peace of mind. But now, she told herself, staring out of the window at the grey, uninspiring view rolling past her, she could consider herself on the road to recovery.

Firstly, she had seen Alessandro and Victoria together in a social situation, and instead of letting her mind drift away into the past she would now have it cemented in her head that Alessandro was half of a couple. She might call it a compromise relationship, but it was still very real and very meaningful for him.

Secondly, she had seen for herself how impatient he could become with her—because really and truly he *had* outgrown her.

Thirdly, she had proved conclusively to herself that she could actually have a normal conversation with him—which surely meant that he was no longer the bogeyman in her head, the guy who had broken her heart, the benchmark against whom all other men fell short.

Fourthly... She couldn't think of a fourthly, but she would.

She thought of him back in his house, looking through her and past her as if she had suddenly become invisible.

The best Christmas present she could give herself would be a gift-wrapped box full of all those reminders of why it was time to finally let Alessandro go.

CHAPTER FIVE

ALESSANDRO stepped out of his car, dispatched his driver, and squinted through the driving rain at Megan's house. There were several reasons why he shouldn't be here—the most pressing one being that he had had too much to drink. It was also gone eleven in the night. A time when most normal people would be tucked up in bed. But he'd banked on Megan not being in the *normal* category, and sure enough there were lights on.

He didn't give himself too much time to think. Lately, thinking hadn't been doing him too much good.

He began walking very slowly up to the front door. He could feel the icy rain slashing against his face, permeating through the thin layers of his trenchcoat and jumper to bare skin.

The three bangs he gave on the front door were loud enough to raise the dead. There was a muffled sound of activity, and the door was pulled open just as he had raised his hand to administer another earth-shaking bang.

'Oh, my God. What are *you* doing here?'

'Developing pneumonia.' Alessandro placed the palm of his hand on the door—at which point Charlotte positioned herself neatly between him and the hallway. 'Let me in.'

'Megan's not here.'

Alessandro pushed a little harder and stepped forward. 'You're as forthright as ever, aren't you?'

'Just looking out for my friend, and she doesn't want to see you.'

'Doesn't want to see me or isn't in? Make your mind up.'

The appearance of Megan hovering on the staircase behind Charlotte answered at least one of his questions. She looked confused and rumpled, as though she had just woken up. Her cheeks were flushed, and her silky blonde hair was a curly cloud around her startled face.

'Alessandro! What on earth are *you* doing here?'

'Have both of you learnt your lines from the same script? I'm getting soaked.'

'Do you know what time it is?'

Alessandro made a cynical pretence of consulting his watch. His head was beginning to throb.

'Just open the damned door, Megan! Please.'

It was the *please* that did it. Alessandro had never made a habit of doing *please*, and to hear it dragged out of him now warned her that something was very wrong. She elbowed Charlotte aside, like a master nudging back a very loyal dog determined to keep all visitors at bay.

'Shall I stay, Megan?' Charlotte's arms were folded, and she was looking at Alessandro's dripping figure with narrow-eyed suspicion.

'No, no. It's okay. I'll just hear what he wants and he'll be on his way.'

'Well, if you're *sure*…' Her voice implied that one false move would have her bounding down the stairs pronto, but she grudgingly left—though not before giving Alessandro an evil look out of the corner of her eye.

Her departure didn't mean that he was warmly welcomed in. In fact, Megan had now adopted her friend's pose, arms folded, her big blue eyes narrowed, her mouth drawn into a tight, suspicious line.

'I need to get out of these clothes.'

'You need to tell me what you're doing here.'

'I thought we'd agreed to a ceasefire, Megan.'

'We have. But that doesn't mean that you can stroll in here at close to midnight. We might have called a ceasefire, Alessandro, but we haven't suddenly become best friends.' She was remembering the way he had looked straight through her two days before—as if she had ceased to exist.

Alessandro didn't answer. Instead he began removing his drenched trenchcoat, which he slung over the banister. Megan immediately removed it, holding it up between her fingers as if wary that it might be contaminated.

'The coat hooks are behind you.'

'I need to get out of these things.'

'Why are you so wet?'

'Have you had a look through your window? It's pouring. And,' he added grudgingly, 'I went for a walk before coming here to see you. If I stay in these clothes, I'm probably going to end up in hospital. Would your conscience be able to deal with that?'

He had played successfully on her greatest weak spot, and Megan hesitated. 'All right. If you wait in the sitting room, I'll go and fetch you... Look, just wait, and I'll be down in a minute.'

'Is there a fire in there?'

'No, Alessandro. No roaring open fire. But you can stand very close to the radiator and hope for the best.'

Her nerves were jangling as she took the stairs two at a time, briefly popping in to satisfy Charlotte's avid curiosity. She wasn't sure what she was supposed to provide by way of clothing for him, but after a few hesitant seconds she pulled out a box from under her bed and removed a pair of his sweats, seven years old, and a rugby shirt, also seven years old. Relics of a time past which she had hung on to.

With both items of clothing in her hand, and a clean towel fetched from the airing cupboard, she flew back down the stairs to find him in the sitting room—where he had stripped down to his boxers.

'Wh-what are you doing…?' she stammered, screeching to a halt in the doorway. It was seven years since she had last seen him like this, and his physique had barely changed at all. She stared, mesmerised, looked away, and then covertly looked back at his magnificent body. Wide shoulders tapered to lean hips and long, muscular legs. He was bronzed from head to toe, and without benefit of clothes every sinewy muscle was evident.

'Taking off my wet clothes.'

Megan cleared her throat and dragged her eyes away from his body to the relative safety of his face. Then she tossed the clothes and towel in his general direction.

'I don't bite, Megan.' Alessandro stooped to pick up the sweats and rugby jumper, which he held up and stared at with open curiosity. 'Bloody hell.'

Megan reddened and stood her ground.

'Are these *mine*?' Alessandro looked past them to her, and for the first time in nearly two days he felt good—really good. Stupidly good.

'They were at my apartment when we broke up. I couldn't face bringing them back to you, and I figured you wouldn't miss them anyway.' She laughed shortly, remembering how she had pressed her face against the fabric, hoping to hold the scent of him. 'I guess I hung on to them for sentimental reasons.'

'What else did you keep?'

'That's all there is, Alessandro. You'd better get dressed.' She turned away and leaned against the doorframe, her profile sideways to him. 'I don't feel comfortable about this…having you here in my house…getting changed…it's not right. I know you've said that Victoria isn't possessive, but I like her and it's not fair on her…'

Alessandro didn't say anything for a while, then, 'It's safe to look now. I'm fully dressed.'

'So why have you come here?' Megan could feel the pulse in her throat beating, mirroring the steady, nervous thump of her heart. She'd been reading in bed, almost ready to switch off the bedside light, when the thumping on the front door had had her flying into her dressing gown. Now she felt wide-awake.

Alessandro strolled over to the sofa and sat down heavily. 'Have you been drinking, by any chance?'

'Stop hovering by the door. I told you. I don't bite. I've come here because I need to talk to you, and I can't talk to you when you're standing there like a sergeant major on duty.'

'I should put your wet clothes in the drier. It'll only take twenty minutes for them to dry.'

She tentatively took a few steps towards the pile of soggy clothes, snatched them up, and then fled to the utility room, where she stuck them in the drier. Twenty minutes on the highest setting. For a few seconds she leaned against the tumble drier, eyes closed, then she took a few deep breaths and headed back to the sitting room.

This time she saw him sprawled on the sofa. He looked bone weary. Megan walked across and stood over him, until he opened his eyes and looked back at her.

'Victoria and I are finished,' he said.

'You're *what*?'

'And, to answer your previous question a few minutes ago, yes, I've been drinking—but I'm not drunk. Two whiskies— admittedly in rapid succession.'

'So you've come here to carry on drowning your sorrows?' Megan said with heavy sarcasm.

'Don't you want to know *why* Victoria and I have broken up?'

'I don't want to get wrapped up in your personal life, Alessandro.' *She did.* Her voice was saying all the right things, but her head was singing a different song. It was telling her that she wanted to sit down and hear every grisly detail of why he had broken up with the perfect woman.

'Well, you don't have much choice. Because you need to know.'

'What are you talking about?'

'Sit down.'

Megan looked around her and pulled up the closest chair to the sofa. It was an ancient nursing chair, with a low seat and a buttoned back, covered in the worst possible shade of mustard-yellow. It had been donated to her by an aunt. Unsightly, but very comfortable.

'That's better.' Alessandro looked at her and wondered where to begin and how much he should say. 'Did you miss me?' he asked, staring at her and watching the colour climb into her cheeks—watching, too, her pointless efforts to appear in control. 'After we'd broken up? Did you miss me?'

'What's the point of these questions?'

'Just answer.'

'What do *you* think? Yes. I missed you. Is that what you wanted to hear?'

Alessandro gave her one of those smiles that had always been able to make her toes curl.

'It'll do. Did you ever imagine that we'd meet again?'

'No, of course I didn't.' The shadows cast by the side light played lovingly on the hard angles of his face, softening them. His eyes were lazy and watchful. Lying there in his old university clothes, Megan could almost believe that time had moved backwards.

'Nor did I,' Alessandro admitted roughly. 'Not that I didn't wonder what you were up to. I never imagined that you would have come down to England, and definitely not to London.'

'I know. Because I was a country bumpkin meant to stay in the country.'

'Because you always made such a big deal about the horrors of city living. If you'd wanted a change, you could have chosen anywhere else—any green and pleasant pasture somewhere on the outskirts of a city. I never imagined you'd dive right in at the deep end.'

'Blah, blah, blah, Alessandro. I've heard it all before. If you came here to offload, then go ahead. Tell me what happened between you and Victoria, and then you'll have to go. How did you get here anyway? You didn't drive, did you?'

'My driver's gone.'

'So you mean you came here and got rid of your driver, so that now you're at the mercy of finding a cab? At this time in the night?'

'We're getting off topic.'

He reached out and took hold of her hand, curling his long fingers around hers. It was a simple, spontaneous gesture that made her freeze. His fingers were softly stroking hers and his eyes were on her face, staring at her with unblinking intensity.

'What are you doing?' Megan whispered. This indistinct question should have been accompanied by her whipping her hand out of reach, setting out once and for all her basic ground rules, which were that she wanted nothing to do with him. Instead, her hand refused to budge.

'What does it look like? I'm touching you. Do you like it?'

Megan cleared her throat. 'I don't think...' she began, but her voice trailed off as he began stroking the soft underside of her wrist with one finger. It sent shivers racing up and down her body and threw her already confused mind into even more of a state of flat-out panic.

'That's good.'

'What is…?'

'Not thinking.' He lowered his magnificent eyes and watched his finger as it traced tiny circles on her wrist. She was wearing an old pink dressing gown, and he would swear that it was the same one that she'd used to wear at university. Same colour anyway. She had always liked pink. 'Just going with the flow. I thought a lot. I thought that Victoria was the perfect woman for me. I thought she complemented me in every way possible. And, more importantly, I thought she was eminently suitable because she didn't stress me out.'

'So I believe you've told me before.'

'What are you wearing under your dressing gown?'

Megan told herself that she didn't want to hear these questions, she didn't want him looking at her like that, and she definitely didn't want his fingers like a branding iron on her skin. But she wasn't pulling away, was she? And this wasn't just about being kind to a fellow human being who was upset. For starters, she couldn't imagine Alessandro ever *being* upset, at least not upset in the way most normal people would be. Nor was he just another *fellow human being*.

'Will you let me see?' he continued.

'See what?'

He didn't answer that one. Instead he raised his hand to push aside the opening of her dressing gown, and Megan gasped as the flat of his hand came into direct contact with her breast and brushed against the nipple, which stiffened and throbbed *and wanted more*.

'Alessandro, *no!*' She pulled back and shot to her feet, but she was shaking all over. 'I'm sorry your relationship with Victoria hasn't worked out,' she said shakily, clutching her gown together as though it might open up of its own accord unless forcibly restrained. 'And now that you're here I guess

I'm willing to hear your sob story. But don't think that you can come here and expect me to be your consolation prize.'

'Come back and sit down,' was all he said.

'I'm not coming anywhere near you!'

'I'll keep my hands to myself.'

Megan looked at him dubiously. He now had his hands behind his head and, God, she couldn't believe how much she still wanted him. He lay there as beautiful as some classical statue, brought to life by a vengeful God who wanted to mess with her head by dangling temptation in front of her.

'You'd better,' she warned him unsteadily. 'Or else I'll scream and Charlotte will come rushing down the stairs....'

'Like a rottweiler on the loose, ready to chew me to bits...? Since when did *you* ever need a keeper? Okay, okay. I'll tell you my sob story and we can take it from there.'

Take what from where? Megan tried to fathom out what exactly he meant by that, but her brain wasn't functioning properly. She gingerly went back to the chair, but pushed it away a couple of surreptitious inches.

'Victoria,' he told her heavily, 'seemed the perfect solution. Intellectually challenging and on the same wavelength as me. I never thought that *you* would come along and throw everything out of joint. I made it my aim to have a life that yielded to my absolute control. I hadn't bargained on the element of surprise.'

Megan fought hard to remain indifferent, but that was sweet, sweet music to her ears.

'Throw everything out of joint?' she encouraged. 'Element of surprise? What do you mean?'

Alessandro raised his eyebrows. The look in his eyes told her that he knew exactly where she was going with her apparently concerned question. 'Fishing?' he drawled, and Megan flushed. 'No matter. You want me to explain—I'll explain. You made me question whether I had overestimated the notion of *suitability*. I'd forgotten how…*stimulating*…you could be. I'd also forgotten how good we were together…sexually.'

The music was getting sweeter all the time.

'Do you like hearing that?'

'I don't care much one way or the other,' Megan lied airily.

'Don't lie. You forget how well I know you. I saw you, and it didn't take me long to realise that there was still something between us. I know you felt it too.'

'You're imagining things.'

'Am I? Why don't you come and sit a little closer to me, and then you can say that again.' He sat up so that they were facing one another, and she could hear her treacherous heart beating like a drum inside her. 'I decided that it was no good pretending that I wasn't attracted to you, and it was no good being engaged to one woman when I was very busy thinking about another one.'

'You were thinking about *me*?'

'Thinking about you,' he confirmed. 'And thinking about what I wanted to do to you.' He smiled another one of those smiles. 'The minute I saw you at that school play you got inside my head and I couldn't get you out. Every time I looked at you, I imagined taking your clothes off and touching you. Everywhere.'

'I don't believe you.'

'Yes, you do—and if you don't, ask yourself this. Why is it that we've managed to meet up so many times since then? I didn't have to come to that football game you were playing. I didn't have to come to your drinks party on Christmas Day.'

'Stop it!'

The silence stretched between them, dangerous and alive.

'You came to that football game with Dominic and Victoria,' Megan told him shakily. 'And you came to the Christmas Day party with Victoria.'

'But I *came*. There was no need for me to. I could just as easily have stayed away from both, but I didn't. The pull to see you was too strong.'

'If I hadn't shown up, Alessandro, you would still be happily engaged to Victoria. You would be making plans for your wedding…' Megan fought to hang on to a bit of sanity.

'Are you telling me that you didn't feel the same pull towards me? That you haven't once thought of me since fate threw us back together?'

'That's not the point.'

Alessandro swung his long body off the sofa and began prowling through the room. Megan twisted round to follow him with her eyes. Every nerve in her body was on fire. Faced with a reality she had never envisaged, she literally didn't know how to respond. She knew, though, that coming here would not have been something he would have undertaken lightly. Alessandro had had his whole life mapped out from the age of twenty-four. He had chosen Victoria because he would have seen her as slotting in with his long-term plans. To have his own predetermined destiny hijacked would have taken a lot, and for that she was prepared to give him credit.

But giving him credit still didn't tell her what she should do. So she remained silent…watching him as he stopped in front of the bookshelves, idly reached down for a book and leafed through it before slotting it back into its space…looking as he paused to inspect the pictures in their frames, of her and Charlotte, of her and her family, of Charlotte and her family…

Her thoughts were all over the place.

Finally he stopped right in front of her and then leaned forwards, his hands resting on either side of the chair and trapping her so that she had to push herself away.

'Tell me that's not the point, Megan, and I'll walk out of that door and you'll never see me again.'

Up until that moment she had managed, more or less, to persuade herself that she was much better off without Alessandro in her life—that the cruel trick fate had played on her could be remedied by just walking away from him or at least taking strenuous efforts to ensure that she didn't bump into him. Then she had told herself that she could do even better than that…she could rise above the situation and be on civil speaking terms with him *just in case* they *did* bump into one another in the course of events. It had all made perfect sense.

Now, though, as she faced his ultimatum, the reality that he would once again disappear was like looking into a deep, black, bottomless hole. He was deadly serious as he looked straight into her eyes. All she had to do was tell him to go and he would. For good.

Furthermore, it would be *her* choice. It had been bad enough when he had finished their relationship the first time, but at least then she had been the wronged party, and even with herself had come out tops with the sympathy vote. In the space of a few heartstopping seconds she had a glimpse of a future filled with never-ending unanswered *what if* questions.

'I came here because you need to know that I still want you, but I'll walk away, Megan, unless you tell me that you feel the same way about me.'

'I… I… Um…' *I don't want to be hurt all over again!*

'Fine,' Alessandro gritted. 'I get the message loud and clear. Whether you're attracted to me or not doesn't matter. You're still wrapped up in the past and you can't forget it.' He pushed himself up while Megan remained frozen in her chair, looking at him as he began dialling into his mobile phone. He would be calling a taxi. Or getting his long-suffering chauffeur back to collect him. Either way, it amounted to him leaving.

'I'll keep these clothes,' he said with a cynical twist to his mouth. 'You can keep the suit. Or you can just chuck it.'

He turned away from her, heading for the door. Seeing him leave galvanised her into action.

'Don't go!'

At that, Alessandro turned slowly around to face her.

'I...I want you to stay,' Megan said.

The words had a familiar ring about them, but she shoved that to the back of her mind. She had been nineteen when she had last begged him to stay! She was twenty-six now, and anyway she wasn't, she told herself, *begging* him to stay. At least not the way she once had when he had been her entire universe and she had wanted to follow him to the ends of the earth.

'But on my terms,' she added, as he began walking towards her.

'Which are...?'

'That...that...it's just about the sex. Okay, I admit I'm still attracted to you, but I don't want to get *involved* with you...' What a joke. She had never *not* been involved with him, but she had learnt a thing or two about self-defence, and the first rule, she thought now, was to keep that vulnerable side to herself. But somehow, some way, she had to get over this incredible pull of attraction between them. An attraction that was driving her crazy.

'Sex without involvement... After my mistakes with Victoria, I'm all in favour of those terms...' He cupped her face with his hands and stroked her cheeks with his thumbs. Her skin was soft, like satin, and touching her was hauntingly and erotically familiar. 'Shall we go up to your bedroom, or is your keeper going to hear us and come out swinging a heavy object?'

'She's not *that* protective!' Megan felt as though she was on the edge of a precipice, with one foot dangling over the side.

'We could always stay down here,' Alessandro murmured. 'Although the sofa might prove challenging for me, and somehow making love after seven years in front of a radiator instead of an open fire just doesn't seem...' for a minute he almost said *romantic enough* '...to fit the bill...'

They went to her bedroom like a couple of teenagers stealthily trying not to wake the adults—although Charlotte wasn't in the room next door. In fact, the bathroom and airing cupboard separated their rooms, and the house, while small, was old, and hence the walls were thick. Unless they made a great deal of noise, there was no chance that she would wake up.

The minute the bedroom door was shut they faced one another, each absorbing the reality of the decision they had made.

'Shall I tell you what I want to do?' Alessandro murmured huskily. 'I want to rip your clothes off and take you right here, right now, against the wall... But God, Megan, I won't— because I want to enjoy every inch of your glorious body slowly...' He stood back, breathing heavily. He had never been so turned on in his life before, and he didn't dare touch her—not yet, not until his body was ready to behave itself.

He removed the rugby shirt. They had switched on the overhead light, but now Megan went across to her chest of drawers and lit the three scented candles which had permanent residence in her bedroom.

'I see you still have that bad habit,' Alessandro admonished, but with a smile in his voice.

She was smiling too when she replied, 'I know, I know. Fire hazard. But don't they smell wonderful?' She looked at him across the width of the small bedroom. It had seemed all wrong before to look at him, to look at him, but now there were no such limits, and she feasted her eyes greedily on his powerful body, like a starving person suddenly offered the vision of a banquet. When it came to male perfection he had broken the mould. His arms were strong and sinewy, his broad shoulders tapering to a narrow waist which led down to…to…

Megan drew in her breath, shuddering, as he began removing the sweatpants and then his boxer shorts.

'Are we taking turns?' Alessandro asked, oozing satisfaction as he watched her helpless reaction to his nudity. His very *turned-on* nudity. Having her look at him was almost as much of a turn-on as having her touch him, and both ranked second place to *him* touching her.

He strolled towards her double bed and lay down with one hand behind his head enjoying watching her watching him.

'Okay. Start with the robe. But do it very, very slowly…'

God, this felt so damned good, lying here on her bed, looking at her as she peeled off the pink dressing gown to reveal the pyjamas she still wore. He had never been able to persuade her to abandon the habit, and he was beginning to think that there might well be something in it—because he was certainly getting a massive buzz, watching her as she took off first the striped drawstring bottoms, and then, oh, so slowly, off came the tee shirt top.

Her breasts had always driven him crazy. They were more than a generous handful, with big, rosy nipples that responded to the slightest sensation. Like now. Even though he hadn't even begun touching her, he could see their nubs, stiff with arousal, as she drew closer to the bed. He knew that if he put his hand where it wanted to go, over the little garter briefs, he would feel her honeyed moistness through the thin cotton, telling him that she wanted him as much as he wanted her.

She sat next to him on the bed and he pulled her down, rolling her to her side so that he could position himself over her, all rock-hard, towering male strength. His kiss was like a release and he lost himself in it, covering her mouth with what started as a lazy exploration but rapidly turned into a blazing assault. She was sweetly, wildly irresistible, and he groaned as their tongues entwined. He felt as uncontrolled now as he had the first time he had ever touched her.

As he brought his questing mouth to her neck, she closed her eyes on a whimper and arched back.

'I've reached heaven,' Alessandro groaned. He fanned out his hands under her breasts, pushing them up, getting them ready for his mouth as he administered his attentions further down, along her shoulderblades and over the gentle pale slopes under which he could feel the rapid beating of her heart.

Unable to stand the exquisite torture, Megan brought his head to her nipples and half opened her eyes to watch as he began suckling on first one then the other, dividing his attention so that neither was spared the abrasion of his tongue as he laved them, or the delicate nipping of his teeth as he drew them deep into his mouth.

Her legs were spread as he straddled her, and his flat, hard stomach rubbed against her, sending her into a giddy, wild response that threatened to have her reaching orgasm when she wanted so badly to wait.

It was almost a blessed relief when he raised himself slightly, as though fully aware of how close she was to the edge. But the relief lasted barely a second as he left her breasts and began to work his way downwards.

His hands slid to her waist.

She had never been much of a believer in working out or going to the gym, but for all that her body had never seemed to need any such attentions. She was soft and feminine where she should be soft and feminine. A man could drown in the glory of her full breasts, and her waist was small, but not so slender that he could feel any protruding hipbones. Just small and soft and rounded, and Alessandro couldn't quite believe how he had managed the past seven years without her body.

He was so much taller and bigger than her, and yet they had always fitted perfectly together.

In comparison, the tall, leggy women he had endeavoured to replace her with now seemed like stiff, unyielding mannequins.

He lifted himself up for a few seconds to gaze at her flushed face, and when she looked back at him, he said roughly, 'Enjoying yourself, my darling?'

'You are *so* smug, Alessandro,' she said, and smiled lazily back.

'I like you being hot for me…' Unbidden came the agonising thought that she might have been equally hot for the other men she had slept with. Sure, they had been losers, or else one of them would still have been on the scene, but still…

Alessandro had never felt a second's worth of jealousy when it had come to any of the other women in his life, but the full weight of it slammed into him now, like a rampaging monster.

He didn't like it, and he steadied himself by remembering that this was simply something of the moment for both of them—sex to be enjoyed without the hassle of commitment. After all, look where his last step to commitment had led him. He would enjoy her, because in some undefined way this was something he had been waiting for. Her eager, pliant body writhing and squirming under his.

He would give her the best sex she had ever had.

He placed his hand between her legs and rubbed. Her soft moans were like music. Then, easing his body back down, he heard the soft moans become more urgent, and felt her body buck against him as he slid his tongue along into her, feeling out her small, sensitive bud. She tasted like honeyed dew, and weirdly it was as though the remembered taste had survived somewhere in his memory bank, waiting for just this moment to come rushing back to him.

He raised his eyes. She was arched back, and her breasts

were bouncing as she moved under him. Her nipples stood up, erect tips standing to attention.

He needed her right now, but he had come unprepared. With a groan of frustration, he asked her whether she was on contraception, and was almost disappointed to be told that she was.

He didn't want any accidents—of course he didn't! But neither did he want this ferocious jealousy at the thought that she might have been readying herself for another man.

It wasn't going to do. She had talked to him about not getting involved. Hell, he *wanted* her involved. He *wanted* her to belong utterly and entirely to *him*. He didn't want her thinking of anyone else. With supreme confidence, he knew that, as always, what he wanted he would get.

CHAPTER SIX

MEGAN propped herself up on her elbows and watched him. He made a great sleeper. He didn't snore, and he didn't thrash around the bed the way she did, so that in the morning the bedsheets were all over the place and at least one bit of her body was hanging over the edge, however big the bed happened to be.

And his was a big bed. Much bigger than her double bed. Big enough, in fact, to throw a party on it.

She sighed, slipped out from under the covers and headed for his bathroom. After nearly three weeks she was familiar with the layout of his house. She wasn't sure whether that was a good development or not.

She had had ample warning from Charlotte. *Have sex in haste*, she had been told, *and repent at leisure*. Even though Megan had told her repeatedly that it was all just about the sex, so there would be nothing to repent over *at leisure*.

What she had tactfully omitted to mention was that small sprig of hope which seemed to have taken root inside her, burrowing in between all her good intentions, finding the little crack where resolution met control and growing every day.

At the back of her mind was the notion that this time they were both different. She was older, and hopefully a little wiser. He had fulfilled his ambitions and maybe, just maybe, was ready for a proper relationship. It wasn't as though she was now standing in the way of him and his dream of conquering the world! He had already conquered it!

And then there was the business of Victoria. Hadn't he tried the path of finding the 'perfect woman' and come up short? Hadn't he told her that the perfect woman had not proved as satisfying as the *imperfect* one?

Maybe not in so many words, but Megan's fertile mind had busily read between the lines, and now...

Now she looked at her reflection in the mirror and sighed again.

'What are you doing in there?'

Megan started. She lived in daily fear that he would somehow read the thoughts in her head. It was one thing thinking the impossible. It was another thing should that weakness be exposed. Would he run a mile? In her crazy daydreams he wouldn't, but daydreams were a far cry from reality, and she was still managing to preserve a healthy scepticism—at least on the outside.

She peered round the door. Alessandro was now sitting up, sprawled amid ivory sheets, the purest of Egyptian cotton. 'I'm going to have a shower,' she told him. 'And then I'm heading home.'

'It's Saturday. Why are you heading home?'

He frowned. Three weeks ago he had considered it a pretty safe bet that she would be running at his beck and call the minute they were lovers. Indeed, Alessandro had taken that as a given. He had also thought long and hard about *why* he still wanted her and had come to the conclusion that it was because, as he had told her, she was his unfinished business. He had broken off their relationship because of circumstances, and of course had been right to do so, but sexually she was without compare, and he needed to *have* her before she cleared his system, so to speak. It made sense.

Unfortunately, whilst they were as rampant as teenagers and the sex was as satisfying as he had ever experienced, he wasn't *reaching* her. They met only on predetermined days, and on the one occasion when a meeting had taken him out of the country, she had smilingly but firmly refused to reorganise her calendar for the following evening. What, he had thought, could be so important in her life that she couldn't shuffle a few things about?

But when they *did* meet he had to admit that he was never disappointed. The sex was everything he could have wanted. It was familiar, and yet blazingly new at the same time. But there was always a part of her that she seemed to be holding back. And, call it a challenge to his male ego, he was determined to reach that part and scoop it out.

'Well?' He tried to pose it as a light question, but the demand was there, just under the surface. 'What's so important that you have to fly off at the break of dawn on a Saturday morning?'

'It's not the break of dawn. It's after ten.'

'That's quibbling over detail.' He patted the side of the bed invitingly. 'Come back to bed and we'll do something.'

'You're insatiable!' Megan laughed. 'I'm beginning to feel like a sex slave!'

'Not precisely what I was thinking of, but are you saying that you don't like the role?'

'I'm saying that even sex slaves need showers.' She looked at his bronzed body, entwined among the sheets, and itched to leap back into bed with him, to spend the whole day wrapped up in his arms, making love until they were too tired to move. When night fell maybe they would stir themselves, grab a take-out, settle in front of the television and watch one of those reality TV shows which he had always hated. Like a normal couple.

This was the forbidden hope and longing which she knew, in her saner moments, she had to fight, but now she compromised. 'We could always have a shower *together*.'

'Tempting…' He slashed a smile and swung out of the bed, as lithe and graceful as a panther.

Megan turned away, already warm at the thought of his hands on her.

'But before we turn on the water…'

Alessandro caught her from behind. In front of the floor-to-ceiling mirror, she watched his big, naked body behind hers. For a second their eyes met and tangled in the reflection. She watched his hand push up under her pyjama top, slowly kneading her heavy breasts. She could see the drowsy flush on her cheeks as he tugged her nipples between his fingers, and when he removed the top the person she was looking at was breathing quickly, chest rising and falling, her nipples turning deep pink as he continued to play with them.

The person in the mirror was not someone in control. She was in the grip of a passion too big for her. But Megan couldn't tear her eyes away from herself, watching as he continued playing with her, teasing her throbbing nipples with his fingers as he leaned down to nip and caress her neck with his mouth.

When he stopped paying attention to her breasts, leaving them full and aching, it was to hook his fingers in the elasticated waistband of her pyjama bottoms and run them delicately under the cotton against her skin—before driving his hand down between her thighs where he, oh, so slowly began to administer his full attention, rubbing the sensitised area with his hand while two fingers deliberately sought out her clitoris, tickling it until she wanted to pass out from the pleasure.

She made a motion to stop him before he took her to a point from which there would be no return, but Alessandro wasn't interested in having his own needs fulfilled. Not yet. No, he wanted to look in that mirror and watch her melt against him. He wanted to see the surrender in her eyes as he brought her to a climax.

He gave a grunt of satisfaction as the hand that had been trying to brush his away fell to her side and she curved back into him, her body twisting as he continued to press faster and harder, until she could no longer help the shuddering release that came in uncontrollable waves, leaving her spent against his hard chest.

If he hadn't been behind her, holding her, Alessandro was sure that she would have sunk to the ground from the power of her orgasm. She had cried out, and at that point had looked beautiful and flushed and helplessly in his control. And that had been immensely satisfying.

She curved round into him and he held her against him, his fingers tangled in her hair.

Gradually he could feel her breathing return to normal, and she laughed a little shamefacedly.

'I didn't want that to happen,' she protested, tilting her face up to his.

'I know,' Alessandro drawled. 'But I did. I wanted to feel you tremble against me as I brought you to fulfilment….'

'It was selfish. Sex is a two-way street.' She reached down and felt the hardness of him pressed against her. 'And don't you think that I'm going to let you get away that easily, mister.' She laughed again—a deep, throaty laugh. 'My turn now….'

But he obviously had more control than she did, because although she lavished as much attention on his arousal as he had on hers, he pulled her onto him and drove deep into her, his head thrown back and his eyes closed as he shuddered to his own climax, bringing her to another.

'I *really* think I need a shower now,' Megan said, when they were finally disentangled from each other. Her body was still tingling all over.

He had a huge wetroom, and it felt strangely natural to have her shower and wash her hair while he stood at the slate basin and shaved. They had fallen into a routine of seeing each other two nights a week. On a Wednesday and a Friday. She only ever stayed over on a Friday, and would leave bright and early on the Saturday morning. Sometimes they would have breakfast together. His chef always kept the fridge laden with delicacies. But she would always make sure that she was out of his house at a reasonable time. Hope might be there, and it might very well spring eternal, but there was no way that she was going to let herself get lulled into a false sense of security. At least not to the point where she would *do* anything about it.

'So…' He was wiping his face on one of the fluffy towels as he turned to face her. 'You never say why you have to rush off. Busy day ahead? Books to mark? Nails to paint? You can't tell me that there's hair to be washed, because you've already done that.'

Megan stepped out of the shower room and looked at him as he lounged indolently against the wide plate of marble that encased the slate washbasin. He had slung a towel around his waist and it hung low, a casual covering that paid token lip service to modesty.

'I always have books to mark. It's a never-ending exercise. Today it's English, and I'm expecting some fabulous stories from Year Four.'

'In other words you are rushing back for no good reason?'

Megan didn't say anything, because this was unfamiliar territory. She had laid down her ground rules and so far he had obeyed them. Sex without involvement. How was she supposed to cling to those ground rules if he started trying to break them?

'Marking books is a very good reason,' she began valiantly. 'I know you probably think that my job isn't as hard as yours—'

'That's not what I meant.' He strolled towards the shower, turned it on and said, casually, 'Don't even think about leaving until we're done with this conversation.'

'Conversation? I thought we were exchanging information about the day ahead.'

Alessandro heard her but chose not to reply, even though he was aware of her dithering by the misted glass.

He was going to take his time, and then—well, it was open to debate whether she would be scuttling off to her house in pursuit of marking 'fabulous stories from Year Four'. He had other plans in mind. Plans which he hadn't had a week ago, when their non-involvement relationship had still seemed a pretty good idea—especially on the back of Victoria.

Megan wasn't in the bedroom when he finally made it out of the bathroom, but she was waiting for him in the kitchen, sitting demurely at the kitchen table, warming her hands around a mug of coffee. Her rucksack was on the ground by her feet and her shoes were on. She was ready and prepared for a swift exit.

He scowled. 'Breakfast?'

Megan shook her head and finished what was left of the coffee in her cup. 'Must dash.'

Alessandro gritted his teeth as he poured himself coffee from the glass jug on the counter. He forced himself to smile. If she was so damned eager to leave, then snarling at her was only going to hasten her departure.

'I've been invited to a company do this evening,' he said conversationally, tugging out a chair with his foot and sitting to face her. 'Theatre and dinner.'

'Oh? That sounds nice. Anything interesting?'

He gave the name of a play which had only just hit the West End. Tickets were like gold dust.

'Lucky you.' Megan sighed. 'I'd love to see that, but the waiting list is probably ten years long. Still, it'll give me time to save up. Have you any idea how much theatre tickets cost?'

'No idea.'

'Well, an arm and a leg.' She stood up and glanced at her watch as she did a mental checklist in her head, to make sure that she had packed up all the stuff she had brought over. She was careful never to leave anything at his house. It was easy to be lazy, and that was a road she had travelled down before. She had reached 'toothbrush'—*tick*—when he interrupted.

'I'm glad you're keen to see that play, because I need a partner and I'm inviting you to come along with me.'

Alessandro could tell immediately that she was appalled by the idea. First off there was her lack of response, and then her face fell. He could snap his fingers and have any woman he wanted leaping at the invitation, but here he was, confronted by the woman he was sleeping with—a woman who, seven years ago, would have squealed with delight at the offer—and she looked as though she was calculating what phony excuse she could dredge up by way of refusal.

'I...I can't.'

'And why would that be, Megan?' he asked with heavy sarcasm. 'Because your social diary is so jam-packed with exciting events that you can't possibly cancel?'

'Because it's not a good idea,' she told him bluntly. She sat back down and looked at him, cupping her chin in her hand.

'And why,' Alessandro asked with laboured patience, 'isn't it a good idea?'

'Because that's not what this deal is all about.'

He clenched his jaw and shoved himself away from the table. 'This so-called *deal* is beginning to get on my nerves,' he said harshly. 'I can't slot my sex life into a diary like a business appointment, and forget about it on the days we don't meet. It's unnatural.'

'It's necessary.'

'Are you telling me that I don't cross your mind on the days when we don't meet?' he demanded. 'If that's the case, then why are we *having* this relationship?'

'It's not a relationship!'

'No? Then tell me what it is.'

'We're attracted to each other and we're…following that attraction…' Yes, she had laid down the rules, but it still felt awful—*cheap* somehow—to refer to what they had as *just sex*. Furthermore, it was a lie. She thought about him *a lot*—analysed what they had over and over again. Did she mean anything to him? Was it really all about the sex for him and nothing else? Now he was telling her that it *was* more than just falling into bed and having fun twice a week. He was branching out from their arrangement. And while she didn't want to go down any slippery slopes, the little hope thing was rearing its head once again, teasing her with scenarios she knew were wrong.

Or were they?

'And would that be like dogs in heat?'

'I don't want you intruding into my life, Alessandro. You seem to have conveniently forgotten that I've been there before. I would have done anything for you back then.'

This, he recognised, was the sound of her raising the stakes, and it was reflected in the determined expression on her face. Take her on board in a full relationship, wherever that might lead, or else they kept what they had in boxes which were brought out on specific days and returned to their shelves as soon as the allotted time was over.

He could, of course, tell her that if the fairy-tale ending was what she was after then it was a promise too far. He could tell her that he had tried the total commitment thing with Victoria. It had crashed and burned, despite the fact that they were so utterly compatible in every way on paper, so there was no hope of it coming to anything with a woman who, theoretically, was the diametric opposite of him. But did he really want to do that? He was enjoying what they had, and when he thought about it it *wasn't* just the mind-blowing sex. Why bring it all to an abrupt end and be left with that sour taste of unfinished business all over again?

That made no sense, and Alessandro prided himself on being someone who was coolly and unequivocally practical.

'I'm not asking you to do anything for me,' he drawled, although the concept was enticing. 'But I'm not prepared to carry on a situation that involves us meeting up like thieves in the night and snatching a few minutes of passion before we slink back to our separate hideaways. I bet you haven't told anyone about us.'

'Charlotte knows.'

'And would that be only because you share a house with her, so it would be virtually impossible to conduct any *situation* without her finding out?' Her silence gave him the answer and he leaned towards her. 'I want more of you, Megan. Why don't we give what we have a chance? See where it leads and stop consigning it to some kind of artificial timetable?'

If she wanted to raise the stakes, then he was willing to go along for the ride.

Megan swallowed. She wanted to tell him that she would need a little time to think it through—that way she could maintain her control—but the way he was looking at her, his dark eyes steady and utterly, utterly mesmeric….

And wasn't this what she had secretly hoped for? That he would begin to consider a proper relationship with her? One that might actually stand a chance of going somewhere? She felt her heart begin to beat quickly. This was a step forwards for them, and, while she would take nothing for granted, she could either agree to relax her rigid timetable or else accept a *situation*, as he had put it, which would eventually end up being stifled by her self-imposed straitjacket.

The fact that he wanted to introduce her to some of his colleagues was also a big plus, because it indicated that at least he wasn't ashamed of her—which was what she had felt seven years ago, when he had dumped her. Ashamed of the girl who had it in her to pop out of a birthday cake in front of his Very Important Business Opportunities, as she had afterwards referred to the pinstriped trio whose meeting she had so rudely gatecrashed.

'When you say that we could give this *a chance*,' she prodded, 'what exactly do you mean?'

Put on the spot, Alessandro refused to concede further ground. 'Do you want to come or not?'

'I'm honestly not sure if I have anything suitable to wear....'

'Which is why I am suggesting we go shopping.'

'Go shopping?'

'It's something people tend to do now and again. Women seem to fall victim to the trend more often than men.'

'I know what shopping is, Alessandro. I just can't imagine it's the sort of thing *you* would enjoy doing on a Saturday.'

Megan savoured this further indication of advancement in their relationship. Hope was shooting up inside her like the proverbial beanstalk from the fairy story.

'It's not how I usually pass my time on a Saturday,' he agreed, 'but needs must.'

'You mean, you don't trust me to buy my own clothes?'

'I mean, I intend to buy whatever you need *for* you. If I tell you to go shopping with my credit card, you'll spend the next five hours arguing why you won't. Don't even think of it, Megan,' he said, seeing her open her mouth as this new thought dawned on her. 'I'm paying because you'll be coming to something at my request. You can wear whatever you want— bearing in mind that there's no green-and-red dress code....'

'Well...I *guess* I'm not doing anything much tonight....'

'Good.' He stood up, his mouth curving into a smile of triumph. 'Then let's go. You can leave that rucksack thing of yours here. No point going back to your house to change. You can come back here. We leave at six.'

Like someone suddenly finding that a gentle fairground ride was turning out to be a roller coaster stomach-churner, Megan was vaguely aware of a certain amount of manipulation. But when she tried to follow through with that suspicion, she found that all she could actually think about was the fact that this was the first really *normal* thing they had done since they had locked themselves away in their little bubble of sexual gratification.

She looked at the rucksack lying on the ground, as if it might just deliver the answer to the question she was asking herself—which was whether she should open this door or not. But she knew that she would. She had fought to be sensible, but the fact that he had broken off his engagement with Victoria *because of her*, because of the attraction he still felt to *her*, must mean something. That was the steady drip, drip, drip continually eroding her good intentions.

'We'll start at Selfridges, shall we?' Alessandro said, before she had a chance to change her mind. Suddenly it was very important that she yield to what he wanted. 'Unless you have somewhere else in mind?'

'I guess I could do Selfridges....'

Several hours later and Megan had discovered that she could do a great deal more than Selfridges. Shopping with a wealthy

Alessandro was a completely different affair from shopping with a broke Alessandro, and although she refused to allow him to buy her anything that wasn't going to be worn that evening to the theatre, she still found herself the owner of a new pair of shoes, a fabulous dress, jewellery which she insisted she would wear just the once and then give back to him—because she couldn't possibly accept a gift with that kind of price tag—a coat of the warmest, softest cashmere, and a selection of make up which she would never have been able to afford in a million years.

Over lunch, she made sure to stress her returns policy. 'That jewellery is ridiculous, Alessandro,' she said, toying with a fat, juicy prawn. 'Anyway, where on earth would I ever wear it after tonight? And the coat... Well, it's beautiful, but it just doesn't feel right to accept stuff from you.'

Alessandro shrugged and declined to mention that he was accustomed to spending far, far more on the women he had dated in the past—women who had never had any qualms about accepting the tremendously expensive gifts that had been lavished upon them. Somehow he didn't think that the observation would have gone down too well. He also declined to tell her that this was the first time he had ever *physically* gone shopping with any woman. It was a task which he preferred to leave to his personal assistant. And he decided to keep to himself the fact that he had actually enjoyed the expedition—enjoyed watching her parade in a selection of outfits for him to see, enjoyed seeing the way her eyes opened wide at the sheer beauty of some of the dresses. It had all given him a kick.

'You can give it all back if it makes you feel better,' he told her 'But if you do it'll all end up stuffed at the back of a wardrobe somewhere. I, personally, have no use for women's clothing or jewellery.'

Megan looked at him. This was a different animal from the one she had known. Urban, sophisticated, blasé about the things money could buy—things that were well beyond the reach of most ordinary mortals. From out of nowhere came the uneasy thought that she was now out of his league even more than she had been seven years ago. At least then they had been broke together.

But she wasn't going to think about that. She was going to enjoy the rest of the day and the evening ahead. So she smiled and didn't say anything—but the prawns no longer looked quite as appetising as they had.

'Who's going to be at the theatre tonight?' She changed the subject and closed her knife and fork conclusively on the remaining sad prawns on her plate. 'Anyone exciting?'

'Aside from me?' Alessandro grinned at her.

'Your ego's showing again,' she teased, relaxing after that brief spell of unwelcome thought. 'Careful, Alessandro. If it gets any bigger then you won't be able to get through the doors to the theatre.'

'Well, my darling, you know you need only concern yourself with me.'

'But what if there's a really fantastic-looking guy there?'

'Are you telling me that you're on the lookout for another man?'

There was a chill note of warning in his voice.

'I'm not your property, Alessandro.'

'When it comes to my women, I don't do sharing.'

'Well, I would never dream of sleeping around, and I'm insulted that you would think that of me.' She looked at him coldly, and eventually he gave her a conciliatory smile.

'You're right—and it's good that we understand one another.'

He called for the bill and she watched as he left a wad of cash, which included a generous tip for the waitress. If there was one thing she couldn't accuse him of being it was stingy, but it still took a little while for the slightly sour end of their shopping day to disappear, and it really wasn't until she was standing in front of the mirror at a little before six that her spirits were once more where they should be.

With the whole outfit put together—the classic jewellery round her neck, the perilously high shoes adding a further four inches to her frame, the dress which clung in all the right places—she felt like a million dollars, and she felt even better when she saw the expression in his eyes as he stood watching her descend the staircase.

'Maybe,' he growled, taking her in his arms, 'we should just keep the taxi waiting a few minutes.'

Megan laughed throatily and touched the extravagant string of diamonds at her neck. 'I'm not missing a minute of this play, Alessandro Caretti!'

'Are you telling me that I take second place in your life to a bunch of actors on a stage?'

'I'm afraid so.' She sighed and shook her head regretfully.

'You know…' he kissed her neck, which she wished he hadn't because now her body was responding, opening up like a flower for him '…you'll have to make up for that terrible insult later….'

'Oh? Will I, really?'

Of course he was expecting her to spend the night at his house! It would be ludicrous to drive all the way out to her place from the West End at some silly time of night! The roller-coaster ride seemed to be picking up speed.

'Yes,' Alessandro told her gravely, 'you will. And if you don't mind, I'll just check to make sure that you're getting in the mood….'

He slid his hand under her dress, up along her thigh, and felt the stirrings of arousal as his finger slipped underneath the scrap of silk he hadn't been able to stop thinking about ever since they'd purchased it in the lingerie department earlier that day. If the taxi hadn't been there he would have yanked up that dress and taken her right there in the hall. He had never been in the grip of such uncontrollable passion in his life before. He removed his hand and smoothed down the dress with an audible sigh of regret.

When he looked at her, her face was flushed, her breathing uneven.

'Stop that,' he said unsteadily, and Megan gathered herself sufficiently to answer.

'Stop what?'

'Looking so damned sexy. An outing to the theatre doesn't stand a chance when your mouth is begging to be kissed… along with every other part of your body….'

His cellphone beeped, and he picked up the call from the taxi driver, telling them that he was waiting outside. He should, he thought, have handed the job to his own driver, but a family illness had seen him off for the week. Now he would have to sit through the entire evening watching a musical in which he had no particular interest, making polite conversation to a bunch of people in whom he had only marginally more interest, when he knew that his woman was right there next to him, hot and eager and desperate to be kissed all over. Worse, they would have to wait at the mercy of a black cab to bring them back to the house late.

'Duty calls,' he said sourly, and Megan tiptoed to give him a fluttery kiss on his mouth—because it gave her a heady feeling of power to have him looking like that. As though she was the only woman in the world, as though he wanted to ravish her senseless on the wooden floor of his hall.

'It's going to be fun.'

'I loathe musicals.'

'This is going to be brilliant,' Megan assured him as he helped her on with the coat. 'The lead singer was recruited on a reality television show.'

'And I loathe reality television shows even more. So put those two things together and I have no idea why I agreed to go in the first place.' He folded her against him as they walked out to the taxi. 'Just as well I shall have something to look forward to when we get back....'

But Megan was excited. It had been ages since she had last been to the theatre. It also made a nice change to be going out. Between seeing Alessandro and doing the routine business of her work, a lot of her extra-curricular hobbies had gone by the wayside. Her football games, which were on a Wednesday, had been ditched in favour of him. Thinking about it, so had a number of her friends outside work—including Robbie, whom she hadn't seen since New Year's Eve.

She frowned and wondered at how quickly her spare time was being eaten away.

She would have to do something about that—give Robbie a call in the week, see what he had been up to, maybe arrange to meet him for a drink.

Alessandro hadn't mentioned the football coach for a while, so hopefully he wouldn't mind her meeting him. Good friends should never be dropped in favour of a relationship, however preoccupying that relationship might be.

He also never spoke of Victoria, and all attempts to get him on the subject had been stillborn. It was as if she had never existed.

She looked at him in the darkness of the cab. Aside from the standard white shirt, he was in black. Black trousers, black jacket, black coat. He looked dangerous, but then he turned to her, smiled, and pulled her towards him, and Megan settled in the crook of his arm with a contented sigh.

'Are you glad I persuaded you to come with me tonight?' he asked softly, and after a moment's hesitation Megan nodded—because what could be better than this? 'And, in case I haven't told you, you look amazing.'

'Is it the sort of thing Victoria would have worn?' The words had left her mouth before she could hold them back, and she could feel Alessandro stiffen next to her.

'It is immaterial what Victoria would have worn or not worn. Don't compare yourself to her. I don't.'

Megan sank closer against him with a contented sound. 'I know, and you don't realise how much that means to me, Alessandro. That you don't compare us. That you broke off your engagement because of me.'

She raised her head to look at him, but he was staring through the window, and in the darkness of the taxi she couldn't make out the expression on his face.

CHAPTER SEVEN

MEGAN had expected the others in their party to be replicas of the pinstriped trio, but in fact, she was pleasantly surprised to find that they were neither old nor boring. One of the women, Melissa, was radiantly pregnant, and was keenly interested to hear everything about the school at which Megan taught—because, as she explained earnestly, although her baby was still only a seven-month bump, names had to be put on registers for private schools as early as possible. Places were so oversubscribed in certain boroughs.

'Ideally, I'd like to move to the country,' she confided, as they were swept along in the crowd to their seats. 'But apparently that's not where the money is. At least not the banking money.'

'I'm going to move back to the country,' Megan said wistfully. 'As soon as I've got enough experience at my school. Maybe in a couple of years' time. Somewhere green and pleasant, as they say. Lots of open fields and trees and rabbits.'

'I don't see Alessandro feeling comfortable around fields and trees and rabbits,' Melissa said, one hand on her stomach.

'Oh, I know! He's definitely a city kind of guy! He enjoys the fast pace, and the cut-throat, watch-out-for-the-knife-in-the-back kind of lifestyle....'

Alessandro, who was right behind her, could hear every

word—even though he was apparently keenly tuned in to a conversation about the stockmarket—and he wasn't sure whether he liked the fact that Megan was discussing a future without him in it. Of course what they had would fizzle out in due course…they were both dealing with the process of successful closure of a relationship. The intensely gratifying sex would inevitably become mundane, at which point they would bid each other goodbye with a little sigh of relief that they were over one another at last. But shouldn't *he* be the one to decide when that point in time came?

'Escape back to the country…?' he murmured, as soon as they were seated, conveniently at the very end of their row.

Megan looked at him with surprise. 'Were you eavesdropping on my conversation?' she asked lightly.

'I prefer to call it taking a healthy interest in what's happening around me. You never told me that you were planning to bolt back to the countryside. Back up to Scotland?'

'You make it sound as though I've already bought the rail ticket and packed my bags. And, no, I don't think I'll be moving back to Scotland any time soon. You could say I've become accustomed to the tropical weather down south.'

Megan watched, entranced, at the people moving between the seats, programmes in their hands. She had forgotten how exciting the atmosphere in a theatre could be—the feeling of pleasant anticipation that hung in the air just before the curtain was raised, the orchestra at the front, trying out a few bars, getting the note just right for when they launched into the first number.

'But London doesn't suit you…' Alessandro murmured.

'It suits me at the moment. But, no, I can't see myself staying here to live for ever.'

'Because it suits people like me? People who enjoy the jungle warfare of the business world?'

Megan looked sideways at the man sitting next to her. In

his dark suit and trademark white shirt, with his gold watch peeping from under the cuffs of the shirt and his dark hair slicked back and curling, slightly too long, against his collar, he should have been just another very rich, very well-dressed, above averagely good-looking businessman. But there was something raw and untamed lurking just beneath the urbane, sophisticated exterior—something that made heads swing round and made people falter in their footsteps. *Jungle warfare?* He couldn't have chosen a better metaphor.

'Guess so,' she told him. 'Don't tell me you don't *enjoy* the fast pace of living in London! You'd go nuts if you were stuck out in the countryside with nothing better to do than laze around watching nature.'

Megan thought how nice it would be just to take time out of the low-level stress that came from being involved with a man when she knew that he would break her heart—just as he had done the first time round. This was what it had been like seven years ago. Fast, furious, sizzling excitement. It had been wild and heady, but it hadn't been relaxing then and it wasn't relaxing now. Her only relaxation came from her private daydreams, in which she constructed a happy ending based on nothing more substantial than the fact that he was with her now and it was his conscious choice.

She hadn't, until right now, even considered the possibility of moving out to the countryside. Melissa had raised the subject and she had replied out of politeness. But, thinking about it, it was beginning to seem more appealing by the second.

She had spent the day on cloud nine, shopping with Alessandro, fighting hard to maintain a cool, detached exterior while her heart had been racing. And just at the moment she was keenly and painfully aware of him next to her, leaning into her so that he could whisper into her ear. His warm breath against her neck made every nerve-ending in her body tingle. Was all of that *desirable*? Moreover, she seemed to have no control over what he *did* to her. Her body and her mind seemed to lose the ability to function normally the minute he was around. Was that a *good* way to be?

'But me,' she said, not looking at him and warming to the idea of a life that wasn't lived in a permanent state of nervous anticipation, 'I'd love the countryside. I'd love to have a little cottage with clambering roses on a white picket fence, and a milkman delivering milk to the door every day. I could teach at a small village school. Maybe,' she elaborated wistfully, 'I would take up knitting.'

Alessandro gave a burst of laughter that had a few eyes turning in their direction. A few, having seen him, lingered a little longer than was necessary.

'I thought you'd already done the rural school fantasy. And *knitting*? You?'

'It's a possibility!' Megan snapped in a low, irritated voice.

'I think your personality might get in the way of such a placid pastime.' Alessandro smirked, thinking of her dressed in that wisp of red and green, with one impractical red shoe sailing through the air. 'I'm not sure if a woman who enjoys running around a muddy football pitch would be content to spend two months in front of a television, knitting a scarf. Seven years ago your dream was to go hang-gliding. How does *that* equate with *knitting*?'

'Okay, maybe not *knitting*,' she said. 'Maybe *rambling*, or…or…'

'Or…or…*bird-watching*…or…or…*embroidery*…or…or… Get a grip, Megan. The picket fence and the clambering roses might sound fine in theory, but in reality you'd be bored stiff. Isn't that why you came down to London? To escape a serious case of open-field syndrome?'

'Maybe now that I've tried the big-city life I'm ready to get back to my *open-field syndrome*!'

'You might just find that's easier said than done.'

Alessandro didn't know why he was getting hot under the collar at Megan's innocent conversation, but it gnawed away at him throughout the whole of the first half of the musical.

He was vaguely aware of dutifully clapping in all the right places—just as he was vaguely aware that the woman next to him was totally absorbed in what was happening on the stage. But he was largely preoccupied with the disturbing suspicion that *he* wanted to be the one calling all the shots. Was that just his male ego talking? From the lofty heights of someone who was used to giving orders and having them obeyed without question, Alessandro had piously thought that he was *not* one of those guys who got off on being always in control.

By the time intermission rolled around, he was in the grip of a pretty foul mood, made more foul by Megan's bubbly chatter and her insistence on getting his thoughts on what he had seen so far. Wasn't the choreography brilliant? Wasn't the singing fantastic? Wasn't that little kid just *so* adorable?

Alessandro was non-committal as they headed for the bar, where drinks had been pre-ordered.

'Not too many musicals in the countryside these days,' was what he heard himself saying. 'Although probably quite a few barn dances.'

'What's it to you whether I bury myself in the countryside to pursue my hobby of knitting and going to barn dances?' Megan asked tartly.

Ahead of them, the other members of their party had become submerged in the chaos of the bar.

This whole stupid conversation seemed to have become a battle of wills, and Megan wasn't going to back down.

'Obviously not much,' Alessandro drawled darkly. 'You

can bury yourself wherever you want to. I merely felt compelled to point out the drawbacks to your master plan.'

'And thanks very much for that. But I'm a big girl now. I think I can work out how to live my life without your advice. In fact—' she furthered her cause for independence '—if you'll make my excuses to everyone, I'm going to join the queue for the Ladies'. I might not be back in time for my glass of wine.'

She wasn't one hundred per cent sure where the restrooms were, and nor did she really need to go, but she needed to put some distance between herself and Alessandro. This should have been a *fun* evening. Instead the fun bit was getting lost in an uncomfortable argument about nothing in particular. If, she thought furiously as she battled through the crowds like a fish swimming upstream, he hadn't wanted to bring her along to the theatre, then he should never have invited her. But he had asked her along and then proceeded to pick a row over her silly, purely hypothetical plan to move out to the country. Just because, she reasoned, he had to be the one whose opinions were always right.

Was she getting on his nerves? Was this his way of showing it?

She reached the restrooms to find the line of people as long as she had expected. Longer. And moving at a snail's pace. But at least it would give her the chance to get back her cheerful frame of mind, so that she could enjoy the second half of the musical.

She was miles away when a familiar voice said from behind, 'Megan? Is that you?'

Megan spun around to find Victoria standing right behind her, exquisite in a pale woollen, long-sleeved dress with a string of pearls around her neck. Her hair, for the first time since Megan had met her, fell in a neat, glossy bob to her shoulders.

'Victoria!'

'Isn't this a surprise? Who are you here with?'

The line was shuffling forwards very slowly. 'I'm with…'
Megan hesitated, guiltily aware that Alessandro's name might
be a depressing reminder to the other woman of her broken
engagement. 'A few…friends. And you? You look tremendous, by the way. And Dominic, I gather, is still head over
heels in love with football! I'm so glad about that.'

'So am I,' Victoria confided with a warm smile. 'And I have
you to thank for that.'

Megan mumbled something in return.

'In fact, I have you to thank for a number of things. Look,
are you absolutely desperate for the loo? We could just slope
off and have a quiet chat before the second half begins. There
are a few things I'd rather like to get off my chest.'

Megan swallowed hard and wished herself back to the
bar—because arguing with Alessandro suddenly seemed more
restful than hearing what Victoria had to say.

'Of course.' She resigned herself to the inevitable and followed Victoria, who seemed to know the layout of the theatre
a lot better than she did. In fact, they managed to avoid the
crowds altogether, and were shown by one of the ushers to a
quiet side room just off the stage.

'Sometimes it's jolly convenient to have connections,'
Victoria explained apologetically. 'My uncle is something of
a bigwig in the field of theatre.' She tapped the side of her nose
and gave a conspirational smile. 'A quiet word in the right ear
and here we are. Far from the madding crowd.'

'I'm here with Alessandro!' Megan blurted out, taking the
bull by the horns rather than waiting for the bull to come
charging at her.

She walked over to one of the small flowered sofas and
stood behind it, her hands resting on the upholstered back.

'Look, I really am so sorry that things didn't work out between the two of you, but I want you to know that the—'

'You're here with Alessandro? I'm *so* glad!'

'You're…what…?' Megan asked faintly.

'So awfully glad.' Victoria looked at her ruefully. 'I felt so dreadfully guilty at the way things ended between us.'

'You felt *dreadfully guilty*?' Her mind seemed to be getting a little clogged up, and now she was repeating language she never normally used! But there was a dull pink tinge to Victoria's face, and she did look very sheepish.

What, Megan wondered, was there for her to feel *sheepish* about? Alessandro had terminated the relationship, had broken off the engagement. Wasn't she entitled to feel a little hard done by?

'Why on earth would *you* feel guilty, Victoria?' she asked in genuine puzzlement.

'I never meant to meet Robbie! And I certainly never meant to—'

Robbie? Megan wondered what Robbie had to do with all of this. She felt as though she was in possession of a jigsaw puzzle, the key pieces of which were missing.

'Dominic absolutely adores him.'

'Good.' Megan tried to work out what was going on. 'It's nice,' she added vaguely, 'for a boy to have a role model, so to speak….'

'And I…' Victoria took her hand in a gesture that Megan suspected was heartfelt rather than customary. 'I felt so terribly awful about Alessandro…but Robbie…'

Pieces of the jigsaw were beginning to mesh together, and even though the picture wasn't as yet comprehensive Megan was slowly realising that she didn't like what she was seeing.

As if to confirm the suspicions forming at the back of her mind, she watched Victoria's face flush with happiness.

'I had to break off the engagement,' she confessed. 'Or rather the matter was taken out of my hands!' She laughed ruefully. 'Freudian slip, I'm afraid. I left my mobile phone at your Christmas party... Actually, I thought I had left it somewhere, put it down, but it turned out to have been in Alessandro's pocket all the while. He found out the worst possible way that Robbie...'

'Found out...?' Megan said in a dazed fashion. Her brain was frantically trying to keep pace with what was being said.

'Of course I never would have dreamt of doing anything!' Victoria exclaimed, misinterpreting the whiteness of Megan's face. 'But Robbie had been texting me...and I did realise that I found him...well...I was absolutely confounded...but...'

'So you told Alessandro?' Megan numbly asked for complete clarification.

'I had to. I couldn't possibly continue the relationship when there had been such a *sea change*, so to speak. You do understand, don't you?' Victoria asked anxiously. 'Of course Alessandro said that he was absolutely fine...' She smiled. 'But I can't tell you how marvellous it is to know that he's here...that you are with him... You *are* with him, aren't you? Darling, I *knew* there was something between you two... Perhaps in the end this is all a question of fate....'

She glanced at her watch and gave a little squeal of dismay.

'Robbie's going to be raging if he gets back to his seat and I'm not there!' She leapt to her feet. 'I've ordered him to get me an ice cream...if I don't rescue it, it will either be dripping down his hand or else he will have polished it off! You know men....'

No, Megan thought as she sprinted behind Victoria to find that the crowds had all returned to their seats for the second half of the play. No, she *didn't* know men. Not at all. She especially didn't know Alessandro.

Those little glimmers of hope that had darted in and out of her mind like fireflies, lighting up a future with promises which she knew would never be fulfilled but which had kept her busy with a little luxury wishful thinking, were now extinguished in a matter of seconds.

Alessandro hadn't broken off his engagement to Victoria *because of her*. He had been on the receiving end of a woman who had fallen in love with another man and had done the decent thing.

No *wonder* Robbie had not been in touch! She'd kept thinking that she should get in touch with him, but she had been so preoccupied with Alessandro that she had barely given anything else a second's thought. He had taken over her daily existence, just as he had seven years previously, even though she had given herself lots of stern lectures about maintaining detachment.

She thought back to the way she had nurtured her hope that this time things would be different between them, and was swamped by a feeling of disgust at her gullibility.

She didn't like to think how long she would have continued seeing him, weaving little dreams in her head about a perfect life with him. Fortunately Victoria had set her straight on that one.

I'm hurting now, Megan thought as she returned to her seat, forcing down the bitter sting of tears at the back of her throat. *But it's all for the best and time is a great healer.*

She could feel Alessandro turn to her in the darkness as she slipped back into her seat next to him, but she kept her head averted.

She didn't know how she managed to sit through the remainder of the play. The dancing which she had thought was so marvellous in the first half barely distracted her from her angry, humiliated, churning thoughts, and she fidgeted, keen to be rid of the intimacy of sitting next to him.

'What's the matter with you?' Alessandro murmured, conclusively sorting out her restless hands by anchoring his fingers around her wrist.

Megan immediately fell still. Only an hour before and she would have leant against him, hotly and wickedly anticipating another night spent in the same bed as him.

'Well?'

'Nothing. I'm just enjoying the play,' she muttered. After a couple of minutes she managed to extract her hand from his and place it on her lap.

There was a standing ovation for the performers, and while she stood up, she made sure to also be gathering her coat and busying herself with her handbag. The clothes which she had enjoyed buying with him now felt tainted on her.

It wouldn't take him long to figure out that something wasn't right. Alessandro was nothing if not adept at sensing nuance. But luckily he had no time to question her because he was caught up in the melee of everyone leaving the theatre. A meal out afterwards had been planned. There was no way on earth that Megan was going to go along.

As soon as they exited the theatre she turned to the assembled group and said, with an apologetic smile, 'I feel awful about doing this, but I'm going to have to cry off tonight's meal, I'm afraid.' She was aware of Alessandro, straight ahead of her and sandwiched between two of the men, looking at her sharply through narrowed eyes. 'Female problems.' She turned to Melissa who glowed with sympathy.

Female problems encompassed a gamut of irrefutable excuses, not one of which any man would ever question. It was an accepted fact that the mere mention of *female problems* sent most men diving for cover.

'Poor thing.' Alessandro moved forwards and took her arm in what could loosely be called a vice grip. 'And not a word to me about them. Such a martyr. But, darling, I couldn't possibly allow you to go back on your own when you're struggling with *female problems*.' He flashed his own apologetic smile all round. 'If you will excuse me? I must cut short this evening which has been so thoroughly enjoyable.'

'There's no need, Alessandro!' Her voice sounded high-pitched and panicked, and she toned it down with a belated smile. 'I just need to have an early night.'

'And I will make sure that you are safely delivered back to your bed.'

'How gallant,' one of the women said, before looking at her own portly husband with an indulgent grin. 'You need to take some lessons from Alessandro, Jamie. Remind me a bit that chivalry isn't dead.' She patted Megan kindly on her arm. 'Such a nuisance for you, my dear, but just so long as you've enjoyed the play. Stunning, wasn't it?'

Alessandro, Megan noticed miserably, kept his hand clamped round her arm as they said their goodbyes. Did he think that she might do a runner if he didn't?

She found herself in the back seat of a taxi while Alessandro gave orders for them to be taken back to his house.

'I want to go back to my own place.' Megan turned to him and edged away ever so slightly.

'You do realise how rude you've been?' He ignored her request and looked at her grimly.

'I'm sorry about that.'

'You don't look particularly sorry.' He raked his fingers through his hair. In the darkness, there was a dangerous glitter in his eyes that would have sent a shiver down her spine if she weren't feeling so *angry*. 'Let's just cut through the crap, Megan. If you've got *female problems,* then I'm the King of England. You were fine today when we were out, and you were perfectly well up until the second half. What the hell's going on?'

'I need to talk to you,' Megan said stiffly, 'and the back seat of a taxi isn't the place.' Nor was his house, for that matter, but there was no way he was going to drop her home, and anyway she had some of her possessions at his place, which she would have to collect.

Alessandro looked first at the distance she had put between them, at her hands which were balled into fists on her lap, and then at her profile as she stared out of the window.

Need to talk? Female problems?

His justified annoyance at her abrupt end to the evening did a rapid U-turn. She had said that she needed to talk to him—correction, that she needed to talk *privately*—and she had said it in a voice that had made him vaguely uneasy. Add to that the fact that she was sitting like an iceberg next to him, and he came up with the one explanation which made sense.

He didn't know how, but it was suddenly clear to him that she had managed to get pregnant. She had disappeared to the restrooms at the theatre, had remained there for an inordinately long time, and then had returned with a personality transplant. Had she taken some kind of testing kit to the loo? Maybe being in the company of Melissa had got her thinking about her menstrual cycle? Made her wonder if it had been as regular as it should have? Who knew? Alessandro wasn't a doctor, but he was pretty sure that he had hit jackpot.

He lapsed into a reflective silence of his own as he began to consider the possibilities of this unexpected event.

He had not considered his relationship with Megan to be a permanent one. She was an itch that he needed to scratch—a fever that roared through his system and needed curing once and for all. A pregnancy would change all that. He thought about becoming a father. Megan wasn't like Victoria. She would see parenthood as a full-time occupation. Broken nights, changing nappies, sterilising bottles—all of that would be, for her, a shared venture. His life would be turned on its head.

Alessandro looked at her. For someone who must be churning up inside, she appeared remarkably calm. In fact, for someone who was perfectly happy to be swept along on an emotional tide, she seemed to be handling the situation with a lot of *sang froid*.

The taxi pulled up outside his house.

'Okay,' he said, opening his front door and standing back to let her walk past him. 'You've had time to try and work out whatever speech you've got prepared…' Alessandro slammed the door behind him and stayed where he was, leaning against it and watching her. 'So what's this *talk* about? Anything to do with those *female problems* you mentioned, by any chance?'

On her way to the sitting room, Megan stopped in her tracks and turned to face him.

'What do you mean?'

'You know what I mean. I wasn't born yesterday, Megan. You're pregnant, aren't you?'

After the ensuing silence, during which Megan tried to gather her scattered wits and not burst into laughter at his wild, inaccurate deduction, Alessandro continued calmly.

'I don't know how it's happened, but it has, and now you're trying to work out how to break the news.'

'Oh, right. Is *that* what I'm doing? And how would you suggest I go about it?' Megan's voice was cool and level. He imagined she was *pregnant*? That, she thought, would have been one complication too far, and she was mightily relieved that she didn't have to deal with it.

Alessandro was a little unsettled by that response. Not a flicker of emotion had crossed her face. 'Just come right out and confess,' he advised. 'You can't skirt round a pregnancy.'

'And how will you react?' Megan tried to tear herself away from a pointless conversation about a non-existent situation. But it was tempting to buy time, and even more tempting to try and find out what he might have felt *had* he been confronted with a pregnant lover.

Part of her knew that she was just shoring up that little twig of hope, building herself a little fantasy that maybe, in a situation like that, he might suddenly be overwhelmed by need and love and race to her side in a supportive way. He wouldn't.

'It doesn't matter,' she told him in an icy voice. 'I'm not pregnant, so you can stop worrying.'

Surprisingly, Alessandro wasn't sure that he *had* been worrying. More contemplating jumping into unknown waters….

'Okay…' he said, moving towards her very slowly and watching her the way he might watch a domestic pet that had suddenly become dangerously unpredictable. 'So what is this all about, then?'

'It's about *us*, Alessandro.'

'What *about* us?'

'I've thought about this arrangement of ours and I've decided that the time has come to end it.' She thought bitterly of that other self—the one who had existed less than two hours ago, the one who had become caught up in all sorts of silly, reckless dreams. She folded her arms and stood her ground while he looked at her in perfect bemusement.

'You don't know what you're saying,' Alessandro told her amiably. 'Did you take a knock to your head when you went to the restroom at the theatre? Maybe you need to lie down?'

'I don't need to lie down. I need to go upstairs and get my stuff, then I'm leaving this house and I won't be coming back.'

The amiable smile dropped from Alessandro's face, but before he could pick her up on what she was saying—which made absolutely no sense whatsoever—she had turned her back to him and was running up the stairs.

After a second's hesitation he followed her, easily catching up with her and blocking the door to his bedroom.

'Just like that?' he ground out. 'You're leaving *just like that*? No explanation? Well, I refuse to allow it.'

'You *refuse to allow it*?' Megan gave a burst of mirthless laughter, but she was trembling.

'Yes, dammit!'

'You can do a lot of things, Alessandro, but you can't stop me walking out on you.'

'What's happened?'

'Nothing happened. I just wised up, that's all.'

'No, it damn well isn't all! I can read people, and you weren't planning on leaving me this morning, when we were out shopping! Nor were you planning to leave me when we were at the theatre—at least not until after the intermission. You disappeared for a while. What happened? Who did you talk to?'

Megan had not intended to go into details. When she had said goodbye to Victoria, she had been in a daze. The second half of the play, which she should have enjoyed but which in reality she would have been hard-pressed to remember, had given her time to try and collect her thoughts, and thought number one had been that she wasn't going to go down the post-mortem route. She was going to be cool and dignified and leave him to stew with unanswered questions.

He probably wouldn't stew for very long, but the thought of him stewing at all might well distract her from her misery at no longer being with him. She couldn't get out of her mind the thought that she had dug herself a hole, jumped in, and proceeded to cover herself with earth. All her crazy hopes had been based on a piece of fiction.

Of course now that she was actually facing his barrage of questions, and staring into those black, intense eyes in which she had happily lost herself, she no longer felt quite so content with a dignified exit.

She had never been able to master the art of being cool.

'Well?' Alessandro demanded. 'Are you just going to stand there, gaping like a goldfish?'

'Let me pass! I want to get my stuff!'

'Not until we've had some kind of conversation about this!'

'You always have to get your own way, don't you, Alessandro?' she responded in a shrill voice, which sent his temper levels up by a couple of notches.

'That's pretty much it,' he agreed. 'And the sooner you start realising that, the better for all concerned.'

'Okay. I'll tell you what you want to know.' She took a couple of deep breaths to calm herself. 'Guess who I bumped into when I was waiting in the queue for the toilet?'

'No idea. Why don't you enlighten me?'

'Your ex! Victoria. Remember her?'

'Of course I remember her,' Alessandro said warily. 'How is she?'

'Oh, she's doing just fine, now that you ask! Better than fine, in fact. Positively thriving.'

Alessandro waited.

'Aren't you going to ask me what we chatted about?'

'Why don't we go downstairs to finish this conversation?' he said in a grim voice. 'You said that you didn't want to talk in the taxi because it wasn't the right place. Well, getting hysterical on the landing isn't the right place for me.'

Megan wanted to tell him that it was the right place for *her*, because that way she might have asserted a little of her will-power, but in actual fact her legs felt wobbly, and while she knew that heading straight towards the question-and-answer session she had wanted to avoid was going to be undignified, collapsing outside his bedroom door because her legs were like jelly would have been even more undignified.

'Fine,' she said in the calmest voice she could muster. 'But once I'm done talking I collect my things and I leave this house for ever.'

CHAPTER EIGHT

ALESSANDRO watched Megan from across the unbridgeable width of the sitting room. She had adopted a defiant pose, perched on the ledge of the bay window. She hadn't removed her coat and she was huddled into it, even though the central heating was still on and the room was warm.

Too warm, in fact. He rid himself of his jacket and rolled the sleeves of his shirt to the elbows.

'Drink?' he asked, and when she shook her head, he shrugged and said, 'Well, I could do with one.'

Megan looked at him with mounting anger as he went across to one of the cupboards which slid noiselessly back to reveal a well-stocked bar.

The man was as cool as a cucumber! She had just threatened to leave him, to walk out of his house for good, and how was he reacting? As though nothing had been said! As though this was just another normal day at the ranch!

'You were saying…?' Alessandro turned back to her and sipped his whisky.

'I was saying that I bumped into Victoria, and she told me what happened between the two of you.' Megan drew in a deep breath and, taking her cue from him, banked down the emotion that was threatening to spiral out of control. Her voice was flat and calm. 'I was under the impression that *you* were responsible for the break-up, Alessandro.'

'Does it matter where the finger points? When it comes to the breakdown of a relationship there is nothing to be gained from apportioning blame.'

'Don't try and twist words,' Megan said bitterly. 'I was led to believe that you broke off your engagement because you wanted a relationship with *me*...'

'You believed what you wanted to believe,' Alessandro told her, his fury mounting at being called to account. He braced himself for the inevitable direction of the conversation.

'So you're not going to deny that Victoria was the one who decided to break off your engagement?'

The last pathetic shred of hope that he might at least try to disabuse her of Victoria's version of what had taken place shrivelled and died in the face of his continued silence.

'She told me about her mobile phone,' Megan continued in a hollow voice. Now that her decision to be cool and to walk away without explanation because he didn't deserve one had been abandoned, she felt driven to expose every little detail of her own foolishness. It was like picking away at a scab. It wouldn't remedy anything but it was still an unstoppable temptation.

And still there was nothing from him. He just stood there, taking small sips of his drink, seemingly at ease with the situation.

'You found out that Robbie had been in touch with her, and I guess before you could—I don't know—try and make her go down the *sensible* route, she decided that she wanted to throw caution to the winds and get involved with someone else. Someone who didn't *make sense*. She and Robbie are an item now. Did you know that?'

If Megan had intended to rile him with that dig then she

failed, because Alessandro simply shrugged and remarked evenly, 'I wish them well.'

A wave of hopelessness swept over her, leaving her small and defeated.

'What do you want me to say, Megan?' Alessandro had been enjoying life, enjoying whatever the hell she wanted to call it—their *relationship, situation, involvement*—but he wasn't enjoying being boxed into a corner. 'That I am prepared to make you promises which I know won't be fulfilled? Do you want to hear the whole love thing?' Every part of him that desired and saw the necessity for absolute control, rejected her directness.

'I never said that!'

'What, then?'

'You used me.'

Alessandro was outraged at that—outraged at her portrayal of herself as a passive victim when she had been as crazy for sex as he had.

However, he wasn't going to succumb to the weakness of raising his voice or getting emotional. 'If that's what you wish to believe, Megan, then there's nothing I can do to stop you. But just think about this: I came to you and you had every opportunity to tell me that you didn't want involvement. If I recall, you didn't do that. In fact, at no point did I get the impression that you wanted out. I might be mistaken...'

This time it was Megan's turn to fall silent as she considered the accuracy of that flatly intoned statement. Yes, he *had* given her the option of backing out.

'I was under the impression—'

'I never once told you that *I* had broken off my engagement with Victoria,' he reminded her, mercilessly driving home his point that she had not been coerced into any situation she hadn't wanted. 'You just went ahead and made assumptions.'

What he failed to tell her was that he would have broken it off with Victoria, anyway. Would have broken it off even if he *hadn't* found those mildly incriminating text messages on her mobile phone. Had been secretly relieved that the onus of ending their relationship hadn't fallen on his shoulders.

'And you never corrected those assumptions because they suited you. You wanted to get me into bed, and the fastest way of doing it was to lead me to believe that you had broken your engagement to Victoria.'

'I didn't need a fast way of doing that. We would have fallen into bed together anyway.' But he flushed, because there was a modicum of truth in what she was saying. He had known that, however much she was attracted to him, she would not have leapt into his arms had she thought for a passing minute that she was a plaything. He resented the fact that she was throwing all of this in his face when she could so easily have accepted the situation for what it was. Two people who had temporarily reconnected.

'Why?' Megan looked at him unblinkingly. 'Why did you bother? Why didn't you just leave me alone?'

'I realised that I still wanted you. I also realised that you still wanted *me*.'

'And so you thought…why not? Is that it?' Yet again, she was good enough to have a romp with, but not good enough for a committed relationship.

It seemed that neither of them had grown up after all. She was still looking for the impossible, and he was still convinced that she didn't fit the bill. The bitter truth, she thought, was that she fitted the bill even less now. In the space of seven years he had become so powerful that the concept of hitching his wagon to a woman who defiantly refused to obey him would be unthinkable.

'You think that you have somehow been insulted? What

you fail to understand is that what's happened between us *needed* to happen!'

Lost in a daze of her own agonising thoughts, Megan barely surfaced to hear his latest piece of wisdom.

Her brain caught up with what he was saying after a ten-second delay, and she looked at him blankly.

'What?'

'I am *saying*,' Alessandro repeated slowly, 'that we needed to get each other out of our systems. I am *saying* that the only way of doing that was to have a relationship, allow this over-powering mutual lust to burn itself out...'

Need? Lust? The words which she knew would have thrilled most women to death when applied to Alessandro dropped like poison into her consciousness.

While she had been blissfully toying with more romantic notions, he had summed everything up in an emotion that blew strong and then faded away. He had allowed her the illusion of pretending that there was more to what they had because he wanted to tire of her, and the only way he could do that was to have her until he no longer wanted her.

'You've said enough.' She forced her wooden body to move. 'I don't want to hear any more. I'm going to go upstairs and get my stuff now.' She reached for the ludicrously expensive jewellery adorning her and carefully removed it. 'You can have this back.'

'Don't be ridiculous.' A dark flush highlighted his sharp, arrogant cheekbones. 'What the hell am I going to do with women's jewellery?'

'I don't know and I don't care.' Since he was making no effort to take what she was offering him *back*, she casually dropped it on one of the side tables in the room. 'You can always give it to your next conquest. Most women adore this sort of thing.'

Alessandro watched her exit the room without fuss. No way was he going to follow her. He had a positive dislike of demanding women, and what could be more demanding than a woman who laid her cards on the table and threatened a walk-out unless her conditions were met?

He hadn't been lying when he had told her that he'd needed to get her out of his system. Whether she wanted to be realistic or not, he also hadn't been lying when he had told her that the same applied to her. If she wanted to ditch what they had, then so be it.

He decided that it just proved beyond the shadow of a doubt how much of a liability a woman like her was. She didn't accept things. She stridently made her opinions felt, even if she could see the opposition all around her. Did he need a woman like that in his life, however good the sex was?

He was assailed by a host of conflicting emotions, but when he tried to pin them down, he found that he couldn't. He could hear her rustling above him, collecting her things. There was a part of him that wanted to try and stop her, but of course, he wasn't going to fall victim to *that* pathetic instinct. Much more overwhelming was his sense of pride, and with pride came a gut-deep certainty that this was a narrow escape.

Finally he heard her half running down the stairs, and she reappeared in the doorway, once more in the clothes in which she had gone out shopping. The dress and all the other accessories had, he assumed, joined the discarded jewellery category.

'I won't tell you that you've blown this out of all proportion,' he heard himself say, in defiance of everything his head was telling him.

'You just did. And if that's your opinion, then you're welcome to voice it.'

'I think you're making a big mistake,' Alessandro said stiffly. For him, this felt like a major concession.

'Oh? And that would be…why? Exactly?'

'What are you going to do when you walk out of this house? Do you imagine that your life is going to slot back to the place it was before we happened to meet? Before we became lovers?'

'No. I don't think it will for a minute, Alessandro.'

Megan looked at him evenly. She was only now really appreciating how different he was from the man she had so stupidly fallen in love with seven years ago, and with whom she was now still so stupidly in love. Alessandro made love like a dream, and could make any woman feel like the sexiest woman on earth, but he was essentially a coldly logical man. He saw only the practicalities of marriage, and didn't shy away from an institution that would further enhance his standing. He was getting older, and how seriously could any man, however brilliant, intuitive and filthy rich, be taken by the People Who Mattered if he approached his forties still with the reputation of being a playboy? For someone whose work was his ruling passion, every scandalous inch in a gossip column would be seen as an erosion into his credibility.

Hence Victoria. She had been his perfect match, because she would never have interfered with his working life.

Realistically, Megan knew that she exercised some power over him—but only in a sexual sense. Her mistake had been to think that he would ever allow passion to rule his life. He hadn't seen her as enhancing his life, more as invading it, and everyone knew what happened to invaders. They were eventually repelled.

It was her misfortune that his role in her life was completely different. If he had been an invading force, then she had been a joyful captive, waving the white flag before he had even had the chance to take up residence. She hadn't so much surrendered before the first tank as begged to be taken on board.

'You said that we needed to get each other out of our

systems.' Megan smiled sadly. 'I think I can honestly say that I've done that. I've got the measure of you, and if my life doesn't go back to the place it was, then I'm hoping that it moves on to an even better place.'

'You've *got the measure of me*?' That sounded very much like criticism to Alessandro, and he was duly outraged. In fact, for the first time in his life he was rendered totally speechless. Not only had she thrown that uncalled-for insult at him, but she was now turning away, clearly seeing no need to follow through with the remark.

'At least,' she said, with a wry smile and one hand on the doorknob, 'there won't be any awkward moments at school. We won't bump into one another.'

For Megan, it had felt dignified to have the last word. She had also succeeded in not making a spectacle of herself. However, those two high points in the evening were lost over the next week or so, as reality set in with a vengeance.

She found it difficult to concentrate at school, and things were made worse when, only ten days after she had staged her walk-out on Alessandro, she was unhelpfully shown a centre spread in one of the tabloids by Charlotte. It featured an extremely riotous-looking Alessandro in the company of several beauties, all of whom were rich young things with family pedigrees coming out of their ears.

He might not be rushing to find another Victoria replacement, she thought bitterly, but he was certainly intent on enjoying himself on the way.

While she had been pining and rehashing their break-up in her head, to the point where she seemed to have a permanent headache, he had been out having fun. She had made her great long speech about putting him behind her and moving on to a better place, but actually all it had amounted to was *blah, blah, blah*.

'Okay.' She looked up from the newspaper to Charlotte, who had tactfully turned away and was reading instructions on the back of a packet of a microwave meal. 'You win. I'm going to get out there and start having some fun of my own.'

Charlotte immediately lost interest in the container in her hand and spun round with a broad grin.

'I know some clubs,' she said, reeling in her fish before it had time to wriggle off the hook. 'I can give you mellow and smoky—not literally, of course, with the smoking ban. Or I can give you *funky*, or upmarket classy… Take your pick.'

Megan, who had always enjoyed going out, and had always seen it as a cure-all for depression, wondered what her friend would say if she were to pick the option of staying in, yet again, with only her thoughts for company. She would probably, Megan thought, throw the microwave meal at her unresponsive head.

After a couple of days of sisterly-style sympathy, Charlotte had adopted the sergeant-major approach to the situation, with lots of bracing advice on moving forward and stirring suggestions on how that might be accomplished. To date Megan had steadfastly ignored them all, because she wanted to enjoy her misery, but now, seeing Alessandro in grainy black-and-white print, laughing, with a drink in one hand and the other hand round the waist of a brunette with legs to her armpits, she decided that it was time to dust herself down and at least make an effort to get on with her life.

'Anywhere,' she said, 'where there are no teenagers. The last thing I need is to feel old as well as miserable.'

'A qualified yes,' Charlotte said, rubbing her hands together in triumph, 'is better than no *yes* at all. We'll start with your hair….'

* * *

It was a form of being managed, and over the next few days, as a particularly hectic week of fractious children eased towards the weekend, Megan was surprisingly relieved to be taken in hand. She spent Saturday morning at the hairdressers, where Charlotte kept a watchful eye on what was being done to her hair like an anxious mother taking her only child for its first haircut. Then they went shopping, where she was made to try on clothes that she would have worn seven years previously but which had gradually morphed into more sensible outfits in keeping with her lifestyle.

'I'm not saying that you need to look like mutton dressed as lamb,' Charlotte assured her, 'but you're not exactly old, so anything in a dark colour, baggy, high-necked or mid-calf is out.'

'I can't afford all of this,' Megan protested half-heartedly.

'It's therapy,' Charlotte informed her, 'of the retail kind, and all therapy comes at a price. Believe me, Megan, the cost of a hairdo and an outfit is a whole lot cheaper than a couple of hours with a shrink....'

But not even an evening of clubbing—or three evenings of clubbing, for that matter—could relieve the dull ache inside her that seemed to be never-ending. Not that she confessed any of that to Charlotte, because her friend's efforts were valiant, and if they weren't entirely successful then it wasn't her fault.

When half-term began looming on the horizon, the week without demanding children that she usually anticipated so eagerly took on the aspect of a nightmare. Enforced leisure time which she didn't want.

Not that there weren't *some* avenues for enjoyment which she could usefully explore.

As an exercise for meeting guys—which was the foundation of much of Charlotte's strenuous efforts in getting her out of the house—the socialising scene hadn't been a total waste of time. True, the men she had met—friends of friends—

hadn't come close to having the sort of dynamic and immediate effect on her nervous system as Alessandro had. But that, she assured herself, was a *good* thing. Remember the motto, she told herself, about frying pans, fires and jumping!

Which was why, in the space of a couple of weeks, she had actually gone out twice with her 'Pick of the Day', so to speak—a lawyer called Stuart, who was a rising star in his firm. He was a tall, good-looking man, with an easy smile and a quiet, affable manner that didn't threaten her nervous system. They had been out once for a meal, which had been fun, and once to the cinema, to see one of those chick flicks which she would have had to have dragged Alessandro to see, kicking and screaming. Megan saw that as a very good omen. A man who would voluntarily sit through a weepie must have a core of sensitivity, and a sensitive man wasn't going to be a heartbreaker.

The Friday before half-term, during which she had decided to get away from London for a few days and clear her head in the Lake District, staying at a B&B she had stayed at years before, on her journey down to London, Stuart phoned to ask her out again. Megan had no hesitation in accepting his invitation. She had already packed her overnight case, which was waiting by the door for her to grab when she left in the morning, and having some fun with a guy who thought she was bright and funny would be just the right start for a relaxing week away from London.

She pulled one of her more glamorous outfits from the batch which she had so optimistically bought when she had been seeing Alessandro, which she had flung into a bin bag and stuffed at the back of her wardrobe the second she'd walked out on him. It was a pale blue dress which was designed to be worn with other soft, falling layers above and underneath, all belted at the waist. At the time it had seemed

a good investment, because layers could be added or sub-
tracted according to the weather. Back then, she had been
thinking *summer*. What a joke that now seemed! They hadn't
even managed to leap into spring!

Stuart came promptly at seven-thirty, and was charmingly
flattering about her outfit. He continued to flatter and cajole
her into feeling happier than she had since she'd walked away
from Alessandro. By ten-thirty, when they arrived back at her
house, she felt at ease about accepting the lips that met hers.

But the kiss wasn't electrifying. Not like… *No! She wasn't
going to go there!* She wrapped her arms around his neck and
really, really tried to inject some passion into returning his
kiss. But her mouth wouldn't oblige, and when he stepped
away from her there was a rueful smile on his face.

'Not working, is it, Megan?' Stuart said.

'It might. In time.'

'And pigs might fly. In time.' He brushed her cheek gently
with one finger. 'Actually, in time but with another guy. I'd
wait around, because you're the kind of girl a man *would* wait
around for, but somehow I don't think I'll ever fit the bill.
So…friends…?'

'Sure. Friends!'

Friends. She could foresee the years stretching ahead,
during which time she would make lots and lots of *friends* and
always end up the bridesmaid but never the bride.

And who did she have to blame? Herself. Alessandro had
ripped her life apart twice, and she couldn't help but think that
whilst once could be excused as an unfortunate event, twice
bordered on downright reckless.

And Stuart would have been such a good catch! She kissed
him regretfully on the cheek, and then hugged him before
waving him off in the direction of the underground.

The house was dark and quiet without Charlotte around.

Megan went to the kitchen, and was gazing thoughtfully at the kettle while it boiled when she heard the sharp peal of the doorbell. Now that Stuart had gone, having had quite a touching farewell, she was a little irritated that he might have returned for a repeat performance. She chastised herself for being so harsh. He was a nice guy, and if he wanted to carry on chatting for a while then she would welcome him in.

She pulled open the door with a smile pinned on her face— and her mouth fell open at the sight of Alessandro, standing on her doorstep. She had been thinking of him only minutes before, as she had waited for the kettle to boil, and she had to blink to dispel the illusion that her feverish imagination had conjured up a ghost.

'I seem to make a habit of turning up on your doorstep,' Alessandro told her wryly, breaking the spell. 'A bit like a stray. I've been trying to work out why that is.'

His inclination was to push past her, get inside the house, demand to find out who the guy was he had seen with her outside only ten minutes before, the guy she had been kissing on the mouth, but he hung back. For starters, since when was it acceptable for an ex to be lurking outside his girlfriend's house, spying? For another, since when did *he*, a man who could have any woman he wanted, *ever* do something as weird as that?

But Alessandro had pretty much given up on finding answers to his behaviour as far as Megan was concerned. The past few weeks had been hellish. He had done his utmost to take the reins by getting out there, reminding himself that there were plenty other fish in the sea. But not only had the plentiful fish been spectacularly disappointing, he had not even been tempted to sample any.

Was this love? He didn't know. He had just reached a point

when he knew that he had to see her. And he had. With another man. Kissing him. But he wouldn't go there.

The knowledge that he might be too late, that she might have moved on, hit him in a tidal rush of urgent panic.

No, he definitely wouldn't mention the other guy, because that would be certain to get her back up and right now Alessandro just wanted to win some Brownie points.

'Forget it.' It took enormous strength to say that, but Megan was rapidly making an assessment of the situation.

Alessandro had been out partying and having fun, had maybe—no, *probably*—slept with some of those beauties she had seen in the newspaper, hanging on to his arm for dear life, but she was still on his mind. And for all the wrong reasons. Sex, lust, unfinished business—not to mention a healthy dollop of flattened male pride because *she* had been the one to do the walking this time. He hadn't had his chance to get sick of her, and now he was back to finish what he had started.

She began closing the door, but he inserted himself neatly into the open space, and pushing against him was like pushing against the Rock of Gibraltar. Megan gave up and glared at him.

'Didn't you hear what I said, Alessandro?' she asked tightly. 'I don't want to see you. I've said everything I wanted to say and I've moved on with my life now.'

Moved on with another man. It was like a punch in the gut. He wondered whether she and the guy had got round to sleeping together yet, and the thought of it sent a red haze of rage through his mind.

'And you've moved on with yours,' she couldn't resist adding.

'What are you talking about?'

'Nothing.' She tried to inch the door shut, but he pushed against it and stepped into the hallway. He didn't know what it was, but this woman drove him to the brink of madness.

'You can't make a statement like that and then refuse to qualify it.'

'You know what I'm talking about!'

Now that he was finally inside, Alessandro felt less like a man teetering on the edge of a precipice. At least he had her full attention. 'I don't.'

'In which case you're stupid. But we both know you're not that!' Megan pressed herself against the wall, her hands behind her back, her eyes blazing with defiant anger. 'I saw all those pictures of you plastered in the newspapers.'

She knew as soon as the words were out of her mouth that he didn't have a clue what she was talking about. He had never, even at university, read the tabloids. He had only ever read the broadsheets. Nothing had changed, and she could have kicked herself for opening herself.

'What pictures?'

Megan took a deep breath and looked at him scornfully. 'Pictures of you having a riotous time with a bevy of beautiful women. And I don't have any objection to that,' she bit out, 'because we're no longer together. In fact, *I've* been having a riotous time of my own, as a matter of fact.' She thought of Stuart and the *riotous time* she had had kissing him and trying to kid herself that it hadn't felt like kissing a slab of wood.

Alessandro felt his spirits soar with satisfaction that she had been following his movements, had been jealous of the women with whom he had pointlessly tried to have a good time. It felt great—until he thought about the riotous time she claimed *she* had been having. Then he crashed back down to earth with supersonic speed.

'You shouldn't read those trashy newspapers,' he gritted. 'And you should know better than to believe that they ever report the truth.'

'Meaning what?' Megan flung at him.

'Meaning that I went out, sure, but if you thought from what you saw that I was having a good time, then you were wrong.'

'Guess what? I don't believe you.' But she *wanted* to.

'I can't blame you.'

Alessandro raked his fingers through his hair and looked at her with unrestrained frustration. He could manipulate any opportunity, had ruthlessly practised the art in many a boardroom, but just at the moment he felt like a man in a straitjacket, desperately struggling to find a way out so that he could swim to shore.

'Look, can we at least go and sit down?'

He could see her struggling with the question, and for a few seconds he wondered what he would do if she refused—if this brand-new life she had apparently found had been a stepping stone for her to move out of his orbit. He cursed himself for not having been more relentless in his pursuit. As it stood, he had let her go, and in so doing had given her a window of opportunity to find herself a replacement.

'I don't see the point,' Megan told him.

'Why?' Natural aggression flowed into Alessandro's veins and he shoved his hands in his pockets. He could feel his resolve to take things easy disappearing fast, like smoke in a high wind.

'Why would I sit down with you when I want you to leave?'

'I should never have let you walk away!'

'You didn't *let* me walk away, Alessandro!' Megan cried. 'I walked away because I *wanted* to!'

'Don't say that!'

'It's the truth.'

'No! The truth is that I...I would have finished with Victoria even if I hadn't found out that there was a third party involved. Or should I say a third party who was *trying* to get involved. I would have finished with her because you were in my head and I wanted to be with you. So you see, Megan, the fact is that my choice would have been for you, but for a mistake in timing.'

'I don't believe you.' Too many disappointments had taken their toll, and Megan looked at him bitterly.

'Then what *do* you believe?'

She drew in one deep, unsteady breath, and her eyes didn't waver as she looked at him, drawing deep from her reserves of courage because even now, after everything, looking at him still made her feel sick and giddy with love. He had said that he had flung himself into having fun, but that he hadn't found the fun he'd thought he would. She believed him. He didn't look like a man who had been out having a good time. In fact, he looked wrecked.

'I think that you do still want me, Alessandro. But I'm not going to bother going down the road of trying to figure out whether what you want is a relationship or not. It doesn't matter. You want me because you know that sooner or later you'll get tired of me, and when that happens you'll be free to move on.'

'And what would you say if I told you that I don't *want* to move on?'

Megan looked at his face, unusually hesitant, and then nodded towards the sitting room.

'Ten minutes.'

Alessandro hadn't realised how tense he had been until he exhaled a deep breath of relief and preceded her into the sitting room, removing his coat en route and resting it on a side table.

'Where's Charlotte?' he asked.

'Out.'

'Is she going away somewhere?'

'Why do you ask?' He had made himself at home on one of the sofas, but Megan still found it hard to relax, and had remained by the door, her arms folded, her defences ready to slam into place at the slightest hint of trouble.

'I noticed a suitcase by the door.'

'That's my case. I'm going away for the half-term week.'

'Your case…'

His mind played with the notion that she might not be going away on her own. Until now he had had an arrogant faith in her dependability on him. Even when they had met again, had resumed their relationship, he had still known that however much she might have hankered for something more she had not been looking around. Now he wasn't too sure. But he shut the door on that meandering, unpleasant thought.

'Whatever you believed about my motivations,' Alessandro said in a raw undertone, 'you were wrong. I've tried to put you out of my mind but I can't, and I want more of you than just an occasional relationship. I know that you're still hankering for a country life, and I have realised that what you want has a pretty high priority in my life. So let's do it, Megan….'

Megan held her breath while frantic hope beat inside her like a drum.

'Let's move in together. A house in the country. Wherever you want.' He hadn't felt dizzy like this when he had contemplated marrying Victoria. For some reason he felt like a man taking a plunge into waters unknown. 'But let's do it soon.'

CHAPTER NINE

ALESSANDRO looked at Megan over the *Financial Times*. She was sitting cross-legged on the sofa, absorbed in a cookery programme. A celebrity chef was giving her tips on how to cook a dish which he knew she would never attempt.

Their move to the country hadn't been quite as dramatic as he had anticipated. She had wanted to still be able to travel to her work, and so they had moved to one of the leafier suburbs of central London, from which she could reach her school on the tube every day. The street was lined with trees, and he had got his people to hunt down the closest he could get to her dream house. It was Grade II listed, with the requisite white fence with roses, and original stained-glass features inside.

Two months ago he had seen this as a highly suitable arrangement. He would have her living with him and his work life would remain largely uninterrupted. His house in central London was empty, and although he had briefly contemplated selling it, he had quickly discarded the idea. It wasn't as though he needed the money.

Now, two months on, he discovered that his work life wasn't what it used to be. He enjoyed being with her, and didn't care to think of her sitting on her own in the house, so he had found himself voluntarily ending his day at a reasonable time so that he could return home. He had even taken to delegating his overseas trips to one of his trusted company directors.

She had asked for none of that. In fact, he thought, looking at her rapt expression as she watched the television, she had demanded nothing from him. He should have been pleased with that, but increasingly he was finding that he wasn't.

He also didn't like the fact that she kept in touch with the loser he had seen her kissing on her doorstep the night he had asked her to move in with him.

It seemed that he was one of Charlotte's friends, and occasionally a crowd of them went out after work for drinks. She made no effort to conceal the fact, and he believed her when she assured him, after some very light questioning, that the man was a nice person and a friend, and they'd both accepted that they were not suited for a relationship.

Alessandro still didn't like it. He wanted her exclusively to himself—by which he meant that he didn't want her to look at another man, talk to another man, far less be *buddies* with another man. Whom she had kissed. It suggested to him that she wasn't giving herself *entirely* to him and he couldn't help wondering if there was a part of her still on the look-out. Had he hurt her so much that he had killed something between them? She was never anything but happy in his company, but niggling doubts were tearing him apart.

He flung the newspaper on the ground. 'You're never going to make that dish, Megan,' he said, shutting the door on the disturbing drift of his thoughts.

'I know, but I live in hope that I might be inspired.' Megan turned to him and grinned. 'It's crazy to have your chef prepare stuff all the time when I'm perfectly capable of cooking. Well, at least of using a recipe book. Now and again.' She went across to him on the sofa, which was a long, very deep, squashy one, quite unlike the cold leather furniture in his Chelsea house.

He was wearing low-slung casual trousers, the ones that had a delicious habit of slipping down his hips, revealing the tightly packed muscles of his torso. Familiarity with his body had done nothing to diminish her craving for him, and she ran her hands over his chest, curling against his body and sighing with pleasure when he pushed his hand under her tee shirt and absentmindedly began caressing her breast. Her nipple predictably tightened into a tight, responsive bud, and she feverishly yanked off the tee shirt, laying herself open to his hungry, dark eyes.

If nothing else, the one thing she knew for sure was that he was greedy for her. Their lovemaking was intense and deeply, deeply satisfying. Right now she wanted him to suckle her nipple, to slip his hand under her panties to where she was hot and wet for him, to send that wonderful fire racing through her veins until she felt giddy and wonderfully out of control.

So much was so good, and this most of all. Two months of pure happiness—although in her quiet moments Megan wondered. He had committed so much, but not once had he even hinted that his commitment might go further. Something held him back. He had never, even in moments of great passion, when every barrier he possessed came tumbling down as his orgasm shuddered through his big body, uttered those three words, *I love you*. Sometimes she figured that there was enough love in her for both of them—although she never let on what she felt, and nor did she ever ask anything of him, mindful of that trait of emotional self-sufficiency which he had found so appealing in Victoria.

Other times, however, there was a dark, destructive voice that reminded her that they might be living together but he still hadn't got rid of his house in Chelsea. She hadn't asked him why that was, and she occasionally wondered whether it was because the bigger part of him, the part that wasn't all wrapped up in touching her, was conscious of the fact that they probably wouldn't remain together. Why ditch his house when he thought he would move back into it sooner or later?

In accepting his offer to move in with him Megan had resigned herself to a life always lived for the moment. With that in mind, she made sure to carry on with her social life, ignoring his frowning disapproval whenever she announced that she would be getting back late. She had also found a firm friend in Stuart, who had slipped into the spot Robbie had held, as a male confidant in whom she had absolute trust. She made sure that she hung on to him—also in the face of Alessandro's frowning disapproval.

In that uncertain place she occupied she would give up a lot, but not everything.

'That feels good.' She sighed, and parted her legs, inviting him to do what he wanted.

Instead, she felt his hand smooth her thigh and resolutely tuck her legs neatly together—which made her sit bolt-upright, because Alessandro, unpredictable in so many ways, was always completely predictable when it came to sex.

'What's the matter?' She drew her legs up and wrapped her arms around them.

'Bad news, I'm afraid. I have to go away on business for a couple of days.'

The surge of bitter disappointment reminded Megan of just how much she had invested in what they had. She had begun to take for granted his daily presence in her life, never once questioning how it was that a workaholic had suddenly become so domesticated. But things would change, and she wondered whether this was the start of it.

'Don't be silly.' She forced a smile. 'Why is that bad news? I do understand that you have an empire to run, you know. As a matter of fact...' she thought quickly, making sure to wriggle out of the box labelled *clingy*, which was anathema to Alessandro '…it's been ages since I met up with all my friends…'

'Ten days.'

'Ten days? Are you sure?'

Oh, Alessandro was sure, all right. She had gone out for a pizza, and amongst their number had been the *good friend* whatever-his-name-was. Alessandro had chosen *not* to actively store that information in his brain.

He was growing more irritable by the second. Was he mistaken, or did she sound *pleased* that she was going to be having a bit of time to herself? He decided to test the water. Yes, he had to be away for two nights—which could easily be extended to four, because there was always a bank of clients with whom he could usefully meet—but really, he wanted to hurry back to her.

'Actually, it's more like four nights. New York.'

To Megan, four nights sounded like eternity.

'Lucky you!' she trilled. 'I've always wanted to go to New York! I don't suppose there's much point asking, but try and take some pictures!'

'You could come with me.' He had never asked a woman to go on a business trip with him—even a business trip which he had only contrived to lengthen on the spur of the moment.

'No chance. School.'

Alessandro scowled. 'A few days away wouldn't result in a generation of drop-outs.'

'True. But I can't.' There was an edginess to his mood that was transmitting itself to her.

'Who are you going to go out with?'

'Oh, just a few friends. Probably a pub.'

That said nothing. Alessandro's mood deteriorated and later, when they made love, there was an aggression that only stopped a little short of savagery.

He told her that he would call. Every day. Megan told him that there was no need, that she would be fine. She was determined to show him self-reliance.

He left for the airport with the ridiculous notion that he had stupidly dug himself a hole by telling her that he would be away at least two days longer than he needed to be.

It left him a hell of a lot of time to wonder whether she would be going out and chatting with the guy she seemed determined to hang on to even though she must *know* that it just wasn't on. At least not in *his* world.

He couldn't concentrate. He repeatedly told himself that it had been a stupid idea to try and tease a response out of her by absenting himself from the scene. And she didn't seem herself when he called her.

Alessandro, who had an office in Manhattan, in one of the seriously tall buildings that dwarfed the street below, swung round in his chair and glared out of the floor-to-ceiling sheet of glass that separated him from a twenty-storey free fall.

He had just got off the phone to her, and although the time difference might have excused her subdued and downright weird response to hearing his voice, he had the sickening feeling that something was wrong.

On the spur of the moment he snatched up the telephone again, drummed his fingers restlessly on the desk as the telephone exchange did its business and connected him through to the landline at the house once again.

It took for ever for her to take the call, making him wonder what he had been interrupting and throwing him into an even darker mood.

'What's the matter?' he delivered tightly, cutting to the chase.

'Matter?' Several thousand miles away, Megan swallowed hard as she bought some time. Of course she should have known that Alessandro would have caught her change of mood. Even when he wasn't looking at her he still seemed capable of reading her like a book.

'Something's wrong. What is it?'

'Nothing. Well…actually, nothing's *wrong*, as such, but… but we need to talk…when you get back…'

'Talk? Talk about what?' Alessandro had bad experiences with Megan's *need to talk* pronouncements, and he was getting a bad feeling now. Suddenly all the meetings he had lined up faded into inconsequence. He would leave New York immediately. He would buy a bloody jet if he had to in order to accomplish that.

'Don't worry, Alessandro…it can wait.'

'Are you sure?'

'Absolutely.'

Wait? She just wished it could wait for ever. She held up the little plastic stick with the prominent positive pregnancy line stamped on it like the decisive hand of fate. A bit of sickness, tenderness in her breasts… It hadn't occurred to her that she might be pregnant until the evening Alessandro had left for New York. She had visited Charlotte for dinner, and after a second dash to the bathroom because she'd felt a little queasy had had the idea planted in her head, when her friend had jokingly asked whether there was 'a bun in the oven'.

Naturally they had been using contraception. Alessandro had taken care of that. But there had been a couple of times when lust had overridden care. And, thinking back, when had she seen her last period anyway? She had always had irregular periods. That absence, in the great scheme of things, hadn't been noticed.

'Don't worry about me,' she told Alessandro now. 'You have fun over there in New York.'

'*Have fun?* I'm here on business, Megan. What the hell do you imagine I'm getting up to?'

'I have no idea,' Megan said waspishly. 'It's your concern!' Tears were gathering at the back of her throat. 'Anyway, I'll see you when you get back, in a couple of days.' At which point she hung up.

He would probably be furious at that, she thought. He would see it as a gesture of defiance—which it hadn't been.

His reaction to the phone call, however, was taking second place to the dilemma raging inside her. All the doubts she had shoved away had crept out of their hiding places and were wreaking long-overdue havoc.

The minute Alessandro found out about this pregnancy he would insist she marry him. After all this time Megan knew him well enough to know that he was a man who was not afraid of committing for the right reasons. Or at least the right reasons *for him*. For reasons that *made sense*. Hence his engagement to Victoria. *She* had made sense. Hence his living with her. It made *sense* to expunge her by having her rather than fight it. A baby would necessitate marriage. That, to him, would make *sense*, because no child of his would be born out of wedlock.

Megan could envisage the Victorian speech even as she sat with the phone in her hand, staring at it.

Did she want to be married to a man who didn't love her? She had agreed to move in with him because she hadn't been able to envisage life without him, because at the back of her mind there had been a thread of hope that she would eventually be able to win him over. But would she be able to face a lifetime knowing that he had married her for the wrong reasons? Connected by a child and in a position where walking away might become an impossibility?

For the first time since she had started her job Megan took the next day off work.

With the silence of an empty house around her, she had

time to really sit down and take stock. Alessandro disliked emotional roller-coaster rides. She had been too much for him seven years ago, and she had tried very hard not to make any demands of him since she had moved in with him. She had never questioned his movements and had maintained her independence. Fat lot of good all *that* had done when he was about to be flung onto the craziest roller-coaster ride of his life. She wondered whether he would resent her for having catapulted him into a situation he would never in a million years have wanted with her. Thinking about that made her feel even sicker than she already felt.

The miserable grey day faded into gathering nightfall, and she drooped around the house, ignoring all phone calls and making sure to switch off her cellphone—because Alessandro would phone again, and she just needed time without hearing his voice.

She hadn't expected to see him. Not when he should have been thousands of miles away. And she was lying on the sofa in the sitting room, nursing the start of a headache, when she felt rather than heard his sudden presence in the room.

He was standing in the doorway and she wondered how long he had been there, looking at her with the strangest expression on his face. The least he could have done was announce his presence by making some noise!

Megan scrambled into a sitting position, the onset of her headache forgotten as she absorbed the deeply sexy man around whom she now felt she had spent *years* orbiting, like a lost little planet trying to fight a gravitational pull that was too powerful for her.

'Wha…what are you doing back here?'

Alessandro looked at her white stricken face and knew that he had been right to have dropped everything and returned.

'You said that you wanted to talk.'

'You flew back here because I said that we needed to *talk*?'

Alessandro was quick to spot the fact that she had replaced *wanted* with *needed*.

'I'm glad,' he asserted, moving towards her.

Before he had left for New York she had been all over him. Now she was watching him cautiously, and he felt a film of perspiration break out over his body. He didn't know what had engineered this change but time apart, not to mention long, hellish hours on the Red-Eye, had put everything into perspective.

'Because I want to talk too.' He swung his long body onto the sofa with her but maintained a certain distance, because he didn't want to be distracted by the proximity of her body. She was looking at him, holding her breath, and Alessandro wondered why it had taken him so long to wake up to the obvious. 'I've been a fool,' he muttered in a low, raw voice, which meant that she had to lean towards him just to catch what he was saying. 'We should never have been apart.'

'You had meetings in New York….'

'That's not what I'm talking about,' he said, waving aside her interruption with an impatient gesture that was so eloquently *him*. 'I mean…' There was a confusing jumble of words inside him, and a panicky desperation for her to hear them. 'Seven years ago…I made a mistake…'

'You did?'

'I was a young, ambitious fool.' He was facing up to a stark truth which he had known from the very first minute she had walked out of his digs at the university, and it felt good to get it off his chest. 'I thought I knew what I wanted.'

'You were never a fool. Maybe young and ambitious, but never a fool.'

'I was a fool to let you walk away from me.' His dark, mesmeric eyes held hers, and Megan felt her heart swoop. This was hardly the conversation she had envisaged, but she was liking it, and hungry to discover where it would lead.

'I thought…'

Alessandro paused, travelling back to a time when he had figured he knew all the answers. From the fluctuations and vagaries of living hand to mouth he would have a life over which he could exercise control—a life which would leave no room for the unpredictable. Megan had been unpredictable. That had been his plan.

'I thought…' He refocused on her. 'I thought that you weren't what I needed. I…I grew up seeing my parents struggle with poverty. It was their constant companion. I was determined never to find myself caught in the same trap, and I thought that the only way to avoid it was to accumulate enough power and wealth to make me invincible. Only then could I be happy. I was wrong. Power and wealth don't bring happiness, and the idea of being in control of every aspect of your life is an illusion. And thank God for that. The thing is, I forgot the one thing I should have had branded in my head from my parents. They might have been broke but they were happy. You were always there, Megan, at the back of my mind and in my heart, and now…'

He shook his head, as if mystified by the inaccurate assumptions he had made. 'I can't live without you,' he told her simply. 'I tried to wrap it all up in something that made sense and I didn't stop to think that when it comes to you—' this time he smiled crookedly '—it's all about winging it. It's not supposed to make sense.' He took her fingers in his hand and idly played with them. 'I know you want to talk about us…maybe tell me that you're having second thoughts about this situation…'

He didn't dare say what else he had thought—that maybe she might want to tell him that he had messed her around just a little too much, that living with him had perhaps opened up her eyes to the fact that she valued her freedom more than she valued his continual presence in her life as a man who refused to commit any further than he thought strictly necessary. Maybe—and this had been the darkest fear of all—she had wanted to tell him that she would rather work on the loser who would probably stick a ring on her finger after the second date than stay around for the man who had resolutely refused to.

Megan was guiltily aware that when it came to second-guessing her motivations he wasn't precisely on cue, but that confession about his childhood had left her breathless. She had only ever had snippets of information about his background, and in a strange way she felt as though a barrier had been breached.

'I don't want to lose you,' Alessandro told her urgently. 'You think I'm a bad bet, but I'm not. I'm…' A *good* bet? Having pretty much told her that he only wanted her around so that he could get her out of his system? Was there a brain cell in his head? 'I'm in love with you, and you can't even think of leaving me.'

'You're in love with me?'

'I think I always have been.'

'You've never, ever said…' Megan was trembling as she looked at his starkly vulnerable face. She felt a lifetime of love swell inside her, and she touched his cheek as if discovering it for the first time.

'Like I said, I was a fool.' He trapped her hand in his and held it tightly. 'I never stopped to ask myself how it was that work became secondary the minute you appeared on the scene. You make me lose focus.'

'And that's a good thing?' Megan asked tremulously.

'It's a very good thing. It's the best thing I've ever known.'

'Are you sure?'

The look he gave her answered that question, and she smiled, her face lit up with joy.

'Because I love you too. I never stopped. Why do you think I agreed to move in with you? It went against reason, but you make me feel...helpless....'

'And that's just the way I like it,' Alessandro told her with immense satisfaction. There was a lot more that he wanted to tell her, and he knew that he would, in time. For the moment he was content to revel in the perfection of the moment. 'But I'd like it even more if you tell me now that you'll be my wife.'

'Yes!' She drew his head towards her and kissed him, and only when she at last opened her eyes once again did she remember why she had needed to talk to him. How on earth could she have forgotten something that had consumed her for the past three days?

'I'm so happy,' she whispered. 'Because...'

'Because...?' Oh, yes, she wanted to have a talk. But Alessandro knew himself to be unassailable. 'You told me on the phone that you wanted to talk to me...?'

'I do...and brace yourself for a bit of a shock... You're going to be a father....'

'I still think that you tricked me when you got me catching the first flight from New York because you wanted to *talk*,' Alessandro told her several months later, as he gazed at her lying next to him in the bed, with their beautiful baby daughter between them. 'You had me worried sick that I might be losing you, and here I am. Not only do I have you, my darling, but I have this miracle lying between us.'

Isabella, whose name they had promptly shortened to Bella, caught his finger and instantly drew it to her mouth.

'If only I was that clever. I would have pulled that trick a lot earlier.' Megan smiled.

It was nearly a year now, and each day was better than the one before. They still lived in the house they had bought in leafy London, and she had continued working right up to the last possible moment—even though he had fussed and fretted like a mother hen, and would have wrapped her in cotton wool for the duration of her pregnancy if he could have. She had stood her ground—something which she now did, safe in the knowledge that it was just one of the things he loved about her. Even more of a revelation had been his admission that he loved her when she was argumentative and stubborn, and he had also told her that if she wasn't possessive with him then he might just be inclined to feel unloved.

So now Megan was the person she was, never hiding anything of herself or editing her personality in any way.

She had even begun buying him the occasional wild item of clothing—and he, a further miracle, had actually worn a few.

'You could, of course, do it again.' He reached across to stroke her face, his dark eyes tender. 'I think it's time I came home and you surprised me with the news that there's another little Bella on the way…'

'Because you're still aiming for that football team…?'

He grinned at her, and they laughed, and Bella's eyes flew open so that she could deliver a glaring reprimand to them both for waking her up.

A private joke. They shared lots of those now, but this one was the dearest held. For Robbie and Victoria had been married around the same time as they had, and they had been the ones to move out to the country, where Victoria had taken up a much less stressed job working for a small firm of lawyers, spending lots of time with Dominic. Right now she was pregnant, with a brother or sister for Dominic, and Robbie had been rash enough to bet that he would be coaching his own personal football team before Alessandro. Something which Megan and Victoria had found very amusing, considering *they* would be the ones giving birth to those amazing prodigies-to-be.

'I would never dare to suggest such a thing, my darling…'
He leant across to kiss her on the lips—a feathery kiss that made her tummy flutter.

'But you're crazy enough to.'

Yes, he thought. This was his life and he loved it. Crazy, in the end, made sense.

* * * * *

THE TIMBER BARON'S VIRGIN BRIDE

BY
DAPHNE CLAIR

Daphne Clair lives in subtropical New Zealand with her Dutch-born husband. They have five children. At eight years old she embarked on her first novel, about taming a tiger. This epic never reached a publisher, but metamorphosed male tigers still prowl the pages of her romances, of which she has written more than thirty for Mills & Boon and more than sixty all told. Her other writing includes nonfiction, poetry and short stories, and she has won literary prizes in New Zealand and America.

Readers are invited to visit Daphne Clair's website at www.daphneclair.com.

CHAPTER ONE

"RACHEL?" BRYN DONOVAN'S grey-green eyes sharpened as he met his mother's cornflower-blue gaze.

Black brows drawing closer together, he sat slightly forward on the dark green velvet of the wing-chair that, like most of the furniture in the room, had been in the family for as long as the big old house. "You don't mean Rachel Moore?"

Pearl, Lady Donovan spread her hands in a surprised gesture. Her slight frame seemed engulfed by the wide chair that matched the one her son occupied on the other side of the brass-screened fireplace.

"Why not?" Her mouth, once a perfect cupid's bow, today painted a muted coral, firmed in a way Bryn knew well. Behind the scarcely lined milk-and-roses complexion and artfully lightened short curls was a keen brain and a will of solid iron.

Bryn said, "Isn't she rather young?"

His mother laughed as only a mother can at a thirty-four-year-old man whose name in New Zealand's business and financial circles engendered almost universal respect. The nay-sayers were mostly competitors jealous of the way he had expanded his family company and increased its already substantial fortunes, or employees who had fallen foul of his rigidly enforced standards. "Bryn," she chided him, "it's ten years since her family left us. Rachel is a highly qualified historian, and I'm sure I told you she's already written a book—in fact, two, I think."

He could hardly tell her he'd tried to expunge all information about the girl from his mind.

Pearl pressed on. "You know your father always intended to write a family history."

"He talked about it." It had been one of the old man's planned retirement projects, until an apparently harmless penchant for the best wines and liqueurs had wreaked a sudden and fatal revenge.

"Well—" the widow's prettily determined chin lifted "—I want to do this as a memorial to him. I thought you'd be pleased." A suspicious sheen filmed her eyes.

Bryn's reputation as a hard-headed though not unprincipled businessman wasn't proof against this feminine form of assault. His mother had emerged from a year and a half of grieving to at last show real interest in something. Her expression today was less strained and her movements more purposeful than since his father's death.

That Rachel Moore's barely seventeen-year-old face under a halo of soft, unruly dark hair, her trusting brown eyes and shockingly tempting, too-young mouth occasionally entered Bryn's dreams, and left him on waking with a lingering guilt and embarrassment, was his own problem. He couldn't in conscience pour cold water on his mother's new project.

He said, "I thought she was in America." Rachel had gone to the States for postgraduate study after gaining her MA in English and history, and had since been teaching university students there.

"She's back." Pearl looked pleased. "She's taking up a lectureship in Auckland next year, but she needs something to tide her over for six months or so because of the different semesters from America. It's ideal, and so nice that we can get someone who isn't a stranger to do this for us. She can stay here—"

"Here? Aren't her parents—" The former estate manager and his wife, who had helped with housekeeping, had left to go sharemilking in the lush green fields of the Waikato district when their daughter started her university studies there. Bryn had vaguely assumed the only contact with his own family since then had been a yearly exchange of Christmas cards and family news. But his mother had always been an inveterate telephone user.

"She's with them now," Lady Donovan told him, "and ready to start in a week or two. She'll need access to our family records, and I wouldn't let them go out of the house." Her expression became faintly anxious. "Of course it will cost, but surely we can afford—"

"No problem," he assured her, reluctantly conceding a rare defeat. "If she wants the job." With any luck Rachel might turn it down.

Pearl gave him her sweetest smile. "Her mother and I have it all arranged."

Rachel had told herself that in ten years Bryn Donovan would have changed, perhaps lost some of his thick, dark hair, developed a paunch from too many business dinners, his aristocratic nose reddened and broadened by the wine imbibed with those dinners if he took after his father. Not that Sir Malcolm hadn't also worked hard and been generous with the fruits of his labours—his knighthood owed as much to his contribution to the national economy as did his public philanthropy.

But his only son and heir was as good-looking as ever.

As she alighted from the bus in Auckland she immediately spotted him among the dozen or so people waiting to greet other passengers or to climb aboard. As if they recognised a man who required more space than ordinary mortals, he seemed to stand apart from those milling around him.

Jeans hugged his long legs. A casual black knit shirt hardly concealed broad shoulders and a lean torso that showed no sign of flab.

If anything had changed much, it was that his habitual understated self-assurance had morphed into a positively commanding presence. Something fluttered in Rachel's midriff and she hesitated on the bottom step of the bus before stepping onto the pavement.

Bryn's eyes seemed silvery in the afternoon light as he inspected the arrivals. When the sweep of his gaze found her and she started towards him, she saw a flash of surprised recognition.

He didn't move, except that his mouth curved slightly into a controlled smile as he watched her approach, while his eyes appraised her jade-green linen jacket over a white lawn blouse, the matching skirt that skimmed her knees, and the Brazilian plaited leather shoes she'd worn for travelling.

He seemed to approve, giving a slight nod before raising his eyes again to the dark hair she'd tamed into a tight knot, which she hoped gave both an illusion of extra height and a mature, businesslike appearance.

Only when she came to a halt in front of him did she

notice the incipient lines fanning from the corners of his eyes, a faint crease on his forehead.

"Rachel," he said, his voice deeper than she remembered. "You look very...smart."

Meaning, she supposed, she was no longer the hoydenish teenager he remembered. "It's been a long time." She was glad her voice sounded crisp and steady, befitting a successful woman. "I've grown up."

"So I see." A spark of masculine interest lit his eyes, and was gone.

Rachel inwardly shivered—not with fear but an emotion even more perturbing. Ten years and he still affected her this way. How stupid was that?

"Your mother...?" she inquired. When Mrs Donovan—Lady Donovan now, Rachel reminded herself—had said on the phone, "But of course we'll pick you up in Auckland... No, you can't struggle onto another bus to Donovan's Falls with your luggage...and a computer, too, I suppose," Rachel hadn't thought "we" meant Bryn.

"She's waiting for us at Rivermeadows," he told her, "with coffee and cakes."

Once they'd collected her luggage and were on their way out of the city in his gleamingly polished BMW, Rachel removed her gaze from the mesmeric, sun-sequined blue of the Waitemata harbour's upper reaches alongside the motorway and said, "Thank you for picking me up. I hope it hasn't inconvenienced you."

"Not at all," he replied with smooth politeness.

"But you don't live at home—I mean, at Rivermeadows now, do you?" she queried, keeping anxiety from her voice. Hadn't her mother said something about Pearl "rattling around alone in that huge house"?

"I have an apartment in the city," he confirmed. "But since my father died I've been spending most weekends with my mother, and occasionally staying during the week. I suggested she move out of the place, but she seems attached to it."

The Donovan estate had once been the centrepiece of a small, scattered rural community, but even before Rachel and her family left, it had become an island of green amongst creeping suburbia, not far from a busy motorway.

"It's only half an hour or so from the city," Rachel reminded him. "Does your mother still drive?" She recalled Pearl Donovan had adored her sporty little cherry-red car, sometimes driving in a manner that caused her husband and son to remonstrate, at which she only laughed, saying they had the common male prejudice about women drivers.

A frown appeared between Bryn's brows. "She's hardly left the house since my father died." He paused, then said with a sort of absentminded reluctance in his tone, "Maybe having you there will be good for her."

If he wasn't overjoyed, it wouldn't have been Rachel's preferred choice, either. When her own mother, so pleased with herself, said she'd found the perfect temporary job for her newly arrived daughter, Rachel had to hide dismay on discovering it was at Rivermeadows.

She'd covered it by saying, "It's…um…so far away from you and Dad." To which her mother replied logically that it wasn't nearly as far as America.

Unable to find a more convincing excuse, especially as the hourly rate was way beyond what she could expect from any other temporary position, Rachel saw no choice but to accept. She didn't intend to sponge on her parents for months.

Hoping she'd mistaken Bryn's decidedly unenthusiastic tone, she said, "I'm looking forward to seeing Rivermeadows again. I have some wonderful memories of it."

He cast an unreadable glance at her that lingered for a tiny moment before he switched his attention back to the road.

Rachel turned to look out of the window, trying not to think about one particular memory, having sensibly persuaded herself that he'd have forgotten the incident entirely. It might have been a defining moment in her young life, but while she'd been a bedazzled teenager with an overflow of emotion, even back then Bryn was already a man, someone she'd always thought of as one of the grown-ups.

She said, "I was sorry to hear about your father." Risking a quick look at Bryn, whose expression now appeared quite indifferent, she added, "I sent a card to your mother."

He nodded. "His death was hard on her."

The frown reappeared, and Rachel said softly, "You're worried about her."

"It's that obvious?"

About to say, *Only to people who care about you,* she stopped herself. He'd think she was presuming on an old acquaintance, and rightly so. Devoutly she hoped he had never realised how closely she'd watched his every movement or expression for a whole year or more every time he came near.

Since then she'd become a different person, and maybe he had too. At twenty-five he'd been handed full responsibility for a new sector of the Donovan business, Overseas Development. And he'd run with it, done spectacularly well at bringing the Donovan name to the notice of international markets and establishing subsidiaries in several countries. Now he was in charge of the entire company. No wonder he gave the impression of a man who had the world securely in his fist and knew exactly how to wring from it every advantage.

The house was as Rachel remembered it, a beautifully preserved, dormered two-storey mansion of white-painted, Donovan-milled kauri timber, dating from the late nineteenth century. Its upper windows were flanked by dark green shutters, and a rather grand front veranda extended into a pillared portico.

Old oaks and puriris and the magnificent magnolia that bore huge creamy, fragrant cups of blossom, cast their benign shadows over the expansive lawn and gardens, and the half circle of the drive was still edged with lavender and roses.

Bryn stopped the car at the wide brick steps leading to the ornate front door sheltered by the portico. Almost immediately the door opened and Pearl Donovan, wearing a pale lemon, full-skirted dress, stood for a moment, then hurried down the steps. Rachel went to meet her and was enveloped in a warm, scented hug, her cheek kissed.

"How nice to see you!" Lady Donovan stepped back with her hands on Rachel's shoulders to inspect her. "And you've grown so lovely! Isn't she lovely, Bryn? Quite beautiful!"

Bryn, having removed Rachel's luggage from the car, had his hands full, the laptop case slung over one shoulder. "Quite," he said. "Where do I put her stuff?"

"The rose room," his mother told him. "I'll go and put on the kettle now, and when you're settled, Rachel, we'll have coffee on the terrace."

Rachel followed Bryn up the staircase to one of the big, cool bedrooms. The door was ajar and Bryn pushed it wide with his shoulder, strode across the carpet to a carved rimu blanket box at the foot of the double bed covered in dusky-pink brocade, and deposited the suitcase on top of the box, the smaller bag holding her reference books on the floor. "Do you want your laptop on the desk?" he asked. "Although you'll probably be working in the smoking room downstairs."

It was many years, Rachel knew, since anyone had smoked in what was really a private library, but it retained its original name within the family.

She nodded. "Thank you," she said, and Bryn placed the computer on an elegant walnut desk between long windows flanked by looped-back curtains that matched the bed cover.

He looked about at the faded pink cabbage roses that adorned the wallpaper. "I hope you'll be comfortable," he said. Obviously he wouldn't have been.

Rachel laughed, bringing his gaze to her face. His mouth quirked in response, and the skin at the corners of his eyes crinkled a little. "My mother's right," he said. "You have grown up beautiful."

Then he looked away. "Your bathroom's over there." He nodded to a door on one side of the room. "You'll have it to yourself. If you don't find everything you need, I'm sure my mother will provide it. I'll see you downstairs."

He crossed to the door, hesitated a moment and turned. "Welcome back, Rachel."

She heard his soft footfalls on the hall runner, then on the stairs, still muffled but faster, as though he were hurrying away from her.

After freshening up and exchanging her shoes for cool, flat-heeled sandals, Rachel went downstairs and crossed the big dining room to the French windows that led onto the brick-paved terrace.

Bryn and his mother were sitting at a glass-topped cane table. A large tray held cups and saucers and a china coffee pot with matching milk and sugar containers.

Bryn got up immediately and pulled out another cushioned cane chair for Rachel. The grapevine overhead on its beamed support shadowed his face, and dappled his mother's dress.

While Lady Donovan poured coffee and talked, he sat back in his chair, looking from her to Rachel with lazy interest that might have been feigned. There was a vitality about Bryn, a coiled-spring quality that didn't fit easily with leisurely afternoon teas. He curled his hand around his cup as he drank, and his eyes met Rachel's with a hint of amusement as his mother opened a barrage of questions about life in America.

When their cups were empty Rachel offered to help clear up. But Pearl, who had insisted Rachel was old enough now to call her by her given name, shook her head. "I'll deal with these. We haven't brought you here to do housework. Bryn, take Rachel around the garden and show her the changes we've made."

Bryn, already standing, raised an eyebrow at Rachel and when she got up put a hand lightly under her elbow, his fingers warm and strong.

"Who does do the housework?" she asked him as they descended the wide, shallow steps that brought them to ground level. Surely it was too much for one person.

"We have a part-time housekeeper." He dropped his hand as they reached the wide lawn. "She comes in the afternoon three times a week but doesn't work weekends."

They crossed the grass, passing the solar-heated swimming pool that had been retiled in pale blue, refenced with transparent panels and was almost hidden among flowering shrubs. Their feet crunched on a white-shell path winding through shrubs and trees underplanted with bulbs and perennials and creeping groundcovers.

The Donovans had allowed Rachel and her brothers free rein in the garden on condition they didn't damage the flowerbeds. She had loved playing hide-and-seek, stalking imaginary beasts, or climbing the trees, and knew all the hidden places under low-hanging branches or in the forks of the old oaks and puriris.

"The fish have gone," she said as they walked under a sturdy pergola—a recent addition—smothered by twining clematis, into an open space paved in mossy bricks. Two rustic seats invited visitors to admire a bed of roses instead of the goldfish pond she remembered.

"Too much maintenance," Bryn told her, "and mosquitoes loved it."

Wandering in the shade of tall trees, they eventually came to a high brick wall. Where there had once been a gate giving access to the house her family had lived in, an arched niche held baskets of flowering plants.

"You know we leased out the farm and cottage?" Bryn asked her, and she nodded, hiding a smile. Only someone who'd lived in a mansion could have called the estate manager's house a cottage.

The path veered away from the wall towards an almost hidden summerhouse, its tiled roof moss-covered and latticed walls swathed in ivy geranium and bare winter coils of wisteria.

Rachel hoped Bryn hadn't noticed the hitch in her step

before they walked past it. She didn't dare look at him, instead pretending to admire the pink-flowered impatiens lining the other side of the path, until they came to another pergola that a star jasmine had wound about, bearing a few white, fragrant blooms.

Rachel touched a spray, breathing in its scent and setting it trembling.

A lean hand reached past her and snapped the stem.

She looked up as Bryn handed the flowers to her. "Thank you," she said, suddenly breathless. They stood only inches from each other. His eyes were on her face, his expression grave and intent and questioning. She ducked her head to smell the jasmine and, turning to walk on, brushed against him, her breasts in fleeting contact with his chest.

Heat burned her cheeks, and when Bryn caught up with her she kept her gaze on the jasmine, twirling the stalk back and forth in her fingers as they walked.

And because she wasn't looking where she was going, a tree root that had intruded onto the path took her by surprise and she tripped.

Bryn's hands closed on her arms, his breath stirring a strand of hair that had fallen across her forehead. "Are you all right?"

"Yes. Thanks." Her bare toes stung but she didn't look down, giving him what she hoped was a reassuring smile.

He drew back, checked her feet and hissed in a short breath.

"You're bleeding." He released her arms to hunker down, his hand closing about her ankle. "Lean on me," he ordered, lifting her foot to his knee so she had no choice but to put a hand on his shoulder to balance herself.

"I'll bleed all over you," she protested. "It's nothing."

His hand tightening as she tried to withdraw her ankle, he glanced up at her. "Looks painful," he said. "Let's get you back to the house." Standing up, he placed a firm hand under her elbow again. Inside, he steered her to the downstairs bathroom and, ignoring her claim that she could manage on her own, sat her on the wide edge of the deep, old-fashioned bath and found a first-aid kit in a cupboard. He let her wash her injured foot, then patted it dry with a towel, dabbed on disinfectant and wrapped a toe plaster around the wound.

"Thank you," she said, picking up her discarded sandal and standing as he put away the first-aid box. She'd dropped the jasmine on the counter next to the washbasin and he picked it up as he turned to her again.

Instead of handing it to her he tucked the stalk into the knot of hair on top of her head, gave her an enigmatic little closed-mouth smile, then ushered her out with a light touch at her waist.

Pearl came out from the kitchen, saying, "Are you staying, Bryn? I've got a nice bit of pork in the oven."

He checked his watch. "For dinner, thanks. But I'll be off after that."

Noticing the sandal in Rachel's hand, and the dressing on her toe, Pearl said, "Oh! Are you hurt?"

"Just a stubbed toe," Rachel said, and after assuring his mother she was fine, left Bryn to explain while she went upstairs to unpack.

When she came down again he and Pearl were in what the family called the "little sitting room", as opposed to the much larger front room suited to formal entertaining.

Bryn held a glass of something with ice, and Pearl was sipping sherry. Bryn rose and offered Rachel his wing-backed chair, but she shook her head and sat on the small, ornate sofa that with the chairs completed a U shape in front of the brass-screened grate.

"A drink?" Bryn said, still on his feet. "I guess you're old enough now."

"Of course she is," Pearl said. To Rachel, she confided, "He still thinks of you as a little girl."

"Not so, Mother," he told her, but his eyes, with a disconcerting gleam in their depths, were surveying Rachel. "Although," he drawled, dropping his gaze to her feet, "the plaster does seem like old times." Transferring his attention back to her face, he teased, "You had a hair-raising sense of adventure as a kid."

Quickly she said, "I've grown out of that. I'd like a gin and bitters if you have it, thanks."

Without further comment, he crossed to the old kauri cabinet that served as a drinks cupboard and disguised a small refrigerator. After making the drink he dropped a half slice of lemon into the glass before presenting it to her.

Pearl asked what Rachel thought of the garden, and when complimented said, "A local man comes once a week to keep it tidy and I potter about with the flowers. We've leased out the farm, so there's only the grounds around the house to look after. Bryn suggested *selling* the place—" she cast him scandalized glance that he received imperturbably "—but I hope to have grandchildren some day, and keep the place in the family. After all, Donovans have lived here since it was built. And owned the land even before that."

"It's a wonderful place for children." Rachel didn't look at Bryn. His older sister had moved to England, was living with another woman and, according to Rachel's mother, had declared she never intended to have children. Obviously Bryn was in no hurry to carry on the family name.

At thirty-four, he still had time and with his looks and his money, probably plenty of choice.

The thought gave her a foolish pang. She wondered if he had a girlfriend, and shook her head impatiently to dislodge the thought.

Bryn said, "Something wrong, Rachel?"

"No. I thought—a moth or something…"

"Maybe some insect you picked up from the garden."

He got up and came near, looking down at her hair. Pearl finished her drink and rose from her chair. "I'll go and check on our dinner."

"Can I help?" Rachel asked. But Bryn was blocking her way.

"No, no!" Pearl said. "You stay here. I have everything under control."

Rachel felt Bryn's touch on her hair. "Can't see any creepy-crawlies," he assured her. "When did you grow your hair long?"

"Ages ago," she told him. "While I was at university." It was easier than trying to find someone who could make something remotely sophisticated of her unruly curls.

Instead of returning to his chair, he sank down on the sofa, resting his arm on the back of it as he half turned to Rachel. "How is the toe?"

"Fine. I told you, it's nothing."

"You always were a tough little thing." His mouth curved. "It's hard to believe you're the same scrawny kid with the mop of hair who used to run about the place in bare feet, half the time with skinned knees or elbows."

"Children grow up."

"Yes. I had noticed before you—" He stopped abruptly, staring moodily at the screened fireplace. His voice altered when he spoke again, sounding a little strained. "What happened, before your family left—I'm sorry if I hurt you, scared you, Rachel. I was…" He raked a hand through his hair and turned to look steadily at her. "I wasn't myself. And that's no excuse. But I do apologise."

Rachel bowed her head. "Not necessary. It wasn't just you."

"You were barely out of high school. I should have—I *did* know better."

"Well," she said, lifting her head and making her voice light and uncaring, "that was a long time ago. I'm sure we'd both forgotten all about it until today." Her gaze skittered away from him as she uttered the words.

One lean finger under her chin brought her to face him again. "Had you? Forgotten?"

In ten years Rachel had acquired some poise. Her smile conveyed both surprise and a hint of amused condescension. "Men *so* like to think they're unforgettable," she said kindly, taking his hand from her chin and laying it on his knee. "Of course it all came back to me when I saw you." She patted his hand before withdrawing hers. "Just as if I were seventeen again, with a schoolgirl crush on an older man." Ignoring the twitch of his brows at that, she shook her head, laughing lightly. "Such a cliché, it's embarrassing."

His jaw tightened. A glint appeared in his eyes as he looked at her searchingly, and for a moment she held her breath, before he gave a short laugh of his own. "All right," he said. "I guess I've got off lightly, at that."

Rachel rather thought she had, too.

At dinner Bryn asked Rachel about her work in America and her research and writing experience.

She realised she was being grilled about her qualifications when he said, "This is a bit different, isn't it? How long do you think you'll need to complete it?"

"I hope to produce a first draft in three or four months," she said. "You have so much raw material, it gives me a head start. I won't have to begin by hunting for all the sources I need."

Bryn looked at Pearl. "Do you know exactly what's there?"

Pearl shook her head. "Supposing we found some old family scandal! Wouldn't that be fun?"

"You may not find it fun if you do," Bryn warned.

His mother looked only slightly quashed. "Oh, don't be stuffy, darling! We don't want some dull list of births, deaths and marriages and profit-and-loss accounts."

Rachel said, "I'm sure there'll be plenty of interesting events to colour the bare facts. By the way, do you have a scanner and printer, or is there someplace I can access one? I don't want to handle old documents more than necessary."

Bryn said, "When do you need it?"

"At a guess, in a few days, when I've had time to see what's here."

"I'll see to it. If you need Internet access, I've set it up in the smoking room because I use it when I'm here."

Bryn left shortly after dinner. He kissed his mother goodbye and said, "Rachel...a word?"

She followed him along the wide, dim passageway to the front door, where he stopped and looked down at her without immediately speaking.

Rachel said, "You needn't worry about the book, really. You—or your mother—are paying for it, and have total control over what goes in, or doesn't."

He smiled faintly. "I'm sure we can trust your discretion, Rachel. It's my mother I'm concerned about. She's always been inclined to go overboard on any new enthusiasm. If she looks like tiring herself out I'd appreciate it if you'd let me know, quietly."

Years ago she'd have blindly agreed to anything Bryn asked of her. But she didn't fancy going behind Pearl's back. "If I see anything to be worried about," she said carefully, "of course I'll do whatever's necessary."

He didn't miss the evasion. "She's not as strong as she likes to pretend."

"If you think she needs a nursemaid—"

Bryn gave a crack of laughter. "She'd skin me alive if I suggested it."

"Hardly." Her tone dry, she let her gaze roam over his tall, strong body before returning to his face.

He watched her, his mouth lifting at one corner, a faint glow in his eyes. "I wasn't suggesting you add nursemaid to your duties. It's good she has someone in the house anyway." He paused. "This scanner-printer. Any particular specifications?"

"A good OCR programme. It needs to read documents." She told him the make and model of her computer. He opened the door, hesitated, then leaned towards her and touched his lips briefly to her cheek. "Good night, Rachel."

After closing the door behind him she stood for a moment, the warmth of his lips fading from her skin, then mentally she shook herself and turned to see Pearl come out of the kitchen at the end of the passageway.

"What did Bryn want?" the older woman asked.

"Oh, it was about the scanner," Rachel said. Then she

added, "And he said he's glad you have someone in the house."

"He worries too much. I love this place, and I intend to stay until they carry me out in a box. Or until Bryn has a family and moves in—should they want to."

"I'm sure he wouldn't want you to leave if he did that."

"His wife might. And I might too by then." Rather wistfully Pearl tacked on, "If it ever happens."

By which time Rachel would be long gone, she told herself. Not that it mattered anyway.

CHAPTER TWO

BRYN DROVE OFF feeling oddly dissatisfied with himself. At least they'd brought that old business into the open, and that should have cleared the air between him and Rachel, as well as easing his conscience. He'd sensed a constraint in her from the moment their eyes met at the bus terminal, and he didn't believe her claim that she'd not given any subsequent thought to their last meeting. A soft, rueful laugh escaped him, remembering the deliberate put-down with which she'd denied it. "Rather overdoing it there, honey," he murmured aloud.

She certainly was different from the rather gauche innocent who sometimes reappeared in his dreams. If she'd never had a similar nocturnal problem he ought to be relieved, but at first he'd felt nothing but chagrin, and had to quell an impulse to exact a sweet revenge on her lovely mouth even as it mocked him.

Instead he'd swallowed the unaccustomed medicine like a man, because she was entitled.

There was an intriguing dislocation between the Rachel Moore he remembered and the Rachel he'd met today. Now and then a glimpse of the ardent, uncomplicated girl peeked through the cool reserve of the woman, arousing in him a capricious desire to probe deeper and find out just how much she had really changed.

A glance at the clock on the dashboard reminded him his departure was later than he'd intended. He'd been seeing a lot of Kinzi Broadbent lately, and he'd half promised to drop in after delivering the historian his mother had hired to Rivermeadows. But he hadn't even thought to call Kinzi.

Already on the motorway, he didn't want to use his mobile phone. For some reason he didn't feel like seeing Kinzi now. Instead he drove home and phoned her from there, saying he'd stayed for dinner with his mother, was tired and wanted an early night. Although she accepted the excuse, her voice was a little clipped as she wished him a good sleep. He'd have to make it up to her.

Three days later Rachel was in the smoking room, sorting through boxes of old letters, diaries and papers and spreading the contents over the big table—made of a single slab of thousand-year-old kauri—that dominated the space.

The door opened and Bryn strode in carrying a large cardboard box. Absorbed in her task, she hadn't heard the car.

"Your scanner," he said. "Where do you want it?"

"On the desk?" She stripped off the gloves she was wearing to handle the fragile old documents and hurried to clear a couple of boxes from the heavy oak desk in a corner of the room where she'd placed her computer. "I didn't expect you to deliver it yourself."

"I wanted to check on my mother."

"She seems fine. Did you see her on your way in?"

He'd taken a paper knife from a drawer and began slitting the tape on the carton. "Yes, busy watering potted plants on the terrace. She's excited about this," he said, nodding towards the documents on the table. "How's it coming along?"

"Deciding what to leave out may be a problem. There's such a wealth of material."

They connected the machine to her laptop and she sat down to test it while Bryn stood leaning against the desk.

A sheet of paper eased out of the printer and they both reached for it, their fingers momentarily tangling. Rachel quickly withdrew her hand and Bryn shot her a quizzical look before picking up the test page and scrutinising it. "Looks good," he said, passing it to her.

"Yes." Rachel kept her eyes on the paper. "Thank you. It'll be a big help."

"Glad to oblige," he answered on a rather dry note.

Looking up, she found him regarding her with what seemed part curiosity and part…vexation? Then he swung away from the desk and strolled to the table, idly studying the papers laid out there, some in plastic sleeves. Carefully turning one to a readable angle, he said, "What's this?"

She went over to stand beside him. "A list of supplies for the old sawmill, with notes. Probably written by your great-great-grandfather." Samuel Donovan had built his first mill on the banks of the nearby falls, using a water-wheel to power it. "You haven't seen it before?"

Bryn shook his head. "I know who's in the old photographs my father got framed and hung in the hallway, they have brass plaques, but I had no idea we'd have original documents in old Sam's handwriting. It's an odd feeling." He studied the bold writing in faded ink. "Intimations of mortality."

"There are letters, too." Rachel pointed out a plastic

envelope holding a paper browning at the edges and along deep, disintegrating creases where it had been folded. "This one is to his wife, before they were married."

"'Dearest one,'" Bryn read aloud, then looked up, slanting a grin at her. "A love letter?"

"It's mostly about his plans to build her a house before their wedding. But he obviously loved her."

His eyes skimmed the page, then he read aloud the last paragraph. "'I am impatient for the day we settle in our own dear home. I hope it will meet with your sweet approval, my dearest. Most sincerely yours, with all my heart, Samuel.'"

Lifting his head, Bryn said, "Quite the sentimentalist, wasn't he? You'd never have thought it from that rather dour portrait we have."

"That was painted when he was middle-aged and successful and a pillar of the community." The man in the portrait had curling mutton-chop whiskers and a forbidding expression. "When this was written—" she touched a finger to the letter "—he was a young man in love, looking forward to bringing home his bride."

"Looks like he's won your heart, too." Bryn was amused.

"I think it's rather touching," Rachel admitted. Bryn would never write something like that, even if he were headlong in love. "There's some wonderful stuff here for a historian. I can't wait to read it all."

He was studying her face, and said, "I remember you had much the same light in your eyes after your dad bought you a pony and you'd had your first-ever ride. You came bursting in at breakfast to tell us all about it."

"And got told off for that," she recalled. Her father had hauled her out of the big house with profuse apologies to his employers. It was then she became conscious of the social gap between the Donovans and her own family, although the Donovans had never emphasised it.

"Do you still ride?" Bryn asked.

"Not for years."

"There's a place not far from here where I keep a hack that I ride when I can. I'm sure they'd find a mount for you if you're interested."

"I'll think about it. But I have a lot to do here."

"Hey," he said, raising a hand and brushing the back of it across her cheek, "you can't work all the time. We hired a historian, not a slave."

She tried not to show her reaction to his casual touch, the absurd little skip of her heart. Her smile was restrained. "I'm certainly not on slave wages. The pay is very generous."

"My mother's convinced you're worth it."

"I am," she said calmly, lifting her chin. She would show him she was worth every cent before she finished this job.

His eyes laughed at her. "You haven't lost your spark. I don't doubt that, Rachel. I trust my mother's judgement."

"I had a feeling that you have definite reservations."

"Nothing to do with your ability."

"Then what…" she began, but was interrupted by his mother coming into the room, offering afternoon tea on the terrace.

"Or actually coffee. Unless you prefer tea, Rachel?"

Rachel said coffee was fine.

A few minutes later over their cups she said, "You really should have the records properly archived and safely stored, in acid-proof envelopes and containers. If you had those I could start doing that as I work."

"Buy whatever you need," Bryn said.

"You won't find anything like that in the village," Pearl

warned. "You'd have to go into the city. I told you, didn't I, there's a car you can use?"

"Yes." It had been one more incentive for Rachel to take this job, not needing to think yet about investing in a car.

Bryn asked her, "You do have a licence?"

"Yes. I need to get used to driving on the left again."

"You'd better go with her," Bryn told his mother, and shortly afterwards said he had to leave. The house seemed colder and emptier when his vital presence was gone.

When Pearl hadn't broached the subject by the end of the week, on Friday Rachel asked if it would be convenient to drive into the city.

"I suppose you don't want to go alone?" Pearl asked.

About to say she'd be quite okay, Rachel recalled Bryn's concern about his mother's reluctance to leave Rivermeadows.

Misconstruing her hesitation, Pearl said in a breathless little rush, "But if you're nervous, of course I'll come."

The garage held a station wagon as well, but the red car that Pearl used to drive had gone, its place taken by a compact sedan.

In the city Pearl directed Rachel to a car park belonging to the Donovan office building, and used a pass card for Rachel to drive the sedan into one of the parking bays.

As they shopped for the things on their list, the older woman seemed ill at ease, sticking close by Rachel's side. After they'd made their major purchases and Rachel suggested they have a coffee and a snack in one of the cafés, Pearl barely paused before agreeing. Waiting for their order to be brought, she looked about with an air of bemusement, as if unused to seeing so many people in one place.

Coffee and the cake seemed to make her a little less

tense. Later, as they stowed their purchases in the car, she paused and looked up at the looming Donovan's Timber building. "Why don't we call in on Bryn while we're here?"

"Won't he be busy?" Rachel wasn't sure how Bryn would feel about being interrupted in business hours.

"We needn't stay long," Pearl said. "Just to say hello."

"I'll wait for you here."

"No!" Pearl insisted. "I'm sure he'll be pleased to see you." Less sure, and wondering if Pearl didn't want to enter the big building alone, Rachel followed her into the marble-floored, wood-panelled lobby.

A silent elevator delivered them to the top floor, where Bryn's secretary, a comfortably rounded middle-aged woman wearing huge, equally round glasses, greeted Pearl with surprised pleasure and ushered them both into his office. Rachel was warmed by the approving glance he sent her after greeting them both and suggesting they sit down in two deep chairs before his rather palatial desk.

"Just for a minute," Pearl said, and proceeded with some animation to tell him about their shopping expedition while Rachel admired their surroundings.

Like the lobby, Bryn's office was wood-panelled, the carpet thick and the furnishings solid and practical but obviously made and finished with expensive care.

The whole building spoke discreetly of prosperity and excellent workmanship—not new but magnificently modernised and maintained without spoiling its original character. While building their little empire from one country sawmill to a huge timber enterprise, and diversifying into paper production and even newspapers, the Donovans hadn't lost sight of their history.

It was fifteen minutes before Pearl declared they mustn't

take any more of Bryn's time. He got up to see them out, Rachel standing back to let Pearl go first. As she made to follow, Bryn closed a hand lightly about her arm, murmuring, "Thank you."

Rachel shook her head to indicate she hadn't done anything, but when he smiled at her she felt a momentary warm fizz of pleasure before they followed his mother through the outer office and he pressed the button for the elevator.

Pearl asked him, "Will we see you this weekend?"

"Not this time, I've made other plans."

"Oh—with Kinzi?" She gave him an arch glance of inquiry.

"Yes, actually."

Rachel, her gaze fixed on the rapidly changing numbers signalling the elevator's rise from the ground floor, was relieved when a "ding" sounded and the doors whispered open.

Rachel worked most of Saturday, but Pearl insisted she take Sunday off, adding, "You're welcome to use the car."

"I'll just go for a nice long walk, see what's changed. I need the exercise." Accustomed to working out at a gym, she had neglected her physical fitness since coming here.

Much of the farmland she remembered had been cut into smaller blocks occupied by city workers who hankered after a country lifestyle or whose daughters fancied a pony. The village of Donovan Falls, once a huddle of rough huts about Donovans' long-vanished sawmill, and later a sleepy enclave of old houses with one general store, had grown and merged into the surrounding suburb.

The little pioneer church the Donovans and the Moores

had attended sparkled under a fresh coat of paint. And the falls named for Samuel Donovan, who had used the power of the river for his mill, were still there, the focus of several hectares of grass and trees donated to the community by Bryn's father, a memorial plaque commemorating the fact. People picnicked under the trees, and children splashed in the pool below the waterfall.

Watching the mesmerising flow make the ferns at its edges tremble as the sun caught tiny droplets on the leaves, Rachel wondered what Bryn was doing.

Whatever it was, he was doing it with a woman called Kinzi. At first she'd thought—not admitting to *hoped*—that "Kinsey" might be male, but Pearl's knowing, interested expression had dispelled any chance of that.

On the journey home from their trip into the city Rachel had suppressed a persistent curiosity while Pearl hummed a little tune to herself in brief snatches and engaged in only small bites of conversation. Rachel had an irrational idea that she was mentally counting potential grandchildren.

And there was no reason to feel ever so slightly irritated about that.

In the afternoon she caught up with her family and friends by e-mail, and on Monday was glad to get back to sorting through the Donovan records.

Pearl helped where she could, explaining family connections or identifying people in photographs. But she was outside dead-heading plants when the phone rang. Rachel picked up the extension in the smoking room and answered.

"Rachel?" Bryn's deep voice said.

"Yes, your mother's in the garden. I'll call her."

"No, I'll catch up with her later. Everything all right?"

"She's fine and the work is going well."

"Did you have a good weekend?" he asked.

"Yes, thank you."

There was a short, somehow expectant silence. Was he waiting for her to reciprocate and ask how *his* weekend was? The thought hollowed her stomach.

Then he asked, "What did you do?"

Briefly she told him, not supposing he was really interested.

He said, "Next weekend I'll take you riding. Unless you've made other plans."

"I haven't thought about it yet—"

"Good. Sunday, around ten. See you then."

He'd put down the phone before she could refuse. And she didn't really want to.

He must have mentioned the plan to his mother, because after talking to him that night, Pearl told her, "Bryn said you're riding together on Sunday. It'll be nice for him to have a companion. I don't think Kinzi rides at all."

"His girlfriend?" Rachel's voice was suitably casual.

Pearl sighed. "Maybe something will come of it this time. They've been seeing each other for quite a long time."

On Sunday Bryn turned up with a long-legged, green-eyed redhead. Her hair was cut in a short, straight, jagged style that would have cost a modest fortune. A primrose cashmere sweater and skinny jeans hugged a figure that most women would give a whole mouthful of teeth for, and high-heeled ankle-boots brought her near to Bryn's height. A short denim jacket finished the deceptively casual outfit.

Kinzi gave Rachel a dazzling smile on being introduced and announced she was here to keep Pearl company while Bryn and "Rachel, isn't it?" went off to "do your horsy thing". On a rueful note she added, "The only time I got on a horse the brute threw me." She laughed, a surprisingly hearty sound. "I know about getting back on and all that, but I thought, why should I? You don't ride, do you, Lady Donovan?"

Pearl shook her head. "It's kind of you to sit with an old lady, my dear. But not at all necessary. And please, let's dispense with the title."

Rachel had to choke back laughter at the uncharacter-istic, almost querulous tone of Pearl's little speech. Meet-ing Bryn's slightly pained expression, belied by the amused appreciation in his eyes, she knew he hadn't missed it, but Kinzi didn't seem to notice.

Whether his bringing Kinzi along had been her own idea or Bryn's, Rachel was very sure Pearl Donovan didn't, and probably never would, think of herself as an old lady.

Perhaps it was the look she turned on her son that made him say, "Ready, Rachel? We'll get going then."

She had put on jeans and sneakers with a sweatshirt and was relieved to see that he, too, was casually dressed, although he wore riding boots.

In the car she told him, "Did your mother mention she had some visitors this week?"

"She asked them to come?"

"I don't think so. They were passing through, I gather." Pearl had invited Rachel to join them for afternoon tea, but she'd declined, not wanting to intrude. Afterwards Pearl had seemed quite animated, describing the middle-aged couple as old friends and saying what a nice chat they'd had.

They were the first visitors Rachel had seen apart from Kinzi. Pearl certainly wasn't doing as much entertaining as she used to. "I think their name was McGill," she told Bryn.

He nodded. "They used to live in Auckland until they retired to a beach community up north. I don't think she's seen them since the funeral. In fact after the first couple of months hardly anyone visited. She hasn't shown any interest in resuming a social life without Dad."

"Give her time," Rachel murmured.

Bryn didn't look convinced. He wasn't used to standing by and letting things happen at their own pace.

The place he drove to offered trail rides and treks, as well as plenty of rolling, open countryside and stands of dark, mossy native bush.

Bryn's big bay gelding seemed pleased to see him, and the owner supplied a pretty, soft-mouthed little mare for Rachel.

They started out at a sedate walk along a broad trail that wound through thick bush, but later when Rachel had got the feel of her mount, enjoyed a glorious gallop across green paddocks under a cloud-dusted sky, ending on a high knoll that overlooked rolling hills and a distant view of the Pacific.

There they rested the horses and dismounted, removing their helmets to admire sheep-dotted paddocks, blue-green stands of old bush in the folds of the hills, and the deep azure line of the horizon.

A few grey rocks seemed to grow out of the ground before them, and they sat side by side on one with a flat, slightly sloping top. Rachel rested her elbows on her thighs, her chin in her hands. At their feet grasses with plumed seed-heads bent before a sudden breeze that stirred her hair, loosening a few tendrils from their confining knot.

For long minutes neither she nor Bryn spoke. Then Rachel said almost to herself, "I never realised how much I missed New Zealand until I came home."

Bryn leaned forward and broke off one of the grass stalks, smoothing the fluffy seed-head in his fingers. "You don't miss the States?"

"Some things, of course. But my heart is here."

"You'll miss your American friends?"

"Yes."

"A man?"

She knew he'd turned to look at her, but kept her gaze on the view. "No one special. If there had been, I suppose it would have been harder."

Abruptly he said, "Kinzi's been offered a promotion—a job in Australia."

She had to look at him then, but couldn't gauge his thoughts. He was staring at the stalk of grass, twirling it backwards and forwards.

"Is she going to take it?" Rachel supposed some response was expected. "What sort of job? I don't know what she does."

"She hasn't decided." He tossed the grass onto the ground. "She edits a fashion and beauty magazine, and the Australian owners want her to take charge of several of their publications over there. It's a big opportunity for her. I don't want to hold her back."

"Would she let you?"

"Maybe," he said, and stood up, looking towards the blue-hazed horizon, his back to her. "If I asked her to marry me."

With a soundless thud something inside Rachel fell from her chest to her stomach. What was he telling her, and why?

Enough of this conversation. Rachel picked up her helmet from the ground beside her and began walking back to where the horses were cropping the grass. "If that's what you want," she said, "you'd better ask her."

She strapped on the helmet, jerking it tight under her chin, and grabbed the mare's reins. The horse turned its head and whinnied as she put her foot into the stirrup and swung her leg over the saddle, then it danced backwards before she'd found the other stirrup.

Bryn caught at the reins and steadied the mare while Rachel took a firmer hold. "That's your advice?"

She looked down at him, exasperated and oddly angry. "I'm not your auntie," she snapped. "It's up to you. Of course if you want to be noble, you could love and let go." Something stuck in her throat, and she jerked the reins from his hands.

He stepped back, black brows raised, his mouth laughing. Then he strode towards his own horse, vaulting into the saddle.

By the time he set the gelding on the downhill path Rachel's mare was well ahead, but he soon drew level.

When she broke into a gallop, the big gelding easily kept pace, but they slowed to a side-by-side walk on the wide track through the bush.

"I don't make a habit of discussing my...affairs of the heart," Bryn said, a sardonic inflection on the final phrase. "Did I offend you?"

"I'm not offended."

"Could have fooled me," he murmured. And then on a note of curiosity added, "Is it a case of female solidarity? Does that weigh more heavily than an old friendship?"

"You and I were never really friends," she argued. "There was such a difference in our ages."

"Our families were close."

"My family were your family's employees."

He frowned. "Surely you're not a snob, Rachel?"

"I'm just stating a fact."

"Why are you angry with me?" He reached out and brought both horses to a halt, their riders knee-to-knee.

"I'm not angry." A half truth. She was annoyed with her-self for caring about Bryn's love-life. Some sort of delayed hangover from a silly teenage infatuation. "Only I can't help you."

"I didn't expect it, just thinking aloud, really."

As if she hadn't even been there. Or was a mere sounding board.

Once she would have been delighted at his confiding in her.

The mare gave a snort and shook her mane. Rachel felt like doing the same. Instead she let the horse break into a canter until they reached the yards and buildings where they'd started out.

Back at Rivermeadows, they found Pearl had prepared a cold lunch and set a table on the terrace.

Bryn said he'd like a short swim first, and although Rachel declined, Kinzi changed into a tiny bikini that showed off her perfect body. Helping Pearl place meats and salads on the table, Rachel could hear the other young woman's giggles and little squeals, and Bryn's laughing voice.

Over lunch Kinzi sparkled, complimenting her hostess on the salad and cold meat loaf, quizzing Rachel on whether she'd enjoyed riding again, and teasing Bryn about his affection for his horse, calling him "my cowboy", which set Rachel's teeth on edge but brought a half grin to Bryn's mouth, that inexplicably made her mad again.

It was a leisurely meal and when the others repaired to the little sitting room Rachel excused herself, went to her room to get a book and then slipped downstairs again and into the garden. There she found a secluded spot under a weeping rimu that brushed the ground, and settled down to read.

She'd been there for some time when low voices, male and female, alerted her that Bryn and Kinzi were strolling nearby. Not wanting to eavesdrop, she scrambled up, closing the book, and got her hair tangled in the sweeping branches of the tree before she escaped its clutching fingers. She was picking narrow leaves and bits of bark out of her hair when the other two appeared round a bend in the path and stopped before her.

Kinzi giggled, then covered her mouth and said, "Sorry, Rachel. What have you been up to?" She stepped forward and plucked a small bunch of lichen and a twig from Rachel's head. "There," she said, dropping them on the ground.

"Thanks," Rachel muttered. She must look a mess.

Bryn was regarding her with a faint smile, the skin about his eyes crinkling as though he too was trying not to laugh.

"I was reading," Rachel said, "but it's getting cool."

Determinedly she stepped forward, and Bryn moved aside. She didn't look back to see them walk on.

Upstairs, she brushed her hair and, leaving it loose, lay on her bed and tried to continue reading, but after a while got up and went to the window that overlooked the back garden, staring at nothing.

After a while she saw Bryn emerge from the trees with Kinzi clinging to his arm.

They stopped under the pergola, Kinzi's face turned up to his as she said something that looked like an urgent plea. Then she slid her arms about his neck and kissed him.

Rachel watched Bryn's hands go to the woman's waist, and Kinzi pressed against him on tiptoe, his dark head bent to hers and their mouths clinging together.

CHAPTER THREE

STEPPING AWAY FROM the window, Rachel drew in a long breath and let it out from pursed lips. Why couldn't Kinzi and Bryn conduct their necking in the privacy of the trees? Or in the little summerhouse…? She unclenched hands she hadn't realised had curled into themselves.

The kiss might be a continuation of other intimacies they'd already shared, she realised bleakly. Even more passionate ones.

Don't think about it.

But she couldn't help it. Couldn't help wondering if Bryn had asked Kinzi to marry him, if that kiss had been the seal on her agreement. She tried to tell herself that if so she would be happy for him—for them both. But all she felt was a leaden foreboding.

Shortly she again heard voices from the terrace. Then silence. They'd moved inside. If they were breaking the news to his mother, she should stay away. It was a family affair.

Later she heard more talk floating up from the entryway, then the sound of the heavy front door echoing as it closed.

She waited twenty minutes before descending the stairs to find Pearl sitting alone on the terrace, and pretended surprise that the other two had left.

"Some time ago," Pearl said tranquilly. "They told me to say goodbye to you."

No hint of anything unusual having happened or an announcement made. Rachel swallowed hard and offered to clear the table.

Rachel spent the following weekend with her parents, a family celebration for her father's birthday. Driving south in the compact but solid car, she wondered what had happened to the dashing red model Bryn's mother used to have.

It was ten days before she saw Bryn again.

Overnight the weather had turned grey and windy with spiteful, spitting showers, and Rachel had foregone the morning jog she'd taken up.

By noon thunder was rumbling intermittently, and the showers had become a heavy, persistent downpour. The lawns about the house were puddled and roof gutters overflowed. The garden looked sodden and woeful, some plants crushed under the force of the wind and rain. Inside, the rooms were gloomy and Rachel had to switch on the lights to read. Pearl's housekeeper phoned to say she wouldn't come in today; there was a severe storm warning on the radio. "They say there might be flooding on the road."

Bryn arrived just before dinner, his hair and his business suit soaked despite the crushed yellow slicker he wore. His hair was flattened, rain droplets streaming from it down his face, and his skin looked taut and cold.

"I went to the village before coming here," he said. "They're bringing in sandbags in case the river overflows."

Rachel said, "Could it breach the stopbanks?" She was sure they were higher and more solid now than before.

"This promises to be what they call a hundred-year

storm," he told her. "No one knows what could happen. I'm staying here tonight. Someone will phone if the town is threatened and I'm needed to help."

Pearl, who had grown more and more nervous and unhappy throughout the day, looked relieved and said in that case she just had time to make his favourite pudding.

When he'd gone upstairs to change, Rachel set an extra place at the kitchen table where she and his mother usually ate, while Pearl put the kettle on to boil and began delving into cupboards.

Rachel was placing salt and pepper on the table when Pearl turned to her with a steaming pottery mug and said, "Would you take this up to Bryn, please, while I get on with dinner? He needs something hot right now."

Given no choice, Rachel took the cup she was handed, which smelled of lemon and the sprinkling of nutmeg on the surface of the drink. Pearl said, "Lemon juice, honey and rum. It'll do him good." And she turned away again to the counter.

After carrying the cup carefully up the stairs, Rachel tapped on the door of Bryn's room, but there was no reply. He must be still in the shower. Not wanting to encounter him emerging from the bathroom, she waited for a short while, and on hearing movement, tapped again.

"Just a moment," his deep voice called, then seconds later he added, "Okay."

She opened the door, stepped into the room and saw he was barefoot and had pulled on a pair of trousers, but the top fastening and belt hung undone, while a dry shirt lay on the navy-blue woven cotton covering the big bed beside him. His torso was bare and he was rubbing a towel over his hair.

Rachel stopped dead, struck anew by the male vitality

that emanated from him. Bryn in a suit or a T-shirt and jeans was stunning. Bryn only half-dressed was positively swoon-worthy.

The towel in his hand stilled; in fact his whole body froze for a millisecond, as if he were posing for a Greek statue—he certainly had the physique for it.

"Rachel!" he said, his voice low and vibrant. He hadn't turned on the light but a flicker of lightning whitened the window and briefly illuminated his face, his eyes reflecting silvery fire. The thunder that followed was a menacing rumble, still far away.

One final swipe at his hair left it standing in spikes, and he dropped the towel about his shoulders and roughly combed his fingers through the damp strands.

"Your mother asked me to bring this," Rachel said, determined to act as if the sight of him hadn't sent a bolt of invisible electricity right through her body. "Where do you want me to put it?"

"On the—" His head jerked towards the bedside table, but as she moved forward he scowled, put out a hand and said, "Give it to me. She had no right to do that. You're not a damned servant."

"I don't mind," she said as he turned to put the mug down himself. Knowing how Pearl treasured the furniture, she asked, "Shouldn't you put something under it?"

He sent her a glance, still frowning, and opened a drawer and removed a folded handkerchief to slide under the mug. "Thanks, but I'll have a word with her—"

"No," Rachel said. "Don't. Pearl asked a favour as a friend and I was happy to oblige. Leave it alone."

His mouth went tight for a moment before he relaxed, but his eyes still probed. "You're sure?"

"Absolutely sure. I'm quite capable of sticking up for my rights if I need to."

He laughed then, and pulled the towel from his shoulders to toss it on the bed. "You always were."

Automatically her eyes had followed the passage of the towel before returning to Bryn. He was still watching her, and although the window remained unlit she thought she saw something flame again in the depths of his eyes before he picked up the shirt and started shrugging into it.

Rachel realised she was staring, pleasantly mesmerised.

As she stepped back, about to leave, another flicker of lightning briefly entered the room and a louder clap of thunder made her flinch.

"Are you afraid of storms?" Bryn asked.

"No. Your mother seems nervous. Is that why you came?"

"And because there's a chance of flooding." His fingers were rapidly buttoning the shirt.

As he tucked it into his trousers she said, "I don't remember floods ever coming this far." Once the river had risen and inundated the village on its banks, but the big house hadn't been threatened.

He opened the door of a huge carved wardrobe and pulled on leather moccasin-style boat shoes. "In the nineteen-fifties the house was surrounded by water that came within inches of the front door, according to my father."

"Really? I'll probably come across some reference to it, I suppose."

Bryn picked up a comb, swiped it through his hair and dropped it back on the dressing table. He seemed ready to leave when Rachel reminded him, "Your drink?"

He picked up the mug, sipped from it, then emptied the contents and said, "Right, let's go down."

* * *

Although Bryn expressed appreciation of the chocolate sponge pudding, he seemed rather preoccupied. As the lightning became more frequent and the thunder louder, Pearl shuddered and paled with each rumble, and when they'd finished eating said she was going to bed.

Bryn offered to take her upstairs but she laughed him off. "I don't need my hand held. I'll just hide under the blankets until it's all over."

Rain still pounded on the roof and gurgled along the guttering, and after the dishes were dealt with Bryn said, "Join me for a nightcap, Rachel?"

They went into the sitting room, where Rachel drew the heavy curtains against the rain streaming down the windows, and Bryn poured her a glass of Irish cream, brandy for himself. Although the house had been fitted with central heating Bryn moved the fire screen aside, exposing paper and kindling laid and ready to be lit.

He took a box of matches and touched one to the paper, waited for the kindling to take hold and added some pieces of manuka from a large brass wood-box beside the hearth.

He had just settled back into his chair when the lights abruptly died.

Startled, Rachel said, "Oh!"

"Does it bother you?" The firelight flickered on Bryn's face. "I can get some candles if you like."

"No, it doesn't matter."

"I'll just check the phone, though the fire brigade chief has my cell number."

He left the room and came back, reporting the telephone was working, then sat down again.

There was an odd intimacy in sitting here in the raggedly shifting pool of firelight with the rest of the room in darkness. Afterwards Rachel couldn't remember what they'd talked about, only that they sat there for a long time, that Bryn refilled her glass more than once, and that his rather brooding mood gradually mellowed. While they chatted in a desultory fashion he leaned back in the big chair, his long legs stretched out and ankles crossed, hands cradling a brandy balloon, and his eyes half-closed.

The fire had burned to embers and the French clock on the mantel was showing past midnight when Rachel stifled a yawn and said reluctantly, "I'd better go to bed before I fall asleep right here."

Bryn gave her a lazy smile, stirred from his comfortable position and, with a long-empty glass still in his hand, stood up and took hers. "Wait," he said. "I'll bring some light." The thunder had died and the rain eased a little, but the lights were still off.

He disappeared into the hallway and Rachel sat for a few minutes staring at the glow of the dying fire, then stood up, arching her back and sleepily stretching her arms out and up. Not hearing Bryn's return, when the light from the electric torch he held fell on her she abruptly lowered her arms, feeling self-conscious.

He stopped in the doorway and she walked towards him, the light making her blink, his face hidden behind it as he handed her an old-fashioned Willie Winkle candle holder with a fresh, unlit candle in it and then led her to the stairs.

At the top they trod quietly past his mother's room and stopped at Rachel's door. Bryn followed her inside, saying, "I don't suppose you have matches here."

"No."

He reached past her to put down the torch, then pulled

matches from his pocket, struck one and touched it to the wick, producing a small, flickering flame. As he waved the match out she placed the candle on the dressing table.

In the mirror her head was level with his strong chin, their shoulders almost touching. For a moment their eyes met in that other, reflected world, and as if the candle flame had leapt and flared, something seemed to pass between them.

She turned as he picked up the torch.

"Keep this, too, if you like," he offered.

Rachel shook her head, unable to speak. Surely she'd imagined that moment of electric awareness. A trick of the night, the dancing candle flame and the mirror.

He said, "Good night, Rachel," and she stood holding her breath when he bent towards her and kissed her cheek. He immediately straightened and turned to leave the room.

She was still standing there and he was halfway across the floor when he abruptly stopped, muttered, "Damn it all," and turned back, the light in his hand dazzling her so that she flinched away. He switched it off before putting it down again with a small thunk as he reached her.

In the candlelight he looked big and dark and dangerous, his mouth set, jaw and cheekbones accentuated, his eyes curiously ablaze.

But his hands were gentle when they framed her face and tipped it upward, and those tightly shut lips were soft when they closed over hers and coaxed her to open them for him.

Her heart was thudding and her hands clenched. She fought the urge to touch him, to wind herself about him and never let go, while her mouth was hopelessly lost in the taste and texture of his, the erotic havoc he was wreaking

with lips and tongue and tiny, tender nips of his teeth, not
hurting but making her shiver with hot, fierce arousal.

Yet while her body urged her to forget everything but
this moment, Bryn and how much she wanted him, her
mind remembered Kinzi doing exactly what she herself
longed to do, and Bryn reciprocating.

She raised her hands and made herself push against him.

He altered his hold from her head to her waist, bringing
her closer even as she pulled back from the kiss.

It was the way he had held Kinzi, kissing her.

Anger came to her aid. She thumped at his chest with
her fists, so that he let go abruptly and she stumbled against
the dressing table, clutching at the wooden edge while
taking a long, ragged breath.

He said, sounding almost dazed, "What is it? What's
the matter?"

Starkly accusing, she said, "Kinzi?"

"Kinzi," he repeated, as if he'd never heard the name
before. He rubbed a hand over his hair. "I did what you
said. She—"

He'd proposed? Her anger ratcheting up several notches,
Rachel interrupted him. "Then, what the *hell* are you doing
kissing *me*?"

"She's going to Australia."

Rachel's mind whirled like a spinning top. She'd told
him to ask Kinzi to marry him if that was what he wanted.
Had the woman actually turned him down?

Then she remembered with a ghastly sinking feeling
that he'd said he didn't want to hold Kinzi back, and her
own flippant paraphrasing of the old saw about letting go
the one you love.

A wounded ego or a classic rebound response, even if

he'd only wanted some kind of comfort, any reasonably attractive female might have been the lucky recipient of that kiss she could still feel on her lips, her tongue. She had just happened to be the handiest.

"So," she said, shaken now by white-hot fury, "you thought, well, good old Rachel's available to fill in—"

"I never thought anything of the sort!" Bryn stepped towards her, his eyes fired with temper. "You know me better than that."

"And you don't know me at all," she flashed. "I'm not a little girl or an impressionable teenager any more."

"That's the truth! If you were I wouldn't have—"

His mouth suddenly clamped shut. Then he said, almost muttering the words, "I wasn't really thinking at all. I wanted to kiss you and—" He stopped, then more normally added, "I didn't think you'd object. You took your time."

"I didn't know you were going to do it," she claimed. True, but if she hadn't exactly given him an enthusiastic response, it was also true that she hadn't fought him off at once.

Bryn's head tipped to one side as he regarded her, the anger fading and replaced by an uncomfortably shrewd appraisal. He said, "Is Kinzi your only problem?"

"No." A lot of things contributed to her wariness and her still-simmering anger. Chief among them a suspicion he'd used her as some kind of substitute for his girlfriend. She couldn't help asking, "Did you ask her to marry you?"

It was a moment before he answered. "No."

Which told her nothing really, but she could see from the jut of his chin and the warning look in his eyes that he had no intention of saying any more on the subject. Bryn wasn't the type to kiss and tell. Whatever had passed between him and Kinzi was not for sharing.

Surprising her, he said after a pause, "I won't be seeing her after Friday night. I've promised her a farewell dinner."

And what else? Rachel wondered, then hurriedly hauled her thoughts back from the direction in which they were heading. "I'm sorry it didn't work out for you two," she said, although wondering if Kinzi might be hoping for a last-minute reprieve. "Your mother will be disappointed. She'd like you to get married."

He shrugged. "So would I, in good time."

His gaze turned speculative again, and she shifted uncomfortably, hoping he hadn't thought she was hinting. "Well," she said crisply, "it's late. And the rain's almost stopped. Surely you can go to bed now."

He gave her a wry smile, nodded and said, "Sleep well."

Then he turned and strode to the open door, shutting it firmly behind him.

Rachel stood staring at the solid wood panels for a minute, then began dragging pins from her hair and flinging them onto the dressing table before she remembered the soft patina of its varnished surface, and guiltily moderated her movements, trying to calm the wildly conflicting emotions that wouldn't allow her mind to rest.

Even after she'd put on pyjamas, slipped under the covers and tried to sleep, anger, indignation, confusion and longing mixed chaotically. Her body was alternately hot and melting, then cold and goose-fleshed as her brain ticked over and reminded her that whatever impulse had moved Bryn, it almost certainly had nothing to do with her personally. It was simply a repeat of what had happened before.

Older and considerably more worldly-wise, she wasn't

going to fall into the same trap she'd embraced—literally—as a misguided teenager. This time Bryn was on his own.

Bryn had dropped onto his bed still dressed, except for the moccasins he'd kicked off. Staring into the darkness overhead, he silently cursed himself for all kinds of a fool. He might be a hotshot businessman and have a gift for negotiating deals and being in the right place in the market at the right time, but at the moment his personal life was in tatters.

Kinzi would have needed very little persuasion to stay in New Zealand if he'd presented her with an engagement ring and set a wedding date. In fact that was exactly what he'd contemplated doing until…well, recently. When it came to the crunch he hadn't been able to bring himself to do it.

He'd come to the conclusion soon after hitting thirty that he was never going to find some dream woman.

He'd known several perfectly nice, perfectly suitable and attractive women, and was aware that the older he got the smaller the pool of unattached females became. In his early twenties he'd thought himself headlong in love once or twice, but none of those affairs had turned into a permanent relationship.

He was resigned to never finding the woman of his dreams—actually the only one who appeared in them with any regularity was Rachel, and he'd long ago declared her off-limits. If her brothers had known what took place when she was seventeen—

Quell that train of thought. But as she'd told him tonight so tantalisingly, she was no longer that innocent child-woman he'd so nearly seduced—his forehead broke out in a sweat at the mere memory. He squeezed his eyes shut and flung an arm over them, assailed by familiar guilt.

But now he remembered how tonight her lips had been soft and sweet and accepting of his kiss. A kiss he hadn't meant to take, drawn back to her by the fire-warmed skin of her cheek when he'd touched his lips to it, and the scent of her hair, like fresh summer apples, and her luminous dark eyes in the light from the candle as he'd said good-night. He could have sworn she was willing him to kiss her.

Damn it, he'd tried to resist, got halfway to the door before his brain surrendered to the urging of his senses, and she hadn't moved, hadn't protested until it was too late, until he'd been drowning in her scent, her luscious mouth, the softness of her hair under his fingers. Until he'd pulled her closer, needing her against him, where he could feel her lovely curves, explore the changes that had filled out her breasts, her hips, brought her to full, ripe womanhood.

Did she kiss you back? his conscience asked sternly.

Maybe not exactly, but neither had she said no when she must have known what he intended. She'd opened her mouth to him, let him do as he willed for all of a minute or two.

She's an employee. He remembered her reminding him that his family had employed hers, as if it mattered.

Maybe it does, to her. Maybe she didn't like to repulse the man who pays her wages. What happened to your rule not to mix business with that particular pleasure? In the office it could be called sexual harassment.

My mother hired her. It's different. Nothing to do with the firm.

He shifted on the bed, dropped his sheltering arm.

Sitting up, he swung his feet to the carpet. He needed a drink.

You've already had a fair bit to drink tonight.

I'm not drunk. Not this time.

He'd never had more than one drink alone since…

Since the last time he'd kissed Rachel Moore. He groaned and headed for the shower, stripped off his clothes and turned on the cold tap, gritting his teeth before stepping under it.

Bryn had left by the time Rachel came down for breakfast.

"He must have gone off very early," Pearl said.

The storm had moved off to the south and was disrupting traffic and flooding small towns, pictures of the devastation forming a large part of that evening's television news. At Rivermeadows the sun reappeared the following day and began to dry up the soaked lawns and gardens.

By Friday, with Pearl's help Rachel had sorted most of the materials she'd been given into roughly date order. On Friday evening she tried to read a historical novel that annoyed her with its minor inaccuracies, while Pearl sat dreamily listening to records and flipping through a magazine.

Pearl looked a little pale and admitted to being tired, having spent the afternoon tying up plants that the storm had battered to the ground, and trimming broken ones while the gardener dealt with fallen tree limbs and shrubs torn up by their roots. For once she hadn't refused Rachel's offer to clean up alone after they'd eaten.

Remembering Bryn's request, Rachel wondered if she should phone him, but this was to be his last evening with Kinzi. The thought wouldn't leave her mind, and after Pearl had opted for an early night, Rachel gave up on her book and went to the smoking room, hoping to absorb herself in work.

After a while she became immersed, and when she heard a car door slam outside and then the sound of a key in the front door, was startled to see the French clock on the smoking room mantel stood at past ten thirty.

Still, surely that was early for Bryn to have left Kinzi. She hadn't expected him to arrive until Saturday.

He pushed open the door she'd left ajar, and said, strolling over to her where she sat at the table, "You're not working at this hour, are you?"

"I'll stop soon," she said, looking up at him. "I had nothing else I wanted to do."

"It's not much of a life for you here," he said. "Is it?" He perched on the edge of the table, so he could examine her face.

"I like it," she said, trying to gauge his mood without being obvious. He looked strong and sexy and his mouth was unsmiling. She thought there were signs of strain about his eyes. "How did your dinner go?"

As soon as the words left her mouth she knew she shouldn't have asked.

His face went wooden, his mouth taut. Then he gave a short, ironic laugh, picked up one of the pens sitting in front of her and tossed it so that it twirled before he deftly caught it. "As well as could be expected," he said. "Very civilized and *triste*."

Sad? Rachel swallowed, watching his hand as he gently replaced the pen on the desk. "You didn't…?" She left the question unfinished. Surely he'd have stayed the night with Kinzi if she'd accepted an eleventh-hour proposal.

But Bryn answered anyway. "No." He got up and strode over to the desk between the long, darkened windows, leaned back on it with folded arms. "She's looking forward to a new job in a new country. She's very excited about it." He paused, looking at Rachel's expression. "What are you thinking?"

"That maybe she's covering up disappointment."

"Kinzi's ambitious. She'll get over it."

"So will you."

"Yes."

His gaze was so steady it was unnerving. She said, "Your mother is rather tired. She's been fixing the storm damage in the garden."

Bryn straightened, black brows drawing together. "I told her to leave it for me and the gardener. That's why we pay these people!"

"She enjoys it, and the gardener was here for the heavy stuff, but I think today she did a bit too much."

He was pacing, hands thrust into his pockets. "If only she'd move—this place is far too big for her."

"She won't do that until—"

He stopped at the other side of the table. "Until she kills herself trying to maintain all this—" He swept an arm in a half circle.

"Your inheritance," Rachel reminded him. Skipping the part about Pearl being carried out in a box, she said, "If you had a family she'd happily move out. That's what she's keeping the place for." As if he didn't know. "It isn't my fault," she added tartly, "so you can stop scowling at me."

"Sorry," he said, but the black brows didn't lift. "Her doctor said—"

When he didn't continue Rachel said, "Does she have a problem?"

Bryn shook his head in an exasperated way. "Blasted man—I've known him for years—wouldn't break patient confidence, but he hinted I should keep an eye on her, and made me swear not to let on he'd said anything. All I could get out of him was she doesn't have cancer or anything immediately life-threatening."

"Then it's probably nothing really terrible," Rachel suggested tentatively.

His mouth twisted. "Ever the little comforter," he said.

Rachel felt her face go still and closed. She stood up and said distantly, "I'm going to bed. Pearl will probably be fine by morning." Then bit her lip because she'd just done it again, offering unwanted comfort.

He caught her before she reached the door, his hand on her arm bringing her round to face him. "I didn't mean to snarl at you," he said. "It's been rather a hell of a day— one of our mill workers had a serious accident, and I'll have to try to explain to the family even though I don't know yet exactly what happened. Tonight I said goodbye to a woman I've grown to…well, that I'd become fond of, and I'm worried about my mother. You just happened to be here when it got on top of me."

Just as she'd happened to be there when he felt like kissing someone, Rachel thought bleakly.

He lifted his other hand and his thumb stroked her cheek, making her insides turn to slush. "Don't look at me that way," he said, "please, Rachel."

She turned her cheek away from his hand. "What way?"

"Like a kitten that's been kicked."

"I *didn't*!" she said, whipping her head back to glare at him.

He laughed, a real laugh of delight. "All right," he said. "A grown-up, very offended cat, ready to spit." He cocked his head to one side, ignoring the childish face she made at him. "A Siamese, maybe…no, they have blue eyes, don't they? Is there a cat that has big chocolate-brown eyes with little gold flecks in them?"

He was examining hers deeply, and she dragged her gaze away with an effort. "I have no idea," she said with determined calm, easing herself out of his hold. "I'll see you in the morning."

Bryn stood in the doorway and watched her mount the stairs, her head high, a small curl lying against the vulnerable curve of her neck, her neat behind moving beneath snug jeans. He leaned against the jamb with folded arms, enjoying the view. After all, if a cat may look at a king....

He'd been called a king of industry. Not a title he particularly relished. It smacked rather of old-time factory owners grinding the faces of the poor into the dust. In these more enlightened times he'd found he got better results from treating his workers well and offering rewards for extra effort. And enforcing safety standards. He hoped today's accident hadn't been caused by slipshod practices.

Frowning, he went to the kitchen to make coffee, then sat there drinking it, his mind going over the day, its ups and downs. Mostly downs. He hadn't been tempted to beg Kinzi to stay. He would remember her with warmth and some regret, but the regret would pass. It always had in the past.

His mother—he suspected her heart might not be all it should be. When he'd first seen Rachel tonight, her head bent so earnestly over some old waybill or business letter, he'd felt the burdens of the day suddenly become lighter. But the news that Pearl had been slaving in the garden and tired herself out brought him back to shouldering his responsibilities.

And he'd hurt Rachel, snapped at her without reason. But she'd never held grudges, and had left him laughing. She had always been able to make him laugh. Until he'd made one of the biggest mistakes of his life, and had no idea how to fix it. She'd had to do that herself. She was strong as well as sympathetic and talented.

He stood up with the coffee cup in his hand and stared out of the kitchen window. A bright moon hung white and aloof over the tops of the trees. He could see nothing but black shadows beneath them, but knew exactly where the summerhouse was. The summerhouse where one dark autumn evening the girl he'd always thought of as the kid next door found him trying to drink himself into oblivion.

CHAPTER FOUR

BACK THEN BRYN had still lived at Rivermeadows, working for the family firm as his father's second-in-command. They'd often talked over business matters there or in the car as they drove to and from the city. The house was big enough for him to have a couple of rooms to himself, and from the age of eighteen he'd come and gone as he pleased.

That night he'd told his parents he was going out with friends, but instead he'd armed himself with a couple of six-packs and a sleeping bag and planned to spend the night in the summerhouse, as he had sometimes with childhood friends or visiting cousins in the school holidays. This time he hadn't wanted company.

So when Rachel unexpectedly turned up, and stifled a small scream on seeing the summerhouse occupied, why hadn't he sent her away immediately, instead of reassuring her, "It's all right, it's only me—Bryn."

She'd seemed to waft like a pale shadow into the small building. For a second, moonlight filtering through the trees outlined her legs under the flimsy, floating white thing she wore—the first time he'd noticed that their childish, sexless contours had become slim ankles, firm and nicely shaped calves, thighs that... He'd stopped there, confounded and confused, and not only by the beer he'd consumed. He didn't remember when he'd last seen her wear a dress.

"Rachel," he said, his voice gruff, "what are you doing here? You should be in bed by now."

She'd laughed, not a little-girl giggle but a low, husky sound that startled him anew. "It isn't that late. I'm not a child, you know."

He didn't know—or hadn't until that moment. Vaguely he recalled she'd had her sixteenth birthday...last year? The age of consent, a voice somewhere deep inside him whispered.

He shoved the thought back where it belonged. He wasn't interested in teenagers. And this was Rachel—he'd known her since she was five years old.

She tripped over the sleeping bag he'd spread on the wooden floor, gracefully righted herself and said, "Are you sleeping here? Why?" Now she seated herself beside him, and pulled her legs up under the white dress, wrapping her arms about them.

"Because I wanted to be alone."

"Oh." The soft syllable expressed disappointment. "I'm sorry, do you want me to go away?"

"No," he said, not knowing what he wanted, but in a slightly befuddled way, unexpectedly glad she was here. "But I should warn you, I'm drinking. Not very good company."

"I wanted to be alone, too," she said, "but I don't mind you being here."

"Good." He reached for another can of beer and pulled off the top. "What's your problem?"

Her shoulders hunched. "Oh, nothing that would interest you."

"Try me." Maybe listening to some teenage storm in a teacup would stop him wallowing in self-pity that alternated with righteous rage.

She stared straight ahead, turning to him a pure young profile. "You know we're leaving soon for the Waikato. Going away."

Bryn nodded. "Are you scared?" Of course, she probably didn't remember any other home but the one belonging to the Rivermeadows estate. He realised he would miss her being around. The tight ache in his gut became tighter. But this wasn't about him. "You'll be okay, make new friends," he assured her, "and you're sure to do all right at university. You're not worried about that, are you?"

"No. A bit nervous." She laid her cheek on her knee as if wondering how far she could trust him. "Only…" Her voice was hushed and shy. "I…I think I'm in love," she said.

Bryn laughed at the irony.

She put her legs down and stood up, ready to flee.

Oh, God, the touchiness of adolescence. He took her hand and pulled her back beside him. "I'm sorry," he said. "I wasn't laughing at you."

"Yes, you were." She was stiff beside him, her head down. But he caught the glitter of tears on her cheek.

"No," he said, hooking a comforting arm about her shoulders. "It's just—well, snap! I have the same problem." His voice had turned rueful.

Only slightly relaxing, she surreptitiously wiped her cheeks before turning to him. "Doesn't she love you back?" As if that were unbelievable.

He swilled down some more beer. "I thought she did, but she's sleeping with my best friend." His fist closed about the can and it crackled.

"I'm sorry," she said, sounding forlorn. And quite fiercely she added, "Then she doesn't deserve you!"

"Thanks," he said sourly.

Her voice was soft in the darkness as the moon sailed behind a tree. "Is she very special?"

"I thought so. I wish she'd told me about…him. Or he had. When I found out another way I felt so… Oh, hell!" He threw the empty can out into the bushes, knowing he'd have to retrieve it in the morning.

"Betrayed," Rachel supplied for him. "Can I have some of that?" she asked as he fumbled out another can.

"No," he said automatically. "You're too young."

"Just a sip or two. I'm allowed it at home sometimes. Please?"

She reached for it when he removed the tab, and dubiously he relinquished it, allowing her maybe a third before taking it back, saying sternly, "No more."

"Was this girl your first, um…"

He gave her a hard look and she ducked her head, looking down at her toes, sheathed in pale leather slippers with tiny bows on the front. "I mean," she said, "have you been in love before?"

"Thought I was when I was—" he stopped there for a moment, cleared his throat as he realised "—just about your age. And a couple of times since. This was…I thought this time was different." It had been his first really serious relationship, that he'd thought might last.

Rachel said fervently, "I don't think I'll ever love anyone else!"

This time he forbore laughing, instead saying gently, "We all think that at the time. Does he know?"

She shook her head. "I can't tell him. He's...he wouldn't want to know."

"Why not? You're a beautiful girl, and smart, and fun..."

"Do you think so? *Beautiful*?" She looked up at him eagerly, sounding breathless.

About to say carelessly, *Of course*, Bryn checked himself and looked at her properly. The moon had shifted up in the sky and a shaft of pale light showed him her smooth forehead, big luminous eyes and a mouth that he realised with a shock was eminently kissable. "Yes," he said, his own mouth suddenly dry. "You are very beautiful, Rachel." She was like one of his mother's perfect, deep-cream dew-kissed roses, with petals just beginning to unfurl.

"Oh!" She breathed it out on a long sigh, her lips parted, her breath feathering his chin. "Thank you, Bryn."

Somehow she seemed to have moved closer, and he became aware of her breast, firm yet tender, against his side.

Breast? Rachel had breasts? Not the little buds he'd sort of noticed she'd started growing when she was...what? Twelve, thirteen—but the real thing!

She's only sixteen, you fool—seventeen? Whatever, she was too young. He eased away from her and grabbed another can to occupy his hands. It was still cold and he wrapped both hands around it as soon as he'd pulled off the tab, thinking he should probably stick it between his legs, where he was uncomfortably hot. But not in front of Rachel. He said, "You'll meet other boys—young men. And one day someone special, when you're old enough." He cleared his throat. "You'd better get back home. Won't your parents miss you?"

"They're out. I told the boys I was going to bed with a

book. They won't go into my room, and I'll be back before Mum and Dad get home."

"Have you done this before?" The beer felt good going down, steadying. He concentrated on the taste of it, the chill. "You shouldn't go wandering around at night on your own. It's not safe."

"I don't wander round. I only come here. It's a good place to think." She wasn't moving, and he was trying to think of a tactful way to send her home when she asked, "Do you think you'll get over…her?"

"I suppose so," he said glumly. At the moment he was too raw to really believe it. "Maybe I wouldn't feel so bad if she'd been cheating on me with someone else. Or if Danny had said something. But it wasn't until I confronted the pair of them, hoping they'd say it wasn't true—"

He stood up, shoving another empty can into the crate. "I didn't mean to go maundering on to you. I was going to get it out of my system on my own."

"I don't mind," she said. Standing, too, she came close to him and put her arms about him, resting her head against his shoulder. "I'm so sorry," she whispered. "I wish I could do something for you, Bryn."

She looked up at him, her eyes sheened with tears—for him! he realised—and her mouth just slightly parted. Her breasts, amazingly full, and hard in the centres, pressed against his chest, and he thought hazily, *No bra*. That thing she was wearing, that made her look like a moonlight nymph, was a nightgown, for God's sake!

He put his hands to her shoulders, ready to push her away, opened his mouth to say something—anything—at the same moment she stood on her toes and touched his lips with hers and breathed sweetness into his mouth.

His body was yelling, "Yes!" His mind squawked a feeble "Oh no," before it stuttered into silence.

And then he lost it completely.

Bryn closed his eyes against the memory, only to abruptly open them again. *Let's not go there.*

He had enough on his plate without reliving that particular episode. Rachel had forgiven—claimed to have forgotten—what had happened that night.

He got up from the bed and impatiently stripped off his clothes, self-prescribing a cold shower that had the desired effect but also brought him wide awake. Tomorrow he'd have to face the family of the injured worker, as well as the government safety inspectors.

The inspection didn't worry him so much, although if they found that the company was somehow at fault it could mean a court case and huge fines. Talking to the family was going to be the worst part. The factory was a three-hour drive away, it was late afternoon and there were no available flights tonight. In any case, the manager had said no one was allowed to see the man yet and he didn't think this was the right time for the CEO to talk with the wife or the man's parents. They were standing by at the hospital, as was the manager.

According to the personnel file Bryn had asked for as soon as he heard the news, the guy and his wife had two young children. The company would make sure they were looked after, but if the father died or remained an invalid for life, there was no way of making up for that.

And dinner with Kinzi had been difficult, preoccupied as he was with wondering if the mill accident had been preventable and whether the man would recover. Kinzi had

smiled too much and spoken in gaily brittle tones of her
new job and finding a place to live in Australia. He'd been
irritated at her manner, and then remorseful, knowing it
was his own mood that caused it.

When he took her home he'd been relieved she didn't
ask him in, instead giving him an eye-to-eye look and
turning her cheek to the kiss he bent to give her before she
said a crisp "Goodbye, Bryn," and stepped inside to close
the door on him.

It didn't make him feel any better that he suspected she
was crying into her pillow right now.

He punched his own pillow and lay back, closing his eyes.
Women.

Kinzi. Would she have stayed if he'd asked? Or would
ambition have won out anyway over the prospect of becoming
his wife and providing heirs for the Donovan dynasty?

His mother. It was no secret she'd like to have grandchildren. She was more anxious than even Bryn's father
had been to see the family name carry on with the family
business. He hadn't told her yet that Kinzi was no longer
a candidate.

Rachel. A smile curved his mouth. Fuming when he'd
compared her to a kicked kitten. All injured dignity when
she went up the stairs, the little-girl curl at her nape reminding him of the unruly child he remembered. She'd had a
temper then, but it never lasted long. Once it was over
she'd be all sunny smiles, her eyes bright and expectant, as
though she knew something good would be just around the
corner. She met life full-on, wholeheartedly, with innocent
openness and confidence in those who cared about her. And
generosity. She'd always been quick to forgive.

People didn't change their essential nature. Underneath

her new grown-up exterior was the Rachel he'd always known…and in a casual, unthinking way, loved.

Rachel…

He went to sleep with the smile still on his lips.

When Rachel descended the stairs in the morning the smell of percolating coffee beckoned her to the kitchen.

Bryn was leaning against the kitchen counter, in a white shirt and dark trousers and sipping from a large cup. Looking relaxed but ready for action.

He took in her T-shirt, shorts and sneakers with a neutral glance, and as they exchanged good-mornings he moved aside for her to pour a coffee for herself. A faint scent of soap and a hint of aftershave teased her, mingled with the more pungent aroma of coffee. Almost sure he was looking at her bent head, she kept her eyes down and sat at the table. Glancing at the clock, she guessed Pearl would be appearing soon.

"Sleep okay?" Bryn asked, still lounging against the counter.

"Fine." She took a sip from her cup. "Did you?"

Bryn shrugged, and she said, "You must be worried about the man who was injured."

"I've phoned the hospital. He's had surgery overnight and he's stabilised. They hope to shift him from intensive care sometime today."

"That's good, isn't it?" She wanted to tell him everything would be all right, remove the strain from his taut cheekbones and jawline. But Bryn wasn't impressed by well-meaning bromides, as he'd made clear last night.

He didn't even acknowledge her Pollyanna-ism. "I'm getting on a plane in—" he checked his watch "—a couple of hours. Maybe I can see him this afternoon. And I have to talk to his family."

He drained his cup, then rinsed it at the sink and placed it on the counter. "I have to go. Tell my mother I'll be back next weekend, will you? It's time you and I went riding again." He gave her a tight little smile on his way out of the kitchen. "And Rachel—sorry I was sore-headed last night."

"Okay." She finished her coffee and followed him to the hallway, where he took a dark jacket from the coat stand before opening the front door for her.

His car sat outside, and they descended the steps together. As Bryn unlocked it and got in, Rachel jogged along the drive, and he slowly passed her, gave her a wave, paused at the gate and accelerated onto the road.

Taking his gaze from the side mirror and Rachel's receding form as she jogged in the other direction, Bryn told himself it would have been more sensible to stay in town last night. Driving to Rivermeadows after dropping off Kinzi had been an impulse he hadn't stopped to analyse.

He'd been keyed up and knew he wouldn't sleep in his apartment, with the muted sound of night-long traffic and the occasional wail of emergency vehicles penetrating the double-glazed windows, and his mind unable to let go of what faced him tomorrow: a hospital visit, a possibly difficult interview with a shocked and worried family, and a meeting with his mill manager and the safety inspectors.

Being with Kinzi had only exacerbated his tension. Not her fault, and Bryn supposed he would miss her, but his only real regret was that he might have given her false expectations.

He'd hoped the drive would help him relax, and that the old house when he reached it would have a calming effect.

But it wasn't until he'd seen Rachel earnestly at work, and she'd turned her big brown eyes on him with a tiny smile curving the corners of her mouth, that he'd began to feel the burdens of the day become lighter.

"What happened to your little red car?" Rachel asked Pearl over lunch.

Pearl looked up from her tomato sandwich. "I sold it years ago. Malcolm wanted me to drive something more 'reliable' as he called it. After I had a teeny little accident, and honestly it wasn't my fault—someone pulled out right in front of me. But he insisted, so in the end I gave in." She sighed. "It didn't stop him having a heart attack though. And since he died…" Her voice trailed off. "I haven't really felt like driving."

"The station wagon…?"

"That was for the farm, really. But after we leased the land I kept it to go to plant nurseries, and collect stuff for things like the annual church fair. Although last year I didn't take part in that…in anything much. Actually I should get some plants to replace the ones we lost in the storm. I suppose the gardener could buy them for me."

"You don't want to go to the nursery yourself?" Rachel queried. And as a flicker of panic crossed Pearl's face, she added quickly, "I could come with you—if that's all right. I can do with a bit of a break."

Pearl said, "But won't you be bored?"

"Of course not. It'll be fun."

"She enjoyed herself," Rachel told Bryn the following weekend as they walked their horses after a good gallop. "We stacked the station wagon with plants, had afternoon tea at the nursery's café. Although she asked me to drive."

"You've been good for her," he said. "I'm grateful to you, Rachel." But she noted the frown on his brow.

"Was she driving before your father died?" she asked.

"Yes, although she complained sometimes that she missed her little red monster. I'm just afraid…" He let the sentence dangle, the frown deepening.

"What?" Rachel asked.

"That she's not driving because the doctor's told her she shouldn't—or she's scared of something happening while she's at the wheel. Maybe a stroke or heart attack."

"Did the doctor hint at anything like that?"

"All he would say was I should keep an eye on her."

Bryn certainly did that. He phoned almost every day. One day the previous week Rachel had answered, and he'd told her the injured worker was on the mend but in for a long rehabilitation. The man had jumped a safety barrier to free a jammed log and got caught in the machinery. He was lucky to have survived. The whole company had been reminded of the strict safety code that operated in all Donovan workplaces, and managers ordered to enforce it to the letter.

"Have you asked her," Rachel said, "if anything's wrong?"

"She said there's nothing to worry about and told me not to fuss." He pushed the gelding into an easy trot as they entered the belt of trees. Rachel let him have a small start before catching up.

When they'd returned the horses and were walking towards Bryn's car he said, "How about we stop for a coffee on the way home? There's a pub along the road with a bistro bar that's not too bad."

Within minutes he drew up outside a country hotel, where dust-covered utility vehicles and smart townies' cars stood side by side in the car park. They sat at a table outside, set on a wide lawn that ended at the riverbank where several people were throwing leftovers to a bevy of ducks and seagulls. On a rock in the middle of the river a grey heron groomed an outstretched wing, its long neck gracefully curved into a half circle.

As she scooped foam from her latté Bryn asked how the book was coming along. He sat back in his chair, a hand curled about his cup of black coffee, a faint smile on his lips and his eyes silvered in the sun. Rachel hadn't seen him so relaxed since she'd arrived at Rivermeadows. In the middle of telling him about a letter she'd found addressed to the first pioneer Donovan by the local Maori chief who had been his landlord, she stopped and said, "I must be boring you."

Bryn shook his head, straightening in his chair to lean his elbows on the small wrought-iron table between them. "I don't remember that you've ever bored me, Rachel." He tipped his head to one side. "I haven't taken as much interest in the family's past as I should."

"Too busy looking after its future?" she guessed. "Although there must be enough money now to keep it going for at least a couple of generations—" She stopped before her tongue ran away with her into *if there are any.*

He looked thoughtful, then shrugged. "That depends on several things."

Like whether he ever has children.

As if she'd summoned it, a child of about four appeared apparently from nowhere. A chubby little boy with olive skin, big blue-grey eyes and cropped fair hair, wearing a T-shirt and jeans.

"Hello," he said, staring at Bryn.

"Hi there," Bryn answered easily. Rachel looked around for the boy's parents, but everyone seemed occupied with their drinks and snacks.

"Have you got a dog?" the child queried, his gaze still fixed on Bryn's face.

"Uh…no, not now. I did when I was a boy, though."

"What was his name?"

"Jet."

"Because he was fast?"

Bryn shook his head. "Because he was black."

The little boy looked puzzled, and Bryn explained, "That's another word for black. What's your name?"

"Toby. I'm going to get a dog when I'm seven. But he'll have to stay at my dad's because my mum doesn't like dogs. I'm going to call him Toa."

"Brave?" Bryn translated the Maori word. "That's a good name."

Toby nodded emphatically. Then he looked up as a man carrying a glass of beer and a soft drink came up to them. "I told you to stay at the table," he said sternly to the boy. And to Bryn, "Sorry, mate."

"No problem," Bryn told him. "We had an interesting conversation."

"You were a long time, Daddy!" Toby explained. "I got bo-ored."

Bryn watched the two of them go off to another table, and Rachel turned her head to follow his gaze. The man put down the drinks and ruffled the boy's hair as he sat down. A cheeky grin lit Toby's face. He obviously adored his father.

When Rachel turned back to Bryn she surprised a strangely pensive expression on his face. Did he envy the other man? Then his eyes returned to her as he said almost defensively, "He's a nice kid. Pity his parents seem to have split up."

"Yes," she agreed, "but his father's still in his life. Some just walk away."

"Some might," he said rather grimly.

Not Bryn, of course. He took his responsibilities seriously. Maybe adding a wife and children to them seemed just too much. She wondered if he'd ever wanted to break away from his family and the Donovan empire as his sister had.

He said, "What are you thinking?"

"Do you like what you do? Your job?" She picked up her coffee cup. "I mean, you didn't really have much choice, did you?"

He sat back as though giving the question some thought. Finally he said, "When I was twelve, thirteen, I desperately wanted to become an astronaut. Like every second boy on the planet." He shook his head. "Otherwise, running the company one day was something I took for granted. And yes, most of the time I like it."

Rachel took another sip from her cup. When she put it down again Bryn reached across the table and wiped a bit of foam from her upper lip with his finger, sending an alarming tingle all the way down her spine.

She used her tongue to remove any further traces, then wished she hadn't as the lazy amusement in his eyes turned to a glint of something much more dangerous. She dropped her gaze to her cup, stirring the remains assiduously.

"Rachel," Bryn said.

Wariness in her eyes, she looked at him. "What?"

He didn't say anything for a moment, then he gave a quiet laugh. "Never mind." A new, probing curiosity in his eyes, he said, "One minute you're the little girl I used to know, the next you're...all grown up."

"I *am* grown up," she reminded him. It wasn't the little girl who had reacted to that casual touch of his finger, it was definitely the adult, sexually aware woman. One who wasn't going to have her head turned by the fact that the great, apparently unattainable object of her foolish adolescent desire had at last actually noticed her new maturity.

Yet she was still haunted by the memory of a night long ago, when for a few ecstatic minutes all her puerile romantic dreams had seemed to be coming true.

Shaking off the memory, and how those dreams had come crashing down on her foolish head, she lifted her cup and drained it, careful that no residue this time would remain on her lips. "Your mother will be expecting us," she said.

The quirked corner of Bryn's mouth and his barely lifted eyebrows told her he recognised a retreat when he saw it. But he didn't comment, instead pushing back his chair and standing. The fact that she stood up too quickly for him to come and move her chair for her was at best a Pyrrhic victory.

CHAPTER FIVE

BACK AT THE HOUSE Bryn suggested a swim. The weather, capriciously, had turned hot and humid despite an overcast sky, and Rachel had planned to shower.

Scarcely hesitating, she said, "Good idea," and went upstairs to get into her swimsuit.

It was low-necked and cut high at the leg, flower-patterned Lycra that she liked for its bold sunset colours, but not nearly as revealing as the tiny bits of cloth Kinzi had worn. When she emerged from her room and ran lightly down the stairs carrying a towel, she was surprised to see Bryn waiting for her below, standing with his legs apart, a towel slung over one bare shoulder, swim shorts low on his hips and showing the muscled strength of his long legs.

For a moment Rachel paused midflight, then slowed her pace of descent to a more decorous one.

Decorous or not, she saw the lazy glimmer in Bryn's eyes as he watched her, taking a leisurely inventory from the top of her head, where she'd tied her hair into a careless knot, to her toes.

She restrained an instinct to hold the towel in front of her, trying to ignore the masculine appreciation in his eyes and her own inevitable response.

Both, the analytical part of her brain reminded her, were natural human reactions with no particular meaning except that we're all wired to continue the species, and an attractive member of the opposite sex stirs primal impulses that civilized people recognise and control.

Rationalising didn't stop her staring at Bryn's near-naked body, or her own from heating, her cheeks from flushing as she neared him.

They walked in silence to the terrace and crossed to the pool. Bryn dived in straight away and Rachel followed. The sunlight at this time of year wasn't strong enough to warm the pool, and the cold water drove everything else from her mind until she surfaced, shaking droplets from her hair.

Bryn had powered away to the end of the pool, and was swimming back. They passed each other midway as she followed his example. A few laps was enough to make her warmer, and they finished eventually at the same end, panting a little.

Rachel turned over and changed to a leisurely back-stroke, and Bryn leaned on the pool's edge, watching for a while before he swam after her, more slowly now, catching her up and then keeping pace. "You haven't forgotten how to swim," he commented when they stopped at the other end.

He'd coached her himself, patiently holding her afloat while she practised the strokes she'd been taught at school, hoping to emulate her brother's prowess in the water. He'd shown her how to turn her head to breathe, and to tuck her chin into her chest when she dived so she didn't belly-flop. "It's not something you forget," she said.

Just as she hadn't forgotten anything about Bryn. Memories she'd tried to suppress—and memories that had been buried for years, overlaid by new experiences with the passage of time—kept coming to the surface, tantalizing her and forcing comparisons with the present.

Sex, she thought, had a lot to answer for. Pearl had once been "Mrs. Donovan", a glamorous, kind though distanced figure, but now she and Rachel had established a comfortable adult relationship. Bryn was diffcrent. There was no denying the undercurrent of awareness that fizzed between them.

After climbing out of the pool and putting on jeans and a sweatshirt she joined Bryn and his mother on the terrace.

Pearl was saying, "Why don't you take Rachel?"

Bryn looked up as Rachel walked towards them. He rose to pull out a chair for her before reseating himself.

"Take me where?" she asked cautiously.

"The annual Donovan's charity ball," Pearl explained. "Without Malcolm," she said, turning to her son, "I'd only be a spare wheel. And I don't want to go on attending year after year like a ghost at the feast until I'm old and doddery. This is as good a time as any to retire from all that."

"People will miss you," Bryn said, with a slightly stubborn air. "I thought you enjoyed these affairs."

"I enjoyed being with your father," she answered. "Nothing is the same without him."

"I know, but—"

"Don't make me, dcar," Pearl said gently. "Please."

Rachel thought he looked momentarily shocked at that. Then he gave his mother a keen, sceptical look. "When," he said, "have I ever made you do anything, my darling mother? I learned long ago not to even try."

She laughed, caught out, and even flushed a little. "Truly, I've had enough of being on my best behaviour for hours on end, trying to remember names and faces and eating too much and dancing with old men who tread on my toes. I wasn't there last year—"

"Everyone understood it was too soon after Dad died."

"Well, I don't want to start fielding condolences again," Pearl said crisply, "and you know that would happen."

"All right." Bryn held up his hands in surrender. "I understand."

Pearl turned to Rachel. "Take pity on him, Rachel. He seems to have somehow lost Kinzi." She cast Bryn a reproving look as though he'd mislaid the young woman through sheer carelessness. "The ball is in two weeks. You might enjoy it."

Bryn laughed. "After your description?"

His mother's lips pursed but her eyes sparkled at him. "She's young and isn't married to the head of the company." As inspiration obviously struck, she added, "You could introduce her to some of the older staff members who might have memories that could go in the book."

To Rachel, she said, "The mayor of Auckland is always there, too, and members of parliament, some people from the arts…"

"I know." Rachel had seen in the Donovan papers the photos of the rich and famous, as well as Donovan employees, who regularly attended one of the social highlights of the year. "I'm afraid it's out of my league."

"Oh, tosh!" Pearl said. "You're as good as any of them, and twice as intelligent as most. Besides being lovely to look at. Bryn would be proud to have you at his side. Wouldn't you, Bryn?"

"Absolutely," he agreed with hardly a hesitation. "But you're bulldozing the girl, Mother. I'm capable of issuing my own invitations, you know. *Will* you take pity on me, Rachel?"

The laughing challenge in his eyes told her the last thing he was in need of was pity.

"Of course!" Pearl told him. "It'll do her good to have a night out. One thing I will say—the music is always excellent."

Rachel protested, "I don't have anything to wear to something like that."

Bryn laughed outright. "The age-old female excuse."

"We'll find you something," Pearl said firmly, and after the briefest pause, added, "Go shopping."

Bryn shot his mother a keen look, the laughter dying from his face. Then he glanced quickly at Rachel as she tried to hide her own surprise. She saw the appeal—almost a demand—in his eyes as he said, "Get something nice, and I'll pay for it."

"You won't!" she shot at him. "I pay for my own clothes."

Pearl said. "Oh, let him, Rachel. Donovan's can afford it. A business expense."

"I can't—" Rachel was certain they couldn't claim that on their tax declaration.

"We can argue about that later," Bryn suggested and said to his mother, "Take her shopping and see what you can do."

"To turn me into a swan?" Rachel asked dryly.

He visibly winced. For effect, she knew. "You know I didn't mean that. You were never an ugly duckling. But as you've pointed out a couple of times—" his eyes gleamed "—you're a woman, aren't you? I haven't yet met one who didn't like to get dressed up occasionally. In fact I seem to remember a pink fairy strutting her stuff around the place for a while...."

Her turn to wince. "I was six years old!" The fairy costume had been a birthday present, her mother's effort to remind her daughter she was a girl, and for a while it was her favourite outfit. But the phase hadn't lasted long. Pink net and gauze wings didn't stand up too well to tree climbing or swinging from tyres strung to a branch. And the wand had broken when she used it as a sword in a play fight with one of her brothers.

She didn't know which was more exasperating, Bryn's frequent reminders of her harum-scarum childhood, or the couple of times he'd shown unequivocally that he saw her as a desirable woman—or at least a stand-in for the one he really wanted.

And here she was again, trapped into taking another woman's place. That the woman was his mother this time didn't much sweeten the pill.

For Pearl's sake she could hardly say no. Offering to take Rachel shopping was another step towards normality for Pearl, a sign that she was ready to break out of the co-coon she'd built around herself after being widowed.

"Well?" Bryn raised his brows.

"All right." Rachel almost glared at him. She was tempted by a sudden notion that she could spend a small fortune and charge it to him in revenge for being manipulated. But to be fair, this was Pearl's idea, and once she'd suggested it he could hardly object without being rude.

If he too felt backed into a corner he didn't show it. "Thank you, Rachel," he said, graciously inclining his head. He sounded so nearly humble she looked at him with suspicion, but he met her gaze with a bland one of his own.

The shopping expedition was an eye-opener for Rachel. Chain stores, no matter how upmarket, didn't even impinge on Lady Donovan's consciousness. She knew by their first names designers whose clientele included American film stars, and celebrities whose names were known across the English-speaking world, and owners of boutiques so exclusive they were almost invisible to the naked eye. In every one of the discreetly sumptuous premises Pearl entered she was immediately recognised and greeted with genuine pleasure.

Rachel tried to assert her independence by declaring she wanted something reasonably priced, but her idea of reasonable seemed at odds with everyone else's.

When one couturier had left them to fetch "something I think will be exactly right for Miss Moore," Rachel murmured in desperation, "Pearl, I really can't spend so much on a dress I'll probably never wear again."

Pearl looked supremely unworried. "You're Bryn's partner for the night and Bryn represents Donovan's. Don't worry about the cost just now. Anyway, you can always sell it afterwards if you like. There's a good market for nearly new designer dresses."

She simply acted deaf to any further attempt at protest, and was obviously relishing her role as fashion mentor. When they eventually settled on a gown Rachel took out her credit card, but Pearl waved it away, saying to the salesperson, "Put it on my account, please."

Rachel knew better than to argue. She'd take it up with Bryn later.

Having inveigled Rachel into new shoes to go with the new dress, Pearl took her to her own hairdresser, who started with a full treatment and then snipped the unruly curls into a lighter, prettier shape.

Pearl also decreed that Rachel should dress for the occasion at Bryn's Auckland apartment, and that Pearl herself would come along—not as a chaperon, but to arrange Rachel's hair for her.

In Bryn's guest bedroom she not only supervised and touched up Rachel's make-up, but also twisted a rope of tiny seed pearls into her hair as she styled it into a Grecian knot, leaving loose curls to frame her face. At the last minute, after Bryn had called that they must leave in five minutes, she took a long leather case from her substantial handbag, and fastened a pearl-and-diamond choker about Rachel's neck.

"Pearl," Rachel said, "I can't wear this!" She had no doubt the gems were the real thing.

"Of course you can. I don't wear it any more—the last thing a woman of my age wants is to draw attention to her neck. And it should be worn. They used to say that you should wear pearls all the time, even in bed, to keep their lustre. It looks wonderful on you, just what that neckline needs."

It would have looked wonderful on anyone. Elegant but not ostentatious, it complemented the satin sheen of the deep gold dress with its intricately pleated bodice showing a hint of cleavage, and the deceptively simple skirt that flared at the hem. "No," Rachel said, "really—"

"Nonsense. It's only a loan, like this." Pearl picked up the incredibly soft, creamy lace wrap that she'd taken from her own wardrobe and dropped it about Rachel's shoulders.

A knock came on the door, and Rachel stood up. Pearl gave her a push towards the door and called, "You can open it."

When Bryn did so, his big form blocking the doorway, in black tie and evening clothes he was more handsome than ever. His eyes darkened as he surveyed Rachel, from the cunningly arranged topknot with pearls peeking from the dark tresses, the jewels that circled her throat and the stunningly designed dress, to the sparkling, high-heeled sandals on her feet.

When the comprehensive gaze returned to her face she saw his jaw tighten, and for a moment feared that he didn't approve.

As he remained silent and unmoving, his mother asked, "Well? What do you think?"

His eyes still on Rachel, he said, "I think she looks... breathtaking."

Rachel said, "Your mother did a good job of the make-over."

"It isn't a makeover!" Pearl scolded. "I just helped enhance your true beauty. Off you go and have fun."

At Pearl's behest Bryn had hired a limo so that Rachel's dress ran no risk of being crushed. The interior was so roomy there was plenty of space between them. Luxurious leather seats and the carpeted floor added to a nervousness Rachel had felt all day. Bryn, sitting with folded arms and appearing oblivious to her, didn't help.

When they arrived the driver pulled up under a pillared portico outside the building, and as Rachel emerged to stand with Bryn on the pavement she was startled by the flash of a camera. After blinking, she forced herself to adopt a slight, composed smile as Bryn's hand on her waist guided her inside.

They were the first to arrive, and Bryn checked with the function manager that everything was going according to plan before other couples and groups began to trickle in. Soon the big room was filled with chattering guests holding glasses of wine and taking canapés from circulating waiters.

Bryn, too, circulated, introducing Rachel to a number of people whose faces she recognised from newspaper photographs or television, and others whose titles or his brief description of their jobs indicated that she would have known their names if she hadn't been out of the country for so long.

"Everyone who's anyone?" she murmured once, as Bryn excused them from one group and moved smoothly across the floor to another.

"Anyone who pays for a ticket," he answered. "Although we make sure that certain people are invited to buy one."

"Certain people" with money or a high profile or more likely both, Rachel deduced as she smiled at a government minister who held her outstretched hand for too long and bent so close she could smell his whisky-laden breath.

Somehow Bryn managed to unobtrusively shift his body so that when the man at last released her hand, his only choice was to face Bryn rather than her, leaving her free to exchange small talk with the MP's wife, a thin, rabbity woman wearing a bright orange dress and too much jewellery.

Other guests, too, glittered with jewels and sparkly dresses under the lights. Some looked elegant, a few had tried too hard, but they all seemed to be having a good time.

She chatted with several of the older employees and noted names for future reference. Then later Bryn introduced her to a group who seemed to be genuine friends of his. They greeted her warmly but with curiosity in their eyes. She supposed they were wondering what had happened to Kinzi, but they were interesting and lively, and she began to relax, the smile that had made her jaw ache becoming real again.

Bryn left her briefly while he made a short welcome

speech and reminded everyone there would be an auction later in support of this year's good cause, the children's hospital.

When he rejoined her he said, "Duty done, now we can enjoy ourselves."

He swept her onto the dance floor, where a few people were either circling or swaying and moving their feet opposite each other. Bryn held her firmly with a hand on her waist and the other holding hers, and she effortlessly followed his lead. A number of young couples were dancing the same way. She recalled Pearl telling her that there had been a resurgence of interest after several TV programmes featured celebrities competing in ballroom dance.

Bryn said, "You like dancing?"

"Yes." She had always enjoyed it, had attended a jazz ballet class as a child, and before her first school ball had attended classes to learn the traditional waltz, foxtrot and some South American dances. "In America," she said, "I took up swing dancing for a while."

"With a partner?" Bryn deftly guided her past another couple.

"A friend," she answered briefly.

For a while they fell silent, their bodies in perfect unison while they moved about the floor. His hand on her waist brought her closer, her spine subtly bent to his will and their thighs brushing when he took another corner. Rachel's spirits began to lift into a dreamy euphoria.

As Pearl had predicted, the music from the live band was good, and Bryn was a great partner.

When the music stopped with a flourish from the drummer, Bryn swung her round in a circle, then caught her close for moment, smiling down at her before escorting her from the floor.

Her cheeks were flushed from the dance and from that brief contact with Bryn's hard, lean body. She was relieved when he noticed her empty wineglass and offered to get her another drink.

"Not wine," she said quickly. "Juice, please." She needed to keep a clear head. The combination of alcohol and spending half the evening with his arm about her and his mouth a tempting few inches away, their bodies touching for tantalising seconds as they danced, was likely to fog her brain and lead to unforeseen consequences.

Bryn wasn't drinking much, either. As the nominal host she supposed he, too, needed to take care.

When he excused himself for a couple of "duty dances" she got up with other men at the table, but they didn't have the same effect.

During the auction that created some exciting bidding for such things as an autographed All Black rugby shirt and an original drawing by a noted cartoonist, Bryn sat beside Rachel with his arm resting on the back of her chair. Earlier they had briefly inspected the goods on offer, and she'd lingered longingly over a papier-mâché box, small enough to fit on her palm, decorated with mother-of-pearl and lined with faded red velvet. Guessing it was Victorian, she'd assumed it would go for at least a few hundred dollars.

She didn't even realise that Bryn was bidding for the little Victorian box until the auctioneer lowered his hammer and called, "Sold to Mr Bryn Donovan! Thank you, sir."

"You bought it?" she said, turning to him in surprise. His signals must have been very discreet.

"You like it, don't you?"

"I do, but you didn't buy it for me?"

"Why not?" He shrugged. "All for a good cause. And there's nothing I particularly want."

"You can't—"

"Shh." He put a finger over her mouth and smiled into her eyes so that her insides turned to mush, before he returned his attention to the stage and the next item on the list.

On the way back to his apartment in a corporate taxi, they hardly spoke. Rachel was tired and yet on edge. The evening behind them had assumed a dreamlike quality.

Bryn at first seemed preoccupied, until he took her hand in his, raised it to his lips and said, "Thank you, Rachel. You were a delightful partner. I hope you weren't too bored."

For a moment she was too occupied with steadying her breath, her heartbeat, to reply. Then the effort to control her voice made her sound woodenly polite. "Of course not," she said. "I had a very nice time."

"Uh-huh," he said on a note of amusement that left her with no comeback. He didn't let go of her hand, holding it on the seat between them until they arrived at the apartment.

Once inside, he switched on the side lights, put a hand into his jacket pocket and drew out the papier-mâché box.

"Here." He took her hand again and placed the box on her palm. "A small thank-you for accompanying me tonight."

"There's no need, Bryn—"

"And for what you've done for my mother." He folded her fingers over the box.

"I'm being very well paid."

"Then look on it as a bonus, if you like."

She shook her head. It might be small but she knew what he'd paid for it. "I can't accept—"

"Rachel." As he had earlier he silenced her with a finger on her lips. "Shut up."

When he moved his finger she stubbornly tried again. "But—"

Bryn made an exasperated little sound in his throat, clasped her shoulders, bared where the lace wrap had slipped down her arms, and bent his head, giving her a hard, quick kiss that effectively robbed her of speech.

"Now will you be quiet?" he demanded, his voice deep and determined, his mouth, his eyes, inches from hers.

She blinked and hastily stepped back. "I'm going to bed," she said flatly, unnecessarily, making herself turn away. She knew he was watching her every step of the way until she closed the door of the room she was sharing with his mother.

Pearl was fast asleep in one of the twin beds.

Rachel went to the dressing table and lifted her hands to remove the pearl-and-diamond choker from her neck. Her fingers fumbled with the clasp but it wouldn't open. Turning it so she could see in the mirror how it was supposed to work didn't help. After five minutes she was still stumped.

She looked at Pearl, but all she could see was the blond curls on the pillow. It would be cruel to wake her. And sleeping with the necklace on didn't appeal.

Reluctantly she took the only alternative, returned the clasp to the back of her neck, left the room and knocked quietly on Bryn's bedroom door.

It opened almost immediately. His shirt was hanging loose, the buttons undone, but he wasn't yet undressed. She saw surprise flare in his eyes, and his lips curved. "Rachel," he said, stepping back as though inviting her in.

Quickly she said, "Sorry to disturb you, but I can't get this thing off," as she touched the choker.

Something flickered across his face, and then it became a wooden mask. "Okay," he said. "Turn around."

She felt him fiddling with the clasp, his fingers brushing her skin, then the small weight was lifted from her neck and she felt something else, the lingering warmth of Bryn's lips where the clasp had been.

She gasped, then turned to take the necklace from him.

He dropped it into her hand, and she parted her lips to say something—anything—but had no chance before his hands at her waist hauled her close and his mouth covered hers. The kiss was of such incredible finesse—a combination of absolute mastery and tender coaxing—that any thought of protest fled from her mind. She was too engrossed in the way his firm lips moved over hers, exploring their contours, and in the scent of his skin, the slide of his hands over her shoulders to her nape, tipping her head farther as his mouth urged hers to open for him, and a thumb settled on the leaping pulse at the base of her throat.

That small touch was unbelievably sexy, and she felt a hot shudder rush through her entire body, the sensation so exquisitely pleasurable that she made a sound like a brief whimper, her hands going involuntarily to his chest, bared by the open shirt, her palms flattened against the beat of his heart.

"What?" Bryn's voice was slurred as he lifted his mouth a fraction of an inch from hers. "Did I hurt you?"

"No," she murmured, barely above a whisper. Hazily she knew she ought to stop this, somehow, but the words wouldn't form on her lips.

He kissed her again, almost roughly, and she felt the scrape of incipient whiskers against her skin but it was more pleasure than pain. Then his mouth went from her lips to her throat and grazed along the line of her shoulder, and his arms brought her even closer as he kissed along the low neckline of her dress until she felt his lips on the curve of her breast.

The breath left her body in a sigh of sheer bliss, and he wrapped his arms about her, then raised his head to stare with glittering eyes into her face, his mouth taut and his cheekbones heated with dark colour. "Come to my bed," he muttered huskily. "I want you there *now*."

She knew he did—she could feel the arousal of his body, and her own was clamouring to do what he wanted, be what he wanted, wherever and as often as he wanted. Because she wanted him, too, with a fierce and almost overwhelming passion.

Almost.

Reason began a slow but inexorable return. She shifted in his arms, pushed ineffectually against his chest, until he got the message and loosened his hold although his arms still held her a few inches from him. "Rachel?" he queried, his eyes narrowing.

Slowly she shook her head. "I'm sorry. I shouldn't have let you… I should have stopped this earlier."

Bryn closed his eyes, and his head went back as he took a long breath through his nose, his mouth clamped tight. Then he abruptly dropped his arms and stepped back. "Your call," he acknowledged with a jerky nod.

He swung round and with a curt, "Good night, Rachel," closed the door on her.

Moments later she realised she was still clutching the necklace in her hand.

In the morning, when she came out of the guest room's en suite bathroom, Pearl was picking up the little box from the dressing table, where Rachel had left it.

"This is pretty," Pearl said. "Did you buy it at last night's auction?"

Rachel hesitated before reluctantly saying, "Bryn did."

"For you? Well, I'm glad to say my son has good taste."

"I can't take it," Rachel told her. "If you like it you'd better have it."

Pearl blinked at her. "It's only a trinket, Rachel."

Rachel stifled a laugh. "He paid a lot of money for it."

"I'm sure he could easily afford it. Even a Victorian lady would have accepted something like this from a gentleman friend without compromising her reputation. There's nothing *intimate* about it. If Bryn wanted to give you a present, don't hurt him by refusing it."

Rachel's eyes momentarily widened. Then she bit her lip. She'd thought he might be annoyed at her rejection of the gift, but even Bryn wasn't immune to ordinary human emotions.

Like hurt and pain—and passion.

How much of last night's unexpected passion had been for her, and how much a reaction to the pain of losing Kinzi?

Or simply a normal male response to a woman who had pulled out all the stops last night to make herself as alluring as possible, whom he'd danced with and smiled at and laughed with for hours, and who had probably been unable to hide her helpless yearning for him. And hadn't even tried to evade his kisses and caresses until he'd suggested the natural progression to his bed.

She grew hot again at the memory, and when Pearl replaced the box on the dressing table and turned, Rachel saw a flicker of surprise on her face, followed by a small, too-innocent smile before she headed to the bathroom.

Inwardly groaning, Rachel flung her overnight bag on her bed and dragged out a pair of jeans.

Over a late breakfast Pearl provided most of the conversation. Rachel didn't want to look at Bryn, after a quick glance had shown her an unsmiling expression that gave nothing away. But they both endeavoured to answer Pearl's questions about the ball and the people who had attended, and assure her they had enjoyed their evening.

Bryn asked if there was anything the women wanted to do or see while they were in Auckland, but after looking from him to Rachel, Pearl laughed and said, "After last night, I think you both need to relax today."

He gave his mother a keen look and said casually, "Okay. Why don't I fetch the Sunday paper, and after we've read it we can have a leisurely lunch before you two head home."

He turned to Rachel and offered, "Want to go for a walk, Rachel?"

Rachel politely declined. Whether he was going to ignore what had happened last night or conduct some kind of post mortem, she didn't want to know. His eyes when she met them were devoid of any emotion, and he shrugged, then left.

The three of them shared parts of the newspaper and the weekend magazine that came with it, swapping them around. Occasionally Pearl commented on some item, eliciting a response from one or both of the others.

It should have been a pleasant, companionable Sunday morning laze. Instead Rachel's nerves were stretching tighter and tighter. She hardly took in anything she read although her eyes moved across the lines, and every time Bryn shifted his feet or turned a page she felt the movement as if he'd reached out and touched her.

Ridiculous, she scolded herself. She knew he'd scarcely glanced at her, seeming absorbed in what he was reading, and when they'd all finished with the leisure section he began filling in the cryptic crossword.

After a while he paused, frowning over a clue, and then read it out, adding, "Any ideas?" Pearl laughed and said she could never work out what those things were about, she had enough trouble with a straight crossword.

Rachel said, "Landmarks."

Bryn gave her a look of respect. "Of course. What about this one?" He held the paper out to her. "Nine across."

Between them they finished the puzzle, and her tension gradually eased. But deep inside she smouldered with what she knew was unreasonable resentment after last night's torrid little episode. He was able to act as though it had never happened. That she was desperately trying to do the same didn't make her feel any more sanguine. Perhaps because Bryn seemed so much better at it.

He took them out to a late lunch, choosing an upmarket café near the harbour. They each had one glass of wine with the meal, and all the food came piled artistically on the plates into mini-towers that had to be dismantled before it could be eaten.

Afterwards they returned to the apartment and Bryn stowed the women's bags in the car before kissing his mother's cheek and telling Rachel, "Drive carefully."

On impulse Rachel said, "Actually, I'm a bit tired still, after the late night. Would you like to drive, Pearl?"

Bryn threw her a sharp glance and Pearl said quickly, "I...I haven't driven for ages. I don't think I could—"

"It's Sunday," Bryn said. "There isn't much traffic—it would be a good time to get back in practice. Do you have your licence with you?"

"Yes, in my bag, but..." Pearl paused, then said, "I had wine with lunch!"

Bryn's gaze turned quizzical. "So did Rachel. One small

glass, just like you did. Not enough to impair either of you behind the wheel. Is there some reason you shouldn't be driving? Something you haven't told me?"

"No." She seemed reluctant to admit it. "Not any more."

Bryn couldn't let it pass. "What exactly does that mean?" he asked. "If you were ill, why didn't you tell me?"

Pearl's surprise couldn't have been feigned. "I was never ill! Not really. The doctor said I'm very fit for my age."

"Then why did he tell me—" Bryn stopped himself there.

"What did he tell you?" Pearl demanded. Her blue eyes narrowed and for the first time ever, Rachel discerned a definite likeness between mother and son. "He had no right!"

"Nothing!" Bryn told her hastily. "He seemed concerned."

"Oh, for heaven's sake!" Pearl said. "I was feeling down after your father died—as anyone would! And very tired, just unable to motivate myself." Bryn nodded, obviously remembering.

"After six months I had a check-up, and there is nothing physically wrong. The doctor suggested antidepressants and I turned them down. I'm perfectly *fine*!"

Rachel let out a breath, sharing the relief she could see on Bryn's face before he frowned. "If he thought you needed medication—"

"I didn't," Pearl said stubbornly. "I got through it."

"In that case," Bryn said, "why aren't you driving?"

CHAPTER SIX

A GOOD QUESTION, Rachel thought, although wondering if Bryn was wise to push the issue. Perhaps she herself shouldn't have asked Pearl to drive, bringing the whole thing to a head.

Pearl cast her gaze about as if looking for an excuse, finally coming up with, "I don't like that car." Even to Rachel, who knew she still missed her red sports model, the excuse didn't sound convincing.

Bryn, too, looked sceptical. "You won't drive *any* car! Even when you're with Rachel you insist on her driving."

Pearl threw up her hands. "Oh, all right." Her cheeks flushed, she said, "I was caught speeding one time too many, not long before Malcolm…went. My licence was suspended for six months. And after that…I don't know," she finished lamely. "I just didn't want to drive. It had been too long and I suppose I'd lost my confidence."

Bryn stared at her, apparently baffled. "Did Dad know?" he asked. "About the suspension of your licence?"

His mother sighed. "I had to tell him in the end. Just before…it happened. The heart attack." Her voice wavered and her eyes filled with tears. "He was very…upset."

Bryn translated, "Angry."

Rachel moved to put her arm about Pearl's shoulders, giving him a warning look.

"What do you mean," he asked evenly, "*just* before he died? Minutes? Days?" Then, his voice gaining force, he said, "You're not *blaming* yourself for his death, are you? It could have happened at any time, the state his heart was in. It was just as well *he* wasn't driving when it happened."

"I know they told us that." Pearl wiped her eyes with her fingers. "But I can't help feeling…if we hadn't quarrelled the day before…we might have had more time."

Bryn stepped forward and took her hands in his. "Listen to me. If he was angry it was because he was worried. You *know* he loved you more than anything in the world."

"Oh, Bryn!" she protested weakly. "You and your sister—"

"He loved us, but he worshipped the ground you walk on."

A shaky smile briefly lit her face before Bryn went on. "He couldn't bear the thought of anything bad happening to you. And after that accident you had—"

"It was *nothing*!"

"It scared him. He wanted you to be safe, and happy. He never tried to stop you driving. If you'd told him you hate that car he'd have bought you another, so why don't you trade it in for something you like? But if I might make a suggestion, get one with a governor—or have one installed."

"A what?" Pearl queried.

Bryn patiently explained. "It limits the maximum speed."

"Oh. I suppose that would be a good idea."

Bryn exchanged a hopeful look with Rachel. Pearl might not sound exactly enthusiastic, but she wasn't dismissing the idea. She hadn't ruled out driving again.

He pulled Pearl forward a little, and Rachel let her pro-

tective arm drop. "Dad would hate for you to make yourself miserable over some kind of misplaced guilt," he said
gently, looking into his mother's eyes. "No time like the
present for getting back on the horse—or into the driver's
seat."

Anticipating his raised glance, Rachel held out the car
key, and he took it and placed it in Pearl's hand.

"Rachel will be with you," he said. "You trust her,
don't you?"

"Of course I trust her." A hint of her old, pert smile
curved Pearl's lip although her voice trembled a little.
"Will she trust *me*?"

"Absolutely," Rachel assured her. Bryn seemed to be
handling his mother's problem with insight and sensitivity
and just the right amount of backbone-strengthening logic.

Pearl looked at the key in her hand, took a deep breath
and said, "All right. Let's do it."

Bryn kissed her cheek. "Go for it," he teased, giving her
a little push towards the driver's seat. "But take it easy, okay?"

Once seated, with Rachel on the passenger's side, she
slid the key into the ignition, and took another big breath
before turning it and carefully pressing the accelerator.
The car moved forward slowly and after entering the flow
of traffic Pearl's driving was unnaturally cautious. But by
the time they'd crossed the harbour bridge Rachel saw that
her white-knuckled grip on the steering wheel had loosened
and her teeth were no longer fastened on her lower lip.

"She was fine," Rachel assured Bryn when he phoned that
evening. Pearl was leafing through fashion magazines in
the little sitting room and Rachel, deciding to make up for
lost sleep the previous night, had been about to go upstairs

when the hall phone rang as she passed it. "A bit nervous at first, but no problems."

"That's great." He sounded relieved. "You've been good for her, Rachel, getting her out of her shell."

"I like your mother. And I haven't really done anything except be around."

"Yes, and I appreciate that. Let me take you out to dinner one evening to show it."

"You've already treated me to a glamorous evening," Rachel said, after a moment's hesitation, "and an expensive present. There's no need—"

"That was business," he said. "And the present was for saving me from an awkward social situation and questions I didn't want to answer."

About Kinzi and the absence of a woman on his arm, he meant. Although Rachel was certain he knew other women who would have jumped at the chance.

Perhaps other women might have been less willing to accept the role of last-minute ring-in.

"Your mother bought me a beautiful dress," she said, "and you both refuse to let me pay for it."

"It was for a Donovan function. Would you have bought it otherwise?"

"No!" *Never in a million years.*

"I rest my case," he said. "Now, would one night this week suit you? Or you name a date."

As if her calendar might be full. "And your mother?"

"Do you feel you need a chaperon?"

"I thought you'd want to get her out, too."

"Let's not push her too fast."

"She'll be on her own."

"For a few hours. She's been on her own most of the

time for almost two years." His voice turned brisk. "I promise I'll get you home by midnight, Cinders. How about
Thursday?"

She knew that tone. He wasn't going to give up, And
further protest would seem like feminine coyness, which
she despised. The stark truth was that the prospect of a
night out with Bryn alone was alluring, even if fraught with
hidden risks.

"All right," she said. "Do you want to talk to Pearl?"

"No need. I'll pick you up at seven on Thursday. There's
a country restaurant I think you'll like, not too far from
Rivermeadows."

Pearl seemed pleased when Rachel told her Bryn insisted on
taking her to dinner, "As a reward for going to the ball with
him, he said." She didn't want Pearl thinking it meant more.

On Thursday she dressed in a cool deep green sheath,
a favourite that she always felt comfortable wearing on any
occasion. Tying a gold mesh scarf about her hips, she
wondered if that was overdoing it, but when she went
downstairs and found Bryn already waiting for her, she saw
he was dressed in dark trousers and a maroon silk shirt that
even without a tie had a semi-formal look.

He gave her an approving once-over and Pearl assured
her she looked very nice, and wished them a pleasant
evening before they left the house.

The restaurant was almost an hour's drive away, attached
to a boutique hotel perched on a hill giving spectacular
views of native bush, with the city lights winking in the
distance across an expanse of satinlike blue-black harbour.

The floor was carpeted and the tables covered in deep
red damask with napkins arranged in fans at each place and

fresh flowers in a low bowl on the table. Everything looked discreetly expensive. The dining room was arranged as a number of spaces holding only three or four tables and joined by wide archways, giving an illusion of intimacy, and easy-listening classical music played quietly in the background.

The maître d' recognised Bryn and led them to a table for two tucked into a lead-lighted bay window that overlooked the darkening landscape. A waiter appeared almost immediately with leather-covered menus and a wine list.

Rachel didn't ask if he'd brought Kinzi here. Almost certainly he had. Annoyed at herself, she studied the list in front of her and asked coolly, "What would you recommend?"

"They change the dishes often," Bryn told her. "The chef is a craftsman. I've never been disappointed."

When they'd made their choices he asked if she had any wine preferences, but Rachel shook her head and left that to him. He ordered wines by the glass, and after two he stopped drinking, saying, "You're not driving. If you'd like something else with dessert, or to finish with, feel free."

Rachel shook her head. As he'd promised, her scallops poached in white wine and the roast lamb that followed were delicious, and the crème brûlée she was now spooning up had been perfectly made with a crisp brown top. They'd talked about Pearl, and Rachel's research, and he'd told her about a timber-treatment company he'd recently picked up in America that had been a family business like Donovan's, then changed hands and went downhill.

"Simply through bad management," he said. "The buildings and plant are sound, though maintenance has been neglected. And they've lost some skilled staff, but with the right person in charge we can bring it back to profitability."

"How do you know when you've found the right one?"

"In the end it comes down to instinct and experience. I've not often been mistaken, but if they don't measure up to expectation, they're out of there with a handsome compensation package before they can do any more damage."

"Can you? Get rid of them just like that?"

"Sometimes the law makes getting rid of a useless, even dishonest employee harder than dissolving a marriage. But our contracts are fair, and I try to avoid legal wrangles."

"By paying them off?"

Bryn shrugged. "The price of my—or a manager's—bad judgement, hiring a dud in the first place. We all pay in some way for our mistakes. Money is the easiest."

"Money won't fix everything," she said.

"Most things," Bryn argued carelessly. "You'd be surprised how easy it is to sway people if you're prepared to part with enough cash."

The old Beatles song "Can't Buy Me Love" came into Rachel's head and haunted her for the rest of the evening.

When they reached Rivermeadows they entered by the front door. Bryn made sure it was locked behind them, saying, "Want a drink or something before we go up?"

"No, thanks." She hadn't known if he meant to stay tonight, but it made sense rather then driving all the way back to Auckland. Turning towards the stairs she said, "Thank you. It was as good as you said it would be."

"My pleasure." He began mounting the stairs beside her. "We should do it again some time."

When they reached the upper floor and her bedroom door he caught at her hand, bringing her to face him. "Rachel?"

His eyes were questioning, expectant, and something in her longed to give him the answer he wanted—perhaps anticipated. Her mouth drying, she made herself take a small step back. "Thank you again, Bryn," she said. "It was nice, although you didn't really owe me anything."

His lips curved, acknowledging the dismissal. "Any time," he said, not letting go of her hand. "Good night, Rachel." He bent forward and gently touched the corner of her mouth with his, lingering just long enough for her to change her mind and kiss him back.

She didn't, although inwardly wavered. When he stepped back and released her hand a pang of regret mingled with relief as she turned to enter her room.

In the following few weeks Bryn seemed to visit more often, sometimes appearing midweek and staying for the evening or even all night. Perhaps, Rachel thought, he was at a loose end with Kinzi gone, and hadn't yet found a replacement. Or was mourning her loss and not ready to involve himself in another relationship.

He'd developed a habit of giving Rachel, as well as his mother, a kiss on the cheek when arriving and leaving. Several times she went riding with him, and on the weekends that she'd gone to visit her family or old friends he commented that he'd missed her.

Sometimes he persuaded his mother to go out for lunch, both of them insisting that Rachel come along, too. Once while she was away in the Waikato he took Pearl to an outdoor concert in Auckland, apparently a great success. He was definitely coaxing his mother back into a more normal life. She had even invited some people over for Sunday brunch once after attending the little church in the village with Rachel. It had become a habit for Pearl to drive them there, but she still hadn't taken the car out on her own.

The day she announced to Bryn over breakfast that she meant to take his advice and buy a new car, Rachel thought for a moment he was going to stand up and cheer. But the glow of gladness in his eyes was extinguished by a certain caution as he said casually, "Good idea. I'll help you choose it if you give me a couple of days to clear some time."

"When I've found what I want," Pearl said firmly, "I'll call you and you can look it over."

Rachel could see Bryn wanted to argue, but instead he nodded. "Okay."

After he left, Pearl asked Rachel rather diffidently if she could take time off to look at cars in Auckland. Guessing she was still nervous of driving in the city alone, Rachel readily agreed.

It wasn't long before Pearl's eye was caught by a new-model silver Peugeot with dashing lines and a steep, raked-back windscreen. A test drive cemented her infatuation, and she asked the salesman to hold it until Bryn had time to confirm her choice.

He said if she liked she could take the car to Bryn for his approval. Hardly hesitating, with Rachel in the passenger seat, Pearl drove to the Donovan building.

Bryn's secretary told the two women someone else was with him, and they waited, flipping through magazines, Pearl impatiently tapping her foot on the carpeted floor.

When the door of his office opened he ushered out a tall, slim, thirty-ish woman, whose superbly cut and shaped blond hair framed an oval face, discreetly made up, and whose fitted skirt and short-sleeved jacket showed off smooth limbs and what Rachel suspected was a salon tan.

The woman held a leather briefcase in a ringless left hand while extending the other to Bryn and flashing him a smile that displayed white, even teeth. "I'll look forward to it," she said, their hands still clasped together. She—or was it Bryn?—seemed reluctant to let go. Even then, she touched his sleeve with her long, ringless fingers and gave him a quick peck on the cheek before turning to leave.

Despising the stab of envy that made her stomach sink, Rachel looked away. The long tanned legs and high-heeled pumps crossed her vision as the woman left and she heard Bryn's voice say, "Hello, Mother. And Rachel. Come along in."

"Who was that?" Pearl asked as soon as she was seated in his office, Rachel taking the chair beside hers while Bryn, as he had before, lounged against the desk, his arms folded.

"A client," he answered. "What have you two been up to?"

"We bought a car," Pearl told him. "Well, nearly. A Peugeot. It's in the car park, so you can look it over if you can spare a few minutes."

"We?" Bryn turned his gaze to Rachel.

Pearl said, "*I* did. Rachel helped."

"Hardly." Rachel shook her head. "I don't know a lot about cars, but your mother is comfortable with it, and it looks very…smart."

He looked with a pained expression from her to his mother and back again. "And I suppose that's important."

Rachel saw the crinkling skin about his eyes that warned he was teasing, and she said with dignity, "It's won awards for fuel-efficiency and it has lots of safety features."

"Are you in love with it, too?" he asked.

No, I'm in love with you! Much to her chagrin.

Of course she didn't voice the unbidden thought. "It's a very nice car. Pearl enjoys driving it."

He duly inspected his mother's acquisition, not saying

much but smiling at her enthusiasm, then took the sales-man's number from the card Pearl handed him, flipped open his cell phone and after asking a few questions said, "Okay. If it's what you want…" Then he looked at his watch. "Have you eaten?"

"Not since breakfast," Pearl told him.

"I'll take you both to lunch to celebrate."

Over salads and seafood, he asked, "What will you do about the other car?"

When Pearl said she hadn't decided, he said, "You won't get much for it, might as well keep it for Rachel's use."

"I can drive the station wagon," Rachel offered.

"It's harder to manage, and a gas-guzzler," Bryn said. "You can go back to Rivermeadows together in the new beast and I'll pick up the old one from the car yard and get it back there to you sometime."

Apparently that closed the subject. Pearl simply nodded. "Who was your client this morning? She's rather striking."

"Beautiful. And smart," Bryn said, causing Rachel another pang. She'd never be able to compete with that kind of svelte confidence coupled with physical perfection.

Bryn continued, "Her name is Samantha and she's Colin Magnussen's daughter. She'd been running her own small business in Australia and came home to take over the family firm a couple of years ago, when he died."

"Magnussen?" Pearl repeated. "The builders?"

"That's right."

Even Rachel knew the Magnussen name. Ever since she could remember, it had been associated with quality public buildings and expensive homes. And the money the family had made.

Samantha was one of the rich list, then. It accounted for

the surely expensive grooming and the air of privilege. There was no faking that. She and Bryn would have a lot in common; both had lost their fathers at a young age and had picked up the reins of the family's business.

Pearl said, "I met Mr Magnussen a couple of times at business functions with your father. A very opinionated man."

Bryn laughed. "Sam left the country and went out on her own because she couldn't work with him, although they were very fond of each other. He'd give her anything she asked for, but they both had very definite ideas about how to run the firm. She's doing a good job, though."

Obviously he admired Samantha Magnussen. For her mind? Rachel wondered hopefully. *Yeah, right.* The woman would make any man's blood run faster.

When they had finished eating Pearl went off to the ladies' room. Left alone with Rachel, Bryn said, "Are you getting your work done? You weren't hired as a chauffeur and lady's companion. Does my mother demand too much? Maybe we should be paying you more."

"The book is on track. And Pearl doesn't demand, she asks, and I'm happy to help. I don't want more money."

He laughed a little. "Then you're a rare being. Most people want all they can get."

Rachel looked at him curiously. Didn't his family have more than they'd ever need? Otherwise how could they afford to so generously support numerous charities and civic projects? Not that they trumpeted every donation to the world, but from the family papers she'd seen that generosity to the community was a Donovan tradition. The amounts they'd given away over the years staggered her. "Is that what motivates you?" she asked. "Making money?"

He seemed to think about it. "No," he said finally. "Not

directly. I suppose it's the satisfaction of adding to, building on, what my forebears began, the challenge of seeing how far we can go. And more urgently, of carrying on our industry in a way that helps maintain and heal the planet."

She hadn't realised he cared. "Sustainable forestry?"

He nodded. "Replanting, growing renewable timber, working with international entities to save rainforests that the world can't afford to lose. Getting products out there to make felling slow-growing, rarer trees unnecessary. Research into things like safer timber preservatives and even paints."

"So money is just a side effect?" she said slyly.

He laughed. "I like the competition of the market, get a buzz from being the best, producing the best. And that's expressed in terms of cold hard cash—or rather, figures in a computer."

"Big figures," Rachel murmured.

"Uh-huh. A measure of quality, and hard, honest work and good judgement."

Unlike his ancestor, Samuel, Bryn had never to her knowledge shoved a log of kauri or kahikatea or even the ubiquitous introduced pine onto a whirling saw to cut it into boards. And Rachel was certain he hadn't handled a ten-foot saw with another man to fell a giant of the forest. But in his own modern computerised world he worked hard, more brain than brawn.

Despite that he was as lean and muscled as any timber man of the nineteenth century. She was glad he hadn't, like those ancestors of his, grown a bushy beard to hide his lean cheeks and determined chin, and camouflage his beautiful masculine mouth. Just looking at him gave her a quiet delight.

Lately Bryn had treated her not very differently from the

way he had when she was the farm manager's brat from
next door. Apart from the kiss on her cheek he bestowed
at meeting and parting, he scarcely touched her.

He talked with her easily, occasionally laughed with her,
shared music or a card game with her and Pearl during evenings at Rivermeadows, discussed the news or challenged
her to Scrabble, or chess, which he played to win, sparing
no quarter, yet was equally sanguine whether he won or
lost.

She ought to be glad that he'd taken her at her word when
she turned down his invitation to his bed. Glad that he'd
backed off and offered no more sexy, difficult-to-resist kisses,
that he apparently was able to forget those few minutes when
she'd been nearly swept away by the power of his sexuality
and her own weakness where he was concerned.

Many women would be happy to enjoy a casual fling
with a man like him—even a one-night stand. Some might
have regarded it as no more than a gesture of comfort to a
friend, like a chocolate bar or a glass of wine.

But Rachel knew that for her, sex with Bryn on that
basis simply wasn't an option. It would alter her life forever.

CHAPTER SEVEN

DAYS LATER BRYN and Rachel stood watching the Peugeot zip backwards out of the garage, turn smartly and head with a discreet roar for the road. "How could I have forgotten what gave my father his first grey hairs?" Bryn said.

"Oh, stop that!" Rachel scolded as they turned to his car, to drive to the riding centre. "Your mother's been driving longer than you have, and her problem with speeding has been solved. She's just a little quick on the accelerator and brake. And you should be grateful she's getting out and about again."

"Ganging up on me?" he grumbled. "My trouble is, I have too many women in my life. Even my secretary's been giving me advice about my…private life. I suspect she's been colluding with my mother."

That surely meant only one thing. Rachel tried to laugh, but something restricted the sound. She dreaded the day Bryn brought another woman to the house. A woman like Kinzi, or like Samantha Magnussen.

Dog in the manger, she admonished herself. That day was surely inevitable. She'd declined to share his bed, and once he got over Kinzi of course he'd find someone else. Not for a temporary balm to a wounded heart, but someone he could love and who would love him back with all her being.

As I would. If only he loved me that way.

Once they'd collected their horses Bryn set a pace too fast for conversation. On the way home they stopped again at the pub for coffee, talked across the table of inconsequentials, and she brought him up to date on the progress of the book, but they didn't touch on anything personal.

The following week Bryn treated Pearl and Rachel to a charity concert. Pearl insisted on lending Rachel the pearl choker again to add glamour to the new dress she'd bought to augment her wardrobe. Another simple style that would suit almost any occasion, it was a dark autumnal red with tiny glints of gold.

Bryn had said he would pick them up rather than having them drive into the city. When Rachel came downstairs to join Bryn and his mother he stood up and gave her a comprehensive, sweeping glance. His face was impassive, and maybe she imagined the quickly doused glow in his eyes before he said, "Very nice, Rachel. Shall we go?"

After the concert, featuring world-renowned New Zealand musicians and singers who held Rachel enthralled, they had supper at an exclusive restaurant with several people she now recognised from the newspapers or TV, even if she couldn't recall all of their places in Auckland arts and society. Bryn did nothing to satisfy the veiled curiosity in their eyes as they discreetly quizzed her. "I'm working for Pearl," she told them, after describing her profession and her present occupation. "And Bryn kindly invited me along with his mother."

Rachel was proud of her family and quietly pleased with her own accomplishments. Yet she was conscious that most of these people were either supremely talented or had been born to money, attended the most prestigious schools, expected the best in everything from food, clothes and entertainment to their homes and the yachts and motor cruisers that several of them owned and regularly sailed. Despite the egalitarianism deeply rooted in New Zealand's colonial history, the world they inhabited was subtly different from the one she had grown up in.

Rachel and Pearl stayed again in Bryn's guest room. In the morning he went off early to the office, and the two women browsed the city shops before enjoying a leisurely lunch in a department store café, and then visiting an art gallery where Pearl bought a small but pricey picture before they returned to the apartment.

There Pearl raided Bryn's drinks cabinet and poured red wine for them both, which in leisurely fashion they drank accompanied by a couple of cheeses Pearl had bought in a delicatessen, and some stuffed olives from Bryn's kitchen. The afternoon was well advanced when she announced she was going to have a nap. "Sorry to be such a bore, Rachel," she said. "I'm not used to late nights any more."

She was sleeping when Bryn arrived home, stripping off his suit jacket and pulling the tie from around his neck as soon as he entered.

Rachel had taken a book from his well-stocked shelves and was curled in a corner of the sofa with her legs tucked under her and her feet bare. Rashly, she'd poured herself another glass of wine and had been intermittently sipping it. Bryn was driving them home tonight and staying for the weekend.

"Hi," he said, eyeing her with an air of amused tolerance. "Don't move," he added as she made to close the book and shifted her legs, ready to get up. "You look very comfortable there." He ambled closer, tossing his discarded jacket and tie onto one of the chairs. Seeing the almost empty glass on the occasional table at her side, and spying the wine bottle, he cocked his head. "And helping yourself to my Ata Rangi Célèbre, I see."

Rachel flushed, stiffening. "Your mother's idea. She's having a nap."

"Hey!" The amusement vanished, his voice gently chiding. "You're welcome to the wine, and anything else you fancy." He turned her face with a hand cupping her chin, sending warm little signals along her nerve pathways. "Surely you know that."

His gaze met hers with perfect seriousness, and she tried to smile. "Thanks. I'm reading one of your books, too."

He smiled back, and removed his hand from her chin to lift the open book she'd dropped to her lap and check the title. It was a New Zealand historical novel by an author who regularly topped the local bestseller lists. "Like it?"

"Yes, she's good."

"Take it with you," he offered. He joined her on the sofa, his elbow resting on the back. He was sitting very close, and his eyes were grey and dark and strangely intent.

Rachel hastily dropped her gaze back to the book, but the words blurred before her eyes.

Bryn got up and lifted the bottle from the table. "Want to finish it?" he queried. There wasn't much left.

"No, I've had enough. Thank you."

He carried the bottle to the kitchen and came back with a half-full glass in his hand. Seating himself on the sofa again, he studied her thoughtfully.

Rachel closed the book, her finger holding the place. "How was your day?" she asked.

"Not bad." He sipped at his glass. "What did you do?"

She told him, adding that Pearl was fine though tired.

"And you?" he queried.

"I'm fine too. We had fun."

"Glad to hear it." His arm rested behind her head, and his fingers began absently playing with her hair, sending darts of sensation up and down her neck. "Don't you have a birthday coming up soon?"

"The fifteenth," she confirmed, not daring to move, although knowing she should. "Why?"

"We should do something special. Or are you planning on going home?"

"The weekend after," she said. "My mother's planned a family party."

He nodded. One finger was tracing a line up and down the side of her neck.

Rachel made an effort to keep breathing evenly. She ought to stop him, but pleasure was feathering down her spine, warming her entire body, no matter how she tried to ignore it.

"Bryn…" she said huskily.

His eyes were half-closed, lambent beneath the dark lashes. "Rachel," he returned, a hint of mockery in his tone, his mouth curving. His hand half circled her neck, bringing her closer as he leaned towards her, and his lips settled on hers.

It was a warm, tender kiss, their lips scarcely parted, and after a few seconds he withdrew, leaving her deliciously tingling all over, also surprised and disappointed.

It had hardly been more than a friendly peck but her head was spinning and her body felt weightless. The wine, maybe. "What was that for?" she asked baldly.

He laughed a little, and drank down some more of his wine. "Impulse," he said. "You're very lovely. Very kissable."

So was he, but she shoved that thought back where it belonged, in the deeper recesses of her brain.

"Do you mind?" His smile was a little crooked.

Wordlessly Rachel shook her head. How could she say she minded when it had been so nice, so…good. And what woman would object to being called lovely? But she said, "You can't go around kissing girls on a whim."

Bryn laughed. "I don't, usually. Only you." Then a strange expression crossed his face, as if he'd just said—or thought—something unexpected. "In fact," he said slowly, "I seem to have made rather a habit of it."

"Well, it's a habit you'd better break," Rachel suggested, but her voice lacked conviction—in fact she sounded to her own ears rather wistful.

"Do you really want me to?"

Rachel glared at him. "I'm not a rubber doll," she said, making him blink, "something you can pick up and put down when the mood takes you, a substitute for the real thing." She uncurled her legs and stood up.

Before she could take two steps Bryn had put down his glass with a thunk on the occasional table and was standing too, grabbing her arm. "Rachel!"

She tried to twist away, but he held her other arm, too, and she stood stiffly, not wanting an undignified struggle.

"Rachel," he said more quietly, "what's this all about? You think I was *using* you?" He gave her a small shake. "It's not like that. I couldn't resist, seeing you sitting there the way you did when you were a kid, but not a kid any more, the *realest* woman I know." A smile hovered on his mouth. "It just seemed right at the time. And you liked it, didn't you?"

"I didn't dislike it," she admitted. Strangely, she was sure that this time he'd been moved to kiss her for her own sake rather than because he missed Kinzi. "But the other times—" she said before cutting herself off.

Darn it, what was the point? She shrugged under his hands and he let her go.

"I can't apologise enough for that first time when you were only a teenager—"

"You already did, and I told you it's okay." It occurred to her that analysing every kiss they'd shared was a useless exercise. "Forget what I said. It was stupid."

"You always were a little firecracker," he said, a faint smile on his mouth, but his eyes were probing, curious. "Only I don't underst—"

Pearl's voice interrupted him from the doorway. "I thought I heard your voice," she told him, walking forward to give him a kiss on his cheek. "You're not quarrelling, are you?" She looked from him to Rachel, her expression a little worried, although her voice was light.

"No," Bryn assured her.

And Rachel said, "Of course not."

They exchanged a glance, both perfectly understanding that Pearl wasn't to be bothered by their private discord.

Back at Rivermeadows Bryn would have liked to continue their earlier conversation, but Rachel went straight upstairs and only came down to help with the dinner preparations.

After they'd eaten he suggested a walk around the grounds and a swim before bedtime, as the weather was warm now, but she declined, saying she was a bit tired, and avoided his eyes.

When he returned from his solitary stroll Pearl told him Rachel had gone up to her room.

"Is she all right?" he asked, taking a seat near the fireplace.

Pearl gave him an alert glance. "She told you she was tired. Is something going on between you two?"

"No." His answer was abrupt. Then he added, "But what if there was?"

His mother's eyes widened for a moment. "Why are you asking me? What happened this afternoon, before I interrupted?"

Bryn shrugged. "I told her she looked lovely. And kissed her. It was only a kiss—hardly even a real one. It barely lasted two seconds."

"And?"

"She didn't object, but afterwards she more or less accused me of using her."

Delicately arched eyebrows rose over Pearl's suddenly piercing blue eyes. "Would she have reason to think so?"

"No! At least—" Bryn rose, and paced away from her before turning. "It's complicated." He shoved his hands into his pockets.

Seeing he wasn't going to confide any more, Pearl said, "Rachel is a very nice girl, everything a man could want, and neither of us would like to see her hurt. So if you plan to kiss her again—or anything else—you had better be serious about her. Because if not you'll be answering to me."

Bryn frowned, meeting her stern gaze with a slightly glazed one of his own. Was he serious about Rachel? He'd never set out to "use" her. But at least once she'd had cause to assume so—when she'd been young and impressionable. And what else was she supposed to have thought now that ever since Kinzi and he had split, he could hardly keep his hands off her?

How could he persuade her otherwise—and make up to her for what he'd done, recently and way back when? That night still made him inwardly squirm with shame.

The answer was suddenly blindingly obvious. Focusing again on his mother, he gave a curt nod, unable to suppress a small smile at the unwonted severity on her pretty face. "You needn't worry," he said, the smile growing a fraction wider when she saw he wasn't going to add anything more, and her tightened lips metamorphosed into a frustrated pout.

The weekend before her birthday Bryn took Rachel to dinner at a club where they could dance. She agreed to go on condition he didn't give her a present, saying the Victorian box was more than enough. He sent her flowers—fragrant roses and lilies and baby's breath, delivered in the morning, with a card saying, "Love from Bryn."

She didn't take that too literally. It was an expression of a fondness he'd had for her since she'd been barely tall enough to reach his waist.

He returned her to Rivermeadows, kissed her cheek and then softly, her mouth, a fleeting caress, before saying, "Happy birthday, Rachel," and leaving.

When he asked her to accompany him again to a business dinner with a group of overseas clients, she said, "Why don't you ask your mother? She might enjoy it, now."

"She says she had enough business dinners when my Dad was alive, and she's old enough to retire from all that. If you help me out here, I promise to make up for it with a proper evening out another time."

"There's no need for that," she said. And that was enough for him to take her company for granted.

She wore the new red go-anywhere dress again and although much of the business talk was over her head, she supposed her role was to keep the partners happy, and played it as best she could. She'd insisted on driving in to Auckland, but agreed to stay at Bryn's flat afterwards with Pearl, who was happy to visit Auckland again and go shopping the next day.

The following weekend they had lunch at a nearby garden café before they went riding, and although Bryn's manner was casual, something in his eyes set off an absurd butterfly fluttering in her midriff and sent some kind of adrenalin rush through her veins.

Then it was a party he'd been invited to by friends. "You met them the night we went to the concert, and they liked you," Bryn told her. "I told them I'd bring you if I could."

"Do go, dear," Pearl said. "They're a nice young couple and I'm sure you'll have a good time."

She did, meeting equally nice new people while Bryn never left her side. This time they drove back to Rivermeadows in the early hours, Bryn having limited his consumption of alcohol while telling Rachel to feel free.

She'd had only one glass more than her usual limit of two, but felt pleasantly mellow by the time she arrived with Bryn at the door of her room. "Thank you," she said. "That was a good party. And your friends are fun."

"They hope to see more of you," he said, and took her face between his hands, making her heartbeat skip.

He smiled into her eyes, then his gaze settled on her mouth, and he kissed her, briefly and sweetly, as if just testing. Before she could even think about responding, he feathered a thumb across her slightly parted lips and then dropped his hands, stepping back. "Good night, Rachel," he said, and strode off to his own room.

Her only consolation was that she thought there was a slight unevenness in his voice before he turned away.

Rachel wasn't quite sure how it happened that they became a couple, but she soon came to realise Bryn's mother was aiding and abetting. Pearl's social life had become busy—visits, lunches and dinners with friends, invitations to other social functions, and her own hospitality to others now filled her calendar. She was frequently out of the house and when Bryn invited her along to some event she often pled tiredness or another engagement and said, "Take Rachel. She'll enjoy that."

Rachel did, and after demurring once or twice decided to go with the flow, make the most of her time with Bryn and try not to imagine a future without him.

One weekend they went sailing with a couple he knew and their baby daughter, a delightfully happy child just starting to walk. Everyone on board kept an eagle eye on the little girl, but she took a particular liking to Rachel, who found the feeling was mutual, returning cuddles with kisses and playing games with her when she got bored.

Her parents were quite open about her conception by in vitro fertilisation. "We'd tried for years," her mother told Rachel, "and in the end we were desperate."

The procedures she described sounded to Rachel invasive, undignified and sometimes painful, but both parents adored their daughter. Perhaps what they'd endured made her all the more precious.

Driving home, Bryn mentioned that his friend had confided in him during the difficult months of tests and procedures. "It was hard on both of them," he commented.

"She's a darling little girl."

"A pet," he agreed, "and I'm glad for them. Still, I'm damned if I'd allow a woman I loved to go through that. And there are no guarantees. If it fails it must be devastating."

"I suppose they knew that was possible but they felt it was worth it."

"Of course, but—" Bryn shook his head "—I'm not knocking their choice, but for myself, I'd never agree to it. Conceiving a baby in a Petri dish—well, I'm happy it works for some and I have to admire them for going through with it all. It's just not for me."

She could understand that. But they hadn't had the experience of wanting to have a baby and not being able to.

At the end of the day his good-night kiss lingered, and when he held her close she knew he was aroused, as she was. But apparently he was satisfied with kisses and didn't press her for more.

Satisfied? Not physically, she knew. But considering his seeming determination to keep their relationship on a near-platonic level, she could only think that he didn't want to get deeply involved.

Maybe the relationship between their two families was a factor. Complications could arise.

Or Bryn might be marking time until someone else turned up—someone who could unleash the passion she knew he was deliberately withholding.

The thought brought a sinking sensation in her stomach. She had begun to hope for the impossible—a future *with*

Bryn. Because wasn't this turning into an old-fashioned courtship? Or was she fooling herself?

Maybe he'd become accustomed to her being his stopgap partner, and didn't want her to get any ideas about permanence or real intimacy.

A flash of anger stopped the hot tears that threatened to spill. If he thought she'd happily put up with being at his beck and call when he needed a woman at his side, and fade into the background when he met someone classier, better-looking, from the same background, she'd…

What? she asked herself derisively. Make a jealous scene about it? The thought made her shudder. Ask him what his intentions were? Hardly better. He knew her time here was almost up. Perhaps he expected their…relationship—if that's what it was—to die a natural death when she left Rivermeadows. If he didn't commit himself in any way, what could be more convenient?

She had a draft of the book on her computer and was working on refining it, cutting, adding and improving, sometimes stopping to recheck a fact or time sequence. Bryn came on her one evening scowling over the screen in the smoking room, and bent from behind her typing chair to kiss her cheek. He gave her hair a tiny tug and whispered in her ear, "'Come into the garden, Maud?' It's a nice evening and there's a spectacular sunset out there."

Scowling even more fiercely because her instinct was to get up and blindly follow where he led, she said, "I'm busy."

Bryn straightened. Then he swivelled the chair around so she was facing him. "Hey, what's the matter?"

"Nothing's the matter. I'm being paid for this job and I can't drop what I'm doing every time you take a notion that you'd like company, or you need a woman on your arm for some corporate bun fight or society do."

"You *are* in a mood," he said, not in the least crushed. Folding his arms, he took a step back, nodding at the computer screen. "Isn't it going well?"

His tone was almost sympathetic, and that was nearly her undoing. The last thing she wanted was to weep on his shoulder. "It would," she said crossly, "if I wasn't interrupted. I only have a few weeks left to get the book printer-ready."

She swivelled the chair again and turned her back to him, staring at the screen without making any sense of the words on the white background.

His hands descended on her shoulders and began kneading the taut muscles. "Relax," he soothed. "No one's going to shoot you if you need more time to get it done. Seems to me you're working too damned hard and too long. It's way after five o'clock. Take a break and get some fresh air." He took her hand to pull her from the chair. "Come on."

Her resistance was short-lived. If only he'd snarled back at her instead of being patient and understanding, she'd have stuck to her guns. As he led her to the door she sighed sharply and said, "Sorry I snapped at you. I had no right."

"My hide's thick," he said, smiling at her crookedly. "And you have every right to tell me if I'm annoying you."

They stood on the terrace and watched the clouds strewn across the pale sky change from fiery red and molten gold to faded pink before turning grey and ghostly, and crickets began to sing in the creeping dusk. Bryn still held her hand and she let it stay, his strong fingers wrapped about hers.

"Let's walk," he said, and tugged her down the steps.

They walked under the archway and strolled beneath the trees that made the air cool and shadowed Bryn's face.

He stopped when they reached the summerhouse, with its festoons of faded jasmine and ivy geranium.

Rachel stiffened and tried to pull away, but he held her hand fast. "You're not frightened of me, are you?" he asked her. His face looked taut and his eyes very dark, a crease in the skin between them. "Not now?"

Rachel shook her head, a definite no. But her mouth was dry and she trembled. Why had he brought her here?

He took her other hand and said, "I scared you, that time. You said you forgave me, but I'll never forgive myself."

"I wasn't scared of you," she said. "I knew I could trust you."

Something crossed his face, like a cloud drifting over the moon. "That was your mistake."

Again she shook her head. "No mistake, Bryn."

He closed his eyes momentarily, squeezing them tight. When he opened them again they seemed brighter despite the deepening gloom all around. "Then you were a naive little fool," he said gratingly. "I was *drunk*. God knows what I'd have done if I hadn't had just enough sense left to send you away. Almost too late."

She had been naive, and foolish. He was right about that. And she was lucky that the man she'd chosen to throw herself at was Bryn. Even drunk he wasn't the type to take advantage of a stupid teenage girl with a serious crush on him and absolutely no experience of men.

She hadn't meant to incite him. Her impulse had been to comfort him in any way she could, and a hug seemed to be what he needed. And to kiss him gently was only natural. She'd daydreamed about kissing Bryn, but had never thought she'd have the nerve to actually do it. Nor the opportunity.

Or that he'd ever welcome it.

But that night was different. Bryn was hurting and she couldn't bear to see it.

He hadn't reacted at first to the kiss. She'd already been pulling away before he moved.

With her arms about him, she'd smelled beer and wrinkled her nose at that, but the hard strong body against hers, his arms coming around her, and another underlying scent she'd never smelt before, but that somehow thrilled her deep down, had woken new sensations.

Her breasts ached in a strangely pleasant way and she felt the centres tighten and harden; her breathing quickened and something shuddered through her like liquid fire, making every part of her—even the most private, intimate parts—feel sensitised.

Vaguely she knew what this was. Sexual arousal. She'd read about it, been told clinical, decidedly unromantic-sounding details in school, experienced odd, undefined stirrings. But nothing had prepared her for this—this overwhelming yearning to be closer, to know how it felt to really kiss a man, hold him, be held by him, let him touch her in places no one had touched her before that she could remember, in ways she'd only ever imagined or read about.

When he wrapped his arms about her, holding her so tight she could hardly breathe, and kissed her almost fiercely, opening her mouth irresistibly beneath his, she'd been both shocked and thrilled. She wound her arms about his neck, holding on to her balance, and tasted beer—and Bryn—in her mouth. She felt his hand on her nape, supporting her head, his fingers in her hair, and then he shifted to tuck her head into the crook of his arm, still kissing her in that desperately sexy way. He touched her breast, setting her on fire, so that she instinctively arched against him, going on tiptoe, her body a taut-stringed bow.

His pelvis thrust against her and she knew what she'd done to him. A flutter of alarm and disbelief mingled with a pagan, primitive triumph that must have been as old as time, when the first man and woman who had ever coupled discovered this marvellous, miraculous need for each other, this wondrous pleasure in each other's bodies.

Bryn lifted her, his hands at the top of her thighs, and staggered a little, then dropped clumsily to his knees so that she tumbled onto the sleeping bag he had spread on the ground and that earlier she'd tripped on. Then he was on her, touching her everywhere, his breathing harsh and heavy as he kissed her mouth, her neck, her shoulder, pulled at the neckline of her nightgown, then found the hem and shoved it upward past her thighs.

Since puberty she'd always been shy about her body, reluctant to wear a revealing bikini or throw off her clothes without thought in the school changing rooms. Now she felt exposed. A cold draught intruded into the summer-house, sent goose-pimples up her arms and along her legs, making her shiver.

She looked up at Bryn's face and saw a stranger, shadowed eyes eerily blazing from deep sockets, cheek-bones with the skin stretched across them, mouth set in a tight grimace. She felt the boards beneath the sleeping bag under her hips, shoulder blades and head. And the heaviness of the body that tangled with hers, all muscle and male strength. She had never known how strong a man's body could feel, that she would be helpless in a man's embrace.

Reality began to seep icily into her consciousness.

She tried to lift him a little, but he didn't seem to notice.

His hand stroked her inner thigh, down and then up, and touched the moist folds between them. The sensation was unlike anything she'd experienced, shooting through her entire body like a lightning bolt—a sharp, bright spear that brought part pleasure and part panic.

Panic and the sudden advent of shame won. She slammed her legs together and gasped, "No!"

Then she began to struggle.

Bryn reacted slowly, muttering, "What?" And when she repeated her repudiation, her voice high and alarmed, he said something explosive that made her wince. But to her relief he rolled over and off her, to lie panting on the bare boards.

"Get out," he said, his voice so thick and gravelly it was unrecognisable. He had one arm flung across his eyes.

"I'm sorry," she whispered. "I didn't mean—"

Gulping, she recalled her private vow not to throw away her virginity easily and early as some of her friends had done, often to their later regret. Romantically, she'd dreamed of retaining that gift that could only be given once, for the man she would love forever. And even in the throes of her immature crush on Bryn Donovan, she'd known in her heart that when she was truly grown up there would be someone else.

"I said," Bryn's voice came louder, harsher, "*go*! For God's sake—and yours."

Wretched, she stammered, "If…if I can do anything—" Boys said they'd be in pain if something like this happened. She swallowed hard, then leaned over to touch him. "I know you wanted—"

He swept her hand off. "I wanted a f— A woman," he said as if speaking through gritted teeth. "Not a bloody schoolgirl. Will you get…*the hell*…out of here before I do something we'll both regret!"

She gave a gulping sob and backed away, then turned and ran stumbling into the dark under the trees, oblivious of twigs snatching at her naked arms, unseen plants whipping at her legs and snagging the hem of her nightdress.

She lost a slipper, snatched it up and ran on with it in her hand; the shells on the path bit into her foot but she didn't care. Incongruously she thought of Cinderella, and even though tears poured down her cheeks she giggled, stifling the sound of hysteria by biting her teeth into her lower lip as she reached the open gate to home.

She had to stop and steady her breath before creeping across the back lawn and climbing through the window into her room, where she slipped under the covers and buried her head in the pillow so no one would hear her crying.

CHAPTER EIGHT

EVEN TEN YEARS LATER, standing at the entrance to the summerhouse with Bryn, the memory of that night had Rachel blinking away tears. She tried to shake them away, her hair falling about her face in the faint breeze as she moved. She pulled her hands from Bryn's clasp and dashed a knuckle against the corner of her eye where one tear had escaped. "I knew you would never hurt me," she said.

Except for that moment of panic when he'd seemed a frightening stranger, as though someone else had taken over his body. Until then the uncontrollable and bewildering physical need that had overpowered her own body made her more tense and nervous than anything Bryn had done.

Then he'd moved away from her, flung himself on his back and snarled at her to go. She knew now that he'd been trying to save her from herself—and him. "You did the right thing," she said. "If I hadn't been so young I'd have realised I was playing with fire. You wouldn't have had to shout at me to make me leave."

"I'm not sure exactly what I said," he admitted. "Only that it was pretty brutal. And you never gave me a chance to say sorry before you went south with your family.

Every time I tried to corner you, you scuttled away. I thought I'd terrified you, that you were afraid I'd attack you. Again."

"You didn't attack me! If anything, it was the other way round. I shouldn't have kissed you. It was stupid."

"It was very sweet," he said. "If only I'd left it at that…."

"Well, it doesn't matter now."

"It does to me. And I haven't been blind to the way you avoid this place. I want to…exorcise the ghost of that night, for both of us. Will you trust me, Rachel?"

"Yes," she said instantly.

He held out his hand and she put her own into it.

Bryn led her inside the little building, where a few fallen leaves whispered under their feet. The light was dim but not yet dark. He took her to the bench where they'd sat so long ago, and kept her hand in his as he sat and pulled her down at this side.

The trees outside cast faint moving shadows on the floor. A couple of curled, dry leaves scurried over the boards.

For several minutes they sat in silence, and gradually the tension she hadn't even registered began to leave her.

Bryn said quietly, "You used to come here often."

Rachel nodded.

"Before that night. And never since."

She didn't answer, but he knew. After a moment he said, "Me too. No one likes to be reminded of making an idiot of themselves. But lately I can't help remembering. And it isn't all about guilt and remorse, though I know it should be." He paused, and his voice lowered. "Does that disgust you?"

Rachel turned to face him. "No! It wasn't your fault I came here—"

"I'm not making excuses, Rachel. If I hadn't deliberately drunk myself out of my mind nothing would have happened. You know that. At least I hope you do."

Of course she knew. "If you brought me here to apologise again—"

"That's not why," he said. "Maybe it was a bad idea. I just thought—it's where we had our first kiss. And if you can discount how it ended… Can you? Or was the whole experience too horrible to think of?"

"It wasn't," she said. "None of it was horrible. But I wasn't ready for an adult sexual…encounter. If I hadn't stopped you I might have found it quite wonderful."

"I doubt it." His voice was clipped. "The circumstances weren't exactly ideal. *Was* your first 'encounter' wonderful? I hope so."

"They hardly ever are," she said carefully.

"I'm sorry," he said. "And I didn't mean to pry. I'd just as soon not know about the men you've made love to."

Of course not. Why would he be interested? She turned her head to stare out through the doorway.

He said, "If you can't stand being here…"

"No, it's all right. I'd forgotten how peaceful it always was, specially at night. Lovely." Tiny stars had begun to glimmer between the now stilled leaves of the trees outside. Other plants were almost indistinguishable in the creeping dusk, but she could smell their mingled aromas. Roses, jasmine, lilies. Perhaps more that she couldn't identify.

Breathing them in, she also breathed a different, closer scent, familiar yet exciting, unique to the man beside her. A combination of clothing and male skin, a hint of soap or perhaps aftershave, and something else—the subtle, alluring scent of Bryn himself.

She closed her eyes, every nerve alert. Bryn's hand

about hers tightened, and then his other hand was on her chin, turning her face to him, and she opened her eyes.

His face looked grave and taut, his eyes darkly glimmering. He fingered away a curling strand of hair from her cheek and tucked it behind her ear. His hand rested now on her neck, the thumb under her chin.

He lowered his head towards her and she didn't move. His mouth brushed hers lightly before he withdrew, studying her reaction.

Rachel swallowed, and her lips involuntarily parted a fraction, her eyes held by his.

He kissed her again, still lightly, though lingering longer, making delicious little forays before he lifted his head and said, "I hope bringing you here wasn't a mistake. That you'll have better memories after tonight."

Poignant ones, Rachel thought. If she let him kiss her again, that would be *her* mistake. Because if she kissed him back, and one thing led to another...

The thought of even one night spent making love with Bryn was far too enticing.

Maybe that was what he had in mind? To erase any negative feelings about this place—and about Bryn himself—by giving her a totally different experience, a gentle seduction as reparation for the past.

A sop, she thought bitterly. Not much different from the Band-Aid he'd insisted on applying after she'd stubbed her toe that first day of her return. Or the chocolate bar he'd given her when she was six and had scraped her knee and he'd taken her to his mother for some first aid.

If she succumbed to temptation now, she'd never get Bryn out of her system. She'd be crying inside for the rest of her life.

She pulled her hands from his and stood up, and he followed suit. "It was a nice thought, and I appreciate it. But if you brought me here to—" *have sex?* "—make love, thank you, but the answer is no."

"Rachel, wait!" She was almost at the door when he caught her hand again and made her face him.

"On a bare floor?" He shook his head. "No. I brought you here because I wanted to ask you to marry me."

She must be asleep—dreaming this whole thing. Her mouth opened but no sound came out. So of course it was a dream.

But surely her eyes were wide open? She blinked hard and widened them again. That seemed real enough. Bryn's hand on hers felt like solid flesh and bone and muscle. The sudden breeze that cooled her skin, and the rustle and plop of a possum dropping from one of the trees and scurrying over the fallen leaves, surely were real. And when Bryn grasped her shoulders and gave her a tiny shake, saying with a hint of laughter in his voice, "Is it such a shock?" the reality of it was unmistakable. "Rachel?" he said.

Finally she found her voice, although it came out in something resembling a squeak. "Yes."

"Yes, it's a shock, or yes you'll marry me?" he demanded. His hands tightened.

She almost said *Both*, but some dimly heard voice of doubt stopped her. "It's a shock," she said. "I had no idea—" *that he had marriage in mind.* "Why?" she blurted. "You're not...you don't love me!"

"Of course I love you! I've always loved you."

Not the way I meant. Not the way I love you, *as if no other man in the world exists for me, or ever will.*

"What do you think I've been doing these past couple

of months, taking you about, spending half my time at Rivermeadows?"

"Marking time," she said dazedly. "Until something—someone—better came along."

"You goose! It didn't take me long to realise I couldn't do better than the girl right under my nose, the girl I've known most of her life and a good chunk of mine. You're beautiful, and smart and kind and honest, and you make me laugh. If you say yes, Rachel, I'll be a very lucky man."

Wanting to fling herself into his arms, saying yes, yes, yes! Rachel reminded herself that if something seemed too good to be true it usually was.

Was this a rebound from his affair with Kinzi? Maybe he'd decided to play safe and settle for the less exciting, familiar girl next door after losing the glamorous, vivacious and high-profile Kinzi.

Bryn said huskily, "I love you, and I want you, as my wife and the mother of my children. You love Rivermeadows, don't you? We could live here and bring up another Donovan family, just as my mother wants."

His mother? Was this for Pearl's sake, because she made no bones about wanting grandchildren? Surely Bryn wouldn't allow her gentle pressure to influence him?

With a small, impatient sound, Bryn pulled her close, his hands going to her waist, and kissed her thoroughly, with skill and tenderness and increasing passion. And when her heart was pounding erratically and her body singing, he lifted his mouth and kissed her at the curve of neck and shoulder, while one hand slid to her breast, exploring the soft curve.

"You won't need to give up your career. I can afford all the help you need with the domestic side. Anything you want, it's yours."

He kissed her temple, and her cheek, and then her mouth again, this time quickly but firmly. He took her head in his hands and tipped her face. *"Anything,"* he reiterated.

She reached up and gripped his wrists, pulling away from him. It was impossible to think while he touched her.

"Rachel? Please say yes."

He stood rigid, waiting for her to answer.

He'd said he loved her. Asked her to marry him, have his babies. What more could she want? If his love was mostly affection left over from their earlier years, and only partly a new awareness of her as a woman, why complain?

Because if he couldn't give her his whole heart, perhaps he'd break hers.

But hers was ready to shatter anyway at the thought of leaving Rivermeadows, of cutting Bryn out of her life.

Either way she risked pain and grief. And if she took the coward's choice she would be turning down the chance of a lifetime—of spending her life at his side.

The chance to make Bryn really love her, and…

"Rachel?" His voice sounded raw, his body emanating tension even with a metre of space between them.

"Yes," she said. If she was dreaming, why spoil it? It was the best dream she'd had in years. "I'll marry you."

There, she'd committed herself.

For a long moment they stood looking at each other, though now she could scarcely make out Bryn's features in the darkness.

Then he stepped towards her and took her hands again, kissing them one by one almost solemnly, as if sealing her answer. "Thank you," he said. "I promise I'll do everything I can to make you happy. Shall we go and tell my mother the good news?"

* * *

If Rachel had held any doubts that Lady Donovan wouldn't approve, they were soon dispelled. Pearl was ecstatic, hugging and kissing them both, and insisting they telephone immediately to inform Bryn's sister over in England, and then Rachel's family. After that she took the phone and spoke at length to Rachel's mother about possible wedding plans, and on hanging up instructed Bryn to open a bottle of real champagne.

They finished the bottle before Pearl went up to bed, leaving Rachel and Bryn to follow.

On the stairs she stumbled a little, and Bryn laughed as he steadied her with an arm about her waist. "Can't hold your drink?" he teased.

"I'm not drunk," she protested unconvincingly. "Just a bit…happy."

He kissed the top of her head. "I hope you're a lot happy. I am."

At her bedroom door he gave her a quick, warm kiss on the lips, said good-night in a husky voice and gave her a little push inside. Then he left her, closing the door behind him.

Surprised but also relieved, Rachel readied herself for bed in a haze, partly due to the champagne. Maybe that was why Bryn hadn't suggested they share a bed—because she'd drunk enough to make her ever so slightly tipsy.

Once under the covers she began to go over what had happened in the summerhouse, reliving those wildly seductive kisses, and his astonishing proposal. Bryn had said he loved her. Maybe he wasn't *in* love with her, but that, according to the people who studied human behaviour, was a transitory condition anyway. In lasting relationships it gave way in time to a deeper and more enduring emotion.

Affection and some sexual attraction might be a better foundation for marriage.

All the same, she thought wistfully, it would be nice if they could share that once-in-a-lifetime experience that had inspired millions of poems, songs and love stories.

She couldn't help feeling just a little cheated.

Bryn presented her with a ring that had been passed down through the Donovan family for generations, but he slipped it on to her right middle finger. "I want to buy you an engagement ring," he said. "Until then, and afterwards, this makes you a Donovan bride." It was a wide band of gold, set with emeralds and a central diamond. He kept his hold on her hand and gently kissed her.

They were in the little sitting room, while Pearl busied herself in the kitchen after dinner.

Rachel looped her free arm about Bryn's neck and kissed him back almost fiercely.

As if taken by surprise, he drew away, then gave a quiet laugh and tugged her to the sofa, where he ensconced her on his knee and kissed her properly until she was breathless and flushed, and his eyes glittered with desire, his cheeks darkened. She was wearing a T-shirt and jeans, and his hand was inside the shirt, exploring the contours of her back, unhooking her bra, finding her breast with a cupped hand and running his thumb over the burgeoning centre.

Rachel gasped, arching in his arms, her head thrown back, and she felt his lips on her throat, burning a passage down to where the T-shirt's V-neck frustrated him.

He made a short, low and primitive sound, roughly pushing up the hem of the shirt, but quick footsteps in the passageway made him pause, and Rachel hastily scrambled off his knee to sit beside him, pulling the shirt down before Pearl entered the room.

She smiled knowingly at them, went to her usual chair and picked up the book that she'd left open on the arm. "I'll take this up to my room," she said, but instead of leaving right away she asked, "Have you two set a date for the wedding?"

"Not yet," Bryn replied. "But for me it can't be too soon. Is six weeks long enough for you mothers to make your arrangements?"

Rachel said, swallowing a nervous flutter in her throat, "Six weeks?"

Bryn turned to her, with raised brows.

Pearl repeated, "Six weeks! Is there a reason to hurry?" she asked, with a tinge of censure.

Bryn gave her a straight look. "Rachel starts lecturing in two months. I'd like to have time for a decent honeymoon."

"Need it be a big wedding?" Rachel asked tentatively.

"Not if you don't want it," Bryn said.

But Pearl looked disappointed. "It's the first Donovan wedding in a generation," she said. "Our relatives and friends will expect to be invited, and Rachel's family must have people they'd like to come."

Rachel supposed a Donovan wedding was always a lavish occasion. And she knew her own mother dreamed of seeing her only daughter married in traditional style with all the usual trimmings.

"Well," Pearl said briskly, "it'll be a stretch, but I daresay we can manage."

Six weeks later Rachel entered the little church at Donovan Falls on her father's arm, and saw Bryn waiting for her in

front of the altar, his eyes dark and intent, his mouth unsmiling. He cast a comprehensive look over the filmy veil
held by a wreath of white flowers, and the simply designed
gown of brocaded satin featuring tiny seed pearls sewn into
the fabric.

When his eyes returned to hers, he gave a small nod of
approval, and as she neared him he held out his hand to take
hers in his strong clasp.

The wedding ring he placed on her finger at the appropriate time was a plain gold band as she'd requested, and
later she replaced above it the diamond solitaire in an in-
tricate, finely wrought gold setting, that he'd bought for her
days after his proposal.

In the last few weeks she had scarcely seen him. Apparently going off for a honeymoon meant he had various
complex matters to take care of first. He hardly ever stayed
at Rivermeadows and, when he did, he always said good-
night to Rachel at her bedroom door.

In the conscientious throes of finishing the manuscript
of the Donovan history while consulting with her mother
and Lady Donovan about the myriad details of the wedding, Rachel had her own reasons for being grateful that
Bryn didn't press her for sex, yet couldn't help wondering
at his circumspection.

Perhaps being in the same house with his mother inhib-
ited him, although Pearl made a point of giving them time
alone. Or maybe he just wasn't that impatient to take their
lovemaking all the way.

When they went out it was with his friends. Bryn said
he wanted her to get to know them. Rachel had lost touch
with most of her friends in New Zealand, so not many of
them were at the wedding.

The reception was held at Rivermeadows, and fortunately the weather was fine, although in case of rain a marquee was pitched on the front lawn.

Rachel fielded congratulations from all the guests and tried to remember their names. Among them she recognised the tall, elegant form of Samantha Magnussen wearing what had to be a designer suit and a wide, conspicuously stylish hot-pink hat.

"We haven't met," Samantha said warmly, smiling at Rachel after introducing herself. Apparently she hadn't noticed the two women waiting the day Rachel and Pearl had watched her leaving Bryn's office. "Bryn's a very good friend." Turning to him, she put a hand on his shoulder and kissed him on the mouth. Just a peck, then she stepped back, smiling again, her hand sliding down the front of his jacket before returning to her side. "Congratulations, darling. I never thought you'd do it. I guess even the tallest tree in the forest has to fall some time."

Bryn laughed. "Very philosophical." He hooked an arm about Rachel's waist and pulled her closer. "I'm a lucky man."

Samantha turned a coolly assessing glance on Rachel before her lips curved again. "You know," she said, "I'm sure you're right. Does she know what she's taking on?"

"I do," Rachel answered firmly. "I've known Bryn since I was five."

Samantha looked a little surprised but the smile didn't waver. "Well, I wish you all the best, and I hope you'll both be very happy." Her gaze shifted to Bryn before she strolled away.

Dying to ask Bryn just what that was all about, Rachel

had to turn to another well-wisher instead, and once the moment had gone there was no way of finding out without making an issue of it.

The day seemed to pass in a dream. Rachel kept reminding herself she was now Bryn's wife. He was by her side, his hand holding hers or guiding her through the throng of guests offering congratulations. Once the temporary tables were cleared from the big formal lounge room and they danced to the three-piece string ensemble, she felt she was floating off the ground.

When it was all over and she'd changed into street clothes, they drove off in Bryn's car to his apartment, where they were staying the night before flying to an exclusive lodge in the far north of the country.

After mentioning other people who had attended the reception, finally Rachel couldn't stop herself. Keeping her voice as casual as she could, she said, "Samantha Magnussen looked very elegant. I didn't realise you and she were close friends."

"Close?"

"That's the impression I had. Does she call all her friends 'darling'?"

A smile momentarily touched his mouth. "Probably. She's one of those women who just can't help using their femininity to advantage, but when it comes down to it, have steel at the core. In some ways she reminds me of my mother."

"Your mother?"

"It isn't a criticism. I love my mother, and I admire her hidden strength."

Rachel fell silent, and Bryn threw a quick glance at her as he slowed for an intersection. "You're not worried about Sam, are you?"

Sam? "Worried?" she asked innocently.

"Jealous." Bryn laughed in a rather pleased, indulgent way that made her hackles rise. "We're too much alike, she and I, both control freaks."

"I'm not jealous!" Rachel denied. She was sure Samantha wouldn't have rebuffed Bryn if he'd shown interest, but reminded herself he'd had plenty of opportunity and not taken it. Instead he'd been wooing Rachel, and it was Rachel he'd married. She'd hold on to that, banish Samantha Magnussen from her mind.

After parking the car they took the elevator to his flat, and he strode to his bedroom, dumped her overnight bag on a curved stool at the foot of the big bed and turned to her.

He seemed remote as his gaze took stock of her. "You look tired," he said.

Rachel tried to smile. She was deathly tired, the strain of the past weeks showing now the pressure was off. "I'm all right." Sounding overly bright, she knew.

She would have liked to walk into his arms, have him hold her, but he made no move and his aloof expression bothered her. Was he already regretting having married her, realising he'd committed himself to life with a woman for whom he felt only a lukewarm kind of love?

"It's late," he said, "And you've had a long day. My...*our* bathroom's there." He indicated the door. "Help yourself."

As if she were a guest. Rachel opened her bag, took out toiletries and the low-cut oyster satin gown she'd bought the previous week, and made her way into the bathroom.

When she returned Bryn was standing by the bed. He was barefoot and had taken off his shirt, loosened his belt. His hair was rather tousled, and he looked lean and handsome and very sexy. His eyes flicked over her and then away. "Finished?"

His voice sounded clipped. When Rachel nodded, he headed for the bathroom.

He'd turned down the bed covers, revealing pristine white sheets and pillowcases. Rachel hesitated and a picture flashed into her mind of Bryn and Kinzi lying there together.

Involuntarily she turned away, a hand at her mouth to stifle an anguished sound, and found herself at the window, staring at the closed curtains.

The room seemed stifling. She pulled back the curtains. There was no balcony, and through the glass she saw a few lights in nearby buildings, and the sky tower that dominated the cityscape of Auckland, lit with red and green floodlights.

She found a catch and pushed open a window, to be met by a roar of traffic noise from the street below, the wail of a police siren passing the building, and when that faded, the sound of music and voices coming from somewhere nearby.

"Hey." Bryn's voice startled her and she turned. "What are you doing?"

"I wanted some fresh air," she said.

"All you'll get there is petrol fumes and noise," he told her. He stood beside the bed, in wine-coloured pyjama bottoms that hung at his hips. They looked brand-new, still creased where they'd been folded. "I'll turn on the air conditioning."

He went to a control on the wall, and Rachel closed the window, but left the curtains a little apart.

Bryn had his hand on the light switch now. He said, "Get into bed."

She moved towards it, and paused. "Which side do you sleep on?" she asked.

His mouth took on a wry grin. "Mostly I sleep in the middle."

Mostly. When he was alone. Rachel took the nearest side, pulling up the sheet and blanket, her head on two pillows.

The light went out and she could see nothing for seconds, but she felt the mattress depress, heard the slight rustle of the sheet as Bryn lay down beside her. The bed was wide and they weren't touching. She could make out the shape of him now, in the bit of light that edged through the opening in the curtains.

He lay with his hands behind his head, apparently staring at the ceiling. Rachel made an effort to relax.

Bryn turned unexpectedly, his face a blur in the darkness, propping himself on one elbow. Rachel stiffened, her emotions a mixture of expectation and nervousness. There was something she should tell him before it was too late.

But with luck he might never know. Maybe she should just keep quiet.

His hand reached out and the back of his fingers touched her cheek in a brief caress. "Go to sleep, Rachel," he said, sounding rather weary himself. "You're exhausted. I'm not going to insist on consummating our marriage tonight."

Blankly she watched him slide down against the pillows again. Had he given her the real reason? Or…he didn't want to make love to her?

She wasn't the only one who was exhausted, she reminded herself. Bryn had been working hard so he could go on holiday without worries or interruptions. Now he'd closed his eyes and was breathing evenly, either asleep already or pretending to be.

Hardly the eager bridegroom she'd expected. She ought to be grateful for his consideration. Instead she felt flat, empty.

Rejected.

You know he wants you! she told herself. He'd said so,

and she'd enough evidence that he found her desirable.
Men couldn't fake that as women might.

Desirable perhaps. But obviously not irresistible.

And on that lowering thought she went to sleep.

CHAPTER NINE

RACHEL WOKE TO the sound of the shower behind the closed bathroom door. When Bryn emerged, a towel tucked about his waist while he dried his hair with another, she was out of bed and rummaging in her bag for clothes.

"Good morning," he said, walking towards her, and as she straightened, her hands full, he dropped a kiss on her cheek. "We have an hour to get to the airport. I'll make coffee and toast while you get ready."

He had everything organised, and Rachel had hardly time to take a breath between leaving the apartment and getting on the plane. It was a small aircraft with only two rows of single seats, and within an hour they had touched down, to be picked up by a courtesy car from the lodge.

Surrounded by native bush and only a short pathway from the sea, the lodge was set in lawns and gardens. Built in Victorian style, with gables and a wide veranda set with a couple of outdoor tables, inside it was discreetly sumptuous.

Their spacious upstairs room, with its own balcony, had two queen beds and in one corner a two-seater sofa and matching armchair, with a round coffee table. There were tea-and coffee-making facilities and a well-stocked bar fridge, and they were given a choice of what they'd like for lunch, served either in their room or the dining room downstairs or, if they preferred, on the veranda with a view of the bay.

They opted for the veranda, and when their host had departed Rachel began unpacking. Bryn quickly did the same, and said, "We have time for a short swim before lunch. The lodge has a pool." From their room they could see a rough, white-speckled sea, with high, uneven breakers laden with seaweed and driftwood that were hurtled onto the beach and left behind by a vicious undertow. Although here the weather was calm, there must have been a storm out in the Pacific.

"Okay." Rachel picked out her swimsuit and hesitated, feeling stupidly shy. Bryn glanced at her with a tiny quirk at the corner of his mouth, and then turned away, beginning to unbutton his shirt. Rachel stripped and had pulled on the swimsuit before he turned around again, wearing shorts.

The pool was clear and sunlit, the temperature just warm. They swam side by side at first, then Rachel floated on her back for a while, contemplating the lazy, apparently unmoving clouds against an intensely blue sky. After a while she stroked for the pool edge and sat watching Bryn.

Eventually he breast-stroked over to her. Standing in waist-deep water, he gripped her waist in his hands and lifted her down.

Rachel gasped and involuntarily steadied herself with her hands on his bare, wet shoulders. He was giving her an oddly tight-lipped smile. "Now, wife—" he said. His head dipped, and his lips, moist and cool with water, found hers in a masterful, questing kiss.

Surprise held her motionless until his arms came about her, bringing their near-naked bodies into contact. Bryn coaxed her mouth open and a surge of joyous, delicious sensation made her shiver. Her arms slid around his neck, and he moved his hands down over the curves of her behind, then cupped and lifted her against him. His mouth travelled down the side of her neck, and nuzzled the soft flesh exposed by her low-cut swimsuit.

Her own response shocked her. She gave a cry as her body was consumed by pleasure, washing over her again and again, accompanied by a need to be closer to him, to experience this moment to the full, the ultimate physical delight. She was dimly aware that Bryn had shifted his stance, moving against her and prolonging the helpless, unstoppable spasms that seemed to go on and on, while she tried to bury her small screams and moans with her mouth against his shoulder.

As the paroxysm faded, she let out a long, uneven sigh, and heard Bryn make a guttural sound before his hold loosened and her feet again found the bottom of the pool.

She rested her bowed head against him, still tingling all over, not wanting to move and almost afraid of looking at him.

"Hey," he said softly. His cheek rubbed against her temple. "You okay?"

Rachel nodded, still not looking up, embarrassed at her loss of control. She moved her head up an inch or so and said, "What if someone had seen us?"

His chest shook with quiet laughter. "We're the only guests and the staff keeps well out of the way unless we want them. It's part of the deal. But we can continue this in our room. Where there are two perfectly good beds."

"It must be close to lunchtime."

And if they didn't turn up the staff would guess exactly why. Rachel moved away, and her eyes widened, a hand going to her throat. *"Oh!"* On Bryn's shoulder were the clear, reddened imprints of her teeth. "I'm sorry! I *bit* you."

Bryn squinted down at the marks, then laughed. "A real little tigress, aren't you? The scars of battle, which I'll wear with pride."

"No, you won't!" Rachel was horrified. "You'll put a shirt on. It's not a battle scar, it's a…a…"

"A love-bite," he finished for her. "All right, I'll cover it up if it embarrasses you." A glint came into his eyes. "But don't think you can make a habit of giving me orders, my sweet. I don't take kindly to them."

"Neither do I," Rachel informed him. The marriage ceremony they'd chosen didn't have any promise to obey. "It goes both ways."

He nodded, but she suspected he had reservations. They might have a few things to work out between them if this marriage was to be a success.

After leaving the pool and dressing they had a lunch of smoked salmon and salad with white wine before the staff disappeared, telling them there was a phone in their room and an intercom in the lobby, should they need any service.

Rachel sat staring at the hypnotic advance and retreat of the shallow waves washing on the curve of reddish sand that defined the little bay. A long way out a white sail dipped and swung on a faint breeze.

Bryn said, "Want to walk on the beach?"

"Yes." She got up quickly, discarding her sandals, and they walked across the buffalo grass that was springy underfoot, and onto the sand. It was gritty with the remains of the orange-red sandstone cliffs and the pulverised shells that had formed it.

Bryn put his arm about her waist as they strolled just above the waterline, defined by glistening clumps of sea-weed and a few stranded jellyfish, to an outcrop of smoothed grey rock that jutted into the sea and defined the bay. He had left his shoes behind, too, and when a rogue wave came in farther and deeper than the others, wetting his trousers, he rolled them up to below his knees.

He helped Rachel climb onto the rock shelf and they explored the tidal pools and watched the seaweed floating back and forth at the end, where the waves smashed against the rock and one sent spray flying into their faces and onto their clothes, making them hastily move farther back.

Rachel's cotton shirt and skirt were soaked with water that felt icy cold, and she tasted salt on her lips.

Bryn eyed her with interest. "You look like a contestant in a wet T-shirt contest," he told her.

Rachel made a face at him. "I suppose you're a regular patron at those."

A disconcerting gleam in his eyes, he said, "You'd win hands down." Then, "We could have our own private one."

His white T-shirt was wet, too. If there were male wet T-shirt contests he'd have her vote every time.

The sea breeze picked up, making her shiver, and Bryn said, "We'd better go and get you out of those things."

Back in their room Bryn stripped off his own shirt as soon as they were in the door, then strode to the bathroom and tossed it onto the marble counter before turning to Rachel.

The look in his eyes told her his intention, and her heart leapt as he grasped the edges of her still damp shirt and pulled it off when she automatically raised her arms.

He threw the shirt aside in the general direction of the bathroom, and looked at her, his mouth curving at the sight of the flimsy lace and satin bra. Rachel bit her lip and felt herself flushing.

His hands went to her waist, resting for a moment on

her skin, before he slid them around the top of her skirt
until he found the zip at the back and it fell around her feet,
revealing the minimal undergarment that matched the bra.

"Very nice," he said, his voice deeply approving. "But
wet." His hands covered the bra, making her breath briefly
halt. Then his thumbs brushed across the erect centres
visible under the thin fabric, and he gently pinched them
with thumbs and forefingers. Rachel closed her eyes and
he said, "I'm not hurting you, am I?"

"No." Far from it.

Bryn lifted her face with both hands and momentarily
she opened her eyes, to see his glittering with desire before
his mouth descended on hers, sending her mindless with
its erotic force and passion.

When he stopped kissing her he took her hand and swept
the covers down on one of the beds, picked her up and lowered
her to the sheet before shucking off the rest of his clothes.

"I've waited far too long for this," he said huskily as he
came down beside her, leaning on one elbow. "But I'll try
to take it slowly, for you."

He kissed her again, while his hand roved her body, and
then he kissed her throat, the valley between her breasts, and
her stomach, her thighs. "Sit up for a minute," he murmured
and unhooked her bra, slid it off and pulled her back against
him as he leaned on the headboard and began exploring her
body with both hands, slipped a finger into her panties and
made a small sound of satisfaction at what he found.

She knew she was about to explode again into ecstasy,
and said, "No! Please…"

"You don't like it?" His questing finger stilled.

On a gasping little laugh she said, "I like it, but—oh,
please, Bryn! I want you."

She heard him—felt him—draw in a breath. "I want you, too," he said. "But I want to see your face, all right?"

Rachel nodded. "Yes."

He manoeuvred her onto her back, and stripped off the flimsy remaining garment, then positioned himself over her, looking into her eyes before she felt him at the entrance to the most intimate part of her body, and she held her breath in anticipation, her hands on his shoulders. He muttered something and as he entered she briefly experienced an uncomfortable stinging sensation. She drew in a sharp breath, and he paused. "You okay?" he asked hoarsely.

"Yes," she breathed, "yes." And raised her hips, inviting him in. "I want you," she said again.

He felt so big, so hard and strong, yet as he moved slowly and gently her flesh parted around him, stretching to accommodate him, holding him snug within, and she started to relax as delicious little thrills ran through her, becoming stronger and more intense when he began moving rhythmically, looking down at her as if checking that she was all right with this.

And she was more than all right, her lips parting while the sensations gathered and spread and engulfed her so that she bucked against him and he released himself to her as the world spun and they were lost in each other.

He rolled over so she was lying along the length of his body, and with the movement she felt an aftershock of pleasure, rocking on him to savour and increase the feeling, while he held her close and whispered encouragement until she lay still and spent, her head dropped against his shoulder as her breathing steadied.

For a long time she didn't stir, and when she did Bryn still had his arms about her. They lay on their sides, face-to-face. He kissed her and said, "You're a wonder, Mrs Donovan."

"Really." *Better than Kinzi?* She pushed the thought away. Jealousy was destructive and unattractive.

He looked troubled. "Something felt…you were so tight. You're not…this can't have been your first time?"

Trying to sound casual, she answered, "Actually, it was." There was nothing to be ashamed of in sticking to a girl-hood vow, no matter that many people would have called it unrealistic.

His shadowy form remained still and the silence stretched.

Finally he said, "Why didn't you tell me? I might have hurt you! *Did I?*"

Rachel shook her head, then realised he wouldn't see. "No. It was a little uncomfortable at first—"

He muttered, "I should have guessed."

"I thought maybe you had. When we were engaged, you didn't…you never suggested we should sleep together."

"It seemed the right thing, with you. Right to marry you, and…I hoped if I didn't press you for sex you wouldn't accuse me again of using you." His voice lowered. "And in a way it was a kind of penance."

"For what?"

"For the past." He paused, and in an almost stricken tone, asked, "Am I the reason you were the last twenty-seven-year-old virgin in the western world? What I did to you—"

"Don't flatter yourself," she said quickly. He seemed determined to cling to his sackcloth and ashes. Cutting down his ego was the only hope of stopping him. "Plenty of women have other things to expend their energy and emotions on. And it saves a lot of angst and complications."

"Hmph." He didn't sound convinced.

"Well, maybe it's harder for men," she conceded. "Although that's debatable. Historically in our culture they've been encouraged to think so, but social and cultural anthropologists have found—"

He laughed and hugged her closer. "I don't need a history lesson, my sweet." After a moment he said slowly, "I'm flattered you thought I was worth it."

Because I love you. She didn't say it aloud. He might have been perilously close to the truth when he asked if he was the reason she'd never slept with anyone else. Not because she'd been traumatised, maybe not even because of the romantic notion that she'd like to share something unique with the special man she hoped was in her future, but no other man had been able to match her memory of Bryn Donovan.

She was Bryn's wife. Even if he didn't feel as she did, he would keep his promises to love and cherish and be faithful to her. And being the man he was, he'd do his utmost to be faithful in heart as well as in body.

Shouldn't that be enough for any woman?

They made love every day, often several times, and at night, getting to know each other's bodies, exploring every plane and hollow and curve, every tiny imperfection, from the jagged scar Bryn carried at the top of his thigh from a childhood fall out of a tree, to the small round mole at the base of Rachel's spine that he said wasn't a blemish but a kissing spot, and set out to prove it.

They swam every day, too, in the sea after it had calmed and become benign and tame, teasing each other with games that turned to foreplay before they raced together, laughing, up to their room. At night they sometimes took a blanket down to the beach and spread it on the cool night sand in a hollowed-out cleft in the cliff, shadowed by plants clinging to its face, and made leisurely love there to the rhythm of the waves.

Bryn hired a car and they travelled to Paihia, where the first missionary settlement from England had been established, fighting an often losing moral battle with the whalers and traders who roistered in ramshackle inns across the water, and who stole girls from the mission with offers of calico dresses for themselves and firearms for their menfolk.

Once Bryn drove along country roads until they found an isolated spot where the thick bush held ancient kauri trees and hid outcrops of huge volcanic or limestone rocks. And on a soft mattress of moss beside a clear, stone-strewn stream, hidden among lacy ferns, he made love to Rachel in a way she would never forget. Afterwards they bathed naked in the stream, and Rachel came out aching from the cold water, but feeling more refreshed than she ever had before.

The time went by too fast, and the day came to return to real life, and Rivermeadows.

Rachel moved into Bryn's room, and persuaded Pearl that there was no need for her to find another home. "Later, maybe," she laughingly told her new mother-in-law. "When the house is full of children and you can't stand the noise."

"My grandchildren?" Pearl said. "I won't care how much noise they make!"

After Rachel began her new lectureship, she and Bryn often stayed in the city overnight, but she always felt that Rivermeadows was home.

The history of the Donovan family was launched at a

crowded, no-expense-spared function attended by local dignitaries and any employees or ex-employees who cared to come along, as well as some of Rachel's university colleagues. Pearl seemed in her element, presiding over it all and proudly introducing her son's wife to anyone who hadn't met her before.

After her first semester Rachel felt ready to cope with a pregnancy, but as time went on she became concerned.

Bryn said he was in no hurry but she couldn't help the nagging feeling that she was somehow at fault, not giving him what he'd expected from his marriage to her.

On the Internet she found all kinds of advice on diet and the things to avoid or to use to make conception likely, and took on board those that seemed to make sense. Certainly a lack of sex wasn't the problem. The opportunities now weren't as available as on their honeymoon, but it was still good, and she had begun to think that Bryn might even be falling in love with her.

Not that he was lavish with endearments or given to showering her with roses. But there was warmth in his gaze when it rested on her, lambent desire lurking in the depths of his eyes. He laughed often, and if business had parted them for a day or two his eyes seemed to light up when he saw her again. And his lovemaking when they were alone would be even more passionate and exciting than she remembered.

Pearl said, "Marriage suits Bryn. I haven't seen him so relaxed and happy for years."

On their first anniversary Bryn booked a table at an exclusive Auckland restaurant, and Rachel drove to the apartment to change into a new dress she'd bought for the occasion. Low-necked and figure-hugging, it was made of rich cream silk shot with amber.

She checked her clothes and make-up in the long dressing table mirror and picked up the pearl-and-diamond choker that Pearl had given her as a wedding present.

Bryn appeared behind her. "Close your eyes," he ordered, taking the necklace from her.

"Why?" But she did as he said.

Bryn's fingers were on her nape and her heart flipped. After a year he still had that effect on her.

Expecting the choker around her throat, she felt something cool and light and involuntarily opened her eyes, lifting a hand to touch the pendant that sparkled deep, deep amber with gold lights, on a delicately wrought gold necklace set with tiny diamonds. "Oh, Bryn!" she breathed. "It's beautiful!"

"I'm not done yet. It's part of a set." Her left hand was taken in his, and he slipped something over her wrist and fastened it.

She saw that the same unusual stone sparkling with more diamonds formed the case of the delicate watch, far too dainty for everyday wear.

Bryn said, "It's a nineteen-twenties cocktail watch. You don't mind that it's second-hand? I thought you'd rather like something with a history. Even though the shop couldn't tell me much about them."

"Mind? No!" He knew her well. "I love it—and the necklace. Thank you, but…"

She'd bought him a gift, too. Fossicking in a rare books shop during her research, she'd found an old map of the area around Donovan Falls and had it framed for him. He'd seemed pleased when she presented it to him earlier, but it cost a fraction of what he must have spent. She touched the necklace and said, "You must have paid an awful lot of—"

"Shh." He put his hands on her shoulders, meeting her eyes in the mirror. "It was worth every cent to see you wear them. Perfect with your eyes." He kissed her shoulder. "You look stunning. Ready to go?"

After a superb dinner, during which she intercepted several envious glances at the necklace and watch, they arrived back at the apartment and after shedding her shoes she went to the dressing table, placed the watch in the antique box he'd bought for her and raised her hands to remove the necklace.

"Don't," Bryn said, and came to stand behind her as he had earlier. He'd taken off his jacket and undone the top button of his white shirt.

Rachel dipped her head for him to undo the clasp of the necklace, but instead he wound his arms about her, pulling her close and kissing her nape, her shoulder. His fingers moved to the zip at the back of her dress and slowly slid it down, then he undid her bra, and slid both dress and bra down her arms.

"Bryn…" It was a feeble protest. His hands cupped her breasts and his eyes glittered.

She closed hers, and he said, "Don't be shy. Watch, darling."

Rachel opened her eyes, at first self-conscious, seeing her own body change under his ruthlessly erotic ministrations, the flush that spread over her skin, the way her breasts peaked between his finger and thumb.

Then she began to feel fascinated, excited, knowing that Bryn, too, was watching her every reaction, his breath like hers becoming uneven, louder.

When his roving fingers caressed her between her legs she gasped and writhed, then leaned against him, silently begging him not to stop. He didn't. Her head went back, her mouth falling open in ecstasy, and he gave a low laugh, pressing his own open mouth to the curve of her neck and shoulder, relentlessly bringing her to an orgasm that left her limp and spent.

She turned in his arms, burying her head on his shoulder until the last shudder left her body, and then he leaned forward, swept the tiny box, a comb, a hand mirror and a bottle of perfume to the back of the dressing table and lifted her to sit on it, before he stripped off his shirt and everything else and came into her while she gripped his shoulders and felt herself beginning to soar again, to that place where nothing mattered but this experience of mutual, uncontrolled pleasure given and received.

After a few moments he said, "Put your legs around me."

Rachel laughed breathlessly but did as he asked, and she laughed again when he lifted her again and staggered to the bed before collapsing on it, but the laughter died when another wave of pleasure unexpectedly washed over her and she had to cling to him, biting her lip and making tiny mewing sounds against the warm, damp skin of his shoulder.

"Go for it," he said, kissing her cheek, her ear, holding her tightly and gently rocking. "Enjoy yourself."

He was still hard inside her, and even as she went limp, dizzy and sated, he, too, came to another climax, holding her afterwards for a long time before they reluctantly parted.

When she finally fell into an exhausted sleep, her cheek resting on Bryn's chest, her last conscious thought was *Surely tonight we've made a baby.*

CHAPTER TEN

SHE WAS WRONG. Weeks rolled again into months, and still there was no sign of a Donovan heir. Pearl had begun to ask discreet questions, and although Rachel's own mother was reassuring, she had no magic fix. "It just takes some people longer," she said. "And if you're anxious about it, that only makes things worse."

Without telling anyone, in the long Christmas break Rachel asked the Donovan's doctor to refer her to a gy-naecological specialist. Sometimes she had to pretend to be visiting friends or going off on an overnight research trip. After a long series of uncomfortable examinations and exhaustive tests she learned that her reproductive system had what the doctor called "congenital anomalies" further complicated by abdominal adhesions from the removal of an inflamed appendix when she was eleven years old.

"Surgery followed by IVF is possible, but the outcome is doubtful," he told her. "The chances of carrying a healthy baby to term are realistically…well, I'm afraid, almost certainly non-existent."

On leaving the doctor's rooms, distraught and shaking, her mind oddly blank, she walked for several minutes in the wrong direction before remembering she'd parked the car at the Donovan building, not knowing how long she'd be in town. In a daze, she turned and walked the several blocks back.

At the car she climbed in, then sat staring at nothing through the windscreen. Part of her wanted to go to Bryn's office, hurl herself into his arms and cry.

But some things even Bryn couldn't fix. She remembered his total rejection of artificial conception. Her own initial feeling was aversion to the whole concept.

She felt disfigured, ugly, as if anyone could see that inside she was what the doctor had called "malformed."

A surrogate? Their child in another woman's body? She wasn't even sure she could produce a normal ovum.

Yet if Bryn really wanted children of his own…

A baby that was Bryn's but not hers? Could she bring herself to accept that? Every instinct screamed no.

They could adopt, but surely what Bryn wanted was a child of his own flesh and blood to carry on the Donovan name and inheritance. To ultimately inherit the business, Rivermeadows, everything he and his forebears had built over time. Which she knew more about than he did himself after her delving into the family archives. There weren't many such dynasties in New Zealand, going back to pioneer days. It would be a tragedy if all of that were lost.

Absorbed in her thoughts, she didn't at first realise that the couple emerging from the office building were Samantha Magnussen and Bryn. Two tall, handsome people with the same air of confidence and success, walking in step with each other, Samantha's blonde head contrasting with Bryn's dark one that was turned towards her as she chatted to him.

Instinctively Rachel slid down in her seat, not wanting

them to see her until she could control her emotions. But she watched as they stopped by a car. Samantha unlocked the driver's door and Bryn leaned forward to open it for her.

Instead of getting in, Samantha turned to him, fingered a strand of hair back into its sleek style, tipping her head, and said something that made Bryn laugh. She laughed, too, looking up at him although he was only a few inches taller, and then he bent and kissed her cheek, and she gave his chest a casual little pat before she curled her long body gracefully into the car and waved as she drove off.

It doesn't mean anything, Rachel told herself. She might have fancied him but he married me. They're friends. Good friends. Though she'd never seen Samantha at Rivermeadows until the wedding, nor had Pearl known her before she and Rachel had seen her in Bryn's office.

Bryn was standing with his back to Rachel's car, seemingly looking in the direction Samantha had taken. Then he turned and strode to the building without looking around, and disappeared through the doorway.

Rachel took a deep breath. She could follow him, casually mention she'd seen him with Samantha.

And then?

Don't be stupid. The last thing he needed was a wife who didn't trust him.

Who couldn't even give him a child.

Bryn would never betray his marriage vows. Even if he were forced to admit he'd made a mistake.

Fear clutched her heart, creating a centre for the vortex of emotions that swirled inside her. Surely this news must make him rethink his commitment to her, to their marriage.

He wouldn't be underhanded about it—he'd be kind and sympathetic and generous—but wasn't continuing the family name his major reason for marrying? And if he wanted a divorce how could she refuse?

She turned the key in the ignition and drove out of the car park, not even sure where she was going until she had left the city and found herself on the road to Rivermeadows.

Halfway there she remembered she was supposed to be going to a business dinner tonight with Bryn, staying the night in the apartment.

Pulling over, she left a message with his secretary, telling the woman not to interrupt him, but "I feel a little sick. Nothing to worry about, only I don't think I can make dinner tonight. Tell him I'm sorry, and I'm on my way to Rivermeadows."

On her arrival she parked the car outside the garage and went in by the kitchen door. Pearl, coming to meet her on hearing the car, took one look, steered her to a chair in the kitchen and sat her down before brewing a cup of hot sweet tea and making her drink it.

When Rachel had finished it Pearl said, "Now tell me what's the matter. It isn't Bryn, is it? Have you quarrelled? That's normal in a marriage, you know. I'm sure it will blow over."

"No. We haven't quarrelled." Rachel had an urge to pour it all out to Pearl, but Bryn should be the first to know. Pearl, too, would be bitterly disappointed, and the longer Rachel delayed putting the devastating news into words, the better. "I'm a bit tired," she said. "And not feeling well."

She recognised the light of hopeful speculation in Pearl's eyes and said sharply in her anxiety to dispel the notion, "I'm not pregnant!" Her eyes stung and she turned away, hurriedly standing up. "If you don't mind I'll go and lie down for a while."

"Of course," Pearl said. "Can I do anything?"

Rachel shook her head. "I'll be all right." Her voice was muffled but steady.

With an effort of will she stemmed the tears before reaching her and Bryn's room and thankfully shutting the door. Then she let go for a few minutes before wiping her face with a tissue, then sat on the bed for a long time, knowing she must eventually break the news to Bryn. And Pearl. It was true she felt sick, nausea churning in her stomach. She rinsed her face in the bathroom, then lay down, trying to think.

What was she going to do? How was she going to tell Bryn? At least he'd be staying in the flat tonight after his business dinner. She'd have until morning…

She didn't remember drifting into an exhausted sleep, but was woken by the sound of the door opening. Daylight had dimmed, shadows filling the corners of the room.

"Sorry," Bryn said. "Did I wake you?" Then he was striding across the floor and taking her hands in his as she struggled to sit up.

He sat on the bed facing her, his face taut and concerned. "You're ill?"

"Not ill, not really. You didn't need to come. What about your dinner?"

He brushed that aside. "I cancelled. You didn't have an accident?"

"No." *Only an accident of birth.*

One hand touched her cheek. "You're pale. My mother said you looked dreadful when you arrived. Do you need a doctor?"

Her brain felt fuzzy. She must have been asleep for at least an hour, maybe more. This afternoon seemed like a nightmare, something that had never really happened.

"I have to tell you something," she said, her voice low.

"Okay, go ahead." When she didn't immediately do so he gave her a tight little smile. "I'm your husband, remember? In sickness and in health, for better or worse, etcetera. It can't be that bad."

She opened her mouth to blurt it out, then closed it again, reeling. *For better or worse...until death us do part.*

Earlier she'd reminded herself that Bryn would never break his marriage vows.

And suddenly she knew he would never ask her for a divorce.

All she had to do was tell him what she'd learned, or even say nothing and let the truth gradually sink in that they were not going to have a family. She could stay married to him, either way.

It was up to her.

She pulled her hands from his, sure she was going to be sick, and gasped, "I need the bathroom." He got up and she fled, a hand to her mouth, locked the door behind her and gagged emptily over the toilet.

"Rachel?" Bryn tried the door. "Are you all right?"

"Yes," she managed to say, finally finished. "Wait a minute."

She turned on the cold tap, drank some water, splashed her face again and dried it. Lowering the towel, she caught sight of her white cheeks and bloodless lips in the mirror, the faint blue shadows under her eyes.

Think. She needed to think. She had never deceived Bryn in her life. She couldn't imagine living with him and keeping her monstrous secret. Cheating him.

Staring into the mirror, she had a clear flashback of watching Bryn walking with Samantha Magnussen across the car park this afternoon, of realising how alike they were, both from the same kind of background, moving in the same world. So easy with each other. Samantha was the sort of woman who could no doubt run a large company with one hand and raise a perfect, healthy and well-behaved family with the other. The sort of woman a man like Bryn should have married. On first sight of her, Rachel had thought they were ideally suited.

Slowly she hung up the towel and opened the door. Bryn reached out to hold her arm and she flinched away. "Please don't touch me."

He frowned. "Are you OK? You'd better lie down again."

"I don't need to." She walked past him, then turned to face him, her hands clasped hard in front of her. He had his hands in his pockets, looking back at her with a baffled expression.

She said, "I…I'm so sorry, Bryn. The thing is, I want—" the last words came in a near-whisper, something clogging her throat "—to end our marriage. A divorce."

For several seconds he seemed turned to stone. Then he shook his head, his brows drawn together. "Divorce?" He stared as if she'd grown horns. "You can't mean that!"

"I do." She had to sound more certain. "I do!" she reiterated. "I made a mistake, a stupid mistake, marrying you. It wasn't right and I…" Her voice sank. "Please try to forgive me."

"What the hell are you talking about? What have I done?"

"Nothing! You've been wonderful."

"Then for God's sake…!" Apparently lost for words, he threw out a hand.

"I th-thought," she improvised, "that friendship and…and sex—" she swallowed "—was enough. We'd known each other forever, and I'd never met anyone else that…anyone I wanted to marry. It's a kind of loving, isn't it?" She couldn't help an ironic, sad laugh. "But not the sort to build a marriage on."

She was twisting the truth, attributing his motives to herself. "It's better to admit being wrong now rather than later."

Disbelief roughened his voice. "You really mean this?"

She could only nod. His expression was one she'd never seen on his face before—holding cold anger, disbelief…and suspicion. At last he said, "There's someone else." As if it were a proven fact.

About to deny it, Rachel hesitated. Would that convince him? She bowed her head, whispered again, "I'm sorry."

In two strides he reached her and gripped her shoulders. *"Who?"*

He looked terrifying, his eyes a dark, thundercloud grey, his face pale with the skin stretched over the bones, his mouth curled into something akin to a snarl.

"No one you know," she said. "Does it matter?"

His eyes narrowed. His fingers dug into her shoulders, and she knew he didn't realise it. In a strange way the small hurt was welcome, something that broke through the sense of unreality that surrounded her like an invisible cocoon.

"Tell me who it is!" he said. "His name."

"No!" But she needed to be more convincing than that. "He's someone I met at university. Another lecturer. But not in my department," she added hastily. If he could narrow the field Bryn might…

Might what? Once he got over the shock of her announcement, he'd calm down and be reasonable. Bryn was always reasonable. He had no real intention of tracking down her phantom lover. And if for some reason he tried, it would be a needle-in-a-haystack exercise.

His hands tightened further and she winced.

He released her, flexing his fingers. "How long have you known him?"

"Not as long as I've known you," she said, "obviously. But quite a while. I...we realised we're in love, and I tried, but I can't go on like this. I'll go somewhere else tonight, take the car if you don't mind, and some of my things. I'll get the car back to you."

"Keep it," he said.

"I can't do that."

He gave a harsh laugh. "But you can walk out on your marriage, just like that?" He snapped his fingers.

"Not like that," she said. "It isn't easy, Bryn, believe me. I don't want to hurt you—" Because he was hurt, she could see that. As any man would be whose wife said she preferred another. If nothing else it wounded his pride, threatened his masculinity. And she was certain Bryn had never thought that Rachel, who had adored him as a child, who had rashly offered him comfort as a teenager, and agreed to marry him as a woman despite knowing he felt little more than fondness for her, would let him down.

He'd get over it. And she...? She'd learn to live with what she'd done. Somehow.

She had to. "Please," she said softly, and she couldn't stop tears burning her eyes. "Please don't make it more difficult for me than it is, Bryn. I have to do this."

He seemed to be trying to see into her soul, with a burning gaze that seared her to the heart. "If that's what you want," he said at last, "you'd better go."

Rachel sagged, less with relief than despair. She'd burned her boats. "I'll…just pack a few things," she muttered. Banal words, the practicality of it seeming monstrously out of place when she had just destroyed the most important thing in her life.

Bryn didn't leave the room, but stood watching as she hauled a few undies and nightclothes from drawers and dumped them on the bed, picked up some other things from the dressing table. She crossed to the big rimu wardrobe and pulled out clothes at random, went back to the bed and only then thought about what she would put them in.

There was a small wheeled suitcase on top of the wardrobe, part of the luggage she'd brought to Rivermeadows. Dully she looked up at it, realising it was too high for her to reach.

Bryn, his mouth a straight, uncompromising line, walked over and brought it down for her, then flung it onto the bed.

"Thank you," she whispered, not daring to look at him. His silent fury seemed to thicken the air in the room, and she switched on the bedside lamp to dispel the gloom that filled it, and so she could see as she hastily stuffed clothing into the suitcase. Then she remembered she'd need shoes, and went back to grab a couple of pairs from the bottom of the wardrobe.

Bryn moved aside when she headed for the bathroom for some toiletries, and came back to add them before zipping the case shut. Automatically she looked around, checking if she should take anything else.

"Do you have money?" Bryn asked, as if the words were forced from him. "Your credit card?"

"In the car," she said. She hadn't even brought her shoulder bag in when she arrived, her single thought to get to

Rivermeadows and hide from the world. Not even a thought really but more of an instinct, like a rabbit pursued by a dog, running to the safe haven of its burrow.

Only it wasn't hers. Rivermeadows belonged to the Donovans and she would never again be welcome within its gracious, timeless homeliness.

She picked up the suitcase, finding it surprisingly heavy, and Bryn stepped forward, his face hard and cold and condemning. "Give me that," he said.

"I'm all right." A helpless longing engulfed her. Even now, he couldn't help his ingrained courtesy getting the better of him. She tried to resist, but when his fingers touched hers she relinquished the case. He held it easily, not immediately moving away.

"I'll see a lawyer," she said, trying to sound as if she knew what to do. "Unless you want to…"

"We'll both need one," he said harshly. "That's how it works. Let me know who yours is and mine will be in touch. It takes two years here, you know. No such thing as a quickie divorce."

She nodded. "Excuse me." He was blocking her way to the door.

He moved aside but she'd taken only a step when he caught her arm. "Goodbye, Rachel," he said. Then he dropped the suitcase, and his hand on her waist pulled her close. Her startled eyes caught a glimpse of his glittering, furious gaze, and the next instant he was kissing her with a raging, pitiless passion.

It took all her will-power to stay still and rigid in his arms. When his hold slackened a little she made an effort to free herself, but the kiss changed. His mouth became tender and coaxing, almost a plea for forgiveness, his hand cradling her head, his hold firm but no longer cutting off her breath, more as though he held something precious that needed to be handled with care, and knew his strength could break it.

He took her head in both his hands, his mouth still moving caressingly, beautifully over hers. She should push him away but was afraid to touch him, afraid that if she did, all her good intentions would fly out of the window and she'd be lost. She felt tears sting her eyes, sliding down over his fingers.

He lifted his mouth away from hers and looked at her, his thumbs stroking her wet cheeks. "Don't cry," he said quietly. His head bent again and he kissed the tears away. Rachel trembled, and raised her hands to his wrists, but tugging at them had no effect. "Bryn," she said. "I ca—"

"Shh." He cut off her feeble protest, and she tasted the salt of her tears on his lips as he claimed hers again, one hand sliding to her waist, the other cupping her nape.

No-o! her mind cried despairingly. But her body had never been able to withstand Bryn's lovemaking. She didn't resist when the kiss became deeper, and his hand found her breast. Her weak, "Please, Bryn," when he kissed her just above the V-neck of her top was hardly a convincing protest. Nor her momentary refusal to raise her arms when he stripped the top from her and kissed her again where her bra dipped in the middle.

By that time her blood was roaring through her veins and when they fell onto the bed together she already had her arms about his neck and had ceased to think at all. She was as eager to strip his clothes off his body as he was to remove hers.

They fell together into ecstasy, breast to breast, thigh to thigh, fused together so closely that his every movement was hers, her every sigh his, everything they felt when they reached the pinnacle of pleasure together was a part of both of them because they were no longer a man and woman but a single being.

Afterwards Bryn lay panting with Rachel's head on his shoulder. Slowly, behind closed eyes, her mind cleared and her heart turned into a cold, hard lump of lead.

Bryn drew a long breath, his chest lifting beneath her cheek, and he said, his voice low and certain, "You can't leave me now."

She wanted to stay within the loose circle of his arm, snuggled against him, never to move again. Reluctantly she began to edge away, but his hold tightened and he kissed her temple. "I'm damned sure you couldn't make love to me like that if you loved someone else."

"Bryn—"

"Don't spoil it," he said roughly. "Whatever the hell that was all about, it can wait."

She turned her head a little and kissed his skin. A reprieve, and she had a bittersweet few more minutes to lie in his arms and pretend everything was all right. But meantime she'd better decide what she was going to say when he demanded an explanation.

Maybe ten minutes later she realised Bryn was asleep. Another five, and she cautiously raised her head from its resting place and looked at him. The bedside light was still on, and he lay on his back, eyes closed and his lips slightly parted. Her heart turned over with love for him, and ached with sorrow. Carefully she edged away, lifted his encircling arm and lowered it to the bed before crawling out almost inch by inch.

She tiptoed to the bathroom and, afraid to turn on the

shower, gave herself a hasty all-over wash before quietly dressing again, retrieving the suitcase and opening the door.

She didn't completely close it before slipping down the stairs like a wraith. In the downstairs hall she paused. There was no sign of Pearl.

Glancing at her watch didn't help in the unlit hallway. Pearl was probably waiting with dinner, and keeping out of the way so as not to disturb her and Bryn.

Hesitating, Rachel saw the notepad on a polished table beside the hall telephone. She picked up the pen lying on top, biting her lip, then scribbled a quick note.

Almost silently she opened the front door, again leaving it slightly ajar, crept down the steps and stowed the suitcase in her car before taking off, her jaw so resolutely set that it ached, and the window wound down, letting the air flow inside, in an effort to stem the tears that stung her eyes.

CHAPTER ELEVEN

RACHEL STRETCHED and got up from her computer, made herself a snack in the kitchen of her flat in Dunedin, the country's southernmost city, and turned on her small-screen TV. She felt heavy and lazy, and when the doorbell shrilled it was a moment before she even realised that it was her bell and not the neighbour's.

Puzzled, she heaved herself from the chair and went to the door, hooking the security chain on before opening up and peeking through the gap.

Then she gasped. Her instinct was to slam the door shut, but Bryn stopped it with a hand on the panel and a foot on the step. "Let me in, Rachel. I'm not going away."

Her heart thumping, she considered for several seconds before giving in. But his stony, determined expression warned her he meant what he said, and she shut the door to remove the chain, then opened it again.

He stepped into the small hallway and Rachel backed to the room where the television was blaring through an advertisement for sporting goods. She crossed the room to switch it off before turning to Bryn, who was standing a couple of steps inside the doorway, staring at her, his face an odd waxen colour.

Automatically her hands went to her midriff, which only accentuated the visible bulge beneath the loose cotton dress she wore.

She saw Bryn's throat move as he swallowed, then he said, hoarsely, "Did the bastard leave you when he found out you were pregnant?"

Rachel's mouth fell open, and she blinked, then shook her head. "It's not like that."

"No?" He looked sceptical. "Why else did you run away, walk out on the university, move as far south as you could get? Did you know you were having his baby when you left me?"

"I didn't walk out—I told the university I had to leave." Pleading a medical condition, not entirely untrue, after she discovered that against all odds she was pregnant.

Bryn said, "I know your mystery lover isn't here. You live alone. What are you doing for money?"

The barrage of questions hit her like blows. She latched on to the last one, the easiest. "I have a job." She'd been lucky to be snapped up as a researcher by a local institute, and was able to do much of her work at home on the computer.

Bryn looked around disparagingly at the minimal furniture and slightly worn carpet that she'd dressed with a couple of cheap, colourful rugs. She hadn't spent much on her temporary home, thinking she'd need money later if…

There were a lot of ifs.

Bryn said, "Does he plan to do anything to help you— and pay maintenance for his child?" His voice was sharp, jagged. A coiled anger showed in his taut face in his eyes, which looked more deep-set than she remembered.

Rachel put a hand to her own eyes, her head drooping. She didn't know what to say to him, tired of the lie she'd been living, battered by his questions. Her knees were watery even though her legs seemed made of lead. "I don't need help. I can't—"

She felt his hand grip her elbow. "For God's sake, sit down," he said and led her to the sofa opposite the TV. He sounded more impatient than solicitous, and he didn't sit, looming over her with hands in his pockets and a scowl on his brow. "Do you want a glass of water or something?"

"No. Nothing." Particularly an angry man firing questions she couldn't answer. She looked up at him. "How did you find me?" Her phone number was unlisted; only her family knew her address and she'd made them promise to not divulge it to anyone, but particularly Bryn.

"Confidential," he replied. "Does it matter?"

Rachel supposed not. "Why did you come here?" she asked.

He didn't answer immediately. "My mother's worried about you," he said at last. "That note you left her didn't explain much. Sorry, thank you and goodbye?"

"Did you tell her…what I told you?"

"She was imagining all kinds of disasters, so I had to tell her in the end. She doesn't believe it."

But he had. Fortunately for her plan, yet that hurt more than anything.

Oh, what was the use of going on with this pretence? She looked away, staring blankly at the empty TV screen for a moment, then said, "She's right, Bryn. There was never any mystery lover. The baby's yours."

The stillness of his body, the silence in the room, were frightening. She didn't dare look up at his face.

From outside came the distant hum of traffic. Somewhere someone was playing rock music with a heavy beat.

Bryn's feet shifted, and he walked rapidly away. She squeezed her eyes shut, thinking he meant to leave.

But when she opened them he was regarding her from across the room. "What did you say?" he demanded, his eyes hard, chilling.

"It's true," she said.

"No." Bryn shook his head. "It makes no sense. You wouldn't have walked out on me—"

"I didn't know then that I was pregnant. In fact, it might have happened that day, when we—" She bit her lip. "The day I left."

"You expect me to believe that?"

"I hope…"

When she faltered, he said, "That I'd be mug enough to accept another man's child as mine? And keep you and… it…in the manner I stupidly accustomed you to?"

"You know me better than that!" The accusation stung unbearably. "I didn't ask—"

"I thought I knew you," he said. "I should have realised you'd changed, become a different person." He looked around again, taking in the less-than-luxurious surroundings, and frowned. "If you need money, I'll write you a cheque. How much do you want?"

"I don't want your money!" It was probably unwise to reject the offer. She might have to give up her job eventually. The specialist who kept an eagle eye on her had wanted her to stop earlier but she assured him the work wasn't strenuous and she'd be very, very careful. "My family will help if I need them to," she told him, hoping it never would become necessary.

Charity from Bryn wasn't an option after his monstrous accusation. Although she could hardly blame him for it.

"I didn't ask you to follow me," she said. "Why did you?" Not because of the baby, that had obviously been a shock.

He shrugged, but the movement was stiff, unconvincing. "We're still married," he said. "I feel some responsibility for you. When your bro— When I found out you were on your own, after all—"

"My *brother* told you?" Rachel's hands clenched. "I'll kill him! Which one?"

"Never mind which one. I practically had to tear out his fingernails to convince him it was in your best interests to tell me where you were and that you live alone. Your whole family is concerned about you. They didn't mention... that." He looked at her swollen stomach. "Do they know?"

"They will soon." She'd have to tell them. In the early stages of the split when she'd first fled they'd expressed shock, offered help, advice, frustrated that she'd say nothing about why she'd left Bryn. So far she'd managed to keep the baby secret, tried to convince them she was okay. Even when her mother flew down to Dunedin and stayed for a week. But if they came visiting now...

"My best interests?" she asked. He'd tracked her down and offered her money because of his overblown sense of responsibility, even though he thought she'd betrayed him in the worst way possible. "We're legally separated—you got the papers from my solicitor? You don't have any obligation to me."

He brushed that aside. "I won't have my wife living in squalor."

"Even though you don't believe the baby is yours? After accusing me of lying to get you—and your money—back? Now you've decided—what? Your pride or your reputation is in danger because I'm not living in a mansion? Make up your mind."

He scowled, running a hand through his hair. "It was a shock," he said, looking again at her body. "I hardly know what I'm saying any more—what to think. I *can't* see you in need, Rachel. We go back too far. You've become a part of me."

His final startling words went straight to her heart, bringing both pain and a small, flickering, feeble flame of hope. There was anger in his voice, his eyes, even in the colour that had returned to darken his lean cheeks, but underlying the anger was something else, something that sounded close to desperation.

Rachel swallowed hard, her eyes stinging. "You're a part of me, too," she said. "And—" she put her hand over her belly again "—so is this a part of you. I swear, Bryn, by everything I hold dear, this is your baby."

For the smallest sliver of a second she thought there was longing in his eyes but it quickly vanished. He looked down at her with hard scepticism, almost hostility. "It doesn't make sense. If that's true why didn't you tell me? You knew I wanted a family."

She had no choice now. "Because," she said slowly, "it was a miracle that I conceived at all, and—"

"Divine intervention? Congratulations."

She tried to ignore the sarcasm. "The day I left I'd just been told that my chances of having a baby were almost zero. I...I still might lose him—" she swallowed before going on "—though so far, thank God, he seems all right."

"He?"

"The scans say it's a boy. But...it might still turn out badly. A late miscarriage, or something wrong with the baby."

"That doesn't explain why you kept its—his—existence from me, if you weren't sleeping with someone else."

"There never was anyone else, Bryn. The only man I ever wanted was you. I lied, and I didn't come back when I found out the impossible had happened because I can't promise you a normal, healthy *live* child."

His eyes didn't leave hers, searching for the truth, and she didn't waver, praying he'd see it. She saw the scepticism, the unwillingness to be taken for a fool, fighting with other emotions—disbelief, anger, even grief.

When he spoke it seemed that anger had won. She heard it in the harshness of his voice. "And you decided not to tell me any of this? To spin some cock-and-bull story about falling for another man? What the *hell* were you thinking?"

She winced at his tone, but at least he might be starting to believe her. Without waiting for her reply he said, "I could shake you until your teeth rattle! What a damned *stupid*, brainless thing to do. And bloody insulting!"

"Insulting?" Rachel queried in a small, startled voice.

"Do you really think I'd not want my own son if he wasn't perfect? Or that I'd stop wanting you, *loving* you, if we couldn't have kids?"

"*I* couldn't. I thought you'd find someone else who could give you—"

"Well think again!" He strode over to her and pulled her to her feet. "I don't want someone else. Only you! Why do you think I married you? You're coming home to Rivermeadows with me, and I'm not letting you out of my sight until this baby is born, with the best specialists in the country looking after you."

"You could have a DNA test after he's born, if—"

"Oh, shut up!" Bryn growled. "I'd have taken you back even if the baby wasn't mine—so long as I had you."

"You wouldn't! You said—"

"Never mind what I said. The only thing I could think about all the way here was that I'd move heaven and earth to make you love me again and come back to me, because no matter how I tried to rationalise, convince myself you'd found a better man, that I was an obsessive, chauvinistic fool, deep inside I always knew you *belong* in my home, my bed, my heart. And in the end I had to at least try to make you see it, too."

Rachel stammered, "In your...heart?"

As if he hadn't heard, Bryn went on, his voice turning grim. "And then...I thought you were having *his* baby, and I wanted to kill him. I've never felt such a primitive, un-civilised emotion in my life."

"Are you saying—" Rachel hardly dared ask, but she had to "—that you're *in love* with me?"

Bryn glared at her, and for a moment she thought he might carry out his threat to shake her. "What sort of question is that?" he demanded. "Of course I'm in love with you! I told you the night I asked you to marry me—"

"That you loved me," she conceded. "But I guess you love my brothers, too, in a way, and—"

"I don't want to go to bed with your brothers!" Bryn drew in a breath. "How could you not *know*? From the moment you stepped off that bus and walked towards me, I was sunk, lost, gone!"

"Huh," she said. "It didn't stop you kissing Kinzi. And more, I suppose."

"All right," he conceded. It was the first time she'd ever seen him look even vaguely sheepish. "So I was a bit slow to realise what had happened to me. But I couldn't stop thinking about you, wanting to touch you, kiss you, be with you. And it was damned difficult to wait until after the wedding to bed you!"

"You didn't seem in a hurry even then."

"You were worn out and I wanted our first time together to be perfect for you. That night wasn't the right time. I shouldn't have rushed the wedding, but I was afraid I might lose you if I didn't get my ring on your finger before you were due to leave Rivermeadows."

Rachel shook her head. "I'd have waited for ever, for you. No other man would do."

"Is that true?" He scanned her face.

"Cross my heart and hope to die."

The old childish vow made him smile. Then he kissed her with great gentleness and great fervour, and said, "Let me take you home. Where you belong."

"Yes, please." Rachel sighed against his chest, already feeling that she had come home. Wherever Bryn was, that was where she belonged.

EPILOGUE

"HE'S PERFECT," Rachel said. Raymond Malcolm Donovan had been born by Caesarean section six weeks prematurely, because the specialists were worried that he'd outgrown his cosy but imperfect home.

He would be in an incubator for a while, but had been thoroughly checked at birth and had all the requisite fingers and toes and the right responses to stimuli.

Both his parents had been allowed to hold him for a few minutes, and now Bryn sat on the bed where Rachel was resting, holding her hand tightly in his.

"Clever girl," he said. "I suppose I have to forgive you for trying to keep him from me. I wouldn't miss this for the world."

"I'm sorry," she said. Now their time apart seemed like a bad dream.

Bryn would make a wonderful father. In the past couple of months he'd been nurturing her, protecting her, making sure she got the very best treatment and every comfort possible. His mother and her own family joked that he was besotted with her. But that was all right, because she was equally besotted with him.

"A Donovan heir," she said. "Your mother will be pleased."

"Over the moon. But I don't want you risking any more pregnancies. I couldn't bear it if I lost you. I waited ten years for you to grow up and come back to me."

She said, "You would have been disappointed if there were no children to carry on the Donovan legacy."

"We both would," he said, "but it wouldn't be the end of the world. I don't give a damn about the Donovan legacy, only about you."

"I thought I was second-best," she confessed. "After Kinzi."

"Idiot," he said, making the epithet sound like an endearment. "You—" he took her face in his hands and kissed her lightly, punctuating the rest of the sentence with more kisses "—will…never…be second-best…to anyone." The last kiss lingered, and she knew he was restraining himself, as if afraid of hurting her, until she slid her arms about him and kissed him back with fervour.

Then she drew away a little and said, "Not even your son?"

"Uh-uh. Not that I don't love him already. Until I saw him, he was an abstract, I'd have given him up in a heartbeat if you were in danger. But when I held him, something happened inside me that I can't describe. He's precious because you gave him to me. And I'll love you both until I die."

"I love you, too," she said simply. "And I'm sorry I was so stupid."

"Yes, well—when you're over this I'll be ensuring you make up for that," he threatened. "You have no idea what hell you put me through."

"Some," she said, remembering the dark, dreary days after she'd left him. And not at all worried about the kind of punishment he planned, knowing it would involve tenderness and passion and wonderful lovemaking.

Everything had come right in her world. Even though the future might hold unknown trials, they'd weather whatever life had in store, because they had each other. And right now, they were in their own heaven on earth.